D1394761

KING'S CROFT

Christine Marion Fraser

COLLINS
London · 1990

William Collins Sons & Co Ltd
London · Glasgow · Sydney · Auckland
Toronto · Johannesburg

ISBN 0 00 223028 3

First published 1986
This reprint 1990
© 1986 by Christine Marion Fraser

Printed and bound in Great Britain by
Billings Book Plan Ltd, Worcester

ACKNOWLEDGMENT

I would like to express my sincere thanks and appreciation to my friend and fellow author, David Kerr Cameron, whose wonderfully descriptive books on the north-east have been such a help to me. I am also grateful for the help and advice he so unstintingly gave.

C.M.F.

To Sarah Molloy, for her enthusiasm and encouragement

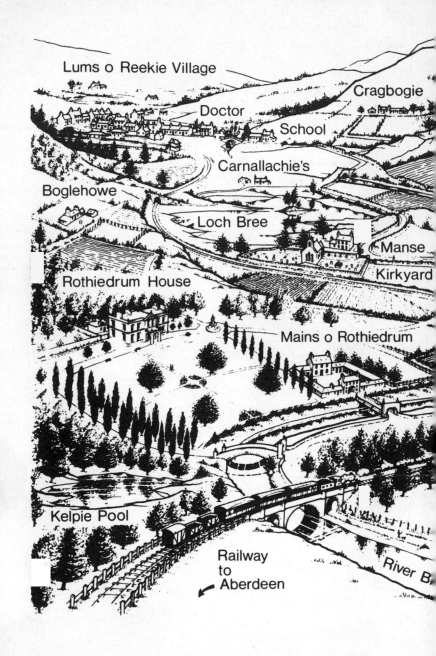

Lums o Reekie Village

Cragbogie

Doctor

School

Carnallachie's

Boglehowe

Loch Bree

Manse

Kirkyard

Rothiedrum House

Mains o Rothiedrum

Kelpie Pool

Railway
to
Aberdeen

River B.

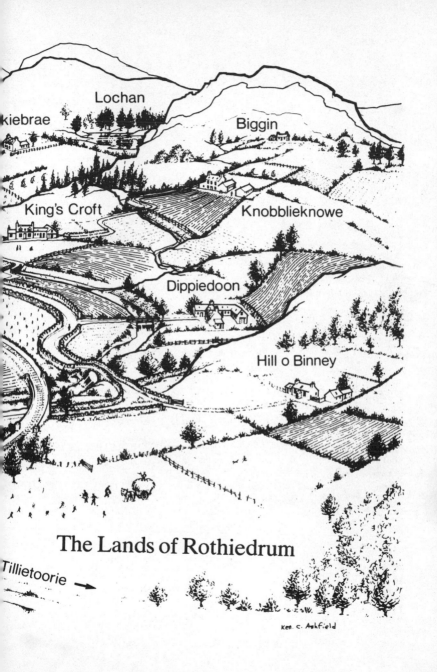

Lochan

kiebrae

Biggin

King's Croft

Knobblieknowe

Dippiedoon

Hill o Binney

The Lands of Rothiedrum

Tillietoorie →

Ken C. Ashfield

ROTHIEDRUM IN ABERDEENSHIRE 1885

It was a good day for a wedding. The summer countryside stretched, a green and golden patchwork for as far as the eye could see, the rich dark green of the firs in the little woods above Mossdyke Croft making a vivid contrast with the azure bowl of the cloudless June sky.

Margaret Innes McKenzie turned away from the window and touched her hot cheek. She felt flustered, excited and unusually nervous. Wedding or no, she had been up at her usual time of five to help her mother with all the tasks around the croft. She had washed and scrubbed till her hands were chaffed and sore, reflecting as she worked how nice it would have been to go to her man with soft, white hands. But then, he might have looked askance at such a rare phenomenon for it was no disgrace for a girl of the farmtouns to have rough hands – more a disgrace if she hadn't – she might have been stamped as a lazy whittrock and no crofter in his right senses would have taken a slut to be his wife.

Still, she reflected as she made butter and cheese, boiled hen's feed and made calfies' stoorum, an oatmeal and water mixture that gave the young beasts strength, how good just for once to be soft and feminine and to smell of roses instead of the byre before it had been mucked.

'I like the smell of you – ' The voice of Jamie King Grant spoke inside her head. 'When I'm near you I'm minded o' the cornfields after rain and I could hold you forever just taking the smell of you to my heart.'

Margaret smiled as she thought of Jamie and his gay, carefree intrusion into a life that had become as sedate for her as that of Miss Beattie, the retired old lady's maid to whom she had been sent as a companion on leaving school at the age of twelve.

Miss Beattie had been a difficult old lady to live with. As

stiff and unyielding as the stays which made her stand ramrod straight, she waved her walking stick about in bayonet fashion to emphasize the demands she barked out imperiously from the moment she rose from bed each morning. The wages she had paid to the young farmtoun lass had been as sparse and as grudging as the gratitude she showed for Margaret's devoted attention to her welfare; thirty shillings annually, seven shillings and sixpence of which was doled out at three-monthly intervals so that Margaret should not keep her mother waiting for her due.

Faithfully Margaret sent the money to her mother at Mossdyke, a great part of her pining to go home to the croft, a smaller, more insistent part content to stay on at Miss Beattie's and absorb all the social graces round which the old lady's days revolved. After the harshness of the crofting life there was a genteel security in refined service, and she was willing to put up with the old lady's crotchety ways in order to learn more about the lifestyle of a society far removed from the rough honesty of the north-east farmtouns.

She was almost twenty when Jamie had come into her life, and a bursting, colourful intrusion it had been too, the travellers encamped on the ley field of Mains of Baldoch, meeting up with the gypsies who had come north of the border for the summer. Most of them had been Grants, all related and inter-related – a happy, laughing throng who bent their backs to the tattie howking by day and gathered to sing round the camp fires by evening.

Miss Beattie had scowled at the noise yet smiled sourly behind her thick glasses as she told Margaret, 'They have their place in society too, Margaret, they have their own codes of behaviour and stick to them. Orderly – you could say that – and I always admire any breed of people who can run their lives in an orderly way.'

Margaret had politely agreed, and in the privacy of her room had laughed with delight as the wild sound of the gypsy fiddles floated over the fields.

Soon afterwards she had met Jamie, velvet-eyed Jamie with the curling dark hair and the smile that melted her

10

heart from the very first moment. He was truly a gypsy king, but it was only coincidence he told her that King was his middle name. He was of true Romany stock; his mother had been a well known fortune-teller among her own people, his father a Seer of great repute. All his life Jamie had travelled country roads. He knew as much about farming as any man in the north-east lowlands. At his mother's insistence he had learned the craft of shoemaking and could stitch as fancy a shoe as any souter in the land. Wherever he went he sold his shoes to the gentry and had earned a good reputation for himself among the rich. More of his time had been spent north of the border than anywhere else, with the result that he had as much of an Aberdeen 'twang' in his voice as Margaret herself.

Soon she was besotted with him, he with her. When the time came for him to move south for the winter she had been desolated, when next he came back he asked her to marry him, ready to give up his nomadic existence and settle down to a more humdrum way of life. By then Margaret's stepfather had been taken ill and she had had to leave Miss Beattie's to return to the farmtouns.

Miss Beattie had tears in her steely grey eyes the day Margaret left her service for good. 'Margaret,' she had said sternly. 'I know you think I'm a bit of an old dragon but that's my way and I can't change it for anybody. I've enjoyed having you in my home – if I may say you have something in you that I could never quite fathom. You're too good to marry a gypsy, but nothing I can say will change that stubborn, proud heart of yours so when the time comes I want you to get married here, in my own drawing room. I insist on it, Margaret – for the sake of a crotchety old maid who has few pleasures left in life but watching other people make a mess of theirs.' She had smiled dourly then and had given Margaret fifty pounds to go to her 'dowry'. On impulse Margaret had hugged her and had promised to come back for her wedding to Jamie.

And now the day had come and the little croft sitting snug in the shelter of the couthy hills shone and sparkled in the morning sunlight. Despite the hours of work that lay behind her, Margaret had rid herself of an excess of energy by polishing the already polished doorstep till her arms ached, had cleaned all the windows till the panes winked among their coverings of crisp white muslin.

She looked at her stepfather sitting in his chair by the fire, a substantial armchair it was, red-varnished, its un-contoured wooden seat black-painted, the armrests polished smooth from untold years of usage. This was Andra McKenzie's chair, his throne, only moved from its place on the left hand side of the fire when the floor was being scrubbed. It was so sacrosanct an object that no one dared use it if it was thought Andra might come in and catch them in it. In days gone by its straight back had forced his work-weary bones into rigid lines, but now he sagged down in it, his eyes gazing unblinkingly into the torpid flames in the grate. Margaret wondered what he was thinking that blithe morning – if he was thinking at all. Once a tough, wiry figure, leathery brown face etched deep with lines from a lifetime of hard work, he was now bent and old looking, surrounded by an aura of loneliness since a stroke had robbed him of speech and much of the power of his body.

'Andra,' she touched his white head gently. 'Andra, it's a good day for a wedding, is it no?'

The silence of the kitchen answered her, broken only by the slow, easy ticking of the pendulum wall clock and the raucous crowing of a cockerel from the yard outside. Margaret drew her hand away from the bowed head and swallowed a lump in her throat. Dear, good Andra McKenzie, she thought, I owe you so much – thanks to you I have a name . . .

Her mother's light step sounded in the lobby. She came into the room and Margaret gazed at her with tears in her eyes. 'I wish he was coming, Mam, I dinna want to get wed without him there.'

Megsie Cameron's tired face didn't waver as she reached out a thin hand to touch her daughter's fiery hair. 'Maggie,' she said softly, 'dinna fret about Andra. He lives in his own wee world now, but once you were all his world and the last thing he would want would be to spoil this day for you. He'll be fine here with Kirsty Keith to see to him – you know how she loves looking after people.'

Maggie thought about the sharp-faced mistress of Dippiedoon and giggled. 'Ay, only too well, the sooner she has bairns to see to the better the rest of us might get some peace from her poking and prying.'

Megsie Cameron sighed and her daughter looked at her quickly, wondering just how much of the curiosity of neighbours had affected her throughout her life. She had been a maidservant at the royal house of Balmoral, an inexperienced girl who had fallen for the flattering attentions of a lordly young creature whose sole purpose in courting her had been to get her into the nearest bed as quickly as possible. Margaret had been the result of that ill-matched mating but she had never had to bear the indignity of being labelled illegitimate. Megsie Cameron had been fortunate to meet and marry Andra McKenzie in relatively far-off Buchan.

Before Margaret's birth, Andra had inherited the old Mossdyke croft and it was here he brought his young wife to bear her child in the attic room upstairs, in the very bed in which he himself had first drawn breath. If anyone in the parish of Rothiedrum suspected that there was disgrace attached to Maggie's birth no one ever said as much, though rumour had a nasty habit of spreading, giving fuel to the busy tongues of people like Kirsty Keith who delighted in proclaiming to her cronies that there was more to Margaret Innes McKenzie than met the eye.

Maggie grew up knowing the true facts about her existence. On one hand she was proud of the blue blood flowing in her veins, on the other she was resentful of the 'idle rich', and over the years had built up quite a hatred against the so-called gentleman who had fathered her with such blithe irresponsibility. To make matters worse she knew who he was, although she had never met him. He had family connections with the House of Rothiedrum and from time to time little snippets of gossip filtered through from the local girls who worked to the laird. Whenever the name of Lord Lindsay Ogilvie was mentioned in her hearing she would purse her lips and turn away, trying to ignore the unwilling yearning she experienced at the sound of her father's name. Yet he was just a name to her, as unreal as the fact that she was a first cousin of his niece, Lady Marjorie Forbes, the attractive new wife of the young Laird of Rothiedrum . . .

'It's time to get ready, Maggie.'

Maggie started out of her reverie and stared at her mother.

'Ay, Mam.' Reaching out she touched her mother's hair, once as rich and red as her own, now dull and streaked with grey. 'Jamie's the right one, isn't he, Mam? You liked him from the beginning.'

She sounded breathless, anxious. Megsie smiled. 'Ay, Maggie, he's a good man – and fitting that a king should marry such a noble lass.'

Maggie joined in her mother's laughter. 'King of the gypsies – my Jamie – he's giving up a lot for me, I just hope he'll be able to settle down after the roving life he's led.'

Megsie nodded wisely. 'Keep his bed warm and his belly full and he'll no stray far from your side.' She took her daughter's hand and held it tightly. 'We need a man about the place again,' she glanced at her husband so still and peaceful by the hearth, 'now that Andra's no as able as he was. Jamie's a Godsend for us all and I bless the day you and he met. Now help me get Andra ben the house and we'll bring the tub to the fire. You must go to your man smelling as pure as the dawn. I have a wee bottle o' rose water I bought from the travellers last year which we'll put in the water.'

Maggie coloured. 'Mam,' she whispered urgently, 'Jamie's the first serious man I've had in my life – I'm a bittie feared of what lies ahead.'

Megsie looked affectionately into her daughter's earnest, flushed face. 'Ah, Maggie,' she nodded, 'would that I had been so innocent when Andra betrothed himself to me. There is nothing to fear, lass. Jamie's a mature man o' thirty, no some callow youth who is all bothy talk and no experience. Loving each other will come as naturally in bed as anywhere else, you mark my words.'

The door rattled and Betsy O'Neil of Cragbogie breezed in. A real sloven of a girl was Betsy whose origins lay in the notorious slums of Aberdeen's Peacock Close. Hard-bitten and as boisterously crude about the facts of life as Maggie was shy of them she more than made up for her shortcomings with her kindly heart and vigorous personality. Her husband, a hard-working, hard-drinking Irishman known as Danny the Fist, had bedded his bride well before their betrothal with the result that she was heavily pregnant after just three months of marriage.

When she had heard that Maggie was marrying a gypsy, she had subjected her to merciless teasing concerning what she called Jamie's hot blood and Maggie, a puritan with a keen sense of humour, caught between Miss Beattie's carefully cultivated gentility and the down to earth world of the farmtouns, could never wait to get rid of Betsy so that she could give vent to her mirth in the privacy of her own room. Despite her swollen girth, Betsy still moved with a certain lithe grace and as soon as Andra was settled in the parlour and the hot tub was brought to the fire she all but yanked Maggie's clothes from her body to throw them willy nilly on the *clickit* rug, the only adornment on the cold, grey stone floor of the kitchen. Backed by hardwearing seed-corn sacks, hooked through with a variety of discarded but colourful variety of old breeks and stockings cut into strips, these rugs littered the floors of the house, but for practical reasons only one was placed at the kitchen fire, rolled up and placed against the wall during morning scrubbing sessions and only put in front of the hearth during the evenings and for special occasions.

Steam from the tub filled the kitchen, the kettle sang on the swee, ready to top up when the water got cold. Betsy lathered soap energetically over Maggie's smooth shoulders and she might as well not have spoken when she protested she could manage fine on her own.

'Ach, wheesht, Maggie,' scolded Betsy, wiping soap from her nose. 'It's no every day a lass gets married, and you'd best take time to preen yourself now for Jamie will no give you a minute's peace for the next few nights.'

Standing back she gazed at Maggie's shapely figure admiringly. 'My, Maggie, it's amazing what secret lies beneath these drab frocks you wear. You're a beauty and no mistake. Ay, Jamie will no go short o' his pleasure wi' you in the feathers beside him, for you're shaped just like the hour glass on my kitchen sideboard . . .'

'Och, be quiet, Betsy,' scolded Maggie, grabbing a towel and wrapping herself in it while her mother and Betsy between them fussed with her hair, rubbing at it, combing it, eventually esconsing her by the fire where little eddies of steam rose from the drying locks. Soon it rippled down her back to her waist, a cascade of rich red waves burnished to gold in the firelight.

Enviously Betsy took the heavy tresses in her hands and let them slide through her fingers. 'Danny says mine are like rat's sookings – ay, Maggie, wi' one thing and another Jamie's in for a fine time. When he's no touching your hair he'll be busy somewhere else – I doubt he'll have no strength left by the time he comes back to farm King's Croft.'

'King's Croft!' Maggie and her mother spoke in unison and dimples dented Betsy's cheeks.

'Ay, that's what folks hereabouts have christened the place already.'

'Daft gowks!' flared Megsie, her eyes darting to the door as if afraid her husband had overheard Betsy's careless words. 'This is Andra's croft and will be till the day he dies!'

'Ay,' Betsy murmured sympathetically and gently pushed Maggie away from the fire and upstairs to help her get ready.

Margaret Innes McKenzie didn't think herself beautiful. She knew the attraction of her face lay in its strength; her features were finely drawn, pride and mischief flashed out of her grey-green eyes, her generous mouth was firm and well set, there was about her an aura of a gentlewoman and a dignity in her bearing that defied her humble surroundings. She knew that people spoke behind her back about what they called her 'uppitiness' but she could no more help her refined ways than she could help breathing.

Staring at herself in her mirror she saw the face of a flushed, bright-eyed girl of twenty-one, framed in a bridal hat trimmed with little flowers and a veil which would later hide her nervous blushes. Her black, full length bridal gown sat well on her slender, small-boned figure. For almost a year she had saved every spare penny to secure the outfit from Esslemont and Macintosh's in Aberdeen and now she was glad she had made all those little sacrifices.

In the rowan trees outside the window blackbirds were singing, laughter drifted from the track leading along to the croft, down below a door banged, voices floated upstairs, among them the masculine tones of Archie McCaskill the travelling vanman who for years had been sweet on Maggie. The house was filling with wellwishers and wedding guests.

Maggie's heart fluttered. She turned to Betsy. 'Do I look alright? My face – it's so hot . . .'

Calmly Betsy applied a powder-saturated wad of cotton to Maggie's red cheeks and flipping up the ruched hem of the dress she tucked a white linen hanky into the rim of the blue silk hose that covered Maggie's shapely legs. Only her petticoats covered her modesty for as yet the fashion for under-drawers had reached only the high society north of the border. She thought wistfully that it would have been rather nice to be in line with the most fashionable on this very important day of her life, but Betsy soon dispelled her thoughts by patting the hanky and saying, 'There, you never know when you might need it. I was glad o' one at my wedding and no for my nose either. Danny was sweating that much at the idea o' losing his freedom I just whipped up my dress in front o' the minister's nose and he was that busy goggling at my bare dowp he forgot to glower at Danny for blowing his nose and nearly forgot the words o' the blessing forbye.'

Maggie burst out laughing and took Betsy's hand.

17

'You've been a Godsend today, Betsy. Sometimes I canna thole the way you go on about Jamie and me, and at others I just shut myself in my room and piddle myself laughing.'

Betsy giggled and holding hands both young women rushed to pull open the door, looked at one another and choking back their laughter walked sedately down the wooden stairs to meet the assembled guests.

It seemed to Maggie as if the whole of Rothiedrum was gathered there in parlour and kitchen to see the wedding guests off in the hired brake which had seating ranged down the sides for more than twenty-four people. Bunty Lovie the postmistress, a round, fat little woman with an inquisitive, bird-like face and bright black eyes, stood at the gate with her cronies, her hanky to her eyes and her tongue going nineteen to the dozen as she hurled hawthorn petals at anyone who happened to pass her line of vision. George the Forge, the village blacksmith, had brought along a barrel of his home-made beer and together with his mates was ensconced under the hedge that lined the track, shouting out a garbled stream of good wishes as the brake passed by. Charlie Lammas the butcher, a tiny little man who wore an old bowler hat both in and out of his shop, was there with Lily, his stout, domineering wife and Maggie waved at them all till her arms ached and she was glad when the horses turned onto the comparative peace of the turnpike. The fifteen mile journey to Miss Beattie's house passed in a dream. In no time at all it seemed they were at their destination and there was Miss Beattie at the door to welcome them, resplendent in black silk, her loud, imperious voice barking out orders to all and sundry.

The minister was ensconced in the heavily draped drawing room, a nervous tic quickening at his eye every time Miss Beattie's voice fell upon his ears. The Reverend Andrew McAuley knew Maggie well. During her time with Miss Beattie she had accompanied the old lady to the kirk every Sabbath, her young face sober as befitted a servant lass imbibing the words preached in the Episcopal church, yet a glimmer of fun sparkling out of her eyes and that air

18

she wore of gracing the establishment with her presence.

'Margaret.' He rose to welcome her, taking her hand courteously.

'Mr McAuley.' Her prim, well-modulated voice with its charming north-east 'twang' fell coolly on his ears and his hand grew perceptibly limp in her firm young grasp, 'It's a fine day for a wedding – is it not?' she queried politely.

He looked directly at her. The grey-green eyes behind the little veil were twinkling and suddenly he lost his resentment at presiding over a marriage ceremony into which he had been bullied by the dragonly Miss Beattie. Never had he thought to be called upon to bless the union of a gypsy to a farmtoun lass but now, seeing the happiness shining our of the girl's refined young face, he felt his heart growing as blithe as the bright June day outside.

'Indeed a fine day, Margaret,' he nodded and was shocked at the realization that it was taking him all his time not to wink at her.

Jamie arrived in as carefree a manner as he had breezed into Margaret's sedate young life. The brake which had conveyed himself and a variety of friends and relatives from a communal meeting point was as gaily and outrageously decorated as the fresh horses which had carried the party from the halfway stage where refreshments had obviously been freely taken. They were all singing as they arrived at Miss Beattie's discreetly genteel front door and from the depths of the throng the untamed notes of a fiddle arose, teeth flashed in sun-drenched faces. Miss Beattie took one look and twitched back into the drawing room to partake of a furtive glass of port wine.

From out of the throng of brown, sweating bodies, a figure detatched itself and walked with dignity up Miss Beattie's spotless steps to her polished front door with its refined display of gleaming brass ornamentation proclaiming her standing in her own peculiarly snobbish society.

Jamie King Grant was not a tall man, but his arresting dark good looks more than made up for his lack of stature.

19

His brown eyes were vividly alive in his sunburned face, its heavy black Kitchener moustache not quite hiding the full sensual mouth that had carried Maggie to heights of shivering ecstasy in their times of courting under the still black trees that shielded Miss Beattie's house from the outside world. Surrounded by a colourful entourage of friends and relations he descended on Miss Beattie, a fine handsome figure in his black, swallow-tailed jacket and lavender coloured shirt, his eyes flashing at sight of his bride and his manner so courteous to Miss Beattie she was soon won over by him.

'A wonderful day for a wedding, Mr Grant,' she beamed, parched skin tautening round her protruding cheekbones as she welcomed each guest in turn, sucking in her breath a little as whisky fumes bathed her and work-roughened hands seized her delicate birdlike fingers in too-hearty handshakes.

Mr McAuley's rather grim countenance was relaxing, smiling even as the spirit of Margaret's wedding day infiltrated his dour soul.

In the middle of all the greetings there came a pause, a perceptible and respectful hush fell over the gathering of travellers and gypsies. Almost automatically they seperated into two rows to make way for a quartet of men who were carrying a rickety object which resembled a sedan chair. On it, ensconced in a cloud of cushions and blankets, was an old woman, dressed to her wrinkled yellow throat in scuffed blue silk, her crown of white hair barely restrained by an enormous black hat decorated with pink birds' wings.

Maggie was glad of the veil that hid her blushes. Out of the corner of her eye she met the devilish, twinkling ones of Jamie and she was seized with an almost irrepressible urge to run to him and hug him. She knew she would remember the agony and the ecstasy of that memorable moment for the rest of her life. She had met Grandmother only once before and had never forgotten the impression the grand old gypsy woman had made upon her. She was the matriarch of the travelling people. All her life she had tramped the highways and byways and now, too old and frail to walk any further, she was carried everywhere in her sedan chair by a willing army of subjects.

The look on Miss Beattie's face was one never to be forgotten. All her hard-won composure failed her in those moments of Grandmother's arrival. Her face sagged, little ringlets of skin curled over the high neck of her dress, her mouth hung suspended for several moments before she took several deep breaths and braced herself for what was to come. Into the elegant drawing room Grandmother was borne in style; her voice, delightfully Highland but no less imperious than Miss Beattie's, barking out orders till she was eventually set down amidst Miss Beattie's softly padded sofas and glass fronted cabinets.

Without preliminary, Grandmother called the minister to her side and made herself known to him, thereupon engaging him in such intricate questions about the Kirk and its functions an audible sigh of relief escaped him when eventually he made good his escape.

Silks and stays rustling and creaking Grandmother arranged herself on her cushions and when she was settled to her satisfaction her bright eyes raked through the gathering, alighting and staying on an aghast Miss Beattie. 'There ye are, my dear,' she cried accusingly. 'Come you here to me and let me look at ye.'

To Maggie's complete surprise Miss Beattie obeyed as meekly as a lamb, her only indication of discomfiture showing in two bright spots of colour emblazoned on each bristling cheekbone.

'Would you look at that,' Megsie whispered in her daughter's ear. 'The old lady is as superior as any Miss Beattie's worked to in her day, she'll be licking her boots before the day is over.'

'If it ever begins,' Maggie replied for it seemed to her that no semblance of order could possibly emerge from the chaos in Miss Beattie's sequestered drawing room. Everyone was talking and laughing, Grandmother and Miss Beattie were engaged in a lengthy conversation concerning the merits of tea, the minister had retired to a corner to gaze rather soulfully from the plush curtained window to the sun-splashed meadows beyond the garden.

'Get me a glass o' port, dear,' Grandmother's high, commanding tones pierced everyone's ears. 'All this talk o' tea has made me drouthy but it's too tame a potion for my needs just now. It's been a long journey and I will no feel like myself without a glass o' the grape inside me.'

Miss Beattie's face was animated as she fetched bottle and glass and bore them to Grandmother's side. A full measure warming in her purple-veined hands, the old lady settled back in her cushions, smiled toothlessly at all and sundry and demanded sweetly, 'What are ye all waiting for? Where's that meenister mannie? Jamie and his bride mustna be kept waiting and the sooner the ceremony is ower wi' the sooner we can get on wi' the feasting.'

Miss Beattie smiled rather nervously at the minister; there was a discreet and decorous positioning of people and chairs round the room. Jamie stood close by Maggie's side, his dark eyes serious now as the minister took his place and the wedding began. Mr McAuley's high-pitched, euphonistic voice rose in the silence; a mistle thrush sang in the deep-shaded sycamore tree by the gate. On the dusty road a rag-and-bone man trundled past on his hot, lethargic way, his little donkey dragging its hooves so that they made trails in the dust, cups and saucers chinking with every turn of the cart wheels, a lolling-tongued dog trailing listlessly behind.

'Any old ra-ags! Any old ra-ags!'

The toneless dirge fell clearly on the ears of the wedding party. Maggie stole a quick look at Jamie. Was it a portent of their life together? Rags and bones with no little riches in between to brighten the way? Jamie half turned. His eyelid came down in a sly, deliberate wink. She straightened. Life with him would always be rich and satisfying, no matter how poor their circumstances.

At the back of the room Grandmother belched softly, a misdemeanour hastily covered by a ripple of respectful throat clearing.

Blessings fell solemly from Mr McAuley's thin lips

followed by prayers and hymns and finally the words of the marriage ceremony itself. The palpable heat of the room enclosed Maggie. She swayed a little. Jamie's hand slipped under her elbow, strong, reassuring. She loved him, oh how she loved her gypsy Jamie. The words uniting them in wedlock fell sweet and dear on her ears. The air lightened, a little whisper ran round the room, breaking the tension that had held everyone stiffly to attention.

And then it was over, chairs scraped, Grandmother's high, lilting voice sang out its congratulations. Jamie took his bride in his arms. The lips that kissed hers were soft and tender, warm with the promise of passion to come.

'Welcome to my life, Mrs Grant,' he whispered softly.

'And you to mine.' Her voice was low, tremulous. Their eyes met and held, wordlessly pledging their love to one another before they were surrounded by wellwishers.

During the feasting and the revelry that followed, the toasts, the dancing, Maggie was aware of her mother's anxiety to be off home to Andra. When it came time to leave she took her mother's hands and squeezed them tightly. 'He'll be fine, Mam, never you fear,' she reassured, then added softly, 'I miss him too. When I was a wee lass I used to think how it would be on my wedding day – you and Andra at my side.'

'He's a good man, Maggie,' said Megsie huskily.

'The best.' Maggie smiled though there was a poignancy in her – for Andra – for her mother who had once been so bonny and who now, at just past forty, was grey and old looking beyond her years though occasionally the young Megsie flashed into the sweetness of her face, a fleeting shadow of the beauty she must have been in her girlhood.

Maggie had changed for the journey to the little fishing village where she and Jamie were to spend a few precious days together in rented rooms. The blue of the tight-bodiced dress with its chaste high neck, was a perfect foil for the upswept tresses of her bright, luxuriant hair upon which sat a blue bonnet tied under the chin, decorated with two gay green feathers.

Megsie looked at her daughter with pride, and her green

23

eyes were shiny when she said, 'My bonny Maggie. You should always be dressed in fine clothes instead o' the drab frocks that hide the pride o' you from the world.'

Maggie laughed. 'A fine bit fool I would look mucking out the byre dressed in velvets and bows.' Gathering her mother to her bosom she held her tightly for a brief moment. 'Goodbye, Mam, I hope you'll manage while we're away. It will pass in no time and then Jamie will be there to take care of everything.'

Megsie drew away. 'Ach, you mustna think yet o' coming back, you make the most o' your time away for it will only happen once in your lifetime.'

She got into the brake that had brought Maggie. It rattled away and Maggie turned back into the house to seek out Miss Beattie to thank her for all she had done.

'It was a pleasure, my dear Margaret,' intoned the old lady with dignity even though she hiccupped discreetly into her hand in the pretence of clearing her throat. She and Grandmother had partaken freely of port wine and had giggled together like schoolgirls in a quiet little corner of the barn where Mains of Baldoch had allowed the dancing to take place. Miss Beattie seized Maggie's hands in her birdlike claws. 'I truly wish you well in your future life with Jamie Grant. I must say I had entertained some doubts about the wiseness of your choice of husband but today I found out he is not only a gentleman, he is quite regal in his own way and thoroughly deserved to be made a king in his own class.'

Maggie hid a smile. Dear old Miss Beattie. She was a snob but an endearing one and Maggie knew she would always have a soft spot for her. As yet she hadn't found another companion to suit her.

'Fools, every one of them,' she told Maggie forcibly. 'Initiative and good manners are so hard to come by – a pity you had to leave my service, Margaret,' she had ended accusingly. 'I could have taught you so much about the finer things in life.'

'Social etiquette is of little use in the byre at five o'clock in the morning,' Maggie had answered lightly, making the old lady smile sourly and mutter, 'Quite, quite, still, I will always regret having to let you go. You'll be wasted, Margaret, wasted, and in time you'll forget all you learned here and become a slave to home and family. The years will settle heavily upon those little shoulders, mark my words, dear.'

The blood of the youth leaping strong in her veins, Maggie hid her smiles and she was still hiding them, though her affection for her former employer was such she gathered her into her arms and planted a kiss firmly on one wizened, bony cheek.

Tears sprang to Miss Beattie's keen grey eyes and transferring her hanky to them from her nose she said huskily, 'Be off with you, girl – and luck go with you. I won't forget you, Margaret, that's a promise. I hope you might find the time to come back and visit me – someday.'

Tears pricking her own eyes, Maggie went quickly outside to the brake that had brought Jamie and his rumbustious following. He was waiting to help her up, his strong arms enclosing her waist briefly, his dark eyes intent and full of warmth as they gazed into hers. Crushed next to him in the packed bench she shivered a little though the cold night air that swept over her had nothing to do with her tremors. He was so hard and warm beside her, so overwhelmingly masculine, she was almost ashamed of how eagerly she anticipated the time when she would be alone with him at last.

His strong brown hand curled over hers and she leaned against him, content to be quiet during the riotous journey. The brake rumbled through a night that would never grow entirely dark during the long northern mid-summer days. The skylarks were still singing in the sky, the ecstatic sound of them seeming to precede the briskly trotting horses along the roads, in the buttercup strewn meadows the peewits were calling in alarm as they ushered their round fluffy babies away from threat of danger, the sun was just below the horizon to the north-west, sending up great unfurling banners of golds and pinks that merged and spiralled upwards like molten smoke.

Grandmother had been transferred from her sedan chair to a well-cushioned seat at the front. She was fast asleep, her silvered head nodding onto her scrawny bosom, quite oblivious to the good-natured ribaldry going on all around her. Whisky had appeared like magic from inner suit pockets and as the drams flowed so did the singing and the earthy jokes, instigated by the cradle which sat between the rows of feet.

'How soon will ye fill it, Jamie?' cried a black whiskered man known as Whisky Jake. Built like a bull with a voice to match, he was Jamie's best friend but Maggie had never taken to him, hating his habit of nudging her roughly and whispering crude suggestions in her ear. She pretended to like him for Jamie's sake, though she was certain if Jamie knew half the things about Jake that she did he would send him on his way in no uncertain terms.

The question started off a whole spate of good-natured taunts concerning Jamie's fertility and it was a boisterous company who rattled into the sleepy little village in the early hours of morning, causing a few windows to be thrown open so that straining eyes could better see what all the excitement was about.

In the hour that followed Jamie was subjected to a whole chain of indignities and when the ribald crew had at last departed into the night, Maggie was left to look at her new husband, trouserless and dishevelled, hands and feet bound and tied to the bedhead. Jake's parting shot rang in Maggie's head. 'The choice is yours, Maggie lass, leave him as he is and get a good night's rest – or let him loose and answer for the consequences.'

A strangled giggle escaped Maggie at sight of Jamie's hangdog look.

'Come on, Maggie,' he said evenly. 'Dinna just stand there laughing. Get me out o' this.'

For answer she untied her hat and tossed it away from her. It sailed through the air to land on top of the wardrobe, its proud cockade of feathers touching the ceiling. Choking back her merriment she put both hands on her hips and surveyed her new husband for a long, considering moment.

'I wonder . . .' she taunted, eyes aglow with mischief. 'I'm tired and needing a good rest right enough. These daft gowks made a fine job of tying you up. I think I'll feel safer if I just leave you the way you are . . .'

'Maggie.' His voice held a warning note. 'It will be the worse for you later if you dinna stop tormenting me now.'

'Ach, Jamie,' she scolded pleasantly, 'and here was Miss Beattie thinking you were so refined. That's no way for a gentleman to speak to his new bride –'

'Maggie! If you don't untie me right this minute I'll start singing at the top o' my voice and fine's the rest you'll get then.'

Breathless with laughter she hastened to free him from his bonds and immediately his arms came round her to draw her close.

'Jamie,' she whispered. 'It was a good wedding, wasn't it?'

'The best. There will never be another like it.' His lips nuzzled her ear, making her shiver anew. 'I love you, Maggie.'

She stroked the dark, curling hair from his brow. 'I hope you'll never regret giving up everything you've ever known – for me.'

'Oh, Maggie,' he crushed her to him. 'If you hadn't come into my life I would have wandered forever – with no one. I'm thirty years old, lass. I've been a man for a long time but never in all my years did I meet anyone I loved enough to marry. I'm not giving up everything – I've found it – so wheesht now – and let me love you.'

Gently he pushed her away and reaching up undid her hair so that it cascaded over her shoulders in a fiery cloud. 'Such bonny hair,' he breathed. 'It was what I noticed first about you – your hair.'

Lifting a thick tendril to his lips he kissed it tenderly and when she saw the burning yearning in his black eyes her heart began to beat swiftly.

'Jamie,' she murmured. 'My gypsy Jamie – we'll have a good future together, you and me – and I'll be proud to bear your children.'

His lips sought hers, roughly, searchingly, so filled with warm passion she felt the heat of it throbbing through her, filling every aching space of her unfulfilled body.

She clung to him, wanting only this now, this night in the arms of Jamie King Grant to last forever. All her tomorrows could wait. The future and all it held was another world away as Jamie carried her with him into realms of an ecstasy she had only just glimpsed in her dreams.

PART ONE

ROTHIEDRUM
CHRISTMAS/NEW YEAR 1908/9

CHAPTER ONE

Evelyn lay in bed, listening to the strange, frightening sounds that intruded into the normally dark, sleeping hours of night. Outside, the December wind was howling, its hoary breath bringing great flurries of freezing snow which rasped against the window panes like snarling demons. She could hear the tormented flailings of the beeches which stood sentinel at the gable ends of the croft, buttressing it from the worst of the winds blowing over from the North Sea.

The house itself stood solid and quiet around its occupants as the snowstorm raved and battered at doors and windows. The cowlings on the lums were rattling monotonously in the teeth of the blizzard, the tortured groans of the trees sounded like lost souls in the last agonies of dying, but King's Croft seemed to hold itself aloof from all inclement threats to its existence. It had always been like that, for as long as she remembered, a safe, protective haven in which there was no uneasiness, only a reassurance that it would remain standing even if the rest of the world collapsed at its feet.

But for Evelyn there was no reassurance on this wild night in December, just two days before Christmas. Her unease wasn't incurred by the black of the night or the viciousness of the storm. She stared into the bitter black shadows of the room, remembering, remembering that awful, terrifying sight she had witnessed just a few hours ago when all was as it had been in her safe, secure child's world.

It had been an evening of gaiety for them all, all seven of the Grants invited to a Christmas ceilidh at Knobblieknowe. There the hearths had blazed in welcome; the buttered bannocks, the crowdie cheese, the tattie scones, had fair made the table groan with good cheer. The

31

whisky and the hot toddies had flown, as unendingly as the songs, the laughter, the banter.

The Keiths of Dippiedoon, the Burns of Birkiebrae, the O'Neils of Cragbogie had all been there with the exception of some of the children made to stay at home to look after younger brothers and sisters. But Johnny Burns and Florrie O'Neil had managed to wangle their way in and Evelyn had had a fine time with them. Kenneth Cameron Mor had been in top form, and he had had good reason to celebrate for just a week ago his bonny Jeannie had given birth to a fine healthy son with golden red hair and big fists on him that had made Kenneth throw back his red head and bellow with delighted laughter.

When Kenneth Cameron Mor first came to Knobblieknowe it was said he was so overjoyed at first sight of his barley fields he did a Highland fling right there in the middle of the dung midden and Jeannie was so disgusted by the smell of him she wouldn't let him in the house but made him sleep in the bothy with the fee'd men till the reek had worn away from him. But that was only talk, for no one could really imagine such a man bowing meekly to the whims of a wife, even such a young and bonny one as Jeannie.

Kenneth Cameron Mor was master of his own house and took no orders from anyone. The house itself seemed full of the same sort of pride that was in its master. It had three storeys to it and stood solid up there on the hill so that at night you could look up to it and see the soft lights shining from the windows and feel the life of Kenneth Mor flowing down the brae and into you. There was a fair number of good sturdy birches growing near the house, yet even so Kenneth went wild when he discovered there wasn't so much as a rowan sapling among them. Off he had gone to find one and plant it in the garden and without the bat of an eyelid had told his neighbours that now his house was safe from witches and all manner of evil things. The young rowan grew up in a walled garden full of roses and wild honeysuckle that filled the clean air of summer with a fragrance that was almost divine.

The road to the farm went along between hedges of broom and hawthorn and went twisting round to a rickety wooden bridge over the burn. It was said that the Witch o' Knobblieknowe lurked here in the shadows of gloaming. Even in broad daylight Eveylyn felt a catch of fear in her throat as she sped between the bushes, putting as much distance as possible between herself and the bridge and wishing that Kenneth Mor had planted a couple of rowans there in order to keep evil creatures at bay.

But there was nothing ghostlike or frightening about Kenneth Cameron Mor. He was a fine big chiel, well over six feet tall with a head of curly red hair and a proud bristling fiery beard that hung over his sark to his great barrel of a chest. His eyes were the cool blue of a Highland loch, filled with a dangerous fire if he was riled in any way. His fine, high-bridged nose had a wee bit of a twist to it as befitted his surname which was Camshron in Gaelic and meant crooked nose.

Evelyn's older sister Murn had had a terrible passion for Kenneth Mor from the first minute she clapped eyes on him. But he was besotted with his bonny Jeannie and had eyes for no one but her. Nellie, the eldest Grant girl, was disgusted at her sister for so openly displaying her feelings.

'You have no right to look that way at a married man,' she told Murn sternly. 'Kenneth Mor is too full o' his own importance to be aware that the likes o' yourself even exists so it's no good your making your sheep's eyes at him.'

Nellie was always being shocked by the things that other people did. Mostly she was shocked at her younger sister Mary who shared a room with her and who jumped out of bed each morning to strip and wash her entire body in cold water from the ewer on the dressing table.

Evelyn had witnessed these punishing douses several times and had ceased to be amazed at the sight of Mary's full breasts glowing pink from brisk washing, had ceased even to wonder at the thick tufts of dark hair sprouting luxuriantly from between Mary's legs.

'Ach, it's only a dowp,' Mary would giggle as Nellie tushed and tutted and turned her crimson face away. 'If you

33

dared to look inside your own breeks you would see the exact same thing, Nellie Grant.'

'Wash your mouth out with soap, Mary!' a scandalized Nellie would flutter, her face twisted in a kind of agony. 'How you can go to kirk on the Sabbath and sit there looking all prim and proper is beyond me.'

Mary could never resist rising to such bait. Her dimples would flash, her dark eyes glint roguishly as she giggled, 'I'm sure a clean dowp sitting on the pews o' the kirk is far more welcome than one which never sees the light o' day. Cleanliness is next to Godliness, just you remember that, Nell. If you don't change those queer spinsterish ways o' yours you will never get a lad to touch any bit o' your body and just think what you would be missing.'

'You're – you're coarse, Mary, no fit to be a daughter o' this house,' Nellie would fling at her sister before flouncing out of the room.

Evelyn watched Kenneth Mor, striding round the kitchen, blasting away at the pipes, his red beard burnished in lamplight, his great booming laugh bursting out of his lungs, his kilt swinging round his hairy knees as he marched up and down, pausing every so often to cuddle Jeannie who blushed as usual and buried her face into the warm layers of fat round wee Callum's neck. Jeannie was as little as Kenneth was big; a tiny, dainty slip of a girl, just eighteen, and so in love with her husband he could never tease her without the crimson staining her soft white cheeks. Her hair was as black as night, a sheaf of silk curling about her shell-like ears and billowing round her slender shoulders like a gossamer curtain.

Murn, jammed into a corner beside Danny the Fist who was playing a Jew's harp as if his life depended on it, couldn't suppress a great pang of jealousy as she watched the exchanges between Kenneth Mor and his young wife.

Kirsty Keith was, as usual, engaged in a verbal battle with Betsy O'Neil whose dark eyes were alive with mischief for she liked nothing better than a wrangle with the sour, wiry mistress of Dippiedoon. Yet they were the best of friends and were always popping into one another's houses for a cup of tea and a blether.

Beside them, little Bunty Lovie watched proceedings with interest, her bird-bright eyes roving ferret-like round the room, not missing a trick. Rob Burns of Birkiebrae, with his devastating good looks, was the focus for quite a few hungry female eyes. Rob had spent most of his life at sea and had often been away from home for days on end leaving his children to be looked after by a semi-invalid wife. The doctor had blamed her arthritic condition on the damp harbour house and so they had moved to the lands of Rothiedrum to rent Birkiebrae which consisted of a big, douce looking house with fine steadings and good fields for barley and corn. To reach Birkiebrae you had to go through a wicket onto a rough track that climbed the hill for a mile through thickets of broom and whin to a reed fringed lochan set in a bowl in the hills.

To this place came Rob Burns, black-mooded and resentful of the sickly wife who had brought him to this god-forsaken place where the distant sea could only be glimpsed if you strained your eyes back over the plains of Rothiedrum. He was big muscled and huge, with fair Nordic colouring and eyes like blue ice. His wife, Catherine Meiklejohn of Braemar, had been a bonny bright lass in her day, but now he had no time for the wan, wishy-washy woman who was wont to lie back and let her ills rule her.

Rob had come from farming stock and he had tried to settle down and make a go of Birkiebrae, working the land with the same sort of vigour he had once applied to fishing. In time the farm came to be one of the best kept for miles around, but Rob never lost his resentment of the ties it had over him.

Always one for a good dram he now took to the bottle with a vengeance, never seeming the worse for it except in temper which he took out on anyone who happened to get in his way. Never with his children though. He loved his bairns did Rob, and lavished them with all sorts of little indulgences. Only with Johnny, his eldest son, was he hard, making him do the same kind of work as the orra loon –

the spare lad – but never teaching him the craft that Johnny pined to be most, to learn to be a ploughman and getting to know how to work with horses which he loved. He itched to get his hands on a plough but Rob would only let him lead horses in the field and in time Johnny came to believe that his father saw him as a potential usurper, for Rob's prowess with horses had fast become legendary though he got the beasts to bend to his will more by brute force than by kindliness.

At one time Johnny had worshipped his big, strong father, but the older he got the clearer his vision became and now threads of contempt were woven into the many emotions Rob wrought in him.

Darkly he watched his father flirting with pretty wee Annie McPherson, Knobblieknowe's kitchen maid, and he thought about his mother lying pale and wan on the couch at home, her eyes following Rob as he washed in readiness for the ceilidh. Johnny had looked forward to this night for weeks but he couldn't help feeling guilty every time he thought about his mother left behind at home with the wee ones who always seemed to take advantage of her when their father wasn't around.

Yet running parallel with those feelings were those others that he tried to push down but which more than ever lately kept coming to the surface. Dark, hateful emotions that seemed to tear the veils of childhood from his eyes and allow him to see his mother for what she really was, a hypochondriac woman who could have made her own and everyone else's lives bearable if only she would try harder. He resented her for leaning on him, for making him nursemaid and guardian to the younger ones when deep down he knew she was perfectly capable of seeing to them herself. He sensed that she was pushing them all to the limits, trying to see how far she could go, how much she could get away with before something or somebody snapped. He had seen her looking at his father in a strange sort of way, with a deep yearning burning in her eyes that he couldn't fathom for she had, of her own choosing, slept alone since the birth of her last child, so he thought, wriggling inside of himself with embarrassment, it couldn't be *that* which made her look so longingly at Rob.

Johnny hated himself when he thought such thoughts about his mother and to make up for such disloyalties he was always specially kind to her afterwards when she would start to take advantage of his good nature again and so it went on, till he felt an invisible net growing tighter and tighter around him.

But that night at the ceilidh he shrugged off his gloom and laughed louder than anyone at the antics of Kenneth Mor and Jamie who had taken up his fiddle and was marching round the room behind Ken, playing it and jigging at the same time.

Florrie had been her usual rosy cheeked, mischievous self. She and Evelyn, together with Johnny and Alan Keith, had ended up under the kitchen table with a plate of buttered scones and a jug of creamy milk which they consumed while all around them the men downed steaming jugs of toddy and the women exchanged gossip and all the while the cats and dogs nosed round, mopping up crumbs and dribbles of whisky.

It was said that Kenneth Mor owned the only drunken sheepdogs in the whole of Rothiedrum and the only reason he got them so obedient to his whistle was because they were 'so leggless wi' the drink they were only too glad to get in among a flock o' yowes for the support they gave'.

But that was the envious tongues speaking, for Ken's dogs were the best for miles around and to compete with them at the trials was just a waste of time and breath.

A few of the fee'd men had come down from the bothy to join in the ceilidh and they played their wild fiddles and their melodeons with Jamie in their midst, his velvet eyes flashing fire in a combination of exuberance and a good few drams of the devil's brew.

From her seat in the ingle Maggie watched him with a certain amount of indulgence, for it wasn't often that he got the chance to enjoy himself so thoroughly, yet even so she sighed a little to herself and wished that he didn't enjoy drinking with such obvious abandon. Her face was pale that night, the flush on her cheeks owing itself to the heat from the fire. A niggle of pain tormented her innards but wasn't serious enough to cause alarm. She was bonny that night.

Jamie, glancing at her, felt a small tug of desire deep in his belly. He had never looked at another woman since Maggie's coming into his life. She had always satisfied him well enough; haughty and proud she might appear to others but he knew the warm, desiring woman that lay under the surface, knew the way her rounded limbs stirred in response to him. Her hair might be white now but her figure was that of a young woman, comely and firm, full of a passion that no one would have guessed at. She was wearing a woollen dress the colour of the heather braes. She had put on a little bit of weight he thought and wondered why he had never noticed it before. But then she was usually happed in shapeless aprons that very effectively hid what was underneath. Her eye caught his, and they threw each other an intimate smile while all around them the music flowed and Kenneth Mor danced with Jeannie, leaving the baby cuddled on Nellie's knee. She held him close to her, smelling the warmth of his soft hair and her features softened and became filled with a radiance that took away their harshness.

Peter Lamont, grieve to the Mains, sat down beside her, his breath warm on her face as he whispered, 'The babby looks right on you, Nellie, lass. Have you never thought o' havin' one o' your own?'

Peter was known as the Wolf o' Rothiedrum and had sent a few tearful young kitchenmaids on their sad, pregnant way, and Nellie didn't deign to answer, her lips folding in characterized disapproval as she edged away from him.

She was a strange girl was Nellie, a born spinster if ever there was one. Folk said she had been born old, for despite her youth, she was mature both in manner and appearance. Her features were angular and hard, yet her glinting fair hair belonged to a young woman and so too did that mouth of hers, large but well-shaped with a sensuousness about it that seemed to promise so much warmth and passion. But she had never shown the least inclination for a young man though her very quality of elusiveness excited not a few of the rich-blooded lads who came and went among the farmtouns.

Peter gave a soft mocking laugh at the haughty look on her face. 'Come on, Nell, let yourself go. There's a passionate woman under that coating of ice. I've always known it, Nell, it runs in that family o' yours. Look at your sister Mary flirting wi' the bothy lads and near driving them crazy. Ay, and Murn sitting there making sheep's eyes at Kenneth Mor. We all know what she would like and the same goes for you. Gie me half the chance and I'll have that prim wee dowp o' yours throbbing wi' wanting. You dinna ken what you're missing but I could show you if you gie me the chance.'

Without a word, Nellie rose, retrieved a jug of piping hot toddy from the hearth and turning she held her arm high and poured the contents of the jug all down the front of Peter's trousers. With a yelp he was up, dancing with pain and enraged shock, holding onto his injured parts, while he glared at her with undisguised hatred.

The room went into an uproar of laughter and no one heard his muttered threat to Nellie. 'I'll get you for this, you frozen-arsed bitch! It might take years, but I'll get you!'

Nellie walked away from him with her head held high to be apprehended by Kenneth Mor, kissing her on the cheek and telling her she was a damned vixen but by God! she knew how to look after herself.

Murn watched the exchange and wished she could do something as outrageous as Nellie in order to gain Kenneth's attentions. His flashing blue eyes swung in her direction but it was only to ask her to go ben the house to fetch another bottle of whisky from the larder. Murn went quickly through to the cold scullery to open the larder door and stand with her brow resting on the shelf. 'Oh, Ken, I love you so,' she whispered, 'and you dinna even see me half the time, yet you know Nellie's there, her wi' a heart in her as frozen and cold as Loch Bree in the clutches o' winter.'

From the kitchen Grace's crystal little voice floated, singing *Rowan Tree*. A few seconds later she was joined by her mother and all other voices fell silent for no sound was more captivating than the combined small sopranos of Maggie and her gentle Grace. Outside the cold panes of the scullery window the wind was rousing, scudding over the moors in all its relentless freedom. Murn raised her head and listened, feeling the bleak echoes of the cold December wind curling round her heart. A movement from the scullery door made her start and look round. Kenneth Mor's hearty voice preceded his entry into the small, confined space. 'Where are you wi' that whisky, lass? The lads out there are gey drouthy yet and the night is still young.'

Murn tried to compose herself. Kenneth's warm hard arm brushed against her breasts and she almost fainted with the shock and delight of that fleeting, accidental touch. He grinned down at her from his great height and laughed. He was being generous with his affections that night, so euphoric was he with his own sense of fulfilled happiness. Bending down his firm warm lips crushed hers briefly before he straightened up, his head almost touching the cramped ceiling of the tiny enclosure. 'There you are lass, a Christmas kiss in return for that bottle you're clutching in your bonny hands.'

Murn couldn't answer him. Her heart was hammering in her throat and even while she struggled to regain her breath she knew that what she had felt for him before was but a mere candle flame to what she felt now. That brief, careless kiss had kindled fires in her that totally consumed all reason. She wanted to tell him, wanted to impress upon him her feelings for him but she knew she never would. He would hate her for it and she couldn't bear the pain of his dislike. She would just have to be content with worshipping him from afar, watching him, waiting for the day when he might really begin to notice her as a woman and not as a silly, half-grown female who was scraggy and thin and who gaped at him as if she could eat him. One day he would look at her, one day . . .

He was eyeing her in some puzzlement. 'You're such a quiet lass, Murn, I never can fathom if you want to talk or run away. You're no' like your sister Mary in that respect, she never stops talking, and Nell for all her reserve is just a buggering wee vixen wi' sharpened claws and a tongue to match. You should have a lad, be a bit more like Mary. You're bonny enough.'

At nineteen Murn was bonny, as skinny as her sister Nellie, but a promise of softness in the coy, tender swelling of her breasts, in the shy burgeoning of her slender thighs. Her round, sweet face with its discontented mouth had a lost, sad look to it and she always gave the impression of being lonely, even when she was surrounded by people. She so obviously wore her heart on her sleeve for Kenneth Cameron Mor it was an embarrassment to her family and a continual thorn in Nellie's reserved side. From the start Murn had had ambitions for her life and had never been much use about the croft, preferring instead to sit about the house reading books even when the corn was ripe in the parks and everyone else out there cutting it. Perseverence rather than a glut of brains had won her a bursary at school and now she attended a college in Aberdeen, travelling there by train every morning, earning money for her expenses by stitching pieces of exquisite embroidery for the rich folk who lived in the numerous mansion houses in the area.

'I – I dinna want a lad,' she told Kenneth seriously. 'They're all so daft and gawky I canna be bothered wi' them.' She forced the words to come out, tried to still her trembling limbs. Outside the wind was rising and the next second it ripped a portion of cladding from the byre roof, sending it clattering and dangling along the close.

Ken's head jerked up. 'Did you hear that?' He raced to the door to open it and peer outside, leaving Murn cursing the intrusion into what had been the most intimate and precious moment of her young life. She heard him shouting to his men to come out with him to fix the roof.

When she got back to the kitchen he was standing in the middle of it, his red head thrown back as he laughed his deep, booming laugh and raising his glass toasted the devil winds o' cauld December whose powers were as naught compared to the fires o' hell in a glass of the bonny malt.

'Put on your coat, we're going home,' Nell greeted Murn, glancing at her sister's red face suspiciously. 'You were a long time wi' Kenneth Mor in the scullery. I hope you weren't being silly again.'

'You've a cheek to talk,' fumed Murn. 'What about you and Peter Lamont? Were you egging him on over in that corner? For all your talk about hating men you seemed to attract their attention well enough.'

'Ach, Murn, it's high time you grew up. Whenever you open your mouth you have nothing better to say than any school bairn.' Nellie tossed her head and flounced away, leaving Murn to put on her coat and to go to wait quietly by the door for the others.

Glowing from the heat of Knobblieknowe's kitchen and well happed up against the weather, the Grants took their leave of the warm, roistering hospitality of Kenneth Mor. By then the snow lay skin deep, fine and white, stretched out over the countryside like a thin layer of cotton wool. It gave off a strange eerie sense of light and distance that went on and on, over the parks and the shallow valleys, broken only by the endless drystone dykes and the black shadows of little woods. The bleak orderliness of the hedgerows marched up over hillocks and braes while tangles of broom shivered on the slate blue skyline. The still cold water of little pools lay undisturbed by the wind tearing over the moor. Bennachie rose up into a mist of snow and wisping yellow-blue cloud, her head buried in a gulping grey swirl, and away to the west, the Hill of Noth crouched like a great black lion through the mists of white.

Evelyn was not dismayed by the biting cold, rather she experienced a bursting sense of such joy she spread her arms and danced along, her boots kicking up snow too new and soft yet to scrunch underfoot. The wind whipped her fiery hair about her glowing face, her breath sang in her throat, heard only by her, the life and strength of it reaching deep down to some inner font that spurted forth and sped through her veins like the Birkie in full spate.

Up on the breast of the brae a herd of deer were flitting out from the trees, dark graceful silhouettes against a backcloth of shimmering white light. The sound of Kenneth Mor's pipes filtered down from the slopes and a Scottish melody burst clean and clear and thrilling upon that wide, white, glittering world, the throbbing passion of it dirling into Evelyn's awakened senses like some lone voice echoing back from the lost reaches of times long gone.

Her green eyes grew wide in a mingling of joy and poignancy, the raw, forgotten emotions of past ages came sharply home to her. She seemed to be looking at the present and into the past at the same time. Three of her sisters were walking together some way in front, behind them her parents plodded along, arm in arm, the quiet murmurings of their voices blending with the whispering of the wind and snow.

Grace was walking beside Evelyn, her face alabaster pale, as if it reflected the virgin landscape, her eyes, black as the sky, were fixed on the herd of deer moving out from the ridge of trees.

Evelyn saw it all, like some silent, beautiful tableau caught in a time warp and yet she felt as if she was being pulled backwards, through deep caverns of space and distance while voices of long ago seemed to whisper to her, borne on the crystal breath of the wind. She stood, immobile and entranced, staring into the bitter night, as if watching scenes from a forgotten age. The fountain within her still spurted but now the joy was replaced by a foreboding so deep she was filled with a dark sense of fear for things that had happened and were about to happen again.

She was warm no longer, the cold of the night curled into her bones and she shivered and gave a little whimper.

'Evie, what ails you?' Grace's voice at her side seemed to come from a long distance.

Everything that was before her vision splintered and shattered like brittle glass; the deer on the hillside scattered and ran; the skirl of the pipes faltered, grew silent; the bulk of Bennachie loomed out of the snowflakes, as if it had uprooted itself and was coming towards her. She felt stifled and terrified.

'Mam!' The name was torn from her lips, yet came out in the merest whisper. In front of her, her mother stumbled and let out an unearthly cry of agony. She bent over, clutching her stomach, one hand fluttering, reaching out to Jamie who instantly bent towards her, his arms tight around her, his voice filled with sudden dread as he asked, 'Maggie, are you ill? What's wrong? What's wrong, Maggie?'

'I dinna ken.' Her voice spurted from her gaping throat, ragged, unsteady. 'My stomach, a pain like a vice.'

Murn had gone on, a dark blob on the ever whitening track between the whins, but Mary and Nellie had halted and were looking back anxiously.

Grace and Evelyn ran forward, their slithering steps leaving ragged gashes in the snow. Evelyn stared at her mother's twisted face and felt the world spinning. Grace went to her mother's other side to put her arms round her in dumb support. Her face was a white blob but Evelyn saw her eyes, moist and wide with a strange kind of fear. Mary and Nellie came labouring back up the slope, their feet slipping and slithering. Everyone stood in a protective circle round Maggie while the wind keened low over the hill and spicules of frozen snow bombarded their exposed flesh.

After a while Maggie took a deep breath and straightened. 'I'm fine, I'm fine, I tell you,' she gasped rather impatiently for she was a woman in whom strength had been bred and who hated to display any sort of weakness in front of others, especially her daughters.

'We'll have you home in no time.' Jamie sounded breathless, as if he had been running and the girls knew he was more concerned than he was making out.

They moved off, keeping together on the track that ran

steeply from Knobblieknowe down to King's Croft. But they had only gone a quarter of a mile when Maggie doubled up again, this time for longer, her breath harsh and uneven, her little whimpers of distress filling the merciless night with dread.

Mary, her black eyes blacker still with uncertainty, lifted her own shawl from her shoulders and tucked it round her mother's. 'Should I go back and get Kenneth Mor to come down, Father?'

'Ay, ay,' Jamie nodded distractedly. 'And best bring Peter Lamont. The three o' us between us can get your mother back up there.'

'Indeed you'll do nothing o' the kind!' Maggie's protest came sharply. 'The last thing I need is three drunken gowks manhandling my person. We'll go down to our own house and under our own steam or my name is no' Margaret Innes Grant!'

And so they went on, through rising wind and blinding snow, a nightmare mile of slithering, freezing night with the tortured bushes throwing out cruel snagging arms that whipped at their legs and tore at their faces and every so often Maggie doubling up in pain till she seemed near to collapsing and would have done if her husband's strong arms hadn't been about her.

When they were but a few yards from the croft Murn announced her intention of going ahead to stir the fire to life and get her mother's bed warmed. 'You come wi' me, Evie,' she said, holding out her hand. 'It's high time you were in your bed.'

'Ay, go wi' your sister,' Jamie supplemented but Evelyn, weary beyond measure yet every nerve starkly on edge, stubbornly desisted and everyone was too worried and tired to force the issue. As Murn hurried away, Maggie stumbled and fell, too weak to get up at once. She sat where she was for a few minutes, getting back her breath then she allowed Jamie to help her to her feet and they moved slowly on.

It was then that Evelyn saw the sight that was to cause her torment for hours to come. The spot where her mother

45

had fallen was stained with red, looking for all the world like crimson cellophane paper pressed into the crumbled snow. Evelyn stood stock still while snowflakes clung to her lashes and the snarling wind whipped her shawl over her shoulders. Her frozen fingers tightened convulsively around the woollen layers at her neck, her numb lips moved but no words came.

The dark shadows that were her family went slowly on and still she couldn't move, couldn't follow. Mary half-turned and saw her little sister, a lone figure buffeted by the storm. She shouted something but the words were torn from her lips and hurled away over the fields.

She came stumbling back to where Evelyn stood, the words of rebuke dying in her throat when she saw what the child was staring at.

'Oh God,' the murmur of dismay came jerkily from her lips.

'Mary, what is it?' Evelyn asked even though she knew the answer. She looked up, her eyes deep pools in the white of her face.

Mary shivered and held out her hand. 'I dinna ken. Father's away down to hitch Fyvie to the gig and then he's away to fetch the doctor. You come wi' me and help us get Mam home.'

CHAPTER TWO

Murn had lit the lamps and stirred the fire to life, shadows of homely things leapt on the ceiling, the warmth and peace of King's Croft was a haven into which Maggie and her daughters dragged their icy feet, their faces white, haggard, afraid. Maggie sat down on the ingle by the fire, hunched up with pain and exhaustion, too weary to make the effort to remove her sodden outer layers. Her daughters gathered round her, chafing her blue hands, taking off her wet boots, setting her feet on a stool by the hearth.

Evelyn wanted to run to her mother and comfort her, but something that was beyond her understanding stayed her and she was glad when Mary picked up the lantern and went back outside. Evelyn followed her, feeling soothed by Mary's calm, reassuring presence as she made the rounds of byre and stable. Normally their father made the last round of the steadings, his stumpy Stonehaven pipe filled with a twist of Bogy roll tobacco clamped firmly between his teeth, his lantern glowing in the dark as he sauntered leisurely across the cobbles.

But tonight wasn't like any other night, tonight he was on the storm-bound turnpike with Fyvie the sheltie taking him on his errand of mercy.

She was glad to get into the byre, to be met by the welcoming warmth made by the breath of Dove and her calf Pinkie. Mostly the summer calves were sold at the autumn mart, but last year's harvest had been good enough to allow Jamie to decide that he had enough feed to see his beasts through the winter. The byre was always a comforting place to which Evelyn often came, sometimes just to be alone to think, sometimes to bring her diary and write into it all the little happenings that made up her day. The peace of the byre was broken only by the rhythmic crunch of turnips and the rattle of chains. Dove gave a gentle little bellow and glanced round, her limpid gaze following the progression of the lantern along the greep.

The stables were steamy and snug with Queenie and Nickum, the Clydesdale pair, peaceful and sleepy in their stalls. Unlike the winter-bed cows, the Clydes were seldom idle as ploughing could go on even when the fields were covered in snow. Not even Queenie, heavy with her spring foal, was allowed to be idle, as a good plough mare could carry her foal and still be yoked every morning ready for a full working day. Jamie fed his Clydes well, three times a day with bruised oats as a rule and crushed linseed cake and raw, whole turnips. If he ran out of neeps, Kenneth Mor could always be relied on to sell him enough to keep him going through the winter.

If it hadn't been for Miss Beattie there would have been no Clydesdale pair for the meagre return of the croft could never have allowed for such an indulgence. On her death some years before, the old lady had bequeathed a small legacy to Maggie with the instructions that it was to be spent on something that would make her life easier. Almost immediately Maggie had purchased a pedigree Clydesdale pair knowing how much Jamie had longed for good plough horses that would almost certainly ease the burden the land imposed upon him.

The benefits of having such beasts came to her in an indirect fashion but it was enough for her to see some of the weariness erased from her husband's face, to observe a spring in his step that had been missing since those blithe, early days of their marriage and she blessed Miss Beattie, the dear old ogre, with a heart of gold whom she had only visited but once since her marriage but whom she had never forgotten.

In the stall next to Nickum, Swack, the extra horse, stood patiently and a little dejectedly, as if she was aware that her standing never quite matched up to Queenie and the lead horse, Nickum, and Evelyn gave her a small extra helping of oat-straw and kissed her velvety nose lovingly. She had ridden the broad backs of the Clydes before she

48

could walk properly, her father lifting her up onto a gelding that could stand a bit over sixteen hands, and leading it over the fields with his small daughter chuckling with joy from her great height.

The hens were blinking and clucking in annoyance from their roosts and Tappit, the best clockin' hen ever to have hatched at King's Croft, fluttered her wings and let out a raucous crow that could have come straight from the throat of a boasting cockerel, a sound that always made Jamie scratch his head and wonder a bit about Tappit's gender. From the loft chaumer, the bothy where the fee'd men had their sleeping quarters, a sleepy voice came floating down. 'What's to do down there? I'm tired and I'm buggered and needin' my sleep.'

'It's only us,' Mary called up, lifting her lantern high as Billy, the orra loon put his feet on the rickety wooden stairs set into a corner of the stable. An orra loon was about the only fee'd help that Jamie could ever afford to hire. Some of the bigger farms had several horsemen or ploughmen as well as a stockman and an orra loon, but Jamie's forty or so acres couldn't support too many hired hands and so he himself was the horseman and the stockman combined. That was why in spring he was only too glad to have his daughters help him in the fields, though he was hard put to ignore the sly sneering of his neighbours who hinted that a man worth his salt wouldn't have woman doing a man's work.

Billy was a big, strapping lad of sixteen or so, gley-eyed and slightly vacant looking, but his strength and willingness more than made up for his lack of good looks which were never counted as much of an asset in the hard life of the farmtouns anyway.

'Go back to bed, Billy,' called Mary softly. 'Father is busy tonight so me and Evie are making the rounds.'

'Aye, well leave the horses be,' grumbled Billy who was fast seeing himself in a horseman's role though he had learnt what he had about the beasts from Jamie who, other than Rob Burns, was reckoned to be the best man with a horse for miles around.

49

'He's getting to be too big for his boots, that one,' said Mary as they made their way out into the frosty night. 'It would do him good to have some older men around him to keep him in his place.'

'Ach, maybe he's gets lonely up there in the chaumer all by himself,' said Evelyn thoughtfully, her heart soft for Billy who always let her in among the horses even when he was busy in the morning getting them fed and yoked. 'I like him fine. Sometimes I go up in the loft with him and he tells me stories about some o' the other places he's worked to. His first fee was up at Mains of Strummie and the men there covered him in dung and rolled him in feathers just because he broke the cut-throat razor that belonged to the second horseman.'

'Life can be gey chancy for these lads,' admitted Mary as they made their way back over the cobbles. 'But still, an orra loon should know his place and it wouldna do Billy any harm to be taken down a peg or two.'

When they got inside Murn was taking the kettle from the fire to fill two 'pigs,' large whisky jars with corks that served well the purpose of warming winter beds, while Nellie set the teapot to warm on the trivet then went ben the scullery to fetch the cups.

Maggie took the tea gratefully, warming her hands on the cup as she drank. The proud arrogance was still there in the deathly pallor of her face but there was a strange look in her eyes, a puzzlement mingling with apprehension.

Nobody spoke or looked at each other. Outside, the wind shrieked, the snow whirled, heavier and heavier. Maggie was resting peacefully enough, her gaze fixed unseeingly on the leaping fire, then suddenly she stiffened and gave a stifled cry, her body thrown back rigidly against the high, wooden back of the ingle.

Evelyn, on the cheekstone by the fire, felt her own body tensing and her grip on Glab, the old retired sheepdog, tightened so drastically he was moved to groan in protest. She saw Nellie and Murn exchange meaningful, disbelieving glances. Nellie's sharply honed face was crimson and wore the same embarrassed look as when the farm beasts were mating and the men standing about watching and winking rudely at her.

Grace was paler than usual, her dark, liquid gaze fixed on her mother's face with a foreboding that seemed to the watching Evelyn to be charged with a thousand unasked questions. She sensed that they all knew something she didn't, that they had seen their mother like this before but couldn't quite believe it was happening again.

'Mary,' Maggie gasped out the name of the daughter she most often turned to for cheery, down to earth comfort.

'Ay, Mam?'

'Go you and fetch Hinney.'

'Hinney!' The elder girls spoke the name in unison, as if they still didn't believe the things their eyes were telling them.

'Ay, Hinney.' Maggie's voice held a note of its old command. She struggled to sit up and in doing so the lamplight caught and shimmered on the white of her hair, giving emphasis to her maturity, giving her daughters further cause to disbelieve the thing that was happening.

Nellie's face seemed to have aged in the last few minutes. It was more sharply angular than ever, twin spots of colour burned high on each cheekbone.

'Mother, it canna be!' she said sharply, in her agitation reverting to the more formal address she had been wont to use as she got older but which she often found hard to maintain when all around her the more affectionate term of 'Mam' was used. 'You're – you're past the age for all that!'

'Hold your tongue, my girl.' Maggie lashed back. 'Do you think I dinna ken that myself?' The anger left her and she sank back once more, a lost, hopeless look about her as she murmured almost to herself. 'It canna be, I know that – there was nothing to tell me – nothing –'

The knuckles of her hands showed white as she gripped the arms of the chair in a spasm of pain. Mary was struggling once more into her outdoor things, shoving her feet into wet boots and pulling her damp shawl over her black hair. 'I'll no' be long, Mam,' she threw the words

51

over her shoulder as she went to the door. 'Maybe Father and the doctor will be here when I get back.' A cloud of snowflakes whirled into the room as she let herself into the hostile night once more.

Nellie stood in the middle of the room, rigid disapproval in every line of her tall, spare figure. For once she seemed at a loss, uncertain of what her next move should be and it was Grace who bent to put her arms gently round her mother's waist. 'Come on, Mam, we'll get you up to bed. Murn has it all nice and warm. The fire is lit and the sheets laid out ready.'

Maggie allowed herself to be helped to her feet. Clinging on to Murn and Grace for support she went slowly out of the room.

Evelyn didn't dare ask Nellie anything, her mind too taken up with thoughts of Hinney, otherwise Hannah Campbell, who lived with her husband Alastair at Hill o' Binney croft one and a half miles east of the road end from King's Croft.

Alastair was a wee wizened crone of a man with a droll face, a bundle of white hair, specs on the end of his nose and a toothless blubber of a mouth. To the children of Rothiedrum he was a perfect match for Hinney who was a small, bent woman with glittering green eyes, blood red hair and a warty nose. In her garden she cultivated herbs which she used in all sorts of potions. She also encouraged weeds to flourish in a patch of ground near the dung midden in an attempt to attract as many varieties of butterflies as she could so that she could study them with a sort of fiendishly delighted enthusiasm.

The children called her the Wee, Wee, Witch Wifie. When they had to pass Hill o' Binney Croft they crept along under cover of dykes and hedges and once safely by they would giggle nervously and dare each other to go into her garden and take some of the herbs they were certain she used to make devilish brews in a big, three-legged iron pot which sat by her door. Hinney's talents were wide and varied. As well as being an excellent gardener, cook and brewer of basic homeopathic medicines, she was also a dab hand at midwifery and it was for Hinney the farm wives sent when they were in labour. She and Alastair had no family left at home though she had birthed nine in her day, every one surviving to strong, robust adulthood with a lust for travel that had taken them far beyond the lands of the north east.

Evelyn sat on the cheekstone and despite the heat from the fire shivered at the idea of Hinney coming to King's Croft at this time of night. It was different during the day when everything was safe and normal and her mother was there to see to things. Maggie liked nothing better than to go over to Hill o' Binney to blether with the old couple and jot down recipes for scones and cakes, and Hinney was forever sprachling down to see Maggie and giggle over some latest gossip about the gentry. But now night shadows were everywhere and Maggie was too ill to be bothered with the fancies of her youngest child. And so Evelyn anticipated the advent of the old woman in a mixture of shivering fear and delight, for in her heart of hearts she knew fine that Hinney was no witch but a homely old soul who happened to be endowed with a few witchlike characteristics.

'Evie, go you up to bed.' Nellie's order came imperiously. Evelyn knew better than to argue with her. Now she lay, her heartbeat drumming in her ears, listening to the sounds of her mother's pain from the room next to that of Nellie and Murn.

A mouse ran across the rafters overhead, squeaking as it went, the tiny, lost sound of a little creature haunting the night.

'Poor wee cowrin' tim'rous beastie . . .' The voice of Mr Gregory dirled into her weary brain and wouldn't go away. Outside her window the storm lashed, beat ferociously at the walls, the cowlings rattled, monotonously and insistently. Despite the heap of blankets her body was cold, her feet like lumps of ice. She pressed her head into her pillow, trying to shut out the alien sounds that invaded the house. Drawing her knees up to her chin she lay for another few minutes, then unable to bear her misery a moment longer she sat up and carefully lit the candle on the table at her bed. Her hand slid under the pillow to retrieve her diary and in it she began to write, stiffly and without enthusiasm. She had started to keep a diary from the day she learned to write, jotting down in it all the little incidents that were of importance to her. It wasn't a proper diary, just a thick, dog-eared notebook with her own handpainted flowers and birds on the front cover. She bit into the end of her pencil, not knowing what to write, everything was so uncertain just then and she was too restless to think straight.

Leaving the book aside she threw back the blankets and padded over to the window. The raw cold seeped through her nightdress, blew on her ears through chinks in the sash. She wiped away the steam from the panes and pressed her face against the glass. Clouds were breaking over the cold Grampian peaks, a dazzling moon rode swiftly in and out of mist vapours. The plains of Rothiedrum were bathed in an ethereal blue glow, the burns frothed down, mercurial, meandering, slashing silver pathways through the tracts of virgin snow. Up at the edge of the corn fields the plough sat crouched in the furrow, breast and share locked in the hoary ground, the rest of it black and stark like the bare bones of some dead creature. Snow was still sweeping over the countryside, tossed down from masses of thick yellow clouds rolling over the sky, the edges of them silvered by the fickle moonlight. It was cold and desolate and bare, yet the stark beauty of it plucked at her heart. The certainty of the seasons was always a solace to her. With her eyes she traced the black branches of the trees standing stark against the winter white, and away over yonder, on the rise of the fields, the tips of the branches touched the frosty stars and made cobwebby patterns against the bright face of the moon.

Three quarters of a mile away the white cold was suddenly pierced by a pin prick of light and she knew that Alan Keith of Dippiedoon was unable to sleep again and had lit his paraffin lamp to draw his pictures by. A slim, gentle lad was Alan, with rusty gold hair and big blue eyes

54

set wide in a face that was as bonny as a girl's. Artistic, long fingers he had, never made for the plough but for the brush and pencil. His paintings and drawings were a marvel. Mr Gregory gave him great encouragement and the walls of the classroom were decorated with Alan Keith's efforts. Just a pity it was that Kirsty Keith made such a broody fuss of his work in front of all and sundry so that strange, sensitive Alan took to being secretive about his talents and preferred to do his drawings in the privacy of his cold attic room rather than at the warm kitchen table with all the family seated round.

He had been at Knobblieknowe's ceilidh and must be dead beat with tiredness yet the drive in him that often gave him a feverish look hadn't allowed him to rest, and no doubt he had rushed up to bed the minute he got home in order to get some new and exciting idea on to paper.

The small needle point of light all at once emphasized the cold desolation of the night and Evelyn drew the collar of her nightgown about her ears and shivered. If only Grace would come up and tell her what was happening, but since the arrival of Hinney and Dr McGregor not a soul had come near. There had been plenty of footfalls up and down the stairs and once she heard her father stopping at her door. For a long time he had stayed there and she knew he was listening for a sign from within, a small voice telling him to come in. Yet no words could she utter though she had sorely needed the comfort of his arms around her. For the first time in her life she knew she couldn't speak to him, for in some strange way she knew that her mother's pain owed itself to him yet she couldn't begin to visualize what it was he had done. Perhaps it had something to do with Nellie's tight-lipped look when his bedroom door was ajar and they glimpsed him taking Maggie into his arms and cuddling her till she protested and pushed away.

At first Evelyn couldn't see a thing wrong with that. He cuddled her in the same way and made her giggle the way her mother sometimes giggled when he whispered nonsense in her ears. Gradually she had come to know that Nellie's most disapproving looks were brought about by the way men and women behaved when they thought no one was looking. The kitchen maids at Mains of Rothiedrum were forever giggling behind the doors of the haysheds and ten to one they weren't laughing to themselves but at something Peter Lamont was doing to them. Other than kissing and cuddling Evelyn had no idea what went beyond, but Nellie knew and so too did Grace who was seldom angry, yet went into a fair tizzy when Evelyn asked her why their father often made strange groaning noises in the night, yet had been in the best of health when he went to bed.

The brittle cold of the dark room enshrouded Evelyn till she could stand it no longer. Going to the door, she opened it a crack and looked out. A lamp on the kist near her parents' door was making flapping phantoms dance on the ceiling while the further corners were cast into mysterious darkness. She flew down the stairs as if all the witches in hell were at her heels and into the kitchen to shut the door and stand with her back to it as if keeping at bay all those weird spooks who wandered the dark lands at night.

Grace was at the table, washing stained towels in a bowl of soapy water. She barely looked up at Evelyn's entry. All night long the door had opened and shut and she was so burdened with weariness it was almost beyond her to remain on her feet. 'Grace, tell me what's happening,' whispered Evelyn, putting her cold fingers to her mouth.

Grace tucked away a coil of hair with a wet finger. She was a beautiful, sweet-natured girl of sixteen, dark-chestnut hair waving softly about her face, her great dark eyes filled with a luminous bright light. All animals loved and trusted Grace, from the great plodding Clydes to the tiniest harvest mouse cowering in abject terror from the lusty swing of the scythe. Grace didn't think it amazing that wild birds came to eat from her hand or that half-wild farm kittens allowed her to handle them when they would have torn the eyes out of anyone else.

Grace attended the same school as Evelyn. Her ambition to be a nurse firmly fixed in her mind, she read every medical book she could get her hands on and often worried Maggie by appearing white faced and drawn at the breakfast table, having read half the night away by the light of a candle.

'I've got to learn, Mam,' was all she would say in answer to her mother's anxious scoldings and Maggie would look at her delicate, lovely daughter and think to herself it was Grace who would need the nursing if she carried on as she was doing.

Coming forward she took her sister's frozen small hands and led her to the fire.

'You're as cold as death, what on earth have you been doing?' Grace's voice was dull and flat as she sat Evelyn down by the fire and threw a shawl around her shoulders. Evelyn looked up and saw the pallor on the creamy skin and the purple shadows under the great dark eyes.

'I couldna sleep, Grace, I heard Mam moaning and everyone clumping up and down stairs. Hinney has feet on her like that cuddy she dotes on, she sounded as if she was wearing tackity boots.'

A smile curved Grace's mouth. 'That was Doctor McGregor. You would have been wearing heavy boots too if you'd had to climb out of drifts up to your lugs.'

'The kitchen is awful empty. Where is everybody?'

'Murn went away to bed hours ago, you know how she needs her sleep and her having to be away early to catch the train. The college is shut for the holidays but she left some books wi' a friend and wants to get them to study a bit over Christmas.'

'She'll never make it to the station,' snorted Evelyn. 'And how could she sleep knowing Mam is ill?'

'Murn could aye sleep through anything.' Grace said quietly though anger burned inside her for the sister, who, of them all, had the least compassion. Not even Nellie, for all her hard, unyielding ways, could turn her back on anyone in distress, far less her own mother whom she worshipped in her own undemonstrative way. 'Mary is ben the parlour setting the table for the doctor's breakfast, Nellie's up wi' Mam and the others. Father's been down

57

here wi' me most of the night but the doctor sent for him just a wee while ago.'

'Couldna the doctor have had his breakfast in here? It's warmer than that stuffed-up old parlour.'

'Ach well, you know how Mam likes things to be done right, just because she's ill doesna mean we've got to be slovenly.'

'Why is Mam so ill?' asked Evelyn in a whisper charged with terrible urgency.

Before Grace could speak a terrible cry from upstairs ripped the night apart and both sisters were silent, each tilting her head upwards to the source of the sound which now faded away like a ghost in the night leaving only its terrifying echoes inside Evelyn's head.

For a long time they sat, one on each cheekstone at opposite sides of the fire. Evelyn stared at her sister's long, slender fingers clasped one over the other, the taut knuckles bluey-white under skin roughened and red from washing and cooking. Oh, she was bonny, so bonny was Grace, with her young sad face and her cloud of shimmering hair swept back over a forehead that seemed honed from marble. The skin on her face and neck was a creamy white and so ought her hands to have been. A sadness enveloped Evelyn for a gentle sister like Grace who should have been born to fine jewellery upon the curve of her breast instead of the tiny cameo brooch she always wore pinned at her throat. Her shadow cavorted on the wall behind her like a spook at play, and Evelyn concentrated hard on it, not wanting to think of the other things that were happening at King's Croft that long, seemingly endless night.

From upstairs there came a feeling of movement, a strange imperceptible lightening of the whole atmosphere. A door opened, footsteps clattered on the stairs, the kitchen door was throw open and Doctor McGregor came into the room, going straight to the fire to throw himself down on a chair.

'Whisky.' He said the word imperatively, and Grace, thinking it was for her mother, went to fetch the Ne'erday bottle from the pantry. The doctor seized the glass and the proffered bottle uncorked it and poured a good stiff dram which he raised to his lips and downed in one gulp.

'I needed that.' He wiped the back of his hand over his mouth and sank back into the chair, 'It's been a long night and a tough one. I'm wabbit, as Hinney would say.'

Evelyn noticed that his long clever fingers were trembling slightly, that his dark brown eyes were heavy with weariness. He was young, was Doctor Gregor McGregor, near thirty maybe, tall and thin with the head of a boy and the wide, strong, sensual mouth of a man. He had just recently come to the area, taking over from old Doc McCrone who had retired to a cottage in Braemar. Doctor McGregor had taken up residence in the rambling, friendly old house about half a mile down the turnpike, just past old Carnallachie's place. A few months only he had been at Rothiedrum but already the folk had gotten over their usual suspicion of a stranger, some even going as far as calling him by his first name. He came from Glasgow and spoke with a bit of a burr that was comforting to the ear. No wife did he have and the amount of healthy young maidens who suddenly found need to visit his surgery was the talk of the place. His speedy consumption of the whisky had made Grace look at him in some astonishment. She turned and caught Evelyn's eye, and both girls burst out laughing for there was a twinkle in his eye that must mean everything upstairs was alright.

Slapping his knee he chuckled as if at some private joke and said to Grace, 'What do you think of that mother o' yours, eh? Thinking she was past having bairns then this – a baby clean out of the blue. She didn't even know she was carrying, would you credit that, Grace, my lassie?'

Grace, coy as yet about the facts of life, cast down her eyes and blushed. Beneath her lashes she keeked over at Evelyn who was agog to hear more but too respectful of the doctor to ask. But he had caught Grace's look and smiled, his eyes crinkling in that nice friendly way they had. 'The bairn doesn't know what's going on, eh?'

Grace looked as if she wasn't too sure either but was

59

saved further embarrassment by Mary's entry together with Jamie who was moving as a man in a trance, his eyes glazed with tiredness and heavy with shock. The doctor sat him by the fire and stuck a glass of whisky into his hand but for once he just sat staring at it as the firelight played on the glass, turning the contents to gold.

'Swallow it down, man,' ordered the doctor. 'It's what you need, doctor's orders.'

Jamie swallowed obediently, coughed, spluttered, lay back with a huge expressive sigh.

The doctor looked at the three girls ranged round the hearth. 'Since your father is in no fit state to break the news I'd better. You have a wee brother, not much more than five pounds at a guess. A mite if ever I saw one. Your mother has come through it well, tired as a ploughman but a good rest will see her fine.'

Grace glanced over at her father, remembering his sadness when his twin sons had died. She had only been four years old then but the tangible sadness of both her parents had never left her. Jamie King Grant had needed boys. If the twins had lived it would have meant another two pairs of hands to do man's work – now, when it had seemed all hope of that was past, there was another son and a dawning of a great rejoicing flooded her heart.

Going to her father she knelt by his chair and put her arms round him. A glaze of tears came to his eyes as he gazed down at the bonny face of this gentle daughter whose sweetness and understanding never failed to move him. 'Ay, lass, I ken fine how you feel,' he said huskily as he stroked her silky hair. 'Just bide by me for a wee whilie – I dinna ken if I'm coming or going.'

His eyes sought out the child who until that strange unreal night had been his youngest. She had come after the twins and was his seventh child, his baby, the one of all his daughters most like himself. There was in her a wildness, a carefree abandon that reminded him of the old days, of gypsy fiddles, and gypsy fires when the moon had sailed high in the heavens and young girls danced in bare feet and laughed to the stars. He knew that his gypsy blood ran free

60

in Evelyn's veins. There was an untamed quality about her, a restless vitality that reminded him of himself as a child. She had Maggie's hair, long, rich, red, flowing down her back to her waist, her eyes were a flashing green, her skin tanned and glowing, bathed as it had been from babyhood with generous helpings of clean, healthy fresh air. But now she looked stricken, her eyes dark and enormous in the sweet pallor of her face, its paleness emphasized by her fiery hair.

He put out a hand to her and she came, half-shy, and when she was near enough he gathered her to his breast and kissed the top of her head. 'You're still my babby, the wee one won't change anything that is between you and me.' His hair tickled her nose. He smelled of soap and disinfectant and something else – the something that was the man of him. It had always been there but tonight it was stronger, a subtle odour of strength and life. He sat in his chair, bewildered, spent, needing only comfort and rest, yet the power that was the man of him strained out of every sinew in his lean, rangy body. She drew away from him, unable to meet his eyes.

'Can I go up and see Mam?' she asked, sensing his hurt at her rejection of him.

He twisted in his chair, seeking the doctor's permission. He was standing in a shadowed corner of the room, just standing beside Mary whose youth and vivacity were still apparent even after a harrowing, wakeful night. She looked vibrant, red roses bloomed in the brown gloss of her cheeks, her eyes were glowing, filled with a strange light that made her appear almost feverish. Mary was small-boned and sweet with a figure that had been full since the age of fourteen. She stood lightly beside the doctor, her head barely reaching his shoulders, not touching him in any way, yet Evelyn sensed the same man power in him that she had just felt so strong in her father. It was as if he was more alive, more aware of life than he had been just a few minutes ago.

'Ay, away you go up, Evie.' His voice was low, soft, a caress in it that Evelyn knew wasn't for her. 'Only for a wee keek at the baby, mind. If your mother's asleep you mustna waken her.'

As she went out of the room Evelyn felt different from the child who had come into it a few hours ago. She felt taller; there was within her a trembling sense of the strangeness of things, of being out of control of everything that had been under her command before.

Nellie was coming downstairs towards her, a spare shape that loomed closer and closer till her face was clearly visible by the lamp she carried. A desperate kind of tiredness was in her odd, rather beautiful, amber-green eyes but Evelyn saw with surprise a softness lying over the angular planes of her face, a smile hovering at the corners of her wide, sensual mouth. Without a word she set the lamp down and gathered Evelyn to her bosom. It was surprisingly soft. Evelyn had always imagined it to be as bony as the rest of her yet the feel of it stirred in her some faraway, half forgotten memories. The kinds of frocks she wore, the bodices severely tight, buttoned always to the neck, were wont to hide feminine curves. She stroked Evelyn's hair and kissed her on the cheek. Her mouth was soft, yielding, not like the hardness of waxed string as Evelyn had imagined.

'I thought you were in bed,' she murmured, so close against Evelyn's ear it made her shiver.

'I couldna sleep so I got up and went down to sit with Grace.'

Nellie rocked her, she felt oddly soothed and comforted. 'Murn's the only one among us who would sleep on such a night.' A familiar note of hardness grated in Nellie's throat but softened again as she went on, 'Oh, Evie, babby, – we have a wee brother. I never thought there would be another to cuddle when you grew out of babyhood.'

This was a revelation to Evelyn, yet those long-buried memories tugged at her till she realized that the gentle loving arms that had held her in babyhood hadn't always belonged to her mother. 'Did you really cuddle me, Nellie? Do you really like babies?'

'Oh, ay, they're so wee and soft and innocent. I was mad

when you grew up and I couldna rock you on my knee any more or wash your smooth wee body in the bath.'

'Why don't you marry and have some of your own?'

Nellie bristled perceptibly. 'Hold your tongue, you nosy wee bitch.' She stood up, pushing her little sister away and she was the Nellie of old, hard, untouchable. 'Away you back to your bed now and just be thankful you're the only one among us able to get a bit o' rest. It's morning and work to be done as usual about the croft. There's the kie to milk, Mother to see to, forbye a new bairn wi' no' a decent wee cloot to his name.'

Evelyn's chin jutted. 'The doctor says I can go and keek at the baby.'

'Did he now? Well, I'll come wi' you and see you don't waken Mother.'

'I can go by myself – I'm a big girl now, Nellie.'

Nellie looked down at her. 'Ay,' she said and her voice had once more lost its harshness. 'You are, aren't you? Away you go ben then, but only for a wee while.'

Evelyn stole silently along to her mother's room to open the door softly. The familiar room seemed all at once different. Mystery and dreams lay soft in the shadows, lit only by firelight which embraced the warm darkness. Raspings of powdery snow sighed against the window panes, but that was all there was to tell of the wild, relentless night. Heavy, thick drapes shut away everything that was alien and made the room a cosy haven which nothing inhospitable could penetrate. Hinney was half asleep by the fire, her black, spindly legs spread wide to the heat, her head lolling on her well happed bosom, her specs swinging gently on the end of her nose.

Evelyn drew in her breath and tip-toed over to the bed. Her mother was fast asleep, lines of exhaustion lying stark across her noble face, her waist-length hair tumbled in silvery strands over the pillow. Evelyn looked at her hands resting on the patchwork quilt. Despite their roughness, they looked frail; a fretwork of purple veins stood out on the backs of them. A feeling of such love overwhelmed Evelyn that she wanted to reach out and gather her lovely

63

strong, proud mother into her young arms – yet she couldn't help thinking that her mother looked neither strong nor proud as she lay there in the exhausted aftermath of childbirth. She looked frail – and – and – old.

She could almost hear the taunts at school. 'Fancy a granny birthing a bairn!' She felt ashamed already and more ashamed still at the idea of thinking such thoughts about her very own mother. She bit her lip and forced herself to look at the small white cocoon at her mother's side. It moved and her heart raced. It was true – after all it was true. There was a baby, a little boy and because of it she was no longer the baby of the family. With quick decision she reached out and drew back the shawl to gape at a cloud of jet black hair above a tiny puckered red face. It looked exactly like one of the wizened little gnomes in the picture book she had had as a very young child. So *that* was what all the fuss was about? A wee wizened old man of a thing with an ugly, gumsy mouth and a tiny, delicate nose. Pushing the shawl back she turned away in disgust just as Hinney grunted and peered through her specs.

'Is that you, Evie?' she hissed and the child hesitated only fractionally before moving away from the shadowed bed to go over to the fire. The old lady smiled at her, a smile that transformed her from a witch into a nice, kindly old woman. 'Are ye still feared o' me, Evie?'

Evelyn sucked her finger and shook her head. 'No, Hinney.'

'And as well. A big lassie like you should be past all that nonsense. Come you to me and get warmed by the fire.' She pulled Evelyn on to her lap and cuddled her like a baby. 'I've given your mother a nice herb tea that will help to relax her and make her sleep away the rest o' this weary night. You bide here wi' me for a whilie, we'll be nice and cosy here by the fire.'

Evelyn allowed herself to relax. Hinney smelt nice, of roses soap and spices with just a hint of mothballs thrown in for good measure. Her lap was a comfortable one, warm and amenable with an ease to it that suggested a long association with childish flesh. Evelyn snuggled closer, resting her head under Hinney's chin so that she could comfortably gaze at the flames prancing up the lum.

'That's right, my wee lamb.' Hinney's voice came soothingly, sleepily. 'You coorie into me and close your bonny een. Whist, do you hear that de'il o' a wind out there?' She gave a wicked chuckle. 'Ay, the witches o' cold December are abroad the night but they canna touch us, bairnie, we're fine and snug in here.'

A stab of shame pierced Evelyn's conscience. She thought of all the times she had laughed at Hinney behind her back and called her a witch wifie. Now, here she was, cooried on her lap, more warm and secure than she had ever been in her life before – except with her father – she had always felt safe with him. But tonight he was different, tonight he had a son and she would have to take second place in his affections. The heat from the fire was making her drowsy. She felt drugged with warmth and a deep, quiet sense of sadness. Hinney was breathing evenly, gently. A new love crept into Evelyn's heart that night. She had lost her fear of Hinney and with it she had lost a small, carefree, ignorant part of her childhood.

CHAPTER THREE

Evelyn woke in her own bed where sometime in the early hours her father had carried her. She was dead tired still but her mind was racing. Raising her head from the pillow she saw that Grace was in bed, the cold fingers of dawn touching her sleeping face, bathing it in a clean, cold glow. Asleep, she looked younger than sixteen – a child still, innocent and unawakened. Evelyn wondered if Grace thought yet about boys, the strange self-conscious strength of them when they were growing up and looking at girls in a half-shy yet wolfish way. She supposed Johnny would be like that one day and she wouldn't like him as much as she did now. Boys became silly and boastful, always showing off in front of other boys. Yet, not all were like that; maybe Johnny would be one of the different ones, quiet about his developing manhood, the kind of quietness that gave those boys a far greater strength than the ones who shouted and strutted.

Evelyn lay back and stared up at the low ceiling, her mind going over the night that had passed. She thought about the new baby, about the dazed, bewildered look on her father's face and about the things Doctor McGregor had said. He said the baby had come out of the blue and something about her mother not knowing that she was carrying. How could she not know? Cows and horses got fat when they were having young, but her mother hadn't looked any different. Maybe that was it. She hadn't been fat so she hadn't known.

The house was dead silent. No one moved or called out the way they usually did in the morning. She turned her head and listened. A funny wailing sound floated from her mother's room, like one of the cats yelling at night from the roof of the byre before Father opened his window to throw an old boot kept specially for the purpose. She smothered a giggle. Maybe he would hurl the boot at that horrible wee gnome of a creature who had come in the night to disturb everybody with its tomcat yells.

Wicked, ay, but it made her feel better to laugh about it, and she roused herself to look to the window. Grace always opened the curtains at night for they both liked to waken in the morning and see the countryside from where they lay. The storm had blown itself out, a red sun was rising over the steadings of Dippiedoon, flooding the world with a ruddy glow, pouring blood over the acres and acres of untouched snow. The sky was a tranquil honey-pink with no trace of cloud to mar its perfection. Beyond the low hills, the peaks of the Grampians stabbed the sky, crystal white they were and sparkling like diamonds in the sun.

A door banged below and she wondered if it was Murn letting herself out. Come hell or high water she never missed a day at college and fretted impatiently if anything at all kept her back from it. She hoped eventually to try for her M.A. for she had it fixed in her head that she wanted to be a teacher, though God alone knew why as she had never been particularly good with the children. But there was status attached to an ambition like that, and of them all Murn liked anything with status attached. There was no real need for her to go out this morning but she jealously guarded her books and must have had her head in the clouds to have loaned them to someone else. Evelyn could picture her struggling through the snow, the hem of her coat already dirty and soaked as she plodded grimly along.

All the family thought she was daft the way she carried on, travelling to college every day when it would have worked out cheaper and with much less bother if she had stayed at student's lodgings in Aberdeen. But of course they all knew why she persisted in remaining at King's Croft. It was to be near Kenneth Mor, to wangle any odd chance she might have of seeing him, so no one said anything.

Sometimes she got a lift along the turnpike from old

Carnallachie, a kindly but moody creature whose horse, Trudge, was nearly as stubborn as himself. When it took it into its head to stop dead in the middle of the road and refuse to move, a mean look came into its eyes as the old man poured vitriol into its ears and slapped his whip to the right and left of it. After a few minutes of this it would get going as suddenly as it had stopped and if Carnallachie had had any sense in his grizzled head, he would have saved his strength and breath on such a self-willed beast. The farm labourers round about maintained that if Carnallachie had learned the horseman's word when he was a young ploughboy he would have had better success with his horses, but he had scorned taking part in a ritual that was as sacred to the ploughmen as the word they heard in kirk on the Sabbath.

But neither Carnallachie or his daft cuddy would be out on the snowbound roads this morning and Evelyn didn't give her stubborn sister another thought, but smiled instead at the idea of the Christmas holidays ahead with no more lessons or homework till after the New Year.

A movement out on the track caught her eye and she saw Tandy striding along, his flock of sheep and his dogs running away in front, heading for Knobblieknowe's turnip fields. Tandy had arrived in Rothiedrum a day or two ago but had stopped off at a relative's croft to while away some time catching up on all the news and also to carry out some other business which couldn't be done in the cramped quarters of Shepherd's Biggin. Evelyn had wondered what that other business was, for word had got around that he was back but she had been unable to find out, not even from Tandy himself who had arrived at King's Croft yesterday morning bearing a large, lumpy, well-wrapped parcel. He stood out there, wrapped in his plaid, a few of his sheep lingering by the dyke, dirty grey against the snow, nothing to cud, a few half-heartedly scraping the ground with tentative hooves.

There was a shout and she saw her father going to greet Tandy, leaving a creel of split neeps by the byre wall and lighting his pipe as he went over to the dyke where he and the shepherd stood talking and smoking amicably.

Mary was out there too, skipping about by the steadings, throwing her rosy smiles at Tandy, the strength and the youth of her making her shout suddenly and throw a great handful of snow at Tandy's well happed figure.

It was as if nothing had changed at King's Croft and for a few joyful minutes Evelyn deluded herself into imagining this to be the case. She was seized with a longing to be out there too, hurling snow in the air, tossing balls of it at Mary who loved such games with all the vigour of a child. And at nearly eighteen she was just that in so many ways – yet woman enough to drive Malcom Keith, Dippiedoon's eldest son, near daft with her smiles and her flirting. Evelyn realized that neither her father or her sisters had been to bed at all yet. It wouldn't have been worth their while for all of them, with the exception of Evelyn and Grace, had to be up every morning at five thirty to see to the beasts.

Evelyn was about to get up and scramble into her clothes but the thought of the new baby stayed her. She wouldn't help with that – that horrible wee hobgoblin. She glanced across at Grace. Nellie had let her sleep on, she was only sixteen after all and they were all aware that she didn't have the same kind of strength that had been born in them. Even in sleep she still looked tired – and rather frail. Evelyn's heart turned over at the realization. Bonny sweet Grace – if anything ever happened to her she didn't know what she would do. Although six years separated them she was closer to Grace than to any of her sisters. Padding softly over to the other bed she slipped carefully in beside her sleeping sister. Grace stirred, sighed. Evelyn cooried into her. She was warm and soft with a faint smell of lavender about her. She always smelt nice, was always washing and bathing herself. Father moaned sometimes about bringing the zinc tub so often to the fire but he would do anything for Grace, she gave so much of herself in return.

Grace half turned, her arm came out to pull Evelyn close. 'I'm glad you came in,' she said sleepily. 'I could hardly settle for the cold. What time is it?'

Evelyn didn't answer. She knew if she did Grace would be at once alert, ashamed to have rested at all when there was so much to do. 'Wheesht,' murmured Evelyn. 'I'm tired yet, just coorie in, we'll keep each other warm.'

The morning was halfway through when they finally wakened. Nellie was clattering about loudly in the kitchen, Mary was singing as she came upstairs to her mother's room. They dressed quickly, the only sensible way to dress in an unheated room with icicles hanging like fangs on the outside sash of the window. Grace hurried downstairs to get on with her neglected duties, apprehensive in case Nellie might meet her lateness with frosty disapproval. But Nellie was singing too that morning, more a hum really, a tuneless one at that but still better than frowns.

The fire was blazing in the grate, a row of napkins and towels were drying on the brass rail of the mantelpiece, the cats were washing contentedly on the ingle. On the fire itself a big clootie dumpling was pushing its swelling breasts against the pan lid, a roast was sizzling in the oven, a mutton roast gifted by Tandy who had bled and dismembered one of his sheep to fill his Christmas larder. He had used every last part of it, from the entrails to the very blood itself, attended by an admiring audience of local farmwives who had watched his clever hands making black puddings and haggis, with something akin to envy, for sheep had never been a mainstay in the mixed farming of the north east. Tandy, laughing at their faces, told them he had learned everything there was to learn about sheep from his Highland parents of whom he was inordinately proud and went home to visit whenever he could.

Grace was reminded suddenly that it was Christmas, that all of them for the past few weeks had been furtively making small gifts for one another out of any bits of scrap material they could lay their hands on. She loved this time of year when the house smelt of delicious festive fare and with work on the farm more or less at a standstill they could all be together such as they never were in the long busy days of summer. She knew her father didn't like it though. He chafed at the enforced idleness the dark days brought but,

70

like her, he loved Christmas and tried to make it special for them, earning extra money with his shoe-making so that he could buy extra food and fuel for the fire.

Grace sniffed the air appreciatively and her eye fell on an almost forgotten sight – a baby's bottle sterilizing in a pan of boiling water on the cheekstone.

'I had to use one o' the bottles we keep for the calves,' explained Nellie blithely. 'Mother threw the others away when Evie didna need them anymore.'

'How is the baby this morning?'

Nellie turned a sparkling face and Grace was struck by her attractiveness. Her fair hair was normally kept under rigid control by numerous pins but she hadn't had time to do it up yet and it tumbled softly and prettily about her face which was pink and lent her eyes a new sparkle.

'He's as good as gold, hardly a murmur out of his wee throat all morning. Mother's a bit tired but managed to eat a bite o' breakfast. Mary took a basin up to her and will help Hinney to get her washed.'

Grace couldn't help staring at her sister. 'Nellie, you look so – so different this morning,' she said impulsively. 'I had no idea you loved babies so much.'

'Well, since he's here we have to make the best o' it.' Nellie said offhandedly. 'Mother's no' able to see to him and I canna just stand back and neglect the wee mannie.'

'You're wasting your time here, Nell.' Grace spoke slowly, trying to choose her words carefully, treading cannily as she always did with Nellie. 'You would make a fine children's nurse – or better still, a fine mother.'

Nellie's lips tightened. 'Ach, dinna blether, Grace, there's time and enough for that. Oh, if a lass could only have bairns without the trachle o' a marriage bed I would be the first to consider it – and dinna look like that, my bonny wee sister, I have no intention of doing such a thing. Mind you, there's those that do it all the time and think nothing o' it but thay're just tramps wi' no shame in them. No, no, I'll bide my time, men are dirty pigs – you should have heard that Peter Lamont last night. A hot blooded lummock if ever there was one. You would have thought at his age he would know that kitchen maids and dirt like that are about all that's good for poor stock like himself but no, always after something better than himself. Well, he'll no' get it from me nor from any o' my sisters. I'd die if that kind of shame was brought upon the good family name. You mind what I tell you, Grace. I'm no' blind, I've seen the way loons look at you. It's all they ever think about – even our own father. Look at what he's done to Mam – seven he gave her and when she thought she was done wi' it this happens. He's a dirty pig and should be ashamed o' himself.'

Grace could hardly believe her ears. She had never heard Nellie saying so much in such a short space of time and the vitriol in her words left Grace in no doubt about her views on men. But to bring their father into Peter Lamont's category was going too far and fire flashed into Grace's placid eyes. 'Don't you speak of Father in that way, Nell. He loves our Mam . . .'

'Love! Is that what you call it? Lust is the word I would have chosen.' She saw her sister's hurt expression and her voice softened. 'Ach, never mind all that now, Grace, go you ben the larder and bring through the milk jug. I'll have to use cow's milk for the bairn, for Mother has none at all to give him. Fancy, Grace, she's forty-four and here she is wi' another baby.'

Both girls forgot their differences and went about the kitchen, talking in low voices, discussing the happening that had stunned them all and had changed the routine of King's Croft in the space of a few short hours.

Upstairs Evelyn had made her way to her mother's room. Hinney was there, her red hair straggling out from under her mutch cap, her little hairy warts outlined in the sharp light pouring in through the window. Evelyn gave a little giggle but smothered it at once when Hinney smiled over at her and she was reminded of last night when the old woman's homely, comforting arms had been about her. She was helping Mary wash Maggie's back and Mary was singing under her breath, not in the least embarrassed at the idea of seeing her mother's exposed flesh. Evelyn tried to keep her eyes averted. With a few exceptions she had hardly ever seen her mother in bed, let alone naked, but she had seen Mary and it was a great surprise to her to note that her mother's breasts weren't all that different from a young girl's. Bigger maybe, a bit slacker but on the main just as proud as the rest of her. She had imagined an older body under the clothes, some wrinkles, but the skin was pink and smooth, the waist well defined – and suddenly she had a picture of her father lying with her mother, touching the pale skin of her body with his big brown hands . . .

'Have you come to see your wee brother?' Maggie sounded tired, unenthusiastic, and it came to Evelyn that maybe she didn't want this strange wee baby who had arrived so unexpectedly, that maybe she was feeling as angry as Evelyn herself was about it.

Maggie didn't feel anger, she felt shock, so deep and frightening she felt she never wanted to get up out of bed and face the world again, face all those women who would talk behind her back about her foolishness and be as nice as ninepence to her face, too nice, the false niceness of women only too pleased to see some of the pride knocked out of her.

God, was there no end to it? She had thought to herself well past the time for conceiving children. There had been no sign of menstruation for almost a year and she had truly believed herself to have come through an early change of life. It had been wonderful, to be free of it all, for herself and Jamie to feel safe together. Not like the nights when she had lain wakeful in the darkness, Jamie satiated and asleep at her side while she worried and wondered what was going on inside her body, if another baby was in the making. Evelyn had been surprise enough, but at least she had known she was carrying her. This time there had been none of the usual signs – she had put on a bit of weight certainly and had experienced feeble flutterings which she'd put down to nerves – and now, in the short space of a few hours she was a mother again, just when she had been rejoicing in her freedom. Still, her daughters were older now, Nellie was showing every sign of taking the baby off her hands – she would have to – somebody would have to! She had neither the strength nor the desire to rear another.

Evelyn was studying the baby who was lying in a drawer hastily lined with blankets. The cradle and pram that had served all five Grant girls had been given away to the travellers only last summer together with numerous items of baby wear that Maggie had carefully saved for years. Evelyn thought the baby didn't look quite so ugly this morning but oh, he was such a teeny, delicate wee thing. His eyes were open, deep blue they were, ringed round with black. His mouth was a slack wet blubber of a thing but his eyes were right bonny – and his hair – finer than the silk Murn used for her needlework and such a blue-black sheen to it, like raven's wings in flashes of sunlight.

Reaching down she plucked him up and held him to her breast. His head lay under her chin, lighter than a sponge cake, his shrimp-like fingers clutched one of hers and held onto it tightly. How light and small he was, like a wee lamb just born. She held her breath as love, sweet and raw and everlasting flooded her being. She hadn't wanted to like him till she had got used to the idea of him about the place, in fact she had felt bitter resentment at him and had thought to herself that an ugly, skinny wee thing like him didn't deserve anybody's love. But it had happened, without any warning of any kind he had simply stolen her heart. Twice in just twenty-four hours she had fallen in love, first with a witch and now with a hobgoblin. She giggled aloud with the sheer daftness of it all and Mary's voice came sharply. 'Evie, dinna you drop that bairn. He's no' one o' your dolls so put him back to his bed.'

'Ach, leave her.' Maggie had noticed the expression on her little daughter's face, changing from indifference to a deep, quiet wonder. 'Bring him here to me, Evie and we'll undress him and change him together.'

Evelyn watched fascinated as the baby was stripped and changed, feeling suddenly sad that his hippens had been hastily made out of an old sheet torn into rough squares. The loose threads tangled round his little stick legs, making

74

him look like a poor orphaned wee thing with nothing in the world to call his own.

Maggie wrapped him in his shawl and put him under the covers at her side and then she looked up at Evelyn, her hand coming out to stroke her silken hair. 'My ain wee lassie,' she said softly. 'You will aye be my youngest, my youngest daughter. This poor wee loon is a stranger yet, and he's going to grow up in a house full of women. We'll have to be good to him, eh, Evie?'

'Ay, Mam,' Evelyn touched her mother's hair. 'Let me brush it, Mam, I'll make it bonny for Father. He'll be up to see you the minute he gets in.

Maggie's eyes flashed. 'Bonny, ay, but you canna change the colour o' it, Evie. How strange it looks, me wi' my frosty pow and a new bairn at my side.' Up went her head, pride took the place of the mockery in her eyes. 'You do my hair, Evie, the sooner I'm back to myself and up out this bed the better. There's things to be done and besides, I dinna fancy Nellie aboot me for any longer than is necessary. A good willing lass she may be but a nurse she is not and never will be.'

Hinney smiled sourly. 'Ay, Nellie wasna made for the bedroom, she's happiest ploutering aboot in the fields or down in the kitchen. She'll make a fine man for some brave chiel one o' these days.'

'Ach, Hinney!' scolded Mary though her dimples were flashing. 'That's no' very fair on Nell. She'll shock the lot o' us one o' these fine days, wait you and see. Nobody knows better than me how prudish she is, but there's fire in our Nell and one day it will flare up and burn everything in its path.'

Jamie came stamping up the stairs, straight from the fields, snow-caked, eyes limpid with tiredness, his black moustache frosted with condensation, his gaze meeting Maggie's in mute, humble appeal, as if asking forgiveness for something he had done. But she didn't meet his glance and he half turned away, his shoulders drooping suddenly. She was blaming him for what had happened, he could hear her silent accusations inside his head, yet he sensed there was more to it than that, and wondered if she would ever tell him what it was.

Tandy came in at his back, looking more unkempt than ever, his hair straggling wetly about his lugs, his plaid wrapped carelessly about his magnificent shoulders. He was an intinerant creature, a man of liberty who wandered the highways and byways, driving his flock before him, owing allegiance only to the man who hired him, the flockmaster who rented grass in summer and turnip fields in winter, so that the sheep were always on the move, roving from one farmtoun to the next, a nuisance on country roads where other travellers could find their way seriously hampered by the wandering shepherd, his sheep and his dogs. Kenneth Cameron Mor had taken to Tandy from the start and whenever his flock came to feed on Knobblieknowe's unwanted turnips Tandy was allowed to sleep in the biggin, no more than a wooden hut with a bed and a fireplace and a kist under the window.

Ay, Tandy came and Tandy went, genuinely liked wherever his voyaging took him. Always when he returned to Rothiedrum he was given the same kind of welcome that might be afforded a favourite uncle. Like Kenneth, Tandy hailed from the Highlands and the two might have been brothers, so alike were they in looks and temperament. Tandy was six feet tall with windblown, rusty fair hair, great ox-like shoulders and a marvellous physique and bearing.

More often than not he wore his kilt and in his spare time played his pipes up there on the windy moors and braes. When folk heard the sound of his pipes drifting down over the plains of Rothiedrum they would tell each other, 'There's Tandy serenading the bottle again. He'll be at it for a night or two then the hills will be as silent as death till the next time.'

Tandy was a man of few words. He maintained that folk wasted their breath in idle chatter and indeed, all the strength of him seemed to go into his work. It was a joy to watch him going about even the most mundane of tasks. Everything he did was slow and purposeful. There was

76

beauty in the way he used his hands. You saw the moulding of ages in their structure, sensed the steely strength in them, thrilled to the whisper of his fingers gliding over a newly smoothed piece of wood. Cosy by the fire in his biggin he spent the long winter nights fashioning things from bits of wood. He had made his shepherd's crook himself, a fine crook it was, fashioned from hazel and horn. He and Kenneth Mor went wild when they got together. If the master of Knobblieknowe had had a row with his bonny Jeannie, he would go and drink with Tandy and the pair of them would stride about the braes, singing in the Gaelic and playing the pipes till the glens of Rothiedrum echoed with untamed skirls and even the very hills, glowering down through veils of mist, seemed to stand to attention and listen.

For a time he and Mary had been seen regularly together till he had gone off voyaging with his flock again. When he had seen fit to return Mary was head over heels in love with a young ploughman, though none of her affairs were of the lasting variety. By the nature of their work the fee'd men were never in any one place for longer than a few months at a time so Mary had a fine time falling in and out of love, delighting in seeing the disapproval on Nellie's face and telling her that variety was the spice of life.

Whenever Tandy came back he spent a lot of his time at King's Croft and now he went to the bed to kiss Maggie soundly on the lips and crush the small shoulders of hers in a bear-like embrace.

There were never any half measures with Tandy, no matter what he was doing, and he laughed wickedly at the bloom of pink on her cheeks. Throwing a cured sheepskin on to the bed he said loudly, 'There ye are, Maggie lass, you can hap yourself in it or use it as a mat for your bedside. It doesna matter which, the auld yowe I took it from has no need o' it now.'

Grinning at Hinney he called her a wily old witch, whereupon she cackled with delight; he squeezed Mary's waist; lifted Evelyn high; keeked briefly at the baby; threw a shiny half crown onto the blankets, then plodded grandly down to the kitchen for a bowl of soup washed down by a steaming toddy.

'I'll tell Father you helped yourself from his Ne'erday bottle.' said Nellie with a sniff. 'Between you and the doctor there's no much left o' it.'

'Well, well now, is that a fact, Nell, lass?' He was up, his kilt swinging as he turned about, the great bulk of him seeming to fill the kitchen. 'I'll see he gets paid back, never you fear, lassie.' He eyed her as she mixed dough in a big yellow bowl on the table. 'You've a new bairn to look to now, eh, young Nell?'

Nellie's back bristled. 'The bairn is Mother's doing, no' mine, Tandy.'

'Hmm – and you're wishing it was, eh? By God, Nell, it's time you were married wi' bairns o' your own. I'd have you in a minute, that I would. If you could thole the kind o' life I lead I would take you away wi' me now. Just think what it would be like, Nell, you and me cooried in bed together. I'd soon show you there's more to life than darning and cooking.'

Nellie almost choked. She had had enough of people telling her she ought to get married and she turned on him like a fury. 'Mind your own business, Tandy McQueen! I'm sick o' gowks like you telling me I ought to be married. Just what do you expect me to say? "Oh ay, Tandy, I'd love to be your wife and have that great hairy mouth o' yours guzzling away at me"'.

'Thank you kindly for the invitation,' he said calmly and without preliminary folded his great arms about her and crushed her wide, sensual mouth against his.

Nellie struggled, kicked, moaned. His mouth was hard, warm, filled with all the heated passion that was the man of him. His unshaven cheek was rough and abrasive against her smooth one, his breath was as clean as a mountain burn, the smell of him was of wet snow and fresh cold and a raw, musky animal smell that was not of the beasts in his care but of himself. When he let her go, he was breathing deeply but evenly and mockery gleamed in his yellow cat's eyes. 'By God, Nell, why do you hide it? Lucky the man

78

that discovers the real you. Your blood boils inside of you, yet on the surface you're pure ice. But remember this, lassie, ice melts, given enough heat it melts and yours is soon for the cracking – I tell you that.'

'Get out – you filthy pig!' Nellie's face was crimson, her eyes wild and staring. Tandy went off whistling and she put her hands on the table to steady herself. Shame, stark and bitter, curled in her belly. She felt sick and wiped at her mouth where his hard lips had been – and yet a small hidden flame burned low down inside of her and she hated herself more than she hated Tandy, for being so weak – for behaving like a woman when a man was the last thing on earth she wanted.

'Is Tandy away, Nell?' She spun round to see her father at the door, watching her with a wary eye.

'Ay, he's away,' she spat. 'And I hope he stays away – he's a dirty pig – just like all the rest. Sit you down, Father, and I'll get you your soup.'

Jamie scraped his chair into the table while Nellie served his meal in a taut silence.

'I'm sorry about all the bother last night,' he said, breaking the silence at last. 'It was a terrible shock to your mother and me. I never wanted her to have to suffer like that again.'

Nellie turned on him. 'Didn't you, Father? Then why did you let it happen? It could have killed her! Have you stopped to think o' that! Have you?'

'Ach, Nell,' he spread his hands in appeal. 'She thought – we both thought she was past all that. I love your mother and I wouldna deliberately hurt her for the world. It was something that just happened.'

'Ay,' Nellie spat the words derisively. 'Just like Evelyn happened and the twins before her. You should have left her alone after the fourth, it was enough, more than enough for any woman to rear in decency.'

'Maybe some day you'll understand, Nell,' he said quietly, scraping back his chair and standing up. He looked into her angry amber-green eyes but found his gaze withering before hers. 'Will you ever forgive and forget,

Nell, will you? It was a long time ago and Jake wasna himself when it happened.'

'No, Father, he was drunk,' she hurled at him scornfully,' and so too were you, too drunk and insensible to hear your very own daughter crying for your help.' Her voice broke. 'I needed you that night, Father, more than I've ever needed you in my life – I was afraid – so afraid and to this very day, thanks to you and your drunken friend – I hate and despise all men.' She paused and seemed not to be looking at him, but at some terrible phantom that leapt at her suddenly out of the past. She sagged and all the anger seemed to go out of her as she said in a soft, low voice, 'You're my father and a good one, God knows that well enough. There are times when I forget and there are times when I remember, you canna blame me for that. And you need never worry that I'll ever tell anyone – I'm too ashamed of what happened ever to put my shame on another living soul. Away you go now, that great gowk will be waiting for you. I suppose you're helping him clear the snow from the field so that his sheep can get at the neeps?'

Jamie nodded and went to the door, a terrible tangible sadness in every weary bone of him. Out in the porch he struggled once more into his wet boots and was about to go outside when Nellie's voice stayed him.

'Take care, Father,' she said softly, almost tenderly. 'We mustna let anything happen to you. Mother will be needing you in the days to come more than she's ever needed you before.'

'Ay, Nellie, I know.' He nodded and went off over the cobbled yard. Plodding beside Tandy along the braes of Binney Hill, the sheepdogs skelping along the snowy slopes in front, he said casually, 'Nell seemed upset by something you did. What was it, man?'

Tandy drew his fist across his nose and grinned. 'I kissed her, man, ay, I did – and I tasted warm blood in the guts of your Nell. She's ripe for it, King Jamie, and the buggering awful thing is she doesna know it.'

Jamie smiled, a dour thin smile as he remembered the

undisguised contempt he had just witnessed in his eldest daughter's eyes. 'The de'il is in her, Tandy, dirling away in thon proud lugs o' hers, telling her that all men are filthy buggers to be watched at every turn,' he sighed and hurled a gobbet of spit to the ground where it made a little pit in the snow. 'Nell's no like the rest o' my girls and maybe she has good reason for being that way. She's seen it all, the birthing, the work, the drudgery. She's determined never to let any o' it happen to her – yet it will, Tandy, it will. I've keeked below the surface o' Nell and seen the wanting there . . .' He paused, seeing her angry face, hearing those terrible accusations pouring from her lips, reminding him of that long ago night of which he could recall very little but which she would never allow him to forget

He was guilty alright, it throbbed inside him now like some deep raw wound which would never heal, guilty of bringing Jake home to the croft, of falling into a drunken sleep in the kitchen while Jake crept up to his daughter's room and . . . He shook his head as if to rid himself of such hateful memories. Maggie didn't know, had never known, she had never liked Jake and was only too glad that he never came back to King's Croft. She had been away at the time, visiting her dying mother in hospital and she had taken Murn with her, so that it was only Nellie left behind to see to things.

Jamie had always hated and despised men who indulged in such ungodly practices, till that one half-forgotten night when he had allowed such a man over his own doorstep, but now he hated himself more for letting the thing happen. It had robbed him of self-respect for may years afterwards. God forgive him, she had only been ten years old at the time, a vulnerable, sensitive child who had known nothing of the lusts of the flesh . . .

He went on talking, more to still the voices in his head than a real desire for talk. 'Ay, Tandy, she'll fight it like a wildcat but in the end it will come to her. There are natural born spinsters, women wi' frozen erses and dried breasts that couldna suckle a harvest mouse. Folk think

81

Nell's like that, but you and me know different, eh, Tandy? Nell will do the natural thing. With all my heart it's what I wish for her most.'

'Ay, she will that, King Jamie, never you fear.' Tandy was tired of the subject. The dogs were running about the field, gathering the flock, and the men set to work, Nellie forgotten in the long busy afternoon that lay ahead.

CHAPTER FOUR

The news of Maggie's baby swept through Rothiedrum like a snowstorm. Cragbogie, the O'Neil's farm, was a favourite place for women to gather and gossip, for though they spoke about Betsy O'Neil behind her back they all enjoyed the warm, carefree atmosphere of the place and truly liked Betsy despite her slovenly ways.

Kirsty Keith was the first to arrive, stamping in through the close, stopping at the door to clump the snow from boots that looked much too large for her spindly legs, before darting into the kitchen like a ferret after a rat.

Betsy had not yet attended to her toilet. Her mousy hair hung in tired strands about the shoulders of her grey, safety-pinned cardigan, her black skirt was longer at the front than at the back and her feet were stuck into a pair of Danny's thick woollen stockings. The skin of her face and neck had a texture to it like course oatmeal and looked as if it hadn't seen water in weeks. She was huddled at the fire, drinking tea while her fourteen-month-old grandson, Pete, played with a heap of cinders on the hearthrug at her feet.

His mother, eighteen-year-old Tina, was reading a cheap penny dreadful at the table, blonde hair straggling about her long thin face with its wide red lips standing out like weals in the fair pallor of her skin. Tina had been pregnant at sixteen and couldn't name the father, there had been so many candidates and so Peter had arrived to swell the ranks at Cragbogie, Betsy maintaining that one more mouth made no difference in the family that so far rated ten. Tina worked at the fish market in Aberdeen, but this morning she had taken one look at the snowy world and had gone promptly back to bed to read her book.

Daniel, a gentle lad of eleven, was trying to do his homework at the table while fifteen year old Maureen squeezed a blackhead from her face at one side of him and youngsters of varying ages squabbled all around him. Out of the melee came Florrie, fair hair cascading down her back, her blue eyes dancing with devilment at sight of the beanpole mistress of Dippiedoon whom she loved to watch and imitate.

'Have you heard the news?' Kirsty darted to the fire to plunk herself down on the cheekstone and hold her damp feet to the blaze. 'I was just passing Hill O' Binney on my way down to Bunty Lovie's for some stamps and who did I meet but Alastair Campbell himself. My, what a strange wee mannie he is.' Kirsty sniffed her disapproval of Alastair who continually riled her with his disparaging remarks about her son, Malcolm, then she rushed on. 'He was fair panting for breath when I came upon him scrabblin' about in the snow and when I asked him what he was looking for he snapped my head off and told me anybody could see he was searching for his specs. Well, there they were on the end of his nose as usual but for his cheek I was no' for tellin' him and would have left him there and then, but auld Hinney came along, supported under the oxters by none other than King Jamie who was looking gey furtive like – the way he looks when he's been at the poaching and trying to look as if there is nothing in his sack but air.'

Kirsty paused for two reasons, to allow Betsy time to absorb her words and to briskly rub at her feet with both hands. Under the table, five O'Neil children watched and listened to every word while Florrie silently mimicked Kirsty's actions, much to the delight of the others who smothered their laughter in the overhang of the grimy tablecloth.

Betsy placidly finished her tea and reached languidly for the teapot which was always perched on a trivet in front of the fire. 'Patsy, fetch another cup,' she yelled and from behind a chair a small tousled boy emerged to run to the scullery and bring back a cracked thick mug into which Betsy poured black treacly tea which she handed to Kirsty. Further orders brought forth a yellowed white sugar bowl and milk jug together with a plateful of biscuits with several suspicious half-moon shapes corroding the already frayed edges.

'Florrie made them,' explained Betsy with a gleam of pride. 'They're a wee bittie scorched but she's only eleven and will get better as she grows.'

Kirsty took the offering with a shudder, glad to note that a scruffy looking mongrel was eyeing her plate with a wolfish expression in its eyes. Behind Kirsty's back, little Pete was methodically filling her boots from the cinder box out of which one of the cats had just emerged with a most self-satisfied expression on its whiskers. Under the table the children were clutching each other in silent rapture while they hoped against hope that nothing would intervene to break the concentration of their little nephew.

Kirsty plunged into a long account of how Jamie had stamped away looking awful red about the gills, leaving Hinney to tenderly help Alastair to his feet and tell him his specs were on the end of his nose. 'He's dottered, the old fool,' she stated forcibly. 'I wonder he hasna been locked away in the asylum years ago. Hinney was for helping him up to the house but I commented on how tired she looked and though she hummed and hawed I eventually got it out of her. She was up all night, it seemed, at King's Croft no less . . .' She folded her lips meaningfully, her ferrety face positively triumphant as she waited for Betsy's reaction. Betsy unwound slowly, a look of anticipation on her long, horsey face.

'Hinney – at King's Croft? Bless me, what on earth was she doing there? Don't you go telling me that one o' the Grant lassies has gone and dropped a bairn.'

Kirsty swelled up, like a great python after swallowing a gargantuan meal. 'Na, na, it wasna one o' the lassies.'

'Then who – you canna mean – Maggie!'

Kirsty pursed her lips and her grey, neat head with its well-pinned bun, waggled up and down. 'Near dropped it in the snow she did, on the way home from Kenneth Mor's ceilidh. I was there myself last night and nary a word did she say to me about expecting again – and right enough there wasna a thing to show for it – you know how Maggie has that awful good shape in her in spite of having seven o' them.'

Kirsty spoke rather grudgingly for Maggie's comely figure was a sore point with her, herself having had only three children and a shape to her like a gatepost.

'But – Maggie's on the change.' said Betsy, her course skin glowing with interest. 'It could be the soul didna ken she was carrying. I've heard o' things like that but never believed it was true.'

'Hmph, it's true right enough. She'll maybe no' be so damt proud after this.'

'Ay, you're right there, Kirsty. Maggie has aye been good to me, but betimes she has looked down her nose at me when I was carrying – and her seven times gone herself – she's no' too proud to enjoy her bit pleasure wi' King Jamie.'

'Ach, seven is decent enough – ten is obscene,' snorted Kirsty, her deceptively benign face filled with self-righteousness.

Betsy's nostrils flared. 'You only had three because you're such a poor wee scrag end o' a thing! Keith must have had a hell of a job trying to find your poor wee wizened dowp. A scraggle o' bones canna be much fun for a chancy chiel like him. I'm sure there are skeletons in the kirkyard wi' more meat to their bones.'

Kirsty's face had turned purple and a battle royal might have raged between the two had not Jessie Blair of the Mains arrived together with Lily Lammas, the butcher's wife. Jessie's face was red with the effort of struggling through the snowbound turnpike and at sight of her the O'Neil children eyed one another with joy because a visit from her meant endless titbits from endless roomy pockets. She was a fat, ponderous woman whose layers of clothing stank and whose round, treble-chinned face, was framed in a grubby white mutch cap. Jessie liked to lie in her bed of a morning, leaving all the work to the kitchen maid who took full advantage of the situation by letting Peter

Lamont, the greive, take advantage of her, not to mention Ewan Blair himself.

Ewan was a round bauble of a man with a fringe of fair hair to the front and back of his otherwise bald head. Big bellied he was, with fat stumpy legs and great plodding feet but he did not allow his appearance to detract from an inflated sense of his own importance as master of the Mains o' Rothiedrum, the big home farm attached to Rothiedrum House. He was also a hot-blooded old goat and was always pawing the kitchen girls and chasing them round the stable yard while his fat, smelly wife snored her time away in bed. But Jessie was a cheery, kindly soul, and was soon sitting comfortably at Cragbogie's fire, a mug of tea in one plump fist, a burnt scone in the other. Kirsty had been careful to move away from her while Lily Lammas placed her own solid bulk on a seat well clear of the fire which was bringing out Jessie's aromas in no mean manner.

The four women wasted no time in discussing the latest piece of news and Cragbogie's kitchen fairly rang with their voices while the children skulked and listened and Florrie wondered quietly how soon she could get over to King's Croft to see what Evelyn thought of having a squalling baby about the place.

'One thing looks certain, King Jamie's gypsy blood is no' for cooling down,' observed Betsy with rude enjoyment.

'Ay, it makes you wonder if that Nellie quine is his.' Jessie lowered her rich fat voice to a merest whisper. 'You couldna say she's got her father's hot blood.'

'Ay, she looks a right frozen snotter,' Betsy poured herself another cup of black tea. 'Yet my Dan says you canna tell a book by its covers. Maybe under that spinsterish look she's hotter than all the rest put together – and she's real stuck on children. If she wants any o' her own she'll have to let a man straddle her sometime.'

Kirsty sniffed her disapproval of Betsy's coarse tongue. 'Well, I'm glad I only had my three – it's quality, no quantity that counts – my Keith has aye maintained that.'

'That's why our Lawrence is such a bonny strong lad,'

Jessie puffed out her huge bosom and fairly bristled with pride. 'All the goodness that was in Ewan and me went into our laddie, bless him.'

The women exchanged glances. Lawrence Bless Him Blair was thirty and one of the biggest show offs ever to spring from Rothiedrum. He thought himself head and shoulders above everyone and had a real knack for riling everybody he met. He had gone to Canada to make good, there to bulldoze his way from one job to the next. On his rare visits home it was his habit to sit with his feet up the lum, bore visitors with tales of his travels, and compete with his father for the attentions of Mary Drummie, the flirting, giggling kitchenmaid of the Mains.

Lily Lammas sniffed disdainfully. 'If Charles and me (Lily always referred to her tiny husband as Charles) had been blessed wi' even the one bairn I wouldna have made him into a sickly sly cratur' wi little to do but lie back and goggle at the quines. Oh no, he would have been good, obedient, and bonny and would never have found the need to leave a home where he was so wanted.'

Jessie was up at this, chins wobbling, skirts flaring, releasing all the smells hitherto kept under reasonable control. 'You're jealous, that's what you are, Lily Lammas. That poor wee downtrodden mannie o' yours couldna mount a mouse, let alone a great slummock like yourself! It's no wonder you never had any children.'

'Agree, women, agree, for I hate to see peace,' laughed Betsy while the children watched the warring pair with bated breath, hoping for a real good fight. But at that moment the door burst open to admit Danny O'Neil with two of his elder sons at his back. He came stamping in, his rusty gold beard flecked with spittle, his hair damp and dishevelled after a morning spent humping feed to his beasts. His great shovel-like hands were the colour of raw meat and of much the same texture, his frightening blue eyes were wild and staring, an expression that was a perpetual one from a lifetime of drink and fiery temper.

At the sight of him an amazing transformation took place in Cragbogie's kitchen. The children scuttled to clear junk from the table and began to run back and forth to set it from an enormous oak sideboard which sat solidly in a walled recess; Betsy took the big black pan of potatoes from the fire and peered at them anxiously while Tina fished in the soup pan for a steaming hunk of hough which she placed in the oven to keep warm. Plates, cutlery, cups and saucers created a frightful din as they made the journey from sideboard to table; the dog-eared cushion on a big ugly wooden armchair was hastily pummelled and plumped; Daniel poured hot water into a basin from a sooty fish kettle and without a word his father stripped off his jacket and shirt and plunged in hairy, sinewy arms.

The visitors were making haste to don outer garments, Jessie Blair puffing and panting, Kirsty muttering as she emptied her boots of cinders and glowered darkly at the giggling children, Lily striving to retain her dignity despite having quite a struggle with her coat owing to a torn sleeve lining.

The women neither liked nor disliked Danny O'Neil, in fact most of them, though speaking about him behind his back, respected him and admired him for the hard-working farmer that he was, but all avoided passing the time of day with him if they could at all help it as his sarcastic and ready tongue was not something to come up against lightly.

By now he had washed and had thrown himself into his chair while little Peter toddled to fetch his warmed slippers and with pink tongue sticking out from the side of his mouth struggled to get them on to the great, solid, wedge-shaped feet.

'You're home then, my poor Dan,' Betsy's rough voice was oddly sympathetic and gentle. 'It must have been a sore struggle out there in the parks this morning.'

'Ay, I'm home,' Dan's bellow might have come from the lungs of an ox. His wild eyes roved over the assembly of womanfolk who were eyeing him warily. 'Home right enough,' he repeated forcibly, 'and wondering bejabbers if I've chanced into the henhouse instead of me own kitchen. What are you all doing clecking in my house instead of being in your own seeing to the needs o' your menfolk? God! If you were mine I'd soon knock you all into shape. By God I would!'

The women glowered at him before beating a hasty retreat out of the door into the hoary day.

Betsy looked across at her husband. 'You'll be ready for your dinner, Danny me boy?'

His red face relaxed, a smile quirked the corners of his thick, cruel mouth and he threw back his curly bull of a head and roared with laughter. 'Bejabbers, Bess, me darlin', I adore frightening the shit out of these gossiping farmwives. Have you ever seen the likes o' that fat old turkey of the Mains trying to move her arse in a hurry? A blabbering jelly she is, a blabbering great sow of a jelly if ever there was one.'

He bellowed with gusto again while Betsy giggled and the children jigged round the table chanting. 'Jessie Blair's a jelly, Jessie Blair's a jelly!'

CHAPTER FIVE

Evelyn and Florrie ran as swiftly as two young hinds up through the snow-covered parks, pelting each other with snowballs, skirling and panting with laughter, rosy cheeked, tumble haired, their flying skirts catching on the stark black fingers of broom and gorse along the way.

'Jessie Blair's a jelly! Jessie Blair's a jelly!' The girls sang the ridiculous chant as they careered along to Birkiebrae, the panting breath in their throats distorting the words. Florrie halted suddenly and pulling Evelyn to her said, 'Promise me, Evie, that you'll come wi' me to the Mains one day. We'll creep up to Jessie Blair's room and just *look* at her lying in bed snoring her great juicy snores.'

Florrie's breath was cold and sweet on Evelyn's face, her face was sparkling, her luminous eyes as blue as the crystal waters of Loch Bree on a sunny day; her nose was red, a cheery bright button of a thing that in summer became peppered with tiny golden freckles. She was taller than Evelyn, two inches at least and her hair against the clear, bright Northern sky was a crown of spun gold. Evelyn felt a strange, sweet sensation washing through her. It was like the love she had for Johnny and her father, only there was more freedom in it, a breathless, wild, exciting thing that curled in her heart and made her pause for a while on that white December day with the earth's scent filtering from the birch woods up on the brae and the tinkling of bells from Hinney's geese chiming far over yon wide, light, blue distance.

'I love you, Florrie O'Neil,' she said simply, her clear child's voice vibrant with the feelings that burst like bubbles from some inner font.

Florrie's bright face became still, and she stared into Evelyn's great green eyes quizzically, the laughter on her lips now a million years in the past. 'Like Johnny?' she questioned solemnly.

'No, different from Johnny, a strange thing, something I'll think about when I'm grown to a woman and will maybe cry a wee bit when I remember.'

Florrie didn't laugh. Instead her eyes misted and she bit her lip. 'I'll remember too.' She put her arm round Evelyn's shoulder and hugged her tightly then they both laughed a trifle awkwardly and Florrie broke away to retrieve a gnarled twig from under a whin bush. Throwing herself on to her knees she began to write in the snow, big, scrawled, laborious letters that read, 'Evelyn McKenzie Grant and Florrie Elizabeth O'Neil. Best friends. Dec. 1908.'

Holding hands, they stood back to survey the handiwork, Florrie mightily pleased with herself, Evelyn a bit sad as she observed, 'Come spring it will get washed away.'

'Ay, but we'll still be here, nothing will wash *us* away.' Florrie said with assurance.

'Ach, you're right enough.' Evelyn giggled suddenly. 'And I promise I'll come and look at Jessie Blair snoring in bed and maybe Ewan Blair scrabbling in the hayshed wi' that silly Mary Drummie.'

Florrie's eyes shone. 'Ay, we'll do it in the spring, that's the best time, grown-up's do awful daft things in the spring, like the animals and the birds. That's when our Tina got caught, I saw her with my very own eyes, over yonder, back of the rigs at old Carnallachie's place, every night wi' a different lad, fleerin' and giggling they were and chaving in the grass like a pair o' big collie dogs. Me and Daniel used to creep over every night and watch from behind the hawthorn hedge but we were feared to get too close and never saw them really *doing* it.'

Florrie ended on a note of disappointment and Evelyn looked at her curiously. 'Florrie , what *is* it that quines and loons do when they're alone?' Her voice was tight, fraught with all the unanswered questions that had drummed in her head since the birth of her little brother.

Florrie stared. 'But you *know*,' she hissed. 'You've seen the bull do it wi' the kie and the ram wi' the yowes often enough.'

Evelyn's face flared to crimson, her eyes grew as big as saucers. 'Ach! Blethers!' she scoffed. 'You're just making it up. People don't do the same things as the animals.'

Florrie's Irish temper flared at that. 'You're just a big tumshy, Evelyn Grant. And if you're too much o' a daftie no' to believe me – well don't.' Up went her head and out went her rounded chin.

Evelyn glanced at her and said fiercely, 'Ach, I knew it all along, I only asked because – because . . .' She faltered and grew quiet, every fibre in her rebelling at the idea of her father doing the same things to her mother that the rams did to the ewes, doing it in the dark, secret shadows of their room, the cries growing in the throat of him as if he was in the throes of some terrible, wonderful agony. She had tried not to think about it all this last week since wee Colin's birth; her father's hand in hers had been the same as it had always been, rough, strong, reassuring. When he ruffled her hair and smiled at her it was the same sunny, flashing smile she had known and loved all her life yet she had looked at him with different eyes and had felt that she had never really known him at all, that he needed more than his beloved fields and his family and home to keep him happy and contented and smiling.

She felt something slipping away from her, something that had been essentially hers all the days of her young life. In the place of sweet ignorance and innocence there came the stirrings of knowledge about people and things around her, and she knew with a trembling sense of poignancy that nothing would ever be the same for her again, that things and people she loved would change and look different the more the years passed, the more knowledge she gained the more of her childhood would slip away till one day it would be no more – and so it wouldn't always be as she had imagined, things would change and so would she.

'I'll never do things with boys – like – like your Tina.' Her voice held a note of defiance even while she knew that she

93

was clinging to an innocence that was past and that now had no substance.

Florrie's dimples flashed. 'Course you will, we all will, and you'll do it right well, Evie, cos your father's hot blood is in you.'

Evelyn stared aghast. 'Did you make that up, Florrie O'Neil?'

'Na, I've heard my Ma saying it often enough to my Da. "The Grants are a hot blooded lot if ever there was one. If Maggie Grant sat her bare erse down on a clump o' heather she'd set the braes o' Rothiedrum that sore on fire the flames would be seen from as far away as Braemar."'

She had mimicked her mother so perfectly that Evelyn looked hastily over her shoulder just in case Betsy O'Neil might be in the near vicinity. But the parks stretched, empty and bare of life save for a few of Tandy's sheep wandering aimlessly along by the dykes. Giggling she reached out her hand. 'Come on, daftie, let's get along to Birkiebrae for Johnny. Mam said he was to come for his dinner and have a keek at wee Colin while he's about it – though I don't think Johnny's all that interested in babies.'

'He's had enough o' them to last him a lifetime,' stated Florrie whimsically, sounding once more suspiciously like her mother, 'Still, your's is different from the rest – fancy him having these fits all the time.' There was a note of morbid curiosity in her tone and she glanced quickly at her friend as if to ascertain her feelings on the matter.

Evelyn was frowning, seeing in her mind's eye the delicate face of her baby brother, blue and convulsed, his tiny body jerking in spasms. She saw too her mother's averted gaze, her father's worried look, Nellie pacing with the child in her arms, endlessly, patiently, her face with that odd soft look to it that made her seem prettier and more feminine than she had ever been. Doctor McGregor had told them not to worry, that a lot of new babies took convulsions in their first year of life, yet Evelyn knew that even he wasn't convinced by his own words and knew within himself that there was something not quite right about Colin James Grant.

The steadings of Birkiebrae loomed, grey and dark against the blue of the sky. The hens were scratching in the snow over the rise, a spiral of smoke rose from the chimneys of the house, the drift of it settling in a grey-blue haze among the rowans and birches which grew in a tight little clump at the northern end of the lochan. Greylag geese were slithering about on the frozen surface of the water, calling in voices that were muted and sweet in the calm, frosty air.

Jimmy and Janet Burns were breaking chunks of brittle ice from the banks and hurling them over the ice-bound lochan, clapping with glee as they shattered into a million pieces, that skated about in every direction. Jimmy dropped the lump that he had just lifted and ran to grin at the visitors. He was a cheery lad of nine with a manly chin and blue eyes shining in an old-fashioned face. Behind him toddled his sister Janet, a tiny doll of a girl, small for four, fair haired and blue eyed. At her back, seven year old Jenny came boldly, pert and cheeky looking, her hand reaching out to drag Janet away so that she could get in front.

'Johnny's in the hoose,' she volunteered readily.

'Makin' the dinner,' added Jimmy cheerily. 'He's been doing everything in the kitchen since Babsie left yesterday.'

'Is it true your new brother tak's fits?' questioned Jenny eyes a-goggle with frank curiosity.

Evelyn poked her chin in Jenny's face. '*You'll* take fits if I pull down your breeks and crack you across the bum.'

'Ay, and maybe die in agony if I take a hazel switch and do the same,' supplemented Florrie, itching to do just that for Jenny constantly irritated her with her bald questions.

'I'll tell my mother,' threatened Jenny aggressively. 'And – and maybe my father as well.'

Florrie pursed her lips disdainfully. 'You'll need a fog horn then for like as no' he's up wi' the lads in the bothy too drunk to listen to the likes o' you.'

Jenny's eyes filled with tears. Nevertheless she stood her ground and called after Florrie, 'Ya, tit for tat! Your father's too drunk half the time even to aim a cow's tit at the milking pail!'

Jimmy poked her with his elbow. 'Be quiet, Jenny Burns! You're getting to be a worse witch than Hinney wi' all your scraichin' and skirling.'

So saying, he took Janet's hand and hurried her up to the house, leaving Jenny stamping her ill temper into the snow.

Johnny was in the kitchen cutting vegetables and putting them carefully into a pan of stock simmering on the fire. At sight of Evelyn and Florrie he reddened with embarrassment and hastily tore off the large apron his mother had insisted he wear.

'Evelyn wants you to come down to King's Croft to see her wee brother.' Florrie spoke quickly, wasting no time on preliminaries.

'Ach, I've seen enough o' scraggy babies,' he snarled, while the blushes ran up over his neck to diffuse the fairness of his face. Viciously he chopped the skin from a potato. 'I'm too busy to be bothered, you shouldna have come.'

'Where's Babsie?' Evelyn stared round the kitchen, her gaze settling on the tiny bed recess set in the wall as if expecting to see Babsie McTaggart, the young kitchen maid of Birkiebrae, lying there ill. Babsie had been with the Burns family since the age of twelve, now she was a strapping, bonny girl of sixteen whom Catherine Burns relied on fiercely to carry out the domestic chores of the farm. Her own home lay in the fishing port of Stonehaven but she had left there at an early age to seek her fortunes in the hiring fairs around Aberdeen, going from one fee to the next till finally coming to Birkiebrae where her willing help had been sorely needed. Babsie was a good, reliable sort of girl but lately she had become flirtatious and giggly and was wont to hang around the fee'd farm lads at the least possible excuse.

At Evelyn's words Johnny's jaw tightened and he remembered again that terrible scene in the kitchen just yesterday morning, witnessed by himself and Jimmy as they had come running downstairs to see what all the shouting was about. His mother had been standing in the middle of the room, supporting herself on the back of a chair, her face ashen, her eyes wild and staring as she looked at the bed recess in which Babsie had slept ever since coming to the farm. It had been very early in the morning, barely six o'clock and pitch dark outside. Babsie had been in the bed, naked and dishevelled, her full white breasts rising and falling while she strove to cover them with the blankets which had fallen to the floor. In particular Johnny remembered her thighs, buxom, creamy white and rounded – and beside her, half on top of her, had been his father, his naked limbs stirring to sluggish life at the intrusion into the kitchen. His fair hair had been tousled, his eyes bloodshot and dazed and he had been breathing heavily as if he had been running and couldn't get back his breath.

Despite his surprise there had been black and bitter resentment in the dark eyes of him as he stared at his wife and heard her rantings and ravings falling about his ears. He had blundered out of the bed, the great unclothed height of him filling the room with its menacing, virile power, and while he was throwing on his clothes he had blundered about the room, no sign of shame in him, nor any word of sorrow for Babsie who had lain in the bed quietly sobbing, her dark hair rumpled about her face and her eyes swollen and red. Soon after that Rob Burns had ranted his way out of the house to be followed an hour or so later by Babsie, her pitiful little bundle of clothes tied in a sack, herself heartbroken and terrified of going home to Stonehaven for fear of what her father would have to say to her. Rob had stayed away all day and all night and Johnny had heard from one of the stockmen that he was lying in a drunken stupor up in the fee'd men's bothy. Johnny knew it wasn't the first time his father had lain with a woman that was not his wife. It happened mostly in the winter when enforced idleness unsettled a lot of the men in the farmtouns, but no one did it unsettle more than Rob Burns who chaved restlessly around the winter wrapped steadings and looked longingly towards the sea lying grey-bellied far, far away over the plains of Rothiedrum. Never though had he brought his cravings and wantings so close to home and even while Johnny hated him for what he had done, some small developing sense in him understood the stark needs of a man like his father who had all but been banished from the marriage bed since wee Janet's birth.

Evelyn was watching Johnny's face, seeing the secrets and the unhappiness lying there and she knew better than to pursue the matter of Babsie any further. Instead she said softly, persuasively, 'Ach, come on home wi' me, Johnny, it's Hogmanay, the end of the old year. Next year – tomorrow – will be better for everybody. It's been awful for me this past week, Mam wi' a new baby and everything and I'd like fine if you could come down to King's Croft. Florrie and me will get on your mother's peenies and do the rest o' the dinner while you go and see to the fowls. They're out there scarting around as if they were trying to dig to Australia.'

A smile hovered at Johnny's mouth. 'Ay, alright,' he conceded gruffly. 'But you'll have to go ben and ask Mother. I'm supposed to stay around till Jessie Blair comes to sit wi' her this afternoon.'

'Jessie Blair's a jelly.' Florrie chanted the words under her breath but even so they were taken up by Jimmy and Janet who began to dance around the table, utterly entranced by this latest description of the ponderous, kindly woman who smiled her fat smiles at them and gave them sweeties from the voluminous folds of her grubby smock.

Catherine Burns granted Johnny's reprieve with a languid wave of her limp white hand. The girls watched the flutterings and were seized with an almost unbearable urge to burst into giggles. She was languishing on a horsehair sofa in front of the parlour fire, an enormous ginger cat cuddled on her lap. The atmosphere was stuffy and foetid yet Catherine snuggled her shawl closer around a neck which hadn't seen daylight in months. In the heat of summer she would venture weakly outside to sit screwing her eyes against the sun's glare but in winter she rarely, if ever, went outside the door. If she hadn't worn such a

98

perpetual expression of hopelessness she would have been an attractive woman, as it was, her sparse brown hair was limp and unkempt, her fine-featured face drawn and woebegone. Once she had loved life and had been frivolous and gay, but her illness, coupled with her unhappy life with Robert, had soured her and so she had taken refuge behind an illness that was neither as painful nor as disabling as she liked to make out.

There was a genteel air about her that owed itself to a Manse upbringing and when visitors came she often harked back to the days of her youth when a faithful servant had tended her every need and her dear, sweet father had filled her life with his goodness and light. Yet she had escaped eagerly enough the strict confines of her orderly upbringing, lured by the good looks and the excitement of a man such as Robert Burns.

The Rothiedrum folk said she had just exchanged one prison for another though, 'a lot o' it is her own doing,' they told one another, 'she enjoys moaning and lying about being ill, as for that lad o' hers, she has made a serf o' him and one o' these fine days she will have cause to regret it. He'll flee the nest as soon as he's able and she'll be forced to rear the younger bairns herself.'

But Catherine could foresee no such future for Johnny. As lacking in foresight as she was in imagination, she saw only a boy whose first duty was to his home and family and who had never indicated by one word his desire for anything else. In many ways Johnny had taken the place of her roving, elusive husband in that he was always there to tend her whims, his loyalty to her never wavering though once or twice she caught him watching her and fancied she saw disdain in his glance – which of course was just her imagination – Johnny loved her and always would.

The door opened and he came in, a glow in his frost-stung cheeks, his tackety boots ringing on the linoleum covered floor. His gaze went quickly to the girls standing awkwardly by his mother's couch. Evelyn caught his eye and her lips widened in a roguishly triumphant grin. Despite himself he grinned back, a warm, good feeling

99

surging into his heart. The sight of her always did that to him, his friendship with her had never earned him the label of cissy, his fists were too hard and too able for anyone to dare use such a word to his face. He had never been one to make a lot of friends with those of his own sex. Alan Keith of Dippiedoon was about the only lad he had ever really confided in, but Alan had that awful mother of his to contend with and Johnny took care never to go near Alan's house if he could help it.

'Are you sure you can manage, Mother?' he asked automatically. 'The soup is on the fire and the tatties peeled. You just have to go ben and keep an eye on things.'

'My mother says Johnny can have his dinner with us,' Evelyn said quickly, seeing Catherine's lips trembling ever so slightly. 'It will save him the trek back seeing Mrs Blair will be along in the afternoon.'

Catherine gathered the cat to her bosom. 'Ay, ay, go you away, Johnny son, and enjoy yourself. The Lord knows you're a good loon and deserve a break. Dinna worry aboot me, I'll struggle ben the kitchen and mind the dinner – though how I'll cope wi' the bairns as well the Lord alone knows.'

She was using her martyred voice, with a whining edge to it that made Florrie draw in her lips and say firmly, 'Never fear, Mrs Burns, Jimmy's old enough to see to the fire and fetch in the water buckets and Mrs Blair will be along soon enough.'

'But there's all the things Babsie usually does,' wailed Catherine. 'Who will take the bothy lads their dinner? I canna sprachle up there wi' milk buckets and the like, you know I'm no able to go outside the door, Johnny.'

'I saw Matt Travers earlier,' said Johnny quietly, 'And he said he would come down for the brose and milk.'

'Ay, Matt's a good man, a good man,' Catherine sighed. 'And from all accounts he's the best ploughman we've had working to us yet.' She lay back and cast a languid, thoughtful eye on the ceiling and the three youngsters crept softly to the door as if afraid to disturb her reverie.

Once outside Johnny seemed to throw off his mantle of

gloom. Blue eyes shining, he ran and rolled in the snow, threw great showers of it in the air so that it cascaded around him in a glistening curtain.

Jenny stood at the gate, arms folded at her back, her chin thrust out aggressively. 'I'm comin' wi' ye, Johnny,' she called threateningly.

'No you're not,' Johnny dusted snow from his sleeved waistcoat, an ancient old thing of his father's which had been handed down to him recently and which sat uncomfortably big on his young shoulders. 'You get back into the house and keep an eye on wee Janet.'

Jenny stuck out her tongue. 'Ya, won't! You canna make me. I want to go wi' you – or else – or else I'll take Jan down to the loch and drown her!'

Johnny's face contorted. With all his heart he loved his tiny, doll-like baby sister and had a continual battle with the rebellious Jenny over her welfare. He stood undecided, torn between his desire to go off on a carefree outing and his responsibility to the younger Burns children. Evelyn and Florrie glanced at one another then as one they made a lunge for Jenny. Her eyes grew big in her pert face and tearing open the gate she flew towards the lochan, Florrie and Evelyn at her back, her shrieks in their ears as they caught her and rolled her in the snow, Evelyn holding her down while Florrie yanked her bloomers to her ankles and delivered several sharp slaps upon the small, pink buttocks.

'I'm tellin', I'm tellin',' sobbed Jenny, sturdy legs flaying the ground, bedraggled hair streaked over her eyes.

'You're telling nothing,' hissed Evelyn. 'Just you give Johnny a bit more peace and do as he tells you.'

Florrie's vivid blue eyes were sparkling in her frost-stung cheeks, her whole being alive with the satisfaction of seeing Jenny squirming under her none too tender administrations. 'Ay, do as you're told, you wee bitch or – or I'll fetch a hazel twig from yon bush and really tan your hide.'

Jenny stiffened and grew still but Evelyn's grip remained firm on her. 'Promise you'll behave yourself or I'll keep your knickers at your ankles till your bum freezes and drops off.'

'Alright,' Jenny's voice came muffled from the snowy ground.

Florrie shook her. 'Cross your heart and hope to die.'

'I canna,' wailed Jenny thickly. 'My heart's squashed in my breest and I canna reach it.'

Without ado, Evelyn yanked her to a sitting position and stood over her while she made the necessary signs, watched in the distance by a delighted Johnny who didn't dare come any closer for fear he would erupt into bellows of laughter which might disrupt the earnestness with which Jenny was obeying orders.

Once released, she scampered back to the house as quickly as her short legs would carry her but as she reached the door her natural defiance spurted forth and she turned and yelled, 'I'm coming wi' ye next time, Johnny, you wait!' So saying she made a hideous face and flew into the house, banging the door triumphantly behind her.

Johnny grabbed hold of the girls and they ran down the snowy fields, keeping to the endrigs as they slithered and rolled and finally stood panting for breath as they dusted the snow from their clothes. A slight thaw was setting in, Johnny could smell it, more a feeling of it in the air than a changing in the earth.

'They'll go soon.' He had spied the writing made by Florrie in the snow and striding over he stood for a long time looking at the childishly scrawled epitaph. Without a word he seized a sharp edged stone and throwing himself on his knees added his own message to that which was already there.

Throwing the stone away he turned an embarrassed face as the girls came up and stared solemnly at what he had written.

'J.B. loves –' Florrie read aloud and glanced slyly at Johnny. 'You havena finished it, Johnny. Which o' us do you love?'

Johnny coloured to the roots of his hair. 'The two o' you.'

'You're blushing, Johnny,' teased Florrie. 'And you canna love two lassies at the one time. Which one is it, me or Evelyn?'

Johnny stood up. He was wearing trousers now, his kilt having been abandoned because it had grown too short for him. He loomed, big and strong and handsome against the cold December sky. Bending forward he brushed the knees of his corduroys with a careless hand and kept his lips tight shut.

'Come on, Johnny, tell us,' persisted Florrie while Evelyn nonchalantly gathered up a snowball and crushed it into smithereens.

'I'm no' telling,' he said at last, a hint of defiance in the gruffness of his voice. Evelyn glanced up sharply, a strange quiet wonder stealing into her breast. Only last month Johnny had celebrated his thirteenth birthday and now there was an occasional and unfamiliar hint of huskiness in his clear child's voice.

Johnny Burns was growing up. The realization wrought in her a sensation of such unexpected sadness she stared deep into his eyes, eyes that had grown suddenly aware and wary . . .

The arrival of The Loon saved him from further embarrassment and brought normality into the situation. Not that The Loon could be described as being normal. He was a wee bent shoochle of a man in thick tweeds and an ancient deerstalker hat under which sprouted a good head of yellow thick hair. Referred to as The Loon behind his back, Pootie to his face, he was an eccentric 'lad' of forty or so who lived with his widowed mother in a But and Ben known as Boglehowe situated half a mile up from Carnallachie's place. As far back as anyone could remember he had been half-witted. 'Wi more wits in that half than some wi' a full head o' brains.'

All the bairns of Rothiedrum liked him though some called him 'Daftie', which was about the only thing that ever seemed to rouse him to rage. A few chickens, a cow, and two horses made up the livestock of Boglehowe but its fifteen or so acres was good corn land and about the only

103

thing that kept Boglehowe from falling to bits round its tenants' ears. Dottie Drummond was hard put to keep her home together and so she put her son out to work on neighbouring farms. The good folk of Rothiedrum always found something that would earn him a few shillings and were glad to have his help at seed time and harvest, for he had good strong hands on him and could be depended upon to work away steadily without supervision. Only two things distracted him, an empty belly and fun-loving children. He loved bairns' play did The Loon, and it wasn't unknown for him to turn his back on work and join the youngsters in their games.

His voice was soft and low; 'Like a calf fresh from a cow's belly,' Betsy O'Neil said, though she as much as anyone was partial to passing the time of day with The Loon, the distraction of hearing him talk in his soft, soothing voice about all the rows and events that went on inside the four walls of Boglehowe was not something to be passed by in a hurry.

He came scrunching towards the children, his beguiling blue eyes lighting his walnut brown face, his stumpy legs and big clairty feet taking him easily through the snow. The size of his feet had always been the focus for much comment. Old Carnallachie had likened them to 'snowshoes wi' the sneezes' for they had a jerky way of moving and the sound of them 'choo choo choo'ing' through grass and snow alike was as distinctive as the screaming of gulls over the spring ploughs.

Maybe The Loon has got wind of all those comments directed at his feet for he always seemed to emphasize the 'choo'ing' of them when he knew folk were near to hand. He emphasized it now as he scrambled up to Johnny and gazed with joy at the writing decorating the edge of the field.

'My, Johnny, that's grand, man,' he nodded in approval. 'Yon dominie at the school has taught ye right well.'

'We did some of it,' interposed Florrie, blowing over her red-tipped fingers, a suppressed excitement in her voice that Evelyn knew well. 'You write something, Pootie,' she urged, turning her most innocent smile on the new arrival.

'I canna, I never learned.' Pootie's soft voice was frayed with frustration for one of the great loves of his life was books, the look of them, the feel of them, the wonderful mystery of all those words which he had never been able to understand.

As a lad he had earnestly tried to master reading but had only managed to learn the alphabet without ever being able to string more than two letters together. His greatest joy was when his mother was in a mood to read to him, but there too he was at a sad disadvantage as Dottie Drummond was not that far ahead of her son in the world of literature, her abilities barely stretching to the large lettered nursery tales she had picked up for a few coppers at one of the hiring fairs.

'Make some letters then, Pootie,' suggested Johnny kindly but Florrie tutted impatiently and grabbing The Loon by one frayed sleeve she implored, 'No, Pootie, make a design in the snow, you know, squiggly marks and things.'

The Loon's face brightened. 'Ay, I could do that. Wait you there and I'll fetch a twiggie.'

'No, Pootie, not a twig – *pee* in it,' hissed Florrie, ignoring Johnny's dark look. The Loon stared at her, taking the request with complete candour since he was far too innocent to regard any human function with distaste. 'Ach no,' he intoned in some disappointment. 'I'm no' needing.'

'Ach, go on, Pootie,' Evelyn joined forces with Florrie, a devil prancing in the green of her eyes. 'Just a wee dribble. It will be a bonny sight – you'll see the steam rising.'

'Turn roond,' ordered The Loon in a burst of decision, fumbling importantly with his fly. Hugging each other, Evelyn and Florrie turned away, half-opened fingers to their eyes as The Loon made his mark, the 'stoor' of his efforts biting its yellow way into the virgin whiteness and even Johnny, who had retired to the other side of the whin bushes in huffed silence, let out a yell of laughter when he saw the initial 'P' carved shakily into the snow.

'I made my ain mark.' The Loon beamed, a burst of pride puffing out his chest. 'I had just enough in me to do it.'

Florrie threw her arms round him and hugged him. 'That's good, Pootie, really good, you're no as daft as folks say.'

'Dinna you call me daft.' The Loon's eyes flashed dangerously and a glimmer of tears shone on his lashes. 'I'm no' daft, I'm no'.'

'Ach, of course you're not, Pootie,' consoled Evelyn. 'Florrie didna mean it. Look, you come along wi' me. You can have a keek at my new wee brother and my Mam will give you something nice for your Ne'erday.'

The Loon wiped his eyes and followed them happily, mimicking every move they made as they tumbled and skipped down through the parks to King's Croft.

Maggie was in the kitchen, pale and drawn after a week spent in bed. There was a lack of sparkle about her, her pride of carriage was gone, she moved listlessly, her eyes lacked the life and lustre that had been so essentially hers. There was an old look about her that tore at Jamie's heart every time he looked at her and wondered if she would ever be the same again.

The week since Christmas seemed unreal to her; sometimes she wondered to herself if any of it had ever happened, then the weak cries of her newborn son brought her back to cruel reality. More for Jamie's sake than her own she had always hoped to have a son. The advent of the twins had plunged her from quiet joy to the depths of sorrow. The arrival of Evelyn had been little surprise to her; she had known it would be a girl, had resigned herself to it and had never regretted Evelyn's birth, but after that she had thought there would be no more – and now this, a son to be sure but such a poor slavering, pitiful wee thing. His convulsions frightened her, she didn't want to look at him – she was past coping – past caring. It was now she thanked God for Nellie, the most omnipotent of her daughters. She had nursed and cared for that poor wee man creature as if she truly loved him . . .

106

Maggie pulled herself up sharply. Didn't she have any feelings for him herself? He was a poor, innocent helpless babe yet – she had to admit – she didn't even like him very much. Jamie did. He had been good and helpful since the birth, pacing the floor with the tiny bundle in his arms, crooning to it, talking to it, his eyes drooping with fatigue, his face twisted in worry as the tiny features of his son contorted and turned a terrifying blue colour . . . She snapped out of her reverie as the children came in, The Loon at their heels. For a moment she stared at Dottie Drummond's son; something about his face was oddly familiar – his eyes . . .

Nellie threw down the napkins she was folding and pulled Evelyn into the scullery to shake her. 'You wee bitch,' she hissed. 'You know Mother's just up, and yet you trip in here wi' the half o' Rothiedrum at your heels.' Lifting her hand, she brought it down heftily on the child's face. Her bony knuckle caught Evelyn at the side of the nose and instantly the blood spurted.

Evelyn stood stock still while Nellie stared aghast at the red marks lying across the child's face, at the thick welling of blood from her nostril.

Grace rushed in to pull at Nellie and sit Evelyn down on a little stool. 'Get a bowl of cold water and a clean cloth,' she ordered, her voice icy with anger.

For once Nellie rushed to carry out someone else's bidding and in minutes they had Evelyn cleaned and the flow of blood stemmed.

Grace turned on Nellie. 'Why did you lift your hand to her?'

'And why no'?' returned Nellie, with a meekness in her tones that surprised Evelyn. 'The wee madam came marching in here wi' half the gowks o' the place trailing at her heels . . .'

'Mam told her to bring the bairns along. Evie hasna had much of a Christmas and I asked Mam if she could have her friends in for a meal – one which *I* prepared.'

'I didna know – I was up wi' the bairn for most of the

morning,' murmured Nellie, looking so shamefaced that Evelyn could do nothing but stare at her openly.

Grace relaxed, composure returned to the sweet stillness of her face. 'Ach, Nell, we're all a bittie on edge. Everything's been so – so strange this past week – and now it's Hogmanay and you can be sure the whole place will be firstfooting come midnight. They're all agog to see the baby – and I canna be bothered wi' any o' them just now.'

Nellie gazed from one sister's face to another, Evelyn white and big eyed, Grace weary and dispirited. An unexpectedly radiant smile lit her strong features. 'I'll tell you what, after dinner you and me, Grace, will hap ourselves and Mam in our warmest clothes and get out in the fresh air for a while. Evelyn and the others can stay here and get the Ne'erday table set between them. They'll enjoy that, especially as there's a nice big sultana cake which I baked yesterday with a wee one to spare for bairns wi' big appetites.'

Grace breathed a sigh of heartfelt agreement while Evelyn let out a suppressed whoop and rushed through to the kitchen to impart the news to Florrie and Johnny who were sitting together on the ingle playing with the cats. The Loon was at the fire, eating black bun and talking in his soft voice to Maggie who was smiling as he described some amusing incident that had taken place at Boglehowe.

Florrie looked at the marks on her friend's face and hissed, 'Did that Nellie slap you? Was that why she rushed you ben the scullery?'

'Ach, you know Nellie,' shrugged Evelyn offhandedly.

'Ay, too well,' agreed Florrie with feeling. 'She slapped me once when I asked her if she had bosoms. I was only a bairn at the time and didna know any better.'

'You've always known better,' snorted Johnny though there was a twinkle in his eyes for he had always admired Florrie's irrepressible nature.

'I know one thing,' said Florrie emphatically. 'That Nellie needs a man to tame her – my sister Tina used to be like her, an irritable old yowe wi' thorns on her tongue till one night she came in – a smile on her face that near split it in two and only left it when wee Pete came along and near split *her* in two.'

At that Johnny threw back his head and bellowed out his hearty laugh while Evelyn giggled into her hand.

Jamie came in, stamping the snow from his boots, a smile at his mouth as the sounds of merriment greeted him. Quickly he looked across at Maggie whose silence and strangeness had worried him of late. Over The Loon's animated head she threw her husband a warm quick glance and said, 'You're back then, Jamie, my man?'

His heart warmed. She only called him 'Jamie, my man,' when she wanted to convey her feelings of love to him. His dark face lit and he nodded, 'Ay, Maggie, I'm back.'

Johnny came over to him, near as tall as him, the fair skin of him reddening a bit as he said quietly, 'There's a thaw coming, Mr Grant, I can feel it in the air.'

Jamie nodded, knowing fine what the boy was hinting at. 'Ay, Johnny that there is.' He threw Johnny a sidelong smiling glance. 'The steel will be off the ground come morning and the earth ready for the turning. I was thinking I might do a wee bittie ploughing, get some work done before the next freeze. Would you maybe come over and gie me a bit o' a hand? If you can get away that is.'

Johnny's eyes were shining. 'I'll get away, never you fear.'

Jamie nodded. 'Good, that's good, man. Evie was telling me you're a big lad of thirteen now. Hmm, well it's shamed you should be that you havna yet put your hand to the plough. Come early enough tomorrow and you can have a wee go, I'll be there to keep you right.' Johnny could say nothing but the affection he had always felt for Jamie King Grant grew just a bit stronger that last bright morning of 1908.

CHAPTER SIX

The Loon gaped down at the baby lying in his makeshift bed by the fire in his parents' room. Florrie and Johnny had had enough of babies in their short lives and were downstairs with Mary who had come back from an errand, sparkling eyed and fresh faced, more of a spring in her step than ever, making Evelyn study her and wonder if she had been over to see Malcom Keith – or if she had set her sights on further horizons this bonny blue last day of the old year. Doctor McGregor had paid several visits to the croft lately, waving away Jamie's protests that he couldn't afford so many calls.

'I'm no' after your sillar, Jamie,' he had grinned. 'Just remember me next time you bring home some of those fine salmon I hear you're so good at catching.'

But, attentive though he was to wee Colin, everyone knew it was really Mary he had come to see, yet strangely enough he and she had almost ignored one another even though their eyes had spoken volumes and their glances had been filled with a sweet yearning – as if they could easily have devoured one another in one big gulp.

Evelyn had seen grown ups looking like that before but not until now she was aware of what it all meant. Mary was in love – and when Evelyn had asked her if she could take The Loon upstairs to see the baby her black eyes had been faraway and she had just nodded her consent – as if she hadn't really heard.

'My, my, he's a poor wee wraith o' a thing.' The Loon's voice brought Evelyn back to earth. The baby's cot was set on two chairs, firelight danced all over the curtained room, splashing warmth on the hearthrug, brushing the baby's white face with gold.

Evelyn tossed back her red head and her eyes flashed

110

green sparks. 'Havers, Pootie, he'll grow up fine and big, I know he will.'

But The Loon shook his head with conviction. 'Na, na, he'll no' grow – yon's a changeling child. I doot the fairies left him here for he looks as if a puff o' wind might blaw him away at any second.'

Evelyn stared down at her brother. Already his tiny puckered face was utterly dear to her, his little grasping fingers so trusting she wanted to cry at the feel of them in hers. With the exception of Nellie and Grace no one else gave him much attention. Murn went about her business as usual and behaved almost as if he didn't exist. Mary tended him but woodenly, Jamie was good to him but often too tired to be bothered – and Maggie – her behaviour was strange, her eyes hooded with a kind of resentment – but there was another look too – a look that could only be described as fear. And now The Loon was saying things that made Evelyn wonder if her mother knew the same things as Pootie – she certainly seemed to believe in fairies as she spoke about them often enough. 'You mustna say things like that, Pootie,' Evelyn scolded, and reaching down she scooped the child to her breast. His head nestled under her chin, he made no protest at the disturbance but drew a deep, shuddering breath before lapsing into wide-eyed silence.

'Wee babby, wee babby,' crooned Evelyn. 'You're my own wee brother, don't be afraid, I'll keep you safe.'

The Loon lowered his head in shame. 'Ach, I'm sorry, Evie, you know I wouldna say things that werena true. He's just too wee and quiet to be real. I was minding something my mother told me.' He spread his big hands. 'She's aye going on at me, tellin' me the bad fairies took her real son and left me instead.' Tears welled in his eyes. 'She blames me for being born. A daftie she calls me, aye a daftie, never her son, yet auld Coulter says it's her own doing. She was an auld bit wife when she had me, too auld Coulter says to make a wise bairn and my faither that long in the tooth he died the year after I was born.

'Coulter's a cruel mannie betimes, but he's aye been good to me and he aye speaks the truth to yer face – no' like some o' the futrets that are nice to yer front and talk at yer back.'

He scrubbed his fists into his eyes and sniffed. 'At least your babby will get good lovin' and plenty o' care and maybe it will no' matter that yer mother was too auld to have him – a daftie needs protecting frae gowks wi' barbed tongues in their heids.'

'You're no' a daftie, Pootie,' Evelyn said softly. 'You've just never learnt like the rest o' us. But I tell you this, wee Colin is not a fairy child, I was in the house the night he was born and though I was downstairs when he came, the doctor and Hinney were up here wi' my mother and saw him being born.'

The Loon gave her a sly look. 'Hinney can work magic – she gies people potions so that they dinna ken what's happening to them. She gave one to my mother when she was ill and she slept for a whole day after.'

Evelyn remembered the herb tea Hinney had given to her mother – and she had slept so soundly she hadn't even heard her coming into the room. With a little shiver she turned away from The Loon and hugged the baby closer.

Mary came in at that moment, her face hot from a good-natured tussle in the kitchen with Florrie. 'Evie,' she cried sharply. 'What have you been told about lifting that baby! Put him back to bed and come you down before Nell gets back or she'll skite me round the lugs for allowing you up here.'

Evelyn laid the child down, wondering if she should tell Mary of the things The Loon had said. But no, she decided quickly, she would never mention them to anyone. The Loon was a daftie anyway; who would believe anything he said – yet she couldn't help wondering if maybe he had been right about her mother been too old to have had a bairn – it would be terrible for them all to have a daftie in the family – her mother would never live it down or be able to hold up her head in pride again.

At half past midnight, the dreaming quiet of King's Croft was invaded. Grace had been right. It seemed the whole of Rothiedrum was agog to see the product of a womb past its first flowerings.

Doctor McGregor was first to bang on the door, his entry preceded by several large lumps of coal and a pair of Finnon haddies that went skiting across the room, straight into the jaws of Ginger, a large, scraggy, opportunist tom. Off he slunk with his prize clamped firmly in his drooling fangs amidst shouts of laughter and New Year greetings. Behind the doctor came Hinney bearing a large pot of heather honey and a whisky pig filled with home brewed ale which was reputed be stronger than any of the beverages concocted in any of the farmtoun kitchens.

Old Coulter arrived with Kenneth Cameron Mor and Jeannie, whose baby was wrapped in a plaid and snuggled in under her shawl. Tandy soon followed, more wild and unkempt looking than ever and behind him came the Keiths of Dippiedoon, Kirsty going straight over to Nellie who sat with the baby on her knee, getting him into his flannel nightgown which had been warming by the fire.

'He's a *wee* mannie,' Kirsty stressed critically, her keen eyes sweeping over the bony little body with something akin to triumph. 'My own were aye padded well at birth – of course, I was a young woman then and didna expect anything else but healthy bairns.'

Neither Nellie nor Maggie had time to make comment for just then a terrible squealing and banging came from the close, making Jamie go and throw open the door to see what was happening. Betsy O'Neil and Danny loomed outside, pushing in front of them a monstrous black object which soon proved to be an ancient pram heaped high with bundles of baby clothes.

'We kent fine you gave yours away to the tinks, Maggie,' Betsy grinned, pushing back a thick wad of newly washed hair and meeting the eyes of the aghast mistress of King's Croft.

Florrie and her sister Maureen slid in at their father's back, going over to squeeze in beside Evelyn. 'They dinna ken we came wi' them,' Florrie breathed in Evelyn's ear. 'Coorie round us and we might no' be noticed.'

Whatever Maggie might have had to say about the pram was lost in a volley of greetings, handshakings and kissings. The room was in a sweating, happy uproar. Murn had turned bright red at sight of Kenneth Mor coming through the door and now she jostled to get to him in the hope that she might be the recipient of a New Year's kiss, the one chance she had of receiving such a rare treasure honestly and openly.

Mary sat in a corner, still and quiet, tanned skin flushed to roses, keeking under her lashes at the handsome, boyish countenance of Doctor McGregor. His brown hair shone in the lamplight, his face was glowing from the bracing air of the countryside. After the first general greetings his eyes sought hers, darkened to unconcealed pleasure as he elbowed his way over and stood looking down at her.

'Mary,' her name was a sigh on his lips. 'I could hardly wait for the bells to come over to see you.'

She dropped her gaze from him and said softly, 'But, I saw you this afternoon.'

'That was last year,' he laughed then unable to contain himself a moment longer he pulled her up and winding his arms about her kissed her long and deeply.

Nellie watched them embracing and turned away to busy herself with the baby, Malcolm Keith also watched and glowered jealously from darkened brows. He was a tall, dark lad of twenty, built for the farm but with little interest in it, much preferring to pass his time socializing at the village inn and pursuing the girls.

Angus Keith had fathered two sons, Alan the gentle one, never fashioned for the farm but for the drawing board, his talent encouraged by Mr Gregory who visualized a day when he would graduate to art college.

Angus was proud of Alan, understood that he was destined for better things – but Malcolm – Malcolm was his despair. His hands had been fashioned for the plough, yet the witless bugger spent all his strength on quines and booze. And worse irony, Chris, his only daughter, bonny, lively and slender as the willows by Birkieside; loved the farm and helped in the fields whenever she could. In fact she was everything that Malcolm was not and Angus often sighed to himself and bemoaned to Kirsty that there had been a gey queer mix-up when Chris and Malcolm were in the making.

Kirsty Keith's lips folded when she saw the doctor and Mary embracing. 'Hmph,' she snorted to Betsy. 'I see that Mary's at it again. Maggie had better watch that one. She'll get herself in trouble afore she's twenty for she's the kind that men just play with. Mind you, I thought the doctor had more sense in him. I liked him fine when he first came but I can see he's no better than the rest.'

Jamie was dispensing drinks and Betsy raised a languid hand as the tray teetered under her nose. Taking a noisy gulp of her whisky she cast a thoughtful eye at Mary. 'Ach, havers, Kirsty,' she said forcibly. 'Mary's too sensible a lass to drop her breeks to just any man. From what I hear, your Malky has only succeeded in yanking down his own. She has her eye on bigger game than Malky but she'll torment both o' them a bittie afore she's through – there's no greater spur than jealousy to prod a man up the aisle – and yon bonny doctor will be on fire wi' jealousy afore this night is over – wait you and see.'

'I'll do nothing o' the kind, Betsy O'Neil,' snapped Kirsty with asperity. 'And dinna you dare insinuate that my Malcolm is no' good enough for the likes o' Mary Grant. She has a queer mixture o' tink blood in her and I wouldna like to think what Maggie has passed on. There have been stories about her you know. Some o' the old ones have long memories and have hinted that there was something fishy about her birth. We Keiths are pure stock and it shows – blood will out, ay indeed.'

Betsy threw back her head and guffawed with laughter. 'By God and it does! Your claws are showing you for the cat you are. Here you sit, snug as a bug at Maggie's fireside – miscalling her for all your worth – which isna much.'

'What about you?' spat Kirsty. 'The other day you cried Maggie for everything – called her a snob – and you turn up here the night pushing a pram that looks as if the tinks themselves had cast it in the junk heap. Well, I'll tell you

115

this, Betsy, Maggie will no use it, you'll never see that poor wee bairn insideof it, not will it be wearing your own bairn's cast offs, for Maggie's that proud she can hardly see over her own bloated breest –'

Maggie came up, a glass of port in her hand, her smile sweetly deceptive as she looked down on Kirsty's upturned, guilty face. 'Am I hearing my name from this cosy wee corner?' she enquired pleasantly.

'Ay – well ay, you did, Maggie,' stuttered Kirsty. 'I was just saying to Betsy that it was kind o' her to bring the pram and the few wee bit things – but I told her I doubted if we would see you pushing it for a whilie yet – you're looking a wee bittie wabbit I thought.'

Maggie took a sip of her port and eyed Kirsty thoughtfully. 'Ay, Kirsty, you're wasted right enough. You know that much about other folks business 'tis a wonder to me you never made a fortune as a Spey wife. Mind you,' she continued contemplatively, 'it wouldna have worked for I doubt there's a body in the land would pay to listen to the kind o' poison you have to say about them.'

Betsy spluttered into her glass while Kirsty grew red and said placatingly, 'Now, Maggie, you mustna say things like that. It's New Year and we should all be neighbourly to one another. Now, how are you keeping, poor soul? No too good from the look o' you – but then, what a shock the bairn must have been, coming unexpected like that. Sit you by us and tell us all about it.'

But Maggie did nothing of the kind. Bunty Lovie had just arrived, together with Lily and Charlie Lammas and Maggie went to see to them, settling them into the few available seats with their drinks. The murmur of voices filled the room and Evelyn sat listening with only half an ear, her attention taken up with her sister Mary who seemed to have abandoned the doctor in favour of Malcolm Keith, who was making the most of the situation by putting his arm round her possessively and holding her too close. Bunty Lovie and Lily were seated behind Evelyn and though they were talking quietly she could hear everything they were saying. They had been discussing wee

Colin but now the talk turned to the circumstances that had led up to his birth.

'Fancy,' Bunty whispered in her clear chirpy voice. 'It is just history repeating itself for I mind fine how it was when Murn came along. Maggie went into labour in the Post Office, right in front o' my very own eyes and what a job we had getting her home for the snow was thick on the ground and she near dropped the bairn in it, it was that quick in coming. And what a state she was in, moaning and greeting and . . .'

Bunty's voice went on but Evelyn didn't hear. She was remembering that eerie sense of premonition she had experienced on the journey down from Kenneth Mor's ceilidh, the feeling that something was about to happen that had all happened before and then her mother's pain and the terrible trauma of getting her home over the snowbound track. A shiver went through her despite the fire's heat and she tried to listen to more of Bunty's conversation, but Florrie nudged her and she started in fright.

'Look at Hinney,' hissed Florrie, 'she's drunk.'

Evelyn forced herself back to reality and glanced at Hinney sitting on the wooden settle in a shadowed corner of the room, a glass of whisky in her hand, her face flushed, her lips moving as she muttered under her breath.

'Do you think she's casting spells on us?' whispered Florrie hopefully. 'She – she looks awful fierce.'

'Ach, no,' Evelyn looked at the old woman affectionately. She hadn't disclosed to Florrie the intimacy she had shared with Hinney on the night of Colin's birth. 'She's only singing to herself. She – Hinney isn't a witch, she's a nice, kind old woman and I truly like her.'

But Florrie wasn't going to have her cherished beliefs shattered so easily and she continued to speculate on Hinney's mysterious powers while Evelyn's attention wandered to her mother who was looking a bit more like her old self. Her shoulders were well back, there was a fine sparkle on her face as she talked to Kirsty and Betsy. Murn was floating about the room, looking lost as usual though she was prettier than she had ever been with a new green

117

dress offsetting the dark of her hair and a bloom of colour on her otherwise pale cheeks. But her eyes were still sad – yet Kenneth Mor had kissed her – a quick, dutiful kiss, like a brother kisses a sister. Grace was lovely that night in a frilly white blouse which lent her a fragile, unearthly quality though her great burning dark eyes were filled with a life that was almost feverish – as if she was absorbing all the vitality of the people around her, storing it up for some future day when her own resources were at a low ebb . . .

Evelyn shuddered at her own dark thoughts. Why, oh why did she think these things about Grace? It was daft – daft. She moved restlessly and concentrated her thoughts on Johnny up there at Birkiebraw while all around her the melodeons, the paper combs, and the fiddles played.

'Would you like me to tell ye a story?' Coulter poked his white-bearded face down to her and she looked up in delight. The very sight of his lean, hard figure filled her with anticipation, for he gave freely of his time to her and often the old man and the young girl would snuggle together in the hayloft, Coulter to tell his tales; Evelyn to listen and perhaps write them down so that she could read them later in the privacy of her room. He was a striking figure to look at, with a face that might have been carved from rock. His jaw was like a gin trap, solid and belligerent, his glittering blue eyes seemed stolen from the winter skies, his shock of white hair and long snowy beard which sprung from the edges of his chin like a whitewash brush, might have been scooped from the sunless corries of Bennachie and plastered round his face.

His voice was his greatest surprise. From such a rock one might have expected a brittle whiplash, but instead there bubbled forth a liquid resonance of sound which fell upon the ears like gentle music. When Coulter told his stories round winter firesides everyone forgot howling winds and blattering rain, and when he stopped talking to light his pipe an eerie silence would descend while the witches of his tales pranced on shadowed ceilings and the dark oblong of the scullery door seemed filled with a waiting menace that was too terrifying to bear. Coulter was too old now to

118

pursue the footloose life of the fee'd man, and the factor allowed him the use of the bothy over by the Mains in return for odd jobs around the estate. At ceilidhs he was much sought after, but it was the children who loved him best and Evelyn eagerly accepted his offer.

'Ay, Coulter, that would be grand.'

'Well, sit ye over a bittie and I'll squeeze doon beside ye. Florrie, coorie in here by Evie and we'll a' be fine and cosy like. I might no' be able to hear myself for a' this din but as long as you twa can make oot what I'm saying it willna matter.'

Placing his big, solid feet on the hearth he slowly lit his pipe then putting an arm round each of the girls drew them in close. 'Noo, I'm thinking o' a fine bright day in summer when the stooks were a' sorted in the parks and the peesies were skirlin' in the sky fit tae burst. I was sitting wi' my back against a nice sunny dyke, enjoying a wee rest like, when I heard this wee voice at my elbow – now – ye'll be thinkin' I'm aboot tae tell ye it was a fairy I was hearin' . . .'

The resonance of his voice filled every space in Evelyn's head, soothing her even while she drew in her breath in anticipation of what was to come. She forgot the world then as the old man's magical tale unfolded, carrying her back to a land filled with summer sun and bird song and terrible wee elves who played havoc with the harvest fields . . .

Jeannie, bonny Jeannie of the shining dark hair, made her way over to the settle to sit herself down by Hinney. The baby was whimpering with hunger and Jeannie pulled apart her blouse to allow one full creamy breast to peep out unobtrusively. The baby's mouth searched for the hard, dark nipple, found it and sucked contentedly.

Kenneth Mor watched and his face darkened. He went striding over, his kilt swirling round his fine hairy knees. 'Are you shameless, woman?' he hissed at his wife. 'The room is full o' men, each one as hungry as the bairn for a suckle at your breest. You're my wife, no' a heedless tink seated at some wild camp fire.'

Jeannie's quiet eyes gazed steadily into his icy blue orbs. 'You're the only one who noticed, Kenneth, and you're the

119

only one jealous enough to think o' such a thing.'

Kenneth Mor's eyes blazed, his jaw tightened and he looked as if he would like to strike her. Damn the woman! She was right! So soft and gentle this bonny lass of his and so wise. He loved her with a love that was stormy and passionate. He was like a ship tossing on stormy seas while she – she ruled the calm, sweet shallows of the shores, tranquil yet restless by a possessive love that was forever threatening to engulf her.

'Ach, leave the lassie be,' Hinney told him sourly. 'You're such a blustering big bairn o' a man ye canna leave her alone for two minutes at a time. Jeannie will no' shame you. She's got more breeding in her wee toe than you've got in the whole o' yer muckle body.'

Kenneth had the grace to look shamefaced. Reaching out one big hand, he stroked the silken hair back from his young wife's sweet face and kissed her brow. 'Ach, Jeannie, I'm sorry I behaved so,' he said huskily. 'It's just – well I'm feart sometimes you might just slip away from me. I canna right believe yet you're mine.'

She smiled at him, calmly, forgivingly. 'Away wi' you, you muckle great bairn. I'll no' leave you if that's what you mean. You surely know that, Kenneth?'

'Ay, I know.' he answered. 'I'd die if you did.'

Hinney sighed. 'What it is to be young and in love. It was like that once for me and Alastair – ay, you can smile but it's true. You would never think to look at the old goat now, but there was a time he was as handsome a chiel you could meet – and myself as bonny as the wild rose on the bough.' She giggled. 'But look at me now, so ugly the bairns will have me a witch and Alastair so blind it doesna matter to him one way or another.'

The O'Neils were taking their leave, calling their goodbyes as they spilled out into the night, Danny for once reasonably sober, but it was early yet and still a lot of places to first foot, Betsy was angry at Florrie and Maureen, clipping them round the ears and turning them both in the direction of home. They went off a little way down the track, waited till the sound of the cart could be heard no

120

more then they turned back giggling to the warmth and hospitality of King's Croft, knowing fine they wouldn't be missed in their own home till morning.

Tandy had picked up his pipes and was striding up and down outside the croft, his great feet crunching in the snow. Kenneth Mor joined him and soon the stirring tunes of old Scotia reeled through air that stung the cheeks and condensed the breath on beards and whiskers. The eaves of the house were overhung with fangs of melting icicles, the moon hung low over Bennachie like a giant dinnerplate rung round with a cold bluish tinge that lit the sky for miles around. The cloying cold of a Northern winter night embraced the world, but inside the snug kitchen of King's Croft the merrymakers sweated and soon followed the sound of the pipes outside where the clouded moon lit the yard, making it ideal for dancing and drinking and generally going wild.

'I wish Johnny was here,' Evelyn confided to Florrie as they swung on the yard gate and watched Bunty Lovie being whirled round and round by Tandy whose whisky-warmed blood made him behave as wildly as his ancestral clansmen of long ago.

'Who do you think he loves?' asked Florrie, holding on to the gate and leaning backwards so that her vivid face was tilted to the stars.

'Don't know,' Evelyn replied with studied indifference. 'But I do know he'll be in bed now with nothing to remind him it's New Year except when that drunken father of his comes home and stumbles about the house swearing.'

'Ach, he's no' that bad,' said Florrie thoughtfully. 'I think he just does it to frighten that wishy-washy wife o' his. My father drinks but it's a different drinking from Rob Burns, he gets happy and kisses my mother and they go to bed giggling and squeezing each other. Your father gets drunk too but in a different way from Johnny's father.'

Evelyn watched her father jigging about in the snow, his fiddle in one hand, a bottle of whisky in the other. 'Ay, he just gets daft. I wish he wouldna – I hate to see men drunk. They're like bairns they act so silly.' She stopped swinging.

'Stay wi' me the night, Florrie. You can come into my bed and we'll tell each other stories. Nobody will miss you at Cragbogie.'

'Ay, alright, but what about Maureen?'

'She can share Grace's bed, Grace won't mind; she never gets angry at things like that.'

A tall dark figure loomed from the corner of the byre and went towards the house.

'It's Mr Gregory,' Evelyn's voice was filled with wonder. 'I wonder why he came. He never usually goes first footing.'

'Maybe he got fed up wi' the ghosts in his house. I hate it there. The pictures stare out at you and give you shivers up the spine.'

Martin Gregory was a fine well-built man of forty with dark hair greying at the temples, a fresh clean skin and piercing blue eyes behind thick glasses. He had lost his wife and only child in the birthing bed and though there were plenty of young maidens in the district eager for his attention, he remained alone. In school he was liked and respected, but there was always an air of sadness in him, as if he had lost his way in the world and could never quite find it again.

'He loved too well ever to think o' casting his een at another woman,' said Bunty Lovie. 'Mary Ann was a bonny lassie and how they looked forward to their firstborn. But ach, it wasna to be, she was never strong and there she went and died on him taking the bairn with her. My, it was sad, ay, indeed.' And Bunty's cheery face would grow sad at the wiles and twists of life.

He went nervously into the house. Jeannie and Nellie were sitting in a corner, talking animatedly about babies. Maggie had gone upstairs, Kirsty Keith and Hinney were snoring together on the settle, propping each other up amicably. Martin Gregory stood nonplussed, his eyes darting round the room, looking as if he would like to turn and walk out again. Grace appeared from the scullery. At sight of the visitor she stopped short, surprise darkening her eyes, a sudden flush of colour diffusing her cheeks. 'Mr Gregory, how nice it is to see you.'

Her low, husky acknowledgement fell on his ears like music in the warm, peaceful heartbeat of the room.

'Grace – I – I hope you don't mind. I – well to be honest I couldna stand bringing in another New Year in that house – alone.'

'Mind? Why should I mind?' She came forward and taking his cold hands drew him in closer to the fire. 'Happy New Year, Mr Gregory.'

'And to you.' Awkwardly he bent towards her and placed a kiss on her cheek. His big frame seemed to tremble, as if seized by some inner trauma, then he grew still and taking her face in his hands, his mouth sought hers. For a moment she melted to him, allowing the kiss to go deeper, then she pulled sharply away to glance quickly and guiltily round the room. But no one had noticed Martin Gregory's arrival, not even sharp-eyed Nellie who was much too engrossed in conversation with Jeannie to be aware of anything else.

'Will you have a dram?' Grace took his proferred bottle and placed it on the table beside the rest.

'If you'll join me.' There was an appeal in the deep timbre of his voice, a lost, lonely appeal that smote Grace's soft heart to the quick.

'I'm too young yet to drink whisky but I'll have some fruit wine,' she murmured, wondering why the nearness of this big, silent man should disturb her so much more than any of the young men who had sought her attentions of late. She was only sixteen after all – not yet ready for any man, let alone one so mature as Martin Gregory.

The mischievous faces of Evelyn and Florrie keeked round the door and watched proceedings with interest. Drawing back, Florrie looked at her friend, her eyes alight with excitement. 'They're all at it tonight, even Mr Gregory and your Grace – look at that Murn, she's practically licking Kenneth Mor's boots – and see, over yonder, there goes Mary and Malcolm into the barn.'

They stared at one another then by mutual, unspoken consent, grabbed each other's hands and sped silently over the cornyard to the dim, secret shadows beside the big barn. The lights of the house, the music, the laughter had receded, it was another world out here under the blue moon shadows. Dried seeds of broom rattled in a faint puff of wind, the horses stamped in the stables, a fox barked way down in the echoing howes, the river gurgled as it slid over the stones.

Heart beating a tattoo in her breast, Evelyn followed Florrie into the silent building where the scents of harvests past hung sweetly. They stood inside the door, backs to the wall as they listened. From somewhere close at hand a mouse scurried and a sigh of human voices breathed down from the loft. Evelyn put the tips of her cold fingers into her mouth. Could she? Dare she? If Mary knew she had been followed, she would be furious. Sweet as a good harvest one minute, fierce as an autumn storm the next, she was a force to be reckoned with and Evelyn began gently to sidle back outside.

'Come on.' Florrie grabbed her hand and pulled her forward and, terrified lest her friend's explosive temper got the better of her, she allowed herself to be led to the loft ladder that seemed to march upwards and onwards into black, endless darkness.

Breath suspended, they ascended the ladder with nerve shattering slowness. Every creak, every muffled footfall were miniature explosions inside Evelyn's head. At last they were at the top, pressing themselves against the rungs, eyes just over the rim of the hatch. Hoarse, passionate mutterings reached their ears but they could make out nothing in the inky blackness. But the moon was coming out, a beam slanted in through the cobwebby skylight – and there were Mary and Malcolm, lying close together in the hay. Mary's full, white breasts were in his hands, his lips were travelling over her neck to come again and again to those ripe, sensual curves which rose and fell and pushed themselves willingly against him.

Evelyn stared, remembering the pinkness of Mary's breasts after she had splashed them with cold water, Nellie's shock, her words of admonishment. It had always seemed to Evelyn that Mary's dark-nippled breasts were just another part of her body that had to be cleansed and cared for – now they took on a different meaning as they were roughly kneaded and kissed and thrust time and again into Malcolm Keith's face – and now her legs were at it too, swaying from side to side – flaying the straw as Jenny Burns' had flayed the snow, only that had been in the passion of temper – not like this, as if they were out of control, the heels scrabbling around, bending, kicking, finally opening wide to allow Malcom Keith to slip in between and seem glad to be captured and held in their grip. He was moaning and snorting, like a gibbering sow that had lost its piglets, saying Mary's name in a queer moist muffled voice as if he couldn't control his spit – and Malcolm Keith always had plenty of that. Evelyn wondered sometimes how Mary could kiss a man with so much spit in his mouth.

Florrie was making strange, strangled sounds into the palm of her hand and Evelyn knew that she was in an agony of silent laughter. The pair of them jumped as Mary's voice through the darkness, so clear she might have been standing on the ladder beside them.

'No, Malky, that's enough now, I canna allow you to go any further.'

Malcolm's voice came in a muffled curse of protest. 'Hell! Dinna stop me now, Mary! Lie back and relax and dinna worry aboot a thing.'

'No, Malky, I must go back. Mam will be wondering where I am and Father too.'

'Bugger your father! He's too drunk to be able to see straight. Na, Mary, it's you, making damned sure you're going to save it for that bloody, mealy-mouthed doctor chiel. Dinna think I'm blind, I saw the pair o' you earlier, all sweet and innocent you were as if he was some sort o' god instead o' a mortal man. You're just playin' wi' me, lass, and I'm damned if I'll have it . . .'

The two didn't wait to hear more. Scuttling down the ladder they tip-toed outside round a corner where they collapsed against each other in explosions of laughter. A short while later Mary came running from the barn, straightening her clothes as she rushed back to the house. Malcolm came blundering outside, breathing heavily, fumbling to light his pipe which he sucked on greedily. Cursing he turned back to the barn to fumble at his still-undone fly and relieve himself against the wall. He took a long time at this and even longer to do up his buttons after which he kicked savagely at the barn door hurling another stream of abuse into the night. After a while his breathing and his temper became easier and tapping his pipe out in the snow he made off in Mary's wake.

The two friends had hardly dared breathe during this interlude but now they exhaled noisily and dancing one behind the other, followed Malcolm's footprints back to the house to find him gone and Mary wandering about rather disconsolately having discovered that the doctor had taken his departure after she had taken hers to the barn with Malcolm.

Kenneth Mor and Tandy were making off down the track to the turnpike, the sound of their pipes carrying over the fields. Behind them went the Keiths of Dippiedoon, old Hinney and Jeannie, Bunty Lovie and Lily and Charlie Lammas, all bound for other farms and crofts along the way. Old Coulter had fallen asleep in the ingle, his frosty brows drawn down over his eyes like hairy blinds, his snowy beard sunk on his sark while he muttered and rambled in his dreams.

Martin Gregory was loth to take his leave. He sat on the settle beside Grace, his face more animated than anyone had seen it since the passing of his beloved Mary Ann. On a worn, deep armchair beside the fire, Jamie was fast asleep, his mouth falling slackly open, his brown, sinewy hands lovingly clutching his fiddle to his breast. The tired look was back on Maggie's face and there was a strange, undefinable expression on her attractive features as she stood looking down on him.

'See to your father, Murn,' she said softly.

'Ay, Mam,' Murn said rather sulkily, a mood that always came on her after a frustrating night in Kenneth Mor's company. Going to the kist she took out two crocheted woollen blankets which she tucked round Jamie's prone figure.

Nellie rose up from the settle, cuddling Colin to her breast, her amber-green eyes glittering with a terrible disdain as she stopped by her father's chair. 'Drunken old pig,' she muttered vindictively. 'Why does he always shame us so?'

'That's enough from you!' Maggie's voice was sharp with warning. 'He's your father – and you will always speak of him with respect. Do you hear me, girl?'

'Ay, I hear.' Nellie flounced to the rail above the fire to retrieve a dry napkin. 'I'll put a clean hippen on the bairn then I'm away to my bed – thank God New Year's done with for it's just an excuse for the likes o' *him* to drink himself into a stupor – and that Kenneth Mor's no better – though at least he can hold his liquor.'

Two bright spots of anger burned high on her cheekbones, her restless gaze lighted on Evelyn and Florrie who were creeping out of the scullery where they had been helping themselves to milk and pieces of cheese.

'What are you doing here, Florrie O'Neil?' Nellie demanded irritably. 'I heard wi' my own ears your mother telling you and Maureen to get back home.'

Florrie's jaw jutted. 'Ach, they'll all be drunk and never miss me – anyway, Evie asked me to stay the night.'

'Oh, did she now?' Nellie began belligerently but Maggie held up her hand.

'Go away upstairs the pair o' you – and dinna let me hear a peep out of you till morning – and take your sister wi' you, Florrie – where is she anyway?'

Faint snorings came from the recess which had once housed a bed for the kitchen maid. Grace got up to investigate and discovered Maureen, sound as a baby, Glab snug and warm to her bosom. Grace gave a little chuckle while behind her Martin Gregory rose up and came over to stand by her so that she felt the heat of him and saw the sweep of his dark lashes as he bent forward to gaze down on Maureen. With a grin he scooped her into his arms as if she was thistledown. 'Where to?' he asked.

'Just follow me.' directed Grace and off she went, the schoolteacher at her heels, Evelyn and Florrie following as meekly as lambs.

'You're too soft wi' that bairn, Mother,' Nellie snapped.

Maggie regarded her eldest daughter steadily. 'And you're a mite too hard, Nellie. She's but a bairn and these are her best years. She'll meet wi' strife in her wee life soon enough, so let her be carefree while she can.'

Murn bent her head into her arms and stared morosely at the hot cinders in the grate. 'Ay, you're right there, Mam. Sometimes I wish I was a bairn again wi' all the world as roses at my feet and all my dreams unshattered and whole.'

'Ach, stop hankering after what's no' yours,' Nellie threw scornfully. 'I dinna ken how you can bear to lower yourself to a man the way you do – it's – it's sickening!'

'Ay, but no' as sickening as a woman who doesn't know how to love anybody – let alone a man.'

'Oh, so you think you are blessed wi' a warm and loving heart, Marion Grant? You that went as usual to bed that night wee Colin was born, never a thought in your selfish head but the college and all your silly dreams about becoming a teacher.'

'That's enough from the pair o' you!' Maggie came ben from the scullery to glare at her daughters who were standing poised as if ready to spring at each other's throats. 'Get away up to your beds – we'll clear this mess in the morning – and give me the bairn, I'll take him up wi' me.'

The pair stamped off, leaving Maggie looking down at Jamie, insensible and almost childlike in his complete repose. 'Ach, my poor man,' she sighed, 'What will become o' you? So gentle and lost and so sore needing a son to take some o' the burden away from your shoulders.'

Bending down she kissed him on the brow. Lamplight shadowed the room, found every hollow on his face, shone on a dew of sweat on his upper lip. Pushing back her soft white hair she straightened up and stole out of the room, her steps growing heavy as she ascended the stairs. The baby lay so lightly in her arms he might have been a dream without substance. Sitting down by the fire in her room, she changed him and happed him in the beautiful creamy wool shawl she had made with her own hands and which had pampered five of her eight babies. He lay wide awake on her knee, his eyes too big in his small, gnome-like face, his forehead puckered as if he was pondering some puzzling problem.

'You're too good, my wee one,' she murmured and her strong voice was husky. 'You dinna greet like a natural bairn.' Gathering him up she rocked him back and forward and the tears that she had suppressed for long, weary days spilled from eyes that were black and wide with sadness.

'I wanted a son,' she sobbed. 'No' for myself but for *him*. I was aye content enough with my daughters, but then the twins came and I saw in my mind two braw pairs o' hands to guide the plough and young men who would walk through the fields wi' their father. But they went – as swiftly as the wind which blows over Bennachie's fair brow and I gave up thinking o' man bairns. And now you, poor, poor wee cratur'. Will you be as my dreams and walk by the side o' that good, bewildered man who smiles at the world and drowns his cares in a bottle?'

Rising she laid the little boy in his bed and going to the window she stared out. It was a clear, star-studded night out of which Bennachie rose, an ethereal black shape with the moon pinned to its breast like a great silver medallion. She loved this dour, couthy, north east landscape, with all her heart she loved it, yet there were times she was afraid of the harshness of a land that could rob a man of so much of his strength. But come the spring, it would give back all that it had taken, blithely and generously, as if it had never laid bare its harshness to the men who put so much of themselves into it during the long, bleak, unrelenting winter.

Remembering Betsy and her ramshackle pram, her head went up and a wry smile touched her firm, determined mouth. She would never use the ugly thing, not because it was falling apart, though God knew that was a good enough reason. No, it was more than that, much, much more. It was the bairn, wee Col, a poor wee mite with a strange wisdom in his eyes and nothing at all inside his head. She knew as surely as she knew night from day that he had been born without blemish on the outside – but inside – God alone knew what he had been given for a brain! Only time would give her the answer to that and she shuddered and choked on the black, bitter sense of shame and guilt that rose like bile into her throat. Guilt had torn her apart since his birth, for she blamed herself for his existence and for her own terrible shortcomings. She of the proud heart and noble spirit was not even woman enough to have given her man healthy sons and that was a terrible burden for any woman to have to bear for the rest of her life. Wee Col had been her last chance to prove herself. She hadn't wanted him but he had come as if to remind her that pride really did come before a fall.

No, she wouldn't ever be seen pushing him in a pram, even if it was the finest carriage ever built, she didn't care to show him to a world in which deviation from normal invited ridicule from the cruel and ignorant.

Perhaps later she would find the strength not to care, but just now she was too mentally and physically weary to worry about the future. The tears of shame and sadness filled her eyes so that the braes of Bennachie touched the sky and the white, cold wastes of Rothiedrum wavered and became a great empty sea in which nothing stirred or lived.

Mr Gregory had long since taken his departure. Grace was in bed beside Maureen, the house slept peacefully under the stars. Evelyn lay on her back, listening to the steady plip plop of icicles melting in the eaves. Grey clouds were meandering across the sky, slowly but surely blotting out the cold face of the moon. She gave a sudden and unexpected little shiver and moved closer to Florrie who was breathing evenly at her side. 'Coorie into me, Florrie,' she whispered.

Obediently Florrie moved closer, her arms coming up to encircle her friend.

130

'Do you ever feel feared – at night?'

'No,' Florrie's voice was heavy with sleep. 'There's always Maureen and Bridie in the bed beside me – I'm too busy kicking them to feel anything but temper.'

'I get feared,' Evelyn stared into the darkness. 'I – I *feel* things.'

'What kind o' things?' Florrie's voice was clearer – more awake.

'I don't really know – I just feel – something, sort of like people beside me that aren't really there.'

Florrie was wide awake now. 'You – you mean – ghosts?'

'Ay, it could be. Forbye that I sometimes feel when something's about to happen – even in broad daylight.' Evelyn spoke cautiously, unwilling to unearth the thing which had always lain like a shadow at the back of her senses. 'Do you ever feel like that? Does everybody?'

Florrie sniggered. 'I know when Father's about to skite me round the lugs. Is that what you mean?'

Evelyn didn't answer. A tremor went through her body. She felt suddenly alone and afraid. She had been wrong. All along she had thought that everyone in the world must experience those strange, eerie premonitions that shook her from time to time. Now she knew she was wrong. Florrie had no earthly idea what she was talking about and something warned her not to pursue the subject. If you showed you were different in these parts it wasn't long before they were talking behind your back and calling you a daftie. For the first time in her life she felt a deep chasm separating her from her friend. Long after Florrie had fallen asleep she lay staring at nothing. She was the only living soul in the world then. Johnny popped into her mind, without any warning at all and she knew – she knew that like her he lay in his bed unable to sleep while all around him Birkiebrae breathed in the deep heartbeat of slumber. 'I'm with you, Johnny,' she thought and an odd sweet contentment flooded her being.

CHAPTER SEVEN

A mild, misty dawn heralded in the first morning of the New Year, with veils of gossamer floating in the hollows and Bennachie trailing frail scarves across her coy pearly face. The harsh cawing of rooks drifted over from the howes and then they rose up in their tattered black droves from the bare branches of the trees above and all around King's Croft as the hooves of Queenie and Nickum clattered on the still-hard ground of the tree lined track that led to the fields. Shafts of watery sun gleamed on harness, slanted through the mist like great torch beams from unseen heavens.

'Hup, hup!' Jamie's voice rose clear in the air, urging the horses forward, but there was no need as they knew well enough the way to the fields and could have found the way blindfolded.

Johnny's heart sang as he ran alongside the horses. He loved the powerful grace of the beasts, the rippling surges of their gleaming muscles seemed to transfer to him so that he felt tall and strong as he walked through that still, tranquil morning. There was something about the Clydesdale's step that wrought in him a great feeling of pleasure. The great bearded feet, the momentary flash of a crescent shaped shoe, seemed lazy and slow but they were clean, clear steps with a surprising swiftness to them and an agility that defied the size of the silk clad hooves.

Jamie was on his lead horse, Nickum, while Evelyn rode on Queenie's broad back. Johnny hadn't wanted her along, for reasons he wasn't too sure about in his own mind. He had hoarded the anticipation of this morning as another might hoard gold. All night long the wonderful knowledge of it had lain in his mind, keeping him from sleep, that and the problem of how to get away from Birkiebrae as early as possible without too much fuss. Towards dawn he had slept fitfully only to awaken suddenly, wondering if he had slept in. His father had thundered into the room, sour of tongue and thick of head after a night of drinking. Curtly he had told Johnny that he was yoking the horses ready for a day in the fields, adding. 'You needna bother coming w' me. Your mother needs you here. There's work to be done, more than ever of that now so shake a leg, my lad, and see to the bairns.'

Johnny knew what he meant. Babsie wasn't around any more and the lot that had been hers was now his. How he got through the next hour he never knew, but somehow he made up fires, fed the hens, prepared the brose for the bothy lads, made breakfast for himself and the others. He had taken his mother hers in bed, told her he had to go out for awhile and leaving the wee ones arguing at the table he had run all the way to King's Croft to arrive panting but triumphant. Jamie had been up at five, getting the horses ready, a quieter Jamie than usual, the dregs of drink still on him, souring his tongue a little, so that Billy kept out of his way, and Johnny slipped unobtrusively into the stables to lend a hand where he could.

By the time the beasts were ready for the road Jamie was more like his old self, a gleam in his eye at the thought of rousing himself from the enforced idleness the last fortnight had brought him. When Evelyn came running up to entwine her arms around him and ask to be allowed to go to the fields he had lifted her up and placed her squarely on Queenie's back. Johnny had glowered a bit at her. He had wanted it to be just himself and Jamie out there in that hallowed morning, had wanted to be quiet and in control of every one of his senses when for the first time he set his hands on the plough stilts. Perhaps he was afraid of making a fool of himself in front of her, he didn't know. It was enough that Billy eyed him darkly all the way to the parks and on one occasion muttered under his breath, 'Why did you have to butt your nose in? We were doing fine the way we were.'

Normally Johnny would have taught him a short sharp lesson but he wasn't going to allow an orra loon to spoil his time of joy so he said nothing but concentrated instead on the horses and the smells of the parks, snow riddled yet throwing up a tangible smell that was earth and dung and the sharp cleanness of melting frost.

The plough lay on its side on the endrigs of the stubble field, bearded with tufts of snow, neglected and rather forlorn looking but between them they soon had it in place. The first pass of the ley land was no more than a scratch, double fine lines of two inch deep furrows twenty inches apart. 'You'd best take the first bout, lad,' Jamie nodded to Johnny. 'Just seize the stilts here and I'll tell you what else to do.'

Evelyn and Billy retired to the edge of the field, the latter muttering under his breath till Evelyn poked him in the ribs and told him sharply to shut up.

'Ach, you're only a girl,' he said sneeringly. 'Why should I heed you?'

'Because I'll tell my father you had a lass from the village up in the chaumer with you – *and* you stole cheese from the milkhouse that was meant for the market. My mother's still wondering where it went. I didna tell – but I will – if you don't leave Johnny be.'

He eyed her warily. She was standing against the sun, her hair a halo of fire, her shadowed eyes studded with green sparks of temper.

'Tell tit!' he hissed, but didn't pursue the matter, avoiding her penetrating gaze by squatting down to adjust the nicky tams at his knees.

Johnny was oblivious to all but the green waves of the ley falling away from the blade of the plough, settling into stillness in his wake. The smell of the newly turned earth was nectar to his keenly awakened senses. He was aware of the sky opening up, of sunlight pouring over the earth, flooding the parks with a great, silvery white light. Gulls drifted like snowflakes in the endless pearly vaults, mewing at first then excitement making them scream and swoop at the turned earth till their frenzy touched the senses, beat inside so that life oozed and bubbled out to meet this great wide, wakening scented world.

Johnny's arms ached yet it was an ache that only served to arouse in him a joy that he felt could never be surpassed. He felt one with the land, his heart beat inside him yet seemed joined to the great, beating life of every ploughman who had ever tread the loamy houghs of Aberdeenshire. Queenie and Nickum plodding in front were part of that life, their gleaming muscles, rippling flanks, power and grace combining into a great oneness that was totally in keeping with the soil.

Billy had got over his sulks and had begun to sing a bothy ballad, soon joined by Evelyn and Jamie who was guiding Nickum. Sweat poured from Johnny's brow, the aching of his fully stretched arms was growing unbearable, yet something about the song and the glory of the day made him forget physical discomfort so that he found the breath to hum and mouth the words. The horses were blasting jets of steam from their nostrils so that great clouds of it drifted backwards and billowed around Johnny at the plough – for the first time in his life at the plough – and a glance backwards let him see that a fair section of the field had turned colour and he thought jubilantly, 'I've done that, I've ploughed all that by myself.'

'Rest, Johnny lad.' Jamie came up, smiled. 'You've done right well for your first furrow.'

'Ay,' Johnny drew a hand across his sweating brow, a trembling hand he was surprised to note. He returned Jamie's smile. 'Ay, Jamie – but it was just the scratch.'

Jamie adjusted the plough wheel. 'I'll take the next bout, Billy the next – then you can have a go. She'll be sunk to her working depth then – six inches for land coming out o' ley – but I'll no work you too hard, you can be sure o' that.'

Johnny went to join Evelyn on the endrigs while Billy went off to join Jamie, throwing behind him a gley-eyed look that said, 'See, I can take a working depth nae bother, the farmer knows he can trust me.'

Johnny looked at Evelyn, she looked at him, for a long time they looked without speaking then a smile broke from Johnny, a radiant triumphant smile that took away the weariness she had noticed in his eyes that morning. His hand came out to touch hers but first he checked to make sure that Billy wasn't watching. Not that he cared what the orra loon thought, it was what he spread about that could be infuriating. Billy had a big mouth for a lad and he had had a big part in spreading the news about Maggie's baby far and wide. He had also been talking, or rather hinting, at the reasons behind Babsie's departure from Birkiebrae and Johnny was always on the lookout for the boy's ferrety eyes. But he was engrossed in his task and Johnny felt safe to reach for Evelyn's hand so that his fingers touched hers.

'You were good, Johnny,' she told him earnestly. 'Good for your first time with the plough.'

'I'll get better,' he said offhandedly, though inwardly he was glowing with a sense of achievement. The warmth of his thoughts transferred to her so that she glowed and took a deep breath of satisfaction.

Johnny was daydreaming as he stood there watching Billy guide the plough clockwise to the feering. The ploughing matches would be starting soon and Johnny imagined the day when he would be able to take part – he could picture it all in his mind, the moving colourful mosaic of men and horses, furrows broad and sleek from the cutter blade, the smells, the colour, the jingle of harness . . . Evelyn's hand had tightened convulsively in his. He glanced quickly at her and saw that her face, pink and glowing moments before, had turned still and white and that her gaze was fixed trance-like on the rolling fields above. Following her eyes he saw Jenny at once, tearing over the snow-dappled field still too far off to be heard but near enough for him to recognize her stocky, untidy figure with her long hair flying behind her in a tangled mane and her stockinged legs a blur of black against the wet snow.

'Jenny,' He whispered the name, before it had left his lips he was moving forward, slowly at first then breaking into a run so that he met her flying figure halfway along the field and was there to catch her as she hurled into his arms to lie against him sobbing, great dry sobs that retched out of her gaping throat and robbed her of speech.

Jamie came running, at his heels Billy and Evelyn, the

Clydes stopped short in the rigs while all around them the gulls birled and screeched in their demented gluttony.

'Jenny, what is it, lass, what is it?' Jamie took her into his arms, his brown fingers gently stroking the hair from her brow, his voice, soothing, cajoling. She lay stiff in his embrace, head thrown back, eyes wide and staring, teeth chattering but no words coming from her wide-stretched lips.

'Jenny, is it Mother?' Johnny knelt by his small sister, trying to put the question gently but unable to keep the harsh fear from his voice.

The little girl shook her head violently, the trembling of her worsening with each passing second. 'Janet,' she got out at last. Just that. She could say no more and with swift decision Jamie ordered Billy back to see to the horses then with Jenny in his arms and Johnny and Evelyn at his back he ran to the stables at King's Croft and with Johnny's help hitched Fyvie to the trap.

They clattered away, down the track to the turnpike, in minutes reaching the wicket gate and the track leading up to Birkiebrae.

When they reached the farm Jenny pulled at Jamie's sleeve and made him drive on till the track petered out and now it was just the rough grass at the edge of the high moorland.

Before Jamie had brought Fyvie to a halt the little girl had jumped down and was running, running to the little lochan lying so blue and serene in amongst the couthy heathery hills. Everyone else followed her, only Johnny walked slowly – for he knew – he knew long before he reached the tiny basin of water what he would see there. And it was true enough. The thing that had leapt into his mind as soon as he realized where Jenny was taking them. Yesterday the ice on the lochan had been diamond hard, today its glittering, blue-grey face was watery and moving, little ice floes bumping each other in the middle, splinters of it crazing the edges where Jenny and Janet had been engaged in a delightful spree of ice breaking.

Wee Babby Burns, as everyone called Janet, was floating face downwards, her golden hair matted, mingling with the

137

ice and the rust coloured reeds, her blue woollen dress lifting rhythmically where the water lapped at it gently. She looked for all the world like an abandoned doll thrown carelessly to land where it would. Jenny was staring in wide-eyed terror at the pitiful bundle that was her little sister, her teeth chattering so much Johnny heard the dull rattle of them inside his head.

She turned beseeching eyes on him, her whispered words rising to a scream, 'She fell in, she fell in – I couldna reach her, I couldna! And Jimmy wasna here, he went to the fields wi' Father.'

Johnny couldn't move, couldn't answer. His world was a terrifying place in those moments. The earth spun, the font of his life rushed in his ears, his heart galloped, pounding in his throat, squeezing, squeezing all the breath from his lungs. Evelyn ran to his side to throw her arms about his waist and he leaned weakly against her, while Jamie lay flat on his belly on the bank and with the aid of a stout branch pulled the child towards him. One look told him that she was gone, but he went through the motions, laying her on her stomach, face to the side while he worked her arms, pumping icy water from her tiny lungs.

Johnny broke away from Evelyn to run to the spot and stare down incredulously on the child's dead face. Only that morning he had plucked her, rosy and warm, from her cot. He had kissed the bright hair of her and she had placed her chubby arms about his neck to stroke his head in her endearing old fashioned way and say his name in her half shy, little voice. 'Joey,' that was the name she had always called him and he had delighted in it just as he had delighted in her laughter, such laughter! Her pearly teeth flashing in the rubies of her lips, joy chiming from her, chiming, chiming, the remembered sound of it dirling in his head even while sadness tolled a deathknell in his heart.

Now, the gold of her hair was matted and dull, her flower-like face as grey as the clouds that had gathered overhead, her lips blue and cold with two of her baby teeth splintered and bloody from her fall against the boulders at the loch side. It couldn't be! No, no,no! Not wee Janet whom he loved more than his own mother – more than himself –

'Come away, lad,' Jamie pulled at him gently. 'There's naught we can do for her – the babby is gone, Johnny, gone.' Stripping off his jacket he placed it quietly round the small body. Johnny stood up, shocked, cold beyond belief. A little way off Evelyn soothed the sobbing Jenny, drawn to her in her sorrow as she had never been in all her self-assured, small girl bravado.

There came a tide of motion up there from the steadings. Billy had done his work well. No sooner was he left alone but he was off, tearing up to the fields where he knew Rob was working. And now Rob Burns burst into the scene, Jimmy at his side, a few of his men bringing up the rear. He stood head and shoulders above them, a bristling, flaxen-haired giant whose stride was such that he left everyone else behind in his rush to get to the lochside. Instinctively Johnny and Jenny made way for him, pale-lipped and red-eyed as they stared at him, waiting, waiting for the inevitable roar of horrified disbelief that would follow. It came, in great waves of harsh sound that echoed and re-echoed all round the lochan and clattered against the couthy, rolling, peaceful hills.

Jimmy took one look at the dead body of his baby sister and running to Johnny buried his anguish into the strong, brotherly shoulder he had always looked to for comfort. The men came fleeing up, stopping short at the sight which met their eyes.

'In the name of God,' muttered one. 'The bairn! What happened to the bairn?'

Rob had dropped on to his knees, speechless now as he wrenched off the jacket to gape in open mouthed incredulity at his baby daughter. 'Jan – Jan – babby.' His lips formed the words before he snatched her up and crushed her to his breast, his mouth buried into the wet tangle of her hair. Straightening up, he wheeled round, his eyes mad and staring.

'What happened?' he roared, then louder. 'What happened, I ask ye?'

Jenny, scared half out of her wits for fear some terrible retribution was about to fall on her, screamed out, 'She fell in, Father! She fell in! I couldna reach her and there wasna anybody here to help!'

Rob seemed to go crazy then. Spinning round on Johnny he ground out, 'And where were you when this happened? Eh, my lad?'

Johnny went whiter than ever and couldn't stop the violent tremors that shook him from head to foot.

'*Where were you, boy*?' The bellow of unleashed fury made both Jimmy and Jenny burst into tears.

'I – I was down at King's Croft – Mr Grant was showing me how to guide the plough.' Johnny at last got the words to come out even though his heart was beating so fast he thought he was going to faint there and then.

Rob's nostrils dilated, his whole face contorted, but his voice came out dangerously calm. 'Oh, so you went on an outing and left the bairns to fend for themselves? Just took a wee turn down to Grants' place to play yourself, eh? In other words . . .' his voice rose to a frightening pitch, 'You buggered off because you felt like it and went down to help that bloody old tink to turn his fields!'

He laid the body of his dead daughter down on the bank and turned to face his son, his fists balled in front of his face. 'Do you know what you've done, you goddammed bastard! You've killed you're wee sister! Ay, just as surely as if you'd pushed her into that bloody loch with your own hands!'

The men muttered amongst themselves, telling each other that Burns was going too far this time, but he heard and saw nothing. White fury blinded him to all but the pale petrified face of his eldest son. Advancing on him he roared, 'I'll pulverize you for this! I'll make sure you never forget this day as long as your miserable life lasts!'

Johnny's head went back; he closed his eyes waiting for the blow that would send him into oblivion – but it never came. A tornado burst into the scene then, in the shape of Jamie, shirt sleeves rolled to his elbows, the rage in his liquid dark eyes more than matching that of Rob Burns.

140

The big man towered above him, easily the strongest and the more brutal of the two. Beside him Jamie looked small and thin and certainly no match for such a demented bundle of steel-like muscle. But Jamie was stronger than he looked, the sinews in his wiry frame toughened by years of working the land – and he was angry just then, an anger that lent him courage and strength and blinded him to the size of his adversary.

'You leave that lad be, Rob Burns,' he said quietly. 'Are you too blind wi' your own guilt to know that it's because o' you that innocent babe lies cold and still over yonder. Can you no see it, even now? Why did your very own bairn no turn to you when she needed help? Even in her terror she wouldna come to you but came fleein' instead to the lad all your bairns turn to when they're demented wi' fear. *You* killed wee Janet, *you*, Burns . . .'

Rob flew at him then, a seething mass of bone and muscle gone wild. There was no control in his movements, none of the lightness of foot, the tactical approach that was in Jamie. Everyone stood around, wide eyed as they watched the two men battling on the soggy ground. The rooks rose up from the trees, their raucous yells inciting the gulls who in turn began to scream as if in rage at the pitiful sight of the two men grovelling and punching.

But the fight didn't last long. Jamie's fists were a blur as they reduced Rob Burns to a bloody, crawling heap, who finally slithered and fell to the ground, blood streaming from nose and mouth. Jamie stood over him, breathing hard but otherwise in full control of himself.

'That's right, Burns,' he panted. 'Grovel a bit more, for the mud is where you've always belonged. And I tell you this. You lay one finger on that lad and I'll be up to finish you off. It's time you got a few things straight. For one, it's high time you got that lazy bitch of a wife of yours off her erse and into the kitchen. *She's* the mother o' your bairns, no some bit lad who doesna ken whether he's coming or going wi' all the filthy jobs you pile on his shoulders.

'Just remember, it wasna him that lay whoring wi' the kitchenmaid so that she had to be sent packing from your

141

house. It was you, Burns, and it's time you woke up to your responsibilities or there will come a day when it will no be me who gies you what you deserve – it will be the lad there and by God! I'll be the first to cheer him on while I'm watching him doing it.'

So saying, he turned on his heel, went over to grip Johnny by the shoulder, then taking Evelyn by the hand he walked unhurriedly away, his dark, gypsy head thrown proudly up and never a glance back at the subdued men left behind at the lochan.

Evelyn looked up at his tight-set face. He wasn't as calm as he was making out, the well-controlled little tremors of him vibrated into her hand and she didn't blame him in the least for stopping when they reached the trap to take from his pocket the little bottle of whisky he always carried around. Steadying himself against the trap he put the bottle to his lips and took a good long draught. With deliberate slowness he corked it, put it back in his pocket and stood looking at her, waiting for her to speak.

'Father, I'm right proud of you.' she said gently. 'And so glad you're my father.' He nodded and forced a smile but it didn't quite take away the sadness in his eyes at the thought of wee Janet Burns lying cold up yonder by the lochan.

Evelyn stroked Fyvie's mane and said slowly, 'Do you think – will Johnny be alright – with him?'

'I'll hear about it if he isna – never you fear, Princess. But dinna underestimate the lad. He's but a bairn yet but he's growing quick and there will come a day when he'll no' need the likes o' me at his back.'

The men drifted away from the scene leaving Rob to scramble painfully to his feet and wipe the blood from his nose with the back of a shaking hand. The children watched in sober silence as he gathered Janet's lifeless body into his arms and made off up to the house. Once at the gate he bade Jimmy and Jenny go on up to their rooms and then it was just himself and Johnny while up above the clouds darkened and the first drops of rain fell coldly about them.

142

'A fine thing to face your mother with,' Rob grated harshly, 'and a hellish burden for her to bear in her state o' health.'

Johnny didn't hear him. Fair head sunk on his chest he was numb with grief for his darling wee sister. He couldn't believe she was gone, he would never believe it . . .

'You will never lay a hand on Grant's plough again, do you hear me, lad?' Rob's brittle voice barely reached through the fog of despair that shrouded Johnny's mind. 'Do you hear me?'

'Ay.'

'And are ye mindin', lad?'

'I'm mindin'.'

Rob glowered at his son's chastened profile. He opened his mouth to say more, thought better of it and strode on up to the house, Janet's body held loosely in his brawny arms so that her small limbs hung relaxed and uncaring, for all the world the way she looked when she had fallen asleep by the fire and Johnny carried her on tiptoe up the wooden stairs to her cot in the room next to his . . .

The funeral was over. Mist happed the kirkyard in a cold grey blanket that made the mourners shiver and think of cosy firesides. The body of the little girl in its tiny coffin lay locked in the wet grip of the earth. The black-clothed figures were moving, dispersing, their quiet murmurings barely disturbing the silence of the old Kirk O' Bree standing coated in dank shrouds on the tranquil banks of Loch Bree. No one expected the funeral repast that was usual procedure after a Burial. Rob had made no mention of any such arrangement, Catherine was too infirm to cope with such things, so everyone went off to their own homes and the comforts to be found in them.

The Rev. Finlay Sommerville, silvered hair beaded with droplets of moisture, stood with his hands demurely clasped in front of him and cast a speculative eye at the tall, silent figure, still standing by the graveside. Clearing his throat he walked over and intoned respectfully, 'You'll be getting a woman in to look to your bairns now, Robert.'

There was no response and he went on, sympathetically but firmer now. 'I think you heard me, Robert, I don't like to intrude on your sorrow at this time, but it is something that has to be discussed. This is no time and place I know. Perhaps if I come and visit you and Catherine tomorrow...'

Rob Burns stirred, the big strong hands of him raw and cold as he took the minister's small soft one and squeezed it hard, so hard the little man winced and drew away slightly. 'Nay minister, I'll no be doing that.' The voice of Rob was as brittle as the ice that had taken his little girl from him.

'Just so, just so.' The minister's silvered head nodded its agreement even while his next words contradicted the action. 'But you'll have to think of it, Robert, you owe it to your bairns, they need a woman's care – as this sad day has so tragically proven.'

Rob's eyes glittered, his hard jaw tightened. 'They have a woman, minister, they have their mother.'

The minister's calm brown eyes did not betray the dark, ungodly thoughts that lay like pebbles in his mind. He knew all about Rob's unsavoury reputation with women and had never wholly approved of him since his arrival in Rothiedrum, not just because of his drinking and womanizing. It was more Rob's attitude to life that he had never cared for and he felt it was high time the master of Birkiebrae stopped behaving like a frustrated child and started facing his responsibilities.

Clearing his throat, he said carefully, 'You will have to watch how you handle Catherine, she is a gentle soul and she treads a lonely path. I knew her father well. He and I had many a talk about his daughter. He knew he was perhaps too lenient with her, but she was an only child and that might explain why she – is as she is. She was a dreamy child, always going off to be by herself in some dark corner. Fortunately her mother was a strong woman and never gave in to Catherine in quite the same way as her father did. Somewhere in Catherine there is a good deal of her mother, only I fancy it has never quite come to the surface.

144

As a child she dreamed of being carried off by some dazzling knight on whose strength she could lean, but real life isn't like that. Whether it needs to be coaxed or bullied out of her I'm afraid I don't know – if only her mother was still alive – she was the only one who could get the best from her daughter – and she got it by firmness. John Meiklejohn was always slightly bemused because he could never, with all his leniency – get Catherine to obey his will.

'She is suffering badly just now, Robert,' he continued gently. 'If your heart is sore with grief think how heavy hers must be – she who bore and lost the wee one. She needs you now more than she's ever needed you – you both need each other – and God knows the bairns need to know that they can turn to both their mother and father in this terrible time – they too have lost a wee body who was very precious to them.'

Rob's eyes grew black and deep at that, raw emotion showed momentarily then the shutters came down, blanking out his innermost thoughts. Taking the minister's hand once more he gripped it briefly. 'Thank you kindly for seeing wee Janet so finely to her rest. I'll be bidding you good day now.'

'I'll be seeing you more often in kirk – after today.' The words dropped from the minister's lips, even and steady but with a crystal hard ring to them. Rob paused, his huge shoulders hunched into his coat. He didn't turn round, didn't speak, and after a few moments strode away, seeing naught before him but a long dark tunnel without end.

'Father,' Johnny was at his side, looking up at him anxiously. 'We'd – we'd best go home now.'

'You go,' Rob said tonelessly. 'Your mother will be needing you – I'm – I dinna ken when I'll be coming back.'

Johnny watched him go, numb with his own burden of sorrow, waiting for the man who was his father to turn round and invite him along. He didn't care how silent they might be in each other's company, he just felt that he needed to be with his father, had to know if there still existed between them a faint glimmer of the understanding they had once shared.

But Rob Burns strode on, seeing not the enquiring glances of his neighbours as he made towards the gate and the sheltie standing patiently in the shafts of the phaeton.

'Father, will you wait for me?' Johnny half shouted the plea at his father's back but it fell unheeded on the ears of Rob Burns. Johnny's head sunk on to his chest, he pushed his cold fists into his pockets, the ground blurred beneath his clouded vision. Hopelessness seared his soul. Wee Janet, his dear little baby of a sister was gone from him and would never come back. Mourning for her clawed at his heart, the black fingers of it squeezing and squeezing till it seemed all the life of him was being wrung from his body . . .

'Come home wi' me, Johnny lad. You can sup wi' us and warm yourself by the fire. This is no day to be alone wi' your thoughts.'

Jamie's firm arm was around him, pulling him in close, guiding him to the roadside where Fyvie stood waiting.

'He – Father said I wasna ever to help you again wi' the ploughing.' Johnny spoke through chattering teeth, hardly aware of what he was saying.

Jamie squeezed his shoulder. 'You're hardly likely to be working the plough inside King's Croft kitchen – are you now? Rob might have forbidden some things, but he can hardly stop you coming to see folks you've known all your life so climb up there and think no more about it.'

Johnny remembered nothing of the journey to King's Croft. He saw not the black tatters of rooks fluttering in the sky nor felt the cold, sweet reality of the January day sweeping over him. The world was unreal to him then, a dark, cold place in which normal things seemed abnormal and out of proportion.

But King's Croft was real enough, the kind of warm, quiet reality that he had often wished he could take away with him up there to the uncertain realms of Birkiebrae.

Evelyn came to him as in a dream, leading him to the fire, taking off his boots, her small hands soothing as she chafed

146

his feet, her pale, quiet face turned down from him, her glorious hair falling sweet and bonny about her cheeks, magnificent and rich, reminding him of the plush drapes the gentry used to cover their windows. She spoke not a word to him but how good it was to have her there, silent and unobtrusive and gentle about the dark, crying river that was the life of him, a river that flowed upwards, as if threatening to drown him and close his throat. Yet that felt dry and hard when everything else in him was moist and moving, and he was forced to swallow again and again so that the river that was in him wouldn't burst and spurt forth.

Then Jamie was making him drink something – and now a fire rushed down to meet the upsurging river, quenching it for a time as he coughed and spluttered and lay back in the chair to catch his breath while all around him the shadows of the Grant girls flitted then one by one floated away till he sensed that he was alone – alone as he longed to be yet feared as he had once feared the black, eerie shadows of night. A sensing of something wonderful came to him then, a strength reaching down to him to hold him close and stroke his hair while a soothing voice crooned in his ears so that waves of calm washed into him, gently, gently. He allowed himself to relax and coorie down into that warm, enveloping breast that was of mother and nurse and wife yet to come. But that was the undoing of him for the river that had abated rose up once more and this time it wouldn't be stilled but welled up and drowned him till the streams ran from the left and right of it. A tidal river it was, for it hurt his eyes and stung his face as it flowed on and on till his muscles went slack for the want of it. He didn't have the strength left in him to resist but gave in to it and the tight, cold stone that was the heart of him melted and ran out of him along with the river that he had thought was his life but which had been slowly killing him for the last few tortured days and nights.

And without his bidding a great sigh trembled out of him and he lay warm against the breast of the woman who was Margaret Innes Grant – such as he had never lain in the

thin, hard breast of the woman who was Catherine
Meiklejohn of Braemar.

It was past midnight when Rob Burns came over the
cobbles and let himself into the kitchen. The oppressive,
dark silence of the room enclosed him, happing itself about
him in cloying folds of stifling nothingness. There was a feel
about the house as if it was holding its breath, waiting for
something to happen that might bring air and life back into
it.

The yawning hole of the bed recess lept out at him, yet
it was blacker than the surrounding walls, black and deep
and accusing, the frilled canopy above it like pale fangs that
slavered out to him as if to clamp him into warm, waiting,
swallowing depths. But there was nothing to be had there
now, no gently breathing Babsie with her still, quiet
beckoning and a coyness that belied the moist demands of
her lips and the creamy, clamouring passion of her stirring
thighs.

For a long time he stood there, a huge, silent figure that
quested the night like some primitive beast waiting in the
shadows. Then he shivered and moved, sitting down to
remove his boots which he placed neatly on the fender,
setting them precisely together as if by so doing he could
arrange his seething emotions as neatly into place.

He hunched up in his chair, his big, fair, handsome head
in his hands, still as the standing stones that crouched in
eternal meditation over by Ythsie in Tarves. After a while
he got up and padded in his stocking soles across the floor
to the door leading in to the lobby. Although he was such
a big man he moved with the stealth of a cat. He reached
the stairs, grace in every gliding movement of muscle and
sinew, assurance in every calculated step. But now he was
a creature bereft of warmth and he shuddered again as he
climbed to the cold upper regions of the house. He gave no
second glance to the small, comfortless room that had been
his for the past four years but went on instead to that other
door behind which Catherine lay upright against her
pillows, the blankets clutched to her neck, held there by

hands that shook and were icy cold despite the sweat that soaked the palms.

All day she had waited – waited for this moment, all day she had lain listlessly in the parlour while kindly neighbours came and went with food and tended to the bairns who sat white-faced and silent beside her.

In her mind she had pictured Rob driving the phaeton to the inn at Tillietoorie, for not even he could be insensitive enough to go drinking at the Lums O' Reekie inn. She knew he would find his solace in drink, it had been the way of things for so long now – ever since he'd had to leave the sea and come to live at Birkiebrae.

But for once in his life Rob Burns had not been drinking, indeed his last dram before wee Janet died was to be the last ever to pass his lips. He had spent the day in torment, leaving his sheltie by the edge of the moors while he walked and walked over vast plains that went on forever. He had neither eaten nor drunk for there was nothing of substance that could fill the empty void that gaped within him. A sickening, bottomless pit it was that ached and gnawed at him yet was numb and cold as the barren wastes he trod. And all the while his thoughts seethed and whirled round in his brain and for a long time he could make no sense of them for what man could tame a whirlpool going round and round, down and down into nothingness. But gradually certain words dirled in his head, then snatches of words and finally the minister's blunt statement ringing round and round, up and down, over and over. 'You'll be getting a woman in to see to your bairns, Robert.'

Damn! Damn if he would! He had a woman, a wife who whined in his ears from dawn till dusk. A woman who lay stinking all day on a sofa and allowed the world to pass her by – like some pallid worm lying white against the earth waiting for someone to come along to pick her up and save her – or else put the bloody boot in her and stamp the useless life out of her for good.

And she had banned him from the marriage bed. Not in so many words, she was to damned clever for that; the headaches; the nausea; the sore and tender bones; the

149

pleas for him to be gentle with her even while her own hands had been rough enough with him. In the end she had driven him to seek his pleasure elsewhere. And dear God! but it had been good with some of those buxom, lusty lassies who might not have had the benefits of a genteel upbringing but who knew well enought how to please a man. Catherine had never let herself go, had never deemed it fitting to be seen enjoying the pleasure of the flesh like a real woman. More fool him! He had gone along with her, had never roughed her up, yet even so she had always managed to convey to him that he was soiling her by touching her bare flesh.

Jamie's words also beat into his head. 'That lazy bitch of a wife of yours . . . That lazy bitch of a wife of yours . . .' Bugger the man! He had shown him up good and proper but he was right, King Jamie had never been afraid to speak his mind . . .

For a long time Rob stood outside the door of his wife's room, head cocked, every nerve stretched as he prepared himself for what was to come. Then at last he put his hand on the knob to turn it slowly, slowly. The hinges creaked, thunderbolts in the silence, his nerves jangled but he kept on pushing, gently, firmly, and finally he stepped inside to close the door and stand with his back to it, eyes staring, adjusting to the dark shapes around him. The room waited, life seemed suspended, an eeriness pervaded the thick, deep silence.

Drapes were pulled across the windows, but its grey oblong was distinguishable from the surrounding walls and reflected itself in the wardrobe mirror opposite. He saw himself in it as he moved forward, a crouching black form that froze and stayed as if afraid of its own menacing reflection.

'Rob – is that you, Rob?' Catherine's voice fell, shivering droplets of sound in the black pool of the night. It was fear-laced, thin and tremulous in her constricted throat.

Soundlessly Rob moved forward to finally stand towering over the bed, a fearful giant separated only from the phantoms of night by the harsh breath that thrust up out of his lungs. 'Ay, it's me, Catherine, me, your husband, come to take what's been due me all those long, miserable years.'

He began to rip off his clothes, first his jacket, then his shirt, throwing them onto the floor without heed nor haste. Seconds later she heard the sounds, first of his braces, then of his fly buttons, one by one, the rustle of his trousers sliding down over his drawers, the whisper of cloth gliding down his long, sinewy legs which she couldn't see but could imagine.

The sweat on her brow felt cold, she lay rigid, her hands fastened on the layer of blanket at her neck. The weight of him rocked the bed, the next instant the covers were ripped from her grasp. She saw him looming above her as he straddled her, a great black bear whose heat enclosed her yet made her shiver. She couldn't speak, her throat was bone dry, yet there was nothing to say anyway, nothing that would stem the rising lust of him as his legs tightened round her thighs, imprisoning her. His hands came out again and in one vicious move he tore her nightdress from throat to navel. A freezing river of cold rushed over her breasts to her belly.

'It's over wi', Catherine.' His voice slashed the silence. 'As from tonight you're going to be a wife to me and a mother to my bairns – do you hear me, woman?'

'Ay, Rob, I hear.' she whispered before the burning flesh of him embraced her, blotting out the cold and the grey, feeble light of the room. His mouth moved from her shoulders to her breasts, his teeth seared her flesh, one knee pushed hers roughly apart and he drove himself into her like the stallion that served the mares in the spring farmtouns. The moving, swelling bulk of him filled every aching empty space in her body, his breath was harsh and swift against her ears, the excited grunts of him sent shivers of delight running the length of her spine. Turning her head on the pillow she gave herself up to rapture and allowed herself to go with him. This – this was what she had waited for all her life. This was the Rob Burns who had incited mad cravings in her from the first moment of meeting. How different he had been from the watery, mild creatures she had known. From the start she had sensed the animal in him and could hardly wait to know what it would be like with him in the marriage bed.

But it hadn't been like that. Her kind of upbringing had never allowed her to show him her true self, but she had thought with him it wouldn't matter. He was the kind of man who must always have taken the lead. But with her he couldn't be himself and so she had waited, hoping always that he would throw off his gentlemanly instincts and behave like the full-blooded man that he was. But it had never worked. He had lain with her, and whored with common servant girls, giving them what by rights should have been hers . . . Pain and pleasure ripped through her. In the darkness she smiled to herself and arching her neck gave vent to her feelings – like a baying hound who has finally cornered its prey.

Johnny lay in bed, his heart hammering in his throat. The sounds of his parents' lust penetrated the night and he imagined the wolves of his childhood nightmares, clawing and slavering at the windows, trying to get in. His father's stealthy footfalls on the creak of the worn stairs had awakened him from a fitful slumber and all at once he was reminded of a tomcat padding the barn slates in the dead of night. He had lain, the tensions back in his belly, feeling that something out of the usual was about to happen. For a long time he had lain listening, hearing nothing, thinking his father had gone as usual to his room along the landing. And just when his eyes were beginning to close once more he had heard *her*, his mother, making fearful sounds which he had imagined at first to be pain. He had been about to get up and go to her when some instinct stayed him, forcing him back on the pillows to lie staring into the darkness, his fists clenched on the edge of the quilt.

How could she? How could *he*? Janet was hardly cold in her grave and they went together in bed as if she had never existed.

The face of his baby sister came to him and he relived

once more that hellish scene that had haunted him day and night. He would never get over it – never – and even if he could have tholed it he could never, never get over the fact that his father blamed him for it – he that had adored that bonny wee thing and would have done anything to save her. But nothing would bring her back now – nothing . . .

'Can I come in wi' ye, Johnny?' Jimmy's voice floated sleepily, the next minute he crawled in and snuggled up.

'Is Father back yet?'

'Ay.'

'Is he in wi' our ma?'

'Seems like it.' Johnny said shortly. 'They're – they're talking.'

Jimmy sniggered. 'Like the bull talks to the kie.'

'Shut up and go to sleep,' snapped Johnny, his face burning.

But Jimmy was already asleep, his quiet little snores tickling Johnny's ears. Johnny stared up at the ceiling and it seemed to him as he lay there in the darkness that the bleakness of winter would never end, and he would never again hear the peewits singing as they tumbled in the brilliant blue skies of a northern summer. Over a great divide the warmth and friendliness of King's Croft came to him; the sympathetic understanding in the eyes of Jamie; the deep, sweet sustaining comfort of a woman who wasn't his mother – and the wonderful tenderness in the deep green eyes of a bit girl who wasn't quite eleven years old. A child yet was Evelyn and already he felt something for her that was deep and good and everlasting . . .

Turning restlessly he whispered into his pillow. 'Goodnight, Evie,' and the tears of his loneliness wet his face . . .

Evelyn tossed and turned and finally reached out to light the candle at her bedside. Fumbling under her pillow she withdrew her diary and wrote; 'Johnny came to King's Croft today. He seemed not to know where he was or what was happening. I took off his boots and rubbed his feet. They were so cold. My heart was sad and I cried inside for

153

him. I wonder if that's what love feels like. Father gave him whisky and we all left the room but I stayed by the scullery door. Mam went in and took him in her arms to cuddle him. He cooried into her and she stroked his hair and looked at him as if he was her own son. It's been a terrible start to the New Year. It might be better when the summer comes and we can all go together to the Kelpie pool in Rothiedrum. Goodnight, Johnny. I love you but I don't know if it's real love. I'll have to wait till I'm older to find out . . .'

PART TWO

SPRING/SUMMER 1911

CHAPTER EIGHT

Jamie strode out to the fields, his step jaunty, chest puffed out as he breathed deeply of the scouring dry March wind which swept in welcome blasts over the peat-black winter rigs stretched out beneath the cold morning skies. But there was nothing dour in the day opening up before his glad vision. The dark, frustrating frost-chilled days of winter were past, the long hours of enforced idleness were already just a memory to horseman and farmers alike. The wraps of winter were thrown back as the world lightened and opened, the sky grew more infinite. Spring was still just a promise on the stark black tree-top tracery etched against the clouds, still just a wisp of yellow on the whins up on the hillocks above King's Croft. But Jamie saw the tender bud on the branch, felt the quickening of the dark earth tingling in his gypsy blood.

The Birkie flashed silver in the fitful sunlight, Bennachie's head was pillowed on cloud, her shoulders a misted shawl of blue, her feet buried in the bleached stubble of last year's harvest.

This was Jamie's favourite time. The promise of it never failed to excite him or stir his heart to hope for everything that was good and sweet. The peesies were on the wing again, tumbling and pirouetting in the vaults above and Jamie paused to listen to the wondrous sound of an Aberdeenshire spring, surprised to discover that while his heart sang his eyes were slightly moist, as if sodden winter still dallied in some part of him and refused to leave.

Stopping to lean on a dyke he took his stubby Stonehaven pipe from his pocket and gave himself up to that most wonderful luxury – anticipation; a looking forward to the long, busy summer ahead. It was a time when joy and weariness ran parallel, for there could never be any let up for a farmer once the growing season got under way. This was the best time, when rest had rejuvenated body and soul during the enforced tedium of the winter fireside. His gaze roved over the bare fields while in his mind he pictured seas of waving corn and fields of sprouting turnip. Always his romantic, idealistic soul allowed him such imaginings, so that if it should be a year of poor harvest he'd had these precious times of fantasy which nothing ever seemed to dim – until this year – when his vision seemed duller, cloudier than it had ever been. It was wee Col of course. He couldn't be happy wondering what kind of future existed for a bairn who couldn't yet walk or talk though he was past the age of two years. He had always been a shrivelled wee elf of a lad. Some of the daft folk from round about had it that he wasn't 'all there', for he had crept close to death through his first year with fits that frightened everybody near silly. But in the last year he had changed, had grown bonny and sweet with big, bright eyes on him and a smile that charmed everyone, even those who said he was a daftie.

Yet his smile and his charm was about all he had yet to his name. He wasn't inclined to play or learn like other bairns of his age. He was quite content just to sit in the wee go-chair Jamie had made him, crooning to himself and giggling when wee Cal, Kenneth Mor's lad, toddled up to talk to him.

Jeannie often brought her sturdy little son down to King's Croft to see Col. Cal and Col, the December twins as they were known, were the greatest of friends. Wee Cal seemed able to make sense of Col's ramblings for he would hold long conversations with him, his baby tongue going on and on while the other laughed in understanding. Nellie was the only other one who understood the wee one and unerringly saw to all his garbled requests. She had nursed and cared for the baby from the start. During his most frightening convulsions her devotion to him had been an inspiration, and not once had she turned away from him though her strong, gaunt face had often been ashen with fear. Twice she had gone out in the middle of the night with Col lying rigid in her arms, first to knock up Doctor

McGregor and stand over him while he administered to the baby, the second to trudge through frozen fields to Hill O' Binney, there to rouse old Hinney from her slumbers. All night long she and the old woman had nursed the little boy and in the morning she had come home exhausted but triumphant, bearing a normally breathing child. After that, she knew what to do for her little brother and had often sat with him in the kitchen through the hours of night.

Jamie loved him; with all the passion in his warm heart he adored the small scrap that was his only son but, he wondered now as he had so often wondered in the past, did Maggie? Oh, she was good to him, saw to his needs, lifted and laid him but rarely had she held him to her breast the way she had held the others. She was a proud one alright, the talk among the other farmwives with her fine, straight figure and an expression on her attractive face that bordered on haughtiness. He often wondered if she was ashamed of her son, but knew there was more to it than that. She hadn't blamed him in any way for what had happened, yet sometimes he caught her looking at him in a certain way – and in the hooded cast of her eyes he fancied he saw resentment.

Jamie took a deep breath and his hand went uneasily to the pocket of his jacket. The hardness of the bottle against his fingers was reassuring, but he had vowed he was done with all that. He had drunk most of the winter away in an excess of self-pity – ever since the knowing that Col wasn't going to be like other children. He had wanted a son – but God! He hadn't wanted a child who was going to be a burden to him! For a long time he hadn't been able to accept the cruel reality of wee Col – but now, now . . . He drew himself up and pushed out his jaw. Now he had come to terms with things as they were. He had his health, he had Maggie and five fine daughters any man would be proud of – and he had a son who would never leave him as another might have left him. He would teach Col about the things that mattered in life, about the spring and the peesies, and the joy of seeing the rainbow flashes of a trout leaping the tumble of an autumn river . . . He patted the bottle nestling

in his pocket, it was there to reassure him, that was all –
but surely one wee taste wouldn't be wrong on a morning
like this – to celebrate the coming of spring . . .

Up on the high fields of Knobblieknowe, figures were
moving about in the sun – the bothy lads were out in full
force, among them Kenneth Mor, his great kilted figure
unmistakable even from this distance – and surely that was
Jeannie with the bairn running at her side. Ay, she would
be out too, letting her bonny, strong son have the freedom
of the opening world.

All over the parks and houghs of Rothiedrum it would
be the same story, the fields alive with life, the Clydes
plodding to the drive of the harrow, dogs frisking and
barking, thousand upon thousand of seed casts fanning
over the ground, acre upon acre of ley ground curling
beneath the plough and all the while the peewits birling and
diving in a landscape misted by the dust of the earth. Jamie
could feel the life of the countryside quickening his heart,
making him forget the bottle and concentrate instead on
the days work ahead. Along the lane from the stables
Coulter was bringing the Clydes; behind him came Nellie
on the cart with Maggie and Col at her side. Evelyn sat on
top of Nickum, her legs barely able to stretch across his
broad back, her hair glinting red in the sunbeams that
slanted through the tracery of branches overhead. The
great feet of the horses were stirring up the sad leaves of
autumn long gone.

Coulter and Evelyn were sharing some private joke; her
glowing face was thrown back, her laughter mingled with
the old man's throaty chuckle. The sight of her did Jamie's
heart good. He was often wont to wonder why he felt such
an affinity with her – but the answer always came readily
– she was like him, so much so he was minded of himself
in those far off enticing days of childhood.

'Man, man, she's an awful lassie that,' Old Coulter
greeted Jamie somewhat breathlessly. 'I canna think where
she gets half her nonsense from.'

'I could tell you that, Coulter,' Jamie returned dryly.
'You and she are aye cooking up mischief between you.'

Coulter grinned unrepentantly and rather worriedly twirled a lock of his snowy beard between sinewy fingers. Evelyn had curled it for him, with a pair of tongs held in the glow of the fire, she had tutted and scolded him and made him stay still while everyone else was getting ready to go out to the fields. Catching her eye they both burst into renewed skirls of merriment that made Nellie tush as she flounced down from the cart. Everyone it seemed had left domestic duties behind on that day of the earth's re-awakening. The majority of them would just linger for a little while as they watched their menfolk going off to the fields. But their turn would come, at tattie lifting, haymaking and harvest when every man, woman and child would be needed.

Jamie watched Maggie making her way towards him. She had regained all her old grace of movement, her back was straight, her head thrown up in that proud, defiant tilt that so set the other farmwives' tongues a-wagging. Col rode on her back, happed up in a tartan plaid. He was cooried in there, warm and snug, his fists balled under his chin, his hair, dark at birth but now a lovely shade of red-gold, glinting under his bonnet. The tenderness of that small frail head caught at Jamie's heart. 'How is our wee lad the day, Maggie?'

'As good as he'll ever be.' She bit her lip at the harshness of her words and caught her husband's arm. 'You mustna fret for him, Jamie. He's stronger than he looks and I havena the time to be pampering him. The others took their journeys to the fields happed at my back and I'll make no difference wi' him.'

Nellie, sleeves rolled to her elbows, hair tied back with a scarf, came up. She was as good as any man with a horse and harrow and had worked alongside the men for as long as she could remember. 'I'll take Col for a while, Mother, your back must be tired.'

'My back is *not* tired,' Maggie's tones were firm. 'You get along wi' the others. I'll watch for a wee while then get along home. I'll send Evie down with your dinner later.'

Nellie turned away, her back rigid with anger at her

161

mother who, lately, had had more to do with the upbringing of her son. Nellie's resentment showed in tight-lipped silences and a tongue so abrasive the rest of the household were careful to give her a wide berth.

'She dotes on the wee one.' Jamie watched his eldest daughter's receding back and bit hard on his pipe.

'Ach, it's no healthy her taking to do wi' a bairn like Col. A young woman like that should have healthy ones o' her own by now.' Maggie's tones were dismissive. Her gaze swept over the landscape. The peesies were in ecstasy, tumbling about, diving to the earth, swooping upwards again into the wind-sculpted clouds. A smile touched her lips. 'Listen to them, Jamie, just listen to the joy of them.' She breathed deeply. 'I feel good today – I feel – life.'

His eyes blurred. Reaching out his strong brown hand, he took hers and squeezed it. 'Maggie, there's something I've aye been meaning to ask – ever since Col was born.'

She glanced at him quickly and he went on slowly, 'It's about you and me, Maggie, how we feel about each other. We used to speak a lot but somehow we don't anymore and I wondered – do you hate me for giving you a bairn like him?'

'Hate you!' She was aghast. 'Not you, Jamie, *me*. I wanted to give you a son who would be a blessing to you but instead I had one who will never be that. Oh no, my dear, dear, Jamie. I hate myself because I failed to bear you one healthy son – and I feel so guilty all the time!'

'Maggie,' he said huskily. 'We've both been blind to one another's feelings. And you're wrong about wee Col, he *is* a blessing. Can you think o' your life without him now?'

'There was a time when I wished for nothing else – but this whilie back he's become – real to me. Maybe because I don't turn away from him like I used to. I look at his wee face and how it lights up when he smiles and I think to myself how lonely the house would be without him in it. When I'm alone wi' him I pick him up and dance round the kitchen with him and I hear such laughter from him I could cry knowing how ashamed I once was of him.'

Col stirred at her back and tickled his face with a strand

162

of her hair. Jamie and Maggie smiled at one another, a lightness in their hearts that took away the years of misery they had endured.

The Loon came scurrying along the lane, yellow hair straggling out from under his cap, big feet scuffing up the drying mud.

'See what I found!' he called, his soft voice raised in excitement. Evelyn rushed up to peer into his cupped hands. A tiny, bedraggled peewit lay gasping in the confines of his sweaty palms and Evelyn prised it from him with great care.

'Two o' them were courtin' up in the sky,' explained The Loon eagerly, 'And this wee mannie got so excited he knocked himself out and plunged straight doon at my heid.'

'He's hurt his wing, Pootie.' Evelyn put the little creature carefully into the pocket of her apron. 'Grace put me in charge o' her injured animals so I'll take it back home. It will be fine in a wee whilie.'

The Loon willingly gave up his prize to the youngest daughter of King's Croft. Grace's menagerie of small animals was a great source of wonder to him and gave him a good excuse to visit the croft when the mood took him.

'Come on, Pootie man,' Jamie called over his shoulder. 'I dinna pay you good sillar to stand around wi' your hands in your pouches.'

Evie ran away home but was soon back. She kissed the top of wee Col's downy head, squeezed her mother's hands and skipped away to the fields.

Maggie stood watching her go. The sun was warm on her face, the scents of the earth strong in her nostrils. At her back Col stirred. His warm, moist little mouth tickled her neck and she giggled.

Leaning against the dyke her eyes roved over the black oblong of the stubble field sloping up to meet the birch wood. The Clydes were on the move, sun glinted on harness, the grubber ripped across the stubble of last year's corn. Gulls swooped, the yellow of the broom splashed gold on the branches. Jamie, Coulter and Pootie moved slowly but purposefully. Evelyn ran, a small dot brimful of

163

life – Nellie's voice floated strongly. A smile touched Maggie's mouth. She was like that, was Nell. A stickler for convention in most aspects of life, but out here in the fields she forgot to be prim and old maidish and exercised her lungs as loudly as the men. Would she ever meet a man she cared for enough to marry? Would Murn, with her discontented mouth and her shameless affection for a married man? She had completed her two year training course at college and having gained her Teacher's General Certificate was now teaching at a primary school in Tillietoorie and seemed to have settled down well in the post.

And what about her bonny gentle Grace with her child's outlook on life and her strange alliance to a man old enough to be her father? She was away from home now, taking her nurse's training in Aberdeen, but whenever she was home on leave she and Martin Gregory were always to be seen together though the relationship appeared to be purely platonic on Grace's part. Not so Martin Gregory. Maggie had seen how he looked at her daughter and she kept hoping that Grace would meet someone nearer her own age before Martin got too enmeshed with his feelings for her.

Only Mary, wholesome, earthy Mary, had pursued a relationship that was entirely normal. She had given Doctor McGregor a run for his money but in the end had succumbed to his persuasions and now they were happily married and living in the rambling old house just outside the village so that Mary was able to visit King's Croft often.

Thank heaven Evelyn was too young yet to worry about. It would be Johnny Burns of course. When the time came it would be healthy and vigorous and wholesome – and it would be Johnny Burns.

Col burped at her back and she smiled. 'Ay, that's what you think o' an auld wife who stands gawping at dreams when I should be home seeing to the house.'

Hoisting him up she turned down the lane, the burbling of the burn humming gently in her ears. 'It's going to be a good summer, Col,' she said with conviction. 'Or my name is no' Margaret Innes Grant.'

164

Several things happened to make it a memorable summer, both for Evelyn and the people of Rothiedrum. George the Forge was up to his usual tricks the day she met Gillan Ogilvie Forbes of Rothiedrum House. It was well into June. Since the middle of May the plough drill had worked at the harrow's tail, spreaders had impregnated the air of the countryside with the rich, warm reek of dung. The travelling people had arrived to help with the neep and potato planting, now that the work was done the countryside seemed to pause to gather breath before the coming of harvest. The travellers would be back then but now they moved in convoy along the turnpike, cart wheels rumbling, the voices of berry-brown children shrill and excited, glad to be back on the road again.

'See you at Hairst, King Jamie,' the men called, waving their caps at Jamie who was standing at the door of the Smiddy, fanning his hot brow with his own cap.

'Ay, ay, we'll have some more work for you then,' he called, adding a few words in traveller's cant which brought a frown to George's sweating, florid face.

'Dyod man,' he said irritably, 'We all ken you're a gypsy but it's ill mannered to be speaking in a language the rest o' us dinna understand. Ye could be saying anything aboot us and us none the wiser.'

Jamie just nodded. George was always kept busy, but at this time of year he was even more so with the farmers bringing in harrows to be sharpened. Jamie had brought two of his horses to be shod and was enjoying a brew of George's ale. Evelyn was inside the Smiddy, fascinated as always with the horses in the stables next door and by the heat and reek of the Smiddy.

'And how's our wee Evie this morning?' George's tone changed at sight of the green-eyed, red-haired child, clean and fresh in a white smock, bare feet and legs burned to a golden brown from long days spent outdoors. 'How would you like a nice big stick o' sugerolly, eh, eh?' He nudged her conspiratorily, one big hand coming to squeeze her waist.

'I'm thirteen now, George.' She ignored his question and his nudgings, niggled because he seemed not to have noticed that she had stretched in the last few months and was no longer wee. With anyone else she wouldn't have minded but somehow it was important to her that he should recognize her increased stature. The feel of his hands on her was no longer the innocent prelude to sweeties and halfpennies and she moved slightly away from him. 'Mam says sweeties are bad for my teeth.'

'Oh, did she now?' George was smiling ingratiatingly. 'And was it no bad for your teeth when you were just a wee bit thing?' He rummaged in a grubby sack and pulling out a strop of liquorice pressed it into her hand, his own lingering on the smoothness of hers. 'That will no' harm ye, it's good for the bowels if nothing else. And, Evie – ye'll no grow away from old George – will ye now?'

His big, amiable smile beamed out and she could do nothing but smile back though she was relieved when Bunty Lovie came bustling over the road with a flatiron grasped in one dimpled fist.

'Will ye be mending this for me, George?' Bunty's beady eyes took in Evelyn's flushed face and George's hastily withdrawn hands. 'The handle's broken and will just need a wee bittie solder.'

'Ach, woman! You and your iron,' he grumbled. 'Can ye no' see I'm up to my een in work . . .'

A clatter of hooves made him pause and groan, 'No another bugger lookin' for a horse to be shod! Well, whoever it is can just wait till I've more time.'

Bunty eyed Evelyn's hot face. 'Was that dirty auld goat up to his tricks again? I ken fine what he does to young lassies round here. It's a wife he should be having, ay, and high time too. The old bugger wouldna get away wi' half . . .'

Looking up she caught sight of Jamie's surprised face turned to the interior of the Smiddy. Everyone stared as a young boy came in leading a sleek and shining chestnut mare with pedigree in every noble line of her. Both the mare and the boy brought with them a tangible presence of the aristocracy and, with the exception of Evelyn, everyone gaped in rude amazement.

'Master Gillan,' George was the first to speak, 'this is a rare surprise and no mistake. Is the stable lad ill?'

'No, I wanted to bring Lady myself. She needs shoeing and Will was busy with other things.'

Although he spoke calmly there was a supressed elation in his voice. Watching him from under her lashes Evelyn thought he would have been as well standing in the middle of the Smiddy and shouting, 'Look at me, everybody. I'm neither mad nor ill and I've brought my horse to be shod because I'm perfectly capable of doing it without Will or anybody else at my back.'

The strop of liquorice was growing soft and squidgy in her hand. The dark, cool gaze of the new arrival flicked over her and, reddening, she stuffed the limp sweetmeat into the pocket of her smock, wondering what Nellie would have to say about the black stains on washday.

George was examining the mare's feet, soon joined by Gillan and Jamie. Evelyn studied young Rothiedrum, thinking, 'So this is the laird's son, the one who's supposed to be daft and kept away from folk for their own good.'

He was about fourteen, a tall, thin boy with dark, waving hair, a pale skin and features that were so fine they might have belonged to a girl. He spoke politely but his manner was somewhat curt, though there was a softness in his tones that was pleasing to the ears, a sort of husky hesitancy that robbed him of a good deal of the arrogance that was in his mother.

Bunty drew Evelyn outside to the sunshine, her bird-bright eyes alive with interest. 'Is that no' a turn up for the books? In all my days I've only glimpsed the lad in the kirk and now he turns up here as if he brought his horse to be shod every other day o' the week.'

Evelyn stood on one foot and looked back into the dim interior of the Smiddy. George and Gillan were busy with the horse's feet, but Jamie was engaged in looking over her, his eyes alight with admiration as he studied every gracious curve of her. 'He must be better now,' Evelyn decided. 'He sounds cheeky enough though he looks as if he's been ill for a long time.'

'Ay, the soul looks a mite too thin,' Bunty was bubbling over with lively curiosity. Her bosom was well puffed out like a preening robin and Evelyn hid a smile as she remembered how often Florrie had imitated the action. 'He looks sane enough to me,' Bunty nodded wisely, a hint of disappointment in her tones. 'I doubt all that gossip about him being soft in the head was just a lot o' rubbish.'

Gillan's arrival in Lums O' Reekie had not gone unnoticed by its residents. Quite a few folk were gathered outside their houses. Mr Anderson Sir had the audacity to step out from his shop and come over the road, wiping his hands on his grubby apron as he came, barging without hesitation into the Smiddy, there to fawn over the laird's son while the old men sitting on the sun-drenched bench outside stretched their ears and nodded to one another sagely.

But Mr Anderson Sir was wasting his ingratiating breath on Forbes the younger of Rothiedrum. With a diplomacy far beyond his years Gillan shook hands politely with the grocer, decanted him from the Smiddy with a few well chosen words of dismissal, and coming outside to shade his eyes from the sun with his hands, he surveyed the dusty street as if he was lord of all he looked upon.

Magically everyone melted back indoors, the retreat being followed by a frantic twitching of curtains which brought an answering twitch to the corners of Gillan's well-shaped mouth. It was a mouth made for laughter, the full firm curves of it fining out to tiny laughter lines though they might just as easily have been the lines brought about by years of illness.

'I'll wait out here for Lady,' he threw back into the Smiddy.

George bustled out, hoisting his leather belt to the lower fatty tyre of his ponderous belly. 'Tis sorry I am, Master Gillan,' he said kindly but firmly. 'Lady will have to wait for a whilie. There are others who were here first and

168

they're the ones I will be seeing to before I do yours.'

George had never pandered to the gentry and never would, for despite his faults he was completely open and honest in his dealings with people and he wasn't going to put his regular customers out just for the sake of appeasing young Rothiedrum.

'But I need her now, man!' Gillan stated emphatically. Then, as George protested once more, 'Goddammit, man! Can't you take a telling? I said I'll wait here for Lady and I mean just that!'

'Suit yourself, sir.' George's florid jowls tightened. 'But you'll have to spend the night in the Smiddy in that case. Of course, I can lend you a spare horse, nothing fancy like, but at least he'll get you home in one piece.'

Gillan opened his mouth to argue further, but just then Jamie came out of the stables, leading Queenie and Nickum. He had spent a lot of time grooming them that morning, helped by the orra loon and Johnny who spent as much time as he dared in the King's Croft stables.

'Queenie will see you home.' Jamie gave Evelyn the reins to hold while he placed a friendly arm on Gillan's shoulder. There was a challenge in Jamie's voice, even more in the impudent eye he cast at young Rothiedrum, a look that said, 'Come on, you young bugger. Let's find out if you're no' too far above yourself to ride the turnpike on a plough horse.'

The boy turned his head slowly, his assessing gaze travelling over Jamie's gypsy brown, face. 'I've always wanted to ride a Clyde,' He spoke the words softly so that only Jamie heard. 'And your Queenie has pedigree – even I know that.'

'Near as much as yourself, Gillan lad, ay, and a mite more manners than some o' the gentry I know. Queenie's a bit frisky the now, mind, she's been running wi' her foal since spring and will be in a hurry to get back to it – but her legs canna be any more frisky than your tongue so you will make a fine team.'

Gillan laughed then, a laugh that gusted up out of his belly and Evelyn laughed just to listen to him while Bunty

169

scuttled away over to regale Lily Lammas with all she had heard and seen.

Gillan disdained George's help on to Queenie's patient back, but his pride was his undoing for his foot slipped and he would have fallen but for Jamie's hands at his back.

'There you go, you proud wee bugger,' Jamie's eyes glinted with mischief as he hoisted the boy up, giving him a whack on the backside for good measure. Queenie wore no saddle, Jamie having ridden to the Smiddy on Nickum with Evelyn at his back and the mare on a rein. 'Your backside will be well warmed by the time you get home so that slap on the erse was just to get it used to the discomfort.'

A quick reprisal sprang to the boy's lips, but one look at Evelyn's delighted face decided him against anything that might bring him further ridicule. They were laughing at him, it was there in the dancing eyes of both father and daughter – and Forbes the younger of Rothiedrum wasn't used to being laughed at.

A moment later Evelyn settled herself at his back and slid her arms about his waist. The feel of her brought a little curl of warmth to his heart. He was surprised at how soft she felt. His first impression of her had been of a skinny bundle of arms and legs but now he realized that there was warmth and softness underneath the loose pinafore she wore. She also smelt nice, not the expensive, overpowering mother smell he was so used to and which often made him squirm away; this was a subtle thing, an echo of bath night, a faint reminder of roses, all mixed up with the smells of the farm . . .

So taken up was he with his thoughts he spoke not a word as they clopped out of Lums O' Reekie and over the bridge to the turnpike. Queenie felt good and solid under him. He was mesmerized by the long, silky mane of her, by the beautiful docile grace that combined so agreeably with her power. The plains of Rothiedrum stretched to the right and left of him, patchwork squares of browns and greens and golds rolling away to misty horizons where phantom-like hills marched in serried ranks, their peaks merging into fluffy clouds which barely moved in the tranquil sky. And overhead the peewits were birling and singing with joy, while far in blue-shadowed houghs the cuckoo's haunting call echoed and re-echoed and blackbirds trilled from cool, hidden woods . . .

Evelyn's breath suddenly tickled his ear. 'You were rude to poor old George back there. It's a wonder to me he managed to keep a civil tongue in his head. I wouldna take snash like that from anyone – gentry or no.'

Inclining his head he said stiffly, 'You've got too much to say for a farmer's daughter. If you were working to my father you'd have to toe the line – like it or no.'

'Ach, I'd never work for the likes of you. Maybe you have been ill all your life but that doesna give you the right to kick people about as if they were bits o' cow dung. I think – I think you've been shut away so long you dinna ken *how* to speak to other human beings.'

The truth of that stung him to the quick. He had spent so much of his life being cossetted and protected he knew only how to converse with adults who, with the exception of the servants, had been of his own class. Yet, how *dare* this skinny girl speak like that to him. 'And you don't know how to speak *at all*,' he threw at her furiously. 'It's – it's like a foreign language. Certainly it bears no resemblance to the King's English.'

Bringing up one bare brown knee she pushed it viciously into the small of his back. '*I* dinna ken how to speak! You're the one who talks funny. How can you even breathe wi' all those marbles you have in your mouth? You sound like a jessie – and if you dinna ken what that means well – it's maybe just as well!'

Jamie listened to the exchanges, a wry smile twisting his mouth. He said nothing. Maybe it was time young Rothiedrum had a taste of his own medicine – and by Dyod, he would get it from that wee spitfire if from no one else. Jamie grinned. The Clyde's hooves beat a peaceful melody on the dusty road. He began to hum a bothy ballad, then as the beauty of the summer's day stirred his gypsy blood, he threw back his head and burst into hearty song.

171

Gillan's back bristled. Noisy beggars. He wouldn't look at them, wouldn't give them the satisfaction of seeing how much they had riled him.

Behind him, Evelyn laughed, her fingers tightened on his waist. 'Smile – Master Gillan! Or are you feared your face will crack!'

His lips twitched. Her breath blew over his neck as she joined in her father's song. A good voice she had too – low and sweet, a surprising strength in it for such a slip of a girl. He began to hum. He knew the bothy ballads, had heard them often enough drifting over from the Mains as he wandered inside the estate. The wild, evocative beat of them had never failed to stir something up in him, a sympathy for the hard-working farm lads, an unexplained yearning to go to the bothies and join them. But he had never dared. He knew he wouldn't have fitted in, his presence would only have brought strain to the informal atmosphere. And now here he was, singing away like a farm hand, such a sense of freedom pervading his being he wanted to do strange things – like taking off his cap and throwing it high in the air . . .

On an impulse he did just that, accompanying the action with such a loud 'Whoopee!' Evelyn jumped behind him and stopped singing. He had thrown the hat with such force it went over a hedge into a field to land somewhere out of sight.

'Whoa!' Jamie reined in his horse and with a grin at both youngsters went off leisurely. He had to go some distance to find the gate into the field and was gone for some time.

Gillan twisted round to look at Evelyn. She noticed that his eyes, deep and brown and hitherto pensive, were now sparkling. 'I couldn't stop myself doing that. Perhaps I shouldn't have!'

'Ay, it was a daft thing to do – but at least you're more like a boy now instead of an old man. Mind you, you should have gone to look for it – my father isn't your servant.'

A quick retort sprang to his lips. He was about to tell her that all the tenants of Rothiedrum were to some extent servants, but there was something about this red-haired

172

gypsy of a girl. She wouldn't have stood for such petty quibbling so he bit his lip and said instead, 'Who are you anyway?'

'Evelyn McKenzie Grant of King's Croft. It's Moss-dyke really but everyone calls it King's Croft because – because –'

'Because what?'

There was a mocking gleam in his eye which made her hesitate before she decided, 'Why not?' He thought himself so grand and he was only landed gentry while she . . . She tossed back her head. 'Because my father's a king – that's what.'

He stared at her incredulously then, as she had expected, burst out laughing. 'A king! A farmer who smells of hay and horses – a king! King who, may I ask?'

'Jamie,' she answered lightly, fighting down her temper.

'Oh, King Jamie, no less. I see. And where is his kingdom?'

'All this.' She made a sweeping gesture that took in the hills and the howes and the wide, stretching plains of Rothiedrum.

'I see.' He wasn't grinning quite so wickedly now. 'And his subjects?'

'My mother, my four sisters, my wee brother and me,' she said quietly. 'We are his subjects and are pleased to do his bidding because we love and respect him and because he works day and night to make our home a happy, safe place to be. King's Croft is our castle – just as much as Rothiedrum House is yours – and I'm thinking it's likely warmer and more contented than your home will ever be – so dinna you dare laugh at my father again – ever!'

Her hands had fallen from his waist to her lap. She sat there, on Queenie's back, eyes brilliant with indignation her soft, sweet mouth trembling with emotion. She had taken his breath away. So passionate in her loyalties, so frank with her opinions, so direct and unashamed of her loves. She was like no one he had ever met before, certainly nothing like the stuffy, boring companions he'd had to thole throughout his short life, the friends and cousins his

173

mother had marched in and out of his life, staid people as befitted his delicate state of health. None had been in the lest beneficial to him. He had much preferred the chance encounters he'd had with various children on his travels abroad. None had lasted however, his mother had seen to that. They were either too boisterous or too common so it was a rare treat for him to meet Evelyn. Evelyn of King's Croft, a breath of fresh air in the dull fog of his life.

On impulse he took her hand. 'I wasn't laughing at your father – I like him – I like you. I'm sorry for acting the way I did. I don't really know what I'm saying today because for once in my life I'm free. My parents are away in England on business and it's just me and my tutor, Frank Thoms. He's a good sport, all specs and brains but a sense of fairness for all that. He comes abroad with us and hates the heat as much as I do. I much prefer it here.' A sweep of his hand took in their surroundings. 'The air is clean and clear and I feel I can really breathe. Thoms is away to Tillietoorie for the day and I have the place to myself.'

He squeezed her arm excitedly, his face so animated she could hardly believe he was the same Gillan who had been pale with temper a short while ago in the Smiddy. 'Why don't you come over this afternoon? I'll show you the house and the gardens and you can ride one of my horses if you like. Afterwards we'll go into the kitchen and have tea. The servants won't mind and they would never tell – I often go down there when Mother thinks I'm in my room. Old Martha the cook is like a mother to me. She saves me bits of marzipan and icing – all the things Mother says are bad for me. How about it? You'll enjoy it – I know you will.'

His face had gone pale after this breathless outburst. Evelyn saw the strain in him and was made suddenly aware of his terrible loneliness, the lonelines of a rich boy who had everything and yet for all that had nothing. Pleading lay stark in his eyes. She bit her lip, tempted to accept his offer – but that very afternoon she was going with Johnny and Florrie to the Kelpie Pool deep in the Rothiedrum estate. All the children of the area were going, grabbing the chance to enjoy themselves before the onset of haymaking and harvest consumed much of their time.

For one wild moment she thought of asking Gillan to join them but no – she couldn't. It would have meant betraying the trust of the others and she couldn't put one lonely boy over the welfare of youngsters she had known all her life – even if it was Gillan's land they were trespassing – or because of it.

He met her refusal ungraciously. His eyes clouded and she saw anger in them mingling with disappointment. He waved off her rebuff rather imperiously. 'It doesn't matter, I'm used to being on my own anyway and girls are nearly always a nuisance.'

Jamie came back then, a smile denting his cheeks as he handed Gillan his hat. Gillan glared at it in distaste. 'But it's filthy – look at it!'

'Ay, lad, you couldna have aimed better if you'd tried. It landed plunk in the middle o' a big cow's plab, but just mind, you threw it, no' me. Never mind, it will maybe bring you luck and if you leave it to dry it will brush off no bother.'

Whistling cheerily, he mounted Nickum and they rode on, Jamie hardly daring to look at his daughter for fear he would see the same sort of sympathetic amusement that was reflected in his own eyes. Gillan sat stiffly, the hat held gingerly in his fingers, his ears red with chagrin, a welter of emotions running so strong in him he couldn't utter a single word but just stared at the road running away between Queenie's ears.

At his back Evelyn sat poker-faced because she knew if she relaxed one muscle she would burst out laughing in Gillan's ears – and she couldn't, just couldn't allow that to happen. In a short space of time she had witnessed many swings of mood in this pampered young Rothiedrum. He was obviously used to getting his own way, yet she realized he had never had what he craved for most – the normal healthy companionship of normal healthy youngsters and even while she felt sorry for him she was glad, so glad that her own life had been natural and free of all the many constrictions the gentry imposed upon themselves.

175

For all that, she instinctively liked him. There was a deep and beautiful sensitivity, a well-controlled passion for life and a sense of humour buried somewhere under a serious facade.

The rest of the journey passed in silence. When they reached the gate opposite King's Croft track, Gillan called on Jamie to halt. 'I'll take the short cut over the fields, the walk will do me good.' He kept his head turned from them. Evelyn noticed the proud tilt to it, yet wasn't taken in by his show of arrogance. He was deeply annoyed at her – hurt too, his eyes gave it away when he half-turned to throw her a last appealing look. Slowly she shook her head. He strode off through the gates, throwing back over his shoulder, 'Thank you for the ride up, Mr Grant and good day to you.'

Jamie turned the horses, a thoughtful frown between his eyes. 'He's a lonely lad is Master Gillan. He tries to hide it but it's there just the same. He needs bairns of his own age to play with. These should be the best years o' his life – mine were – but then I was a lad born to freedom. There was aye plenty of fun to be had – poor and hardworked though we were.'

They topped a rise in the track. Evelyn looked back. A blue, smoky haze lay in the woods that densely surrounded Rothiedrum House. Her gaze rested on the treetops and she allowed her mind to wonder what beauty lived beyond them. There was a deep silence in the thickets and she could picture Gillan trudging along that lonely road to home, the chimneys of which she only just glimpsed in the blue mysterious yonder between the fronds of summer greenery.

She had been looking forward to that long awaited Saturday afternoon but now she felt guilty and ashamed to think that because of his position young Rothiedrum wasn't allowed to join in the delights to be had in the grounds of his own estate.

CHAPTER NINE

The tree-shaded pool was calm and deep and so cold it took a great deal of control for the lads and lasses of the farmtouns not to scream too loudly as they plunged and splashed in ecstasy. Evelyn and Florrie, naked and self-conscious about it as they had never been before, hugged one another on the bank and Florrie whispered, 'Yours are beginning to grow. Maybe we should get dressed before Dirty Wullie starts goggling at us.'

Evelyn looked down quickly at her chest, surprised to see tiny bumps appearing on what had hitherto been a flat, uninteresting part of her body. Florrie too was showing the same earth-shattering development and Evelyn glanced round in embarrassment, certain that all eyes must be on her. But Dirty Wullie, named so because of his aversion to soap and water and lately, his earthy comments about girls, was too engrossed in keeping most of himself out of the water to be much bothered about anything else. Johnny, a magnet for several pairs of female eyes with his smooth, tanned body dressed in nothing but a pair of swimming trunks, was taken up in practising the various strokes at which he was so good. Nevertheless Evelyn withdrew a little from the scene, only to be grabbed by Florrie and pulled into the water before she could utter one word of protest.

'This is the best hiding place,' Florrie giggled gleefully, splashing herself with handfuls of water, her golden hair tumbling down her creamy back so that it touched the surface of the pool.

The Loon was on the opposite bank, splashing about in his semmit and drawers, his big shaggy yellow head thrown back in delight as the youngsters ducked him. Alan Keith was on the bank, his back to a tree, his painting pad open on his knees, tongue sticking out in concentration as he

177

tried to capture the essence of that halcyon summer's day by the Kelpie Pool; the shafts of dusty sunbeams slanting through the trees; the needle-strewn red earth; the deep blue of the sky glimpsed above majestic spires.

It was the sudden silence which drew Evelyn's attention to the fact that something out of the ordinary had happened. Glancing up, she saw Gillan sitting astride a horse in the little clearing, his look of triumph directed at her. If she hadn't been so taken aback she would have found something comical in the open-mouthed stillness of the others. Like statues they were, just staring at young Rothiedrum, he looking back at them with a slight arrogance on his face that told of his feelings of superiority.

In her surprise Evelyn forgot all about her new found embarrassment of her body. Scrambling out of the water she looked desperately round, her gaze alighting for no reason on Will, the youngest stable boy at Rothiedrum. His eyes were directly on her and she saw the unmistakable stain of guilt reddening his face. Will had told, possible goaded into it by Gillan anxious to find out where he was going on his afternoon off. Johnny had seen her state of agitation and he was at her side, his arm all at once possessive and intimate on her bare flesh. Gillan was watching her again and now there was enjoyment on his face, for her embarrassment, for the same thing that Johnny was finding so attractive? She didn't know. The whole episode seemed timeless to her, but in fact only a few moments had elapsed since Gillan's unexpected appearance. His intrusion had brought unease to the tranquil day. Everyone looked as if they didn't know whether to stay and brazen it out or whether the best course would be to gather up their clothes and run.

Gillan took the matter into his own hands. With a wild whoop he was off his horse and peeling off his clothes so that in seconds he was as naked as everyone else there. With the removal of his immaculate riding habit he seemed also to shed the aura of the distant young aristocrat. His horse wandered away, bent on seeking out the sweet cool grasses growing nearby and after only a brief hesitation

Gillan was in the pool, paddling around, shoulder to shoulder with village bairns and farmer's sons and daughters.

'Can ye swim, Maister?' Jenny's cheeky inquiry brought normality to the situation. Gillan admitted that he was a hopeless swimmer and was immediately surrounded by an eager mob, all willing and eager to help. Evelyn and Florrie joined in the melee, flesh touched flesh, no one was different then. In the gliding silken caress of the Kelpie Pool, they were all just children enjoying themselves on a hot summer's day in mid-June.

Later, when everyone else had dispersed, Gillan walked with Florrie, Evelyn and Johnny to Rothiedrum House. Will led the horse away to the stables while Gillan led his new-found friends into the kitchen to beg tea from Martha. Plump, good natured and devoted to the son of the house, the old cook batted not one eyelid at the intrusion into the kitchen and soon all four were enjoying a feast of home baked scones and cakes.

Gillan talked a lot that first day of unusual happenings and unusual friendships. It was as if he had bottled everything up all his life till now, this time with sparkling eyed Florrie, strong, silent Johnny, pensive, attentive Evelyn. He told them of his years of being dogged by childhood illness, his mother's efforts to make him well by taking him abroad which he detested, his love of Rothiedrum, his growing conviction that the years of enforced confinement were behind him and he could now begin to live a normal and active life.

Florrie was dazzled by him. 'I hope he asks us back,' she said when they at last stood outside in the glaring sunshine.

'He will,' Johnny said with conviction and Evelyn wondered why he looked at her when he said it.

A few days later, Rothiedrum woke up to the spectacle of The Loon streaking stark naked along the turnpike, Dottie Drummond hard on his heels, brandishing a broom and screeching at the top of her voice. Dottie was a placid enough soul in the normal way of things and was quite a respected character in her own right. It was a common enough sight to see her sitting at the Boglehowe road end contentedly sucking on her clay pipe as she raised a languid hand to the traffic coming and going. In her own way she was fairly religious and every Sabbath was to be seen in kirk, The Loon at her side whether he liked it or no', her sharp elbow digging into his side if he dared to fidget or show anything else but an avid attention to every word that came from the Rev. Sommerville's lips. It mattered not to her that she usually nodded off to sleep in the middle of the sermon. She was there, in the Lord's house, and on that account her conscience was as clear as crystal.

She had a good sense of humour too, cackling and laughing at the coarsest of jokes, many of them heard in Lums O' Reekie inn. For to that establishment she actually dared to go, the only female in the parish to take such an astounding liberty. At first Andrew Dalgliesh and his customers had been shocked at such a thing and debated long and hard whether they should evict her from the premises for once and for all. But so entertaining was she, sitting there downing ale, smoking her pipe as good as any man, and cracking the coarsest jokes of all, that in time the men came to accept her presence and even to look forward to it.

But to Dottie there was a time and place for everything and when she had come upon her son that morning, bathing stark naked in the little burn that ambled along by Boglehowe, her sense of outrage had been such that she hadn't waited for any explanation but had rushed into her house, there to seize a broom and charge with it to the burn, her high-pitched yells of rage enough to frighten away any of the bogles which were reputed to haunt the area. The Loon, with the delights of the Kelpie Pool still fresh in his mind, had arisen that hot, still morning before his mother was astir to take himself off to the burn, there to sample the ecstasies of cold hill water on sweating naked flesh. His mother in a rage at any time was enough to make him jump to her bidding but to see her at that time of the morning, just risen from her bed, her spiky grey hair

180

standing on end, the broom held like a lance in front of her, was too much for his simple heart to face. And so he had taken off, down past Carnallachie's, hellbent for the turnpike.

Carnallachie was coming along the road from the Mains with a barrowload of dung which he had somehow managed to scrounge from the miserly Peter Lamont. Dung was a precious commodity in the north-east, and to get a farmer to part with it was almost akin to extracting a gold filling from a back molar. But Carnallachie was a crafty old rogue and knew certain things about the grieve of the Mains which wouldn't have gone well for him if they had reached the ears of the laird.

So Carnallachie was feeling right pleased with himself that blithe morning in mid-summer up until Trudge, that daft cuddy of his, stopped dead in the middle of the road, his eyes rolling as the sound of screeching reached his ears. The demented intrusion of The Loon and his mother into the scene soon put paid to the old man's pleasant musings and it was with no great difficulty that he reverted to the Carnallachie everyone knew best. Strings of oaths issued from his twisted lips, his leathery countenance screwed into a snarl and there he sat fuming, his precious heap of dung steaming behind him, his whip cracking to the right and left of his cuddy and all to no avail.

To make matters worse, who should come along at his back but Tandy, pleased at having made so early a start he had made good time on the comparatively empty roads. His bewilderment at meeting so many obstacles in such a short space of time resulted in a temporary loss of command over his flock and his dogs. Sheep and sheepdogs spewed over walls and into ditches, between them making a terrible din and further blocking the already blocked road.

Down the track from King's Croft several of the Grants came running to see what all the noise was about, soon joined by Kenneth Cameron Mor who had been coming down anyway and shortly after that by Kirsty and Angus Keith from Dippiedoon. They stood in a knot, for there

181

was no other way to stand with crazed sheep and dogs milling around, watching proceedings and asking one another what on earth The Loon was thinking about and even more eagerly what had possessed his mother to behave in a manner so out of keeping with her normal introverted self.

The Loon came tearing along, foaming at the mouth, eyes rolling with terror, not a pretty sight to behold at that ungodly hour. Even the dogs barked at sight of him and bared their fangs as his great clairty feet stamped on their paws and his untrammelled private parts flopped up and down and slapped themselves about. One of the dogs stood and bared its teeth at them and between one thing and another all hell seemed to have been let loose.

Carnallachie glowered blackly as the birthday-suited Pootie, his screeching mother hot on his cracked, dirty heels, came steaming up towards him. Out shot Carnallachie's horny hand to grab the Drummond lad by the scruff of his hair, the only handhold available to him, and drag him up on to the cart beside him.

'Hup! Hup!' he roared at Trudge who snapped out of a terrified trance, for once only too glad to obey a command in order to escape the melee of sheep and dogs and bawling humans. Back went his ears, his eyes rolled right into his blinkers and with a flash of his yellow teeth he was off, dung and dust flying everywhere, leaving Dottie shaking her fist far on the road behind and a bewildered Tandy to deal with her, the sheep, and the dogs and to ward off a barrage of questions shot at him by the insatiably curious Kirsty.

Carnallachie had never arrived at his place so quickly yet even so, before he could bring the snorting Trudge to a halt, The Loon was down, tearing pell mell for the pig pen into which he jumped to cower down. A new kind of pandemonium broke out then. Terrified pigs ran in circles, squealing and grunting, The Loon in their midst, the bluey pink of his nakedness mingling with pink, hairy pig hide.

When Carnallachie realized what had happened his face turned blue and his eyes bulged. If there was anything he had ever loved in his life he loved his pigs, and ten to one,

182

if he wasn't to be found howking tatties or spreading dung on his few acres, he was in the sty with his pigs, rubbing their ample backsides, talking to them as if they were children. But his sentiments never stood in the way of his fondness for silver and he thought nothing of carting a fat pig off to market after a summer of talking sweet talk into its lugs.

The sight of the Rothiedrum daftie, crawling about among his pigs nearly sent him wild and he danced around, ranting and raving and was all for climbing into the pen to get The Loon out when Coulter chanced upon the scene.

'Leave that laddie be!' the old man commanded, dusting the stour of the road off his trousers. 'Can you no' see he's so feared he doesna ken if he's in a pigsty or a hayloft?'

Carnallachie glanced at The Loon cowering in abject fear just inside the door of the shed, his arms clasped round his knees in an effort to stop them shaking. Compassion settled heavily on both old men. Coulter tore off his hairy tweed jacket and tossed it gently at The Loon but he was too dazed and weary to lift a hand to take it and in seconds the pigs had trampled it into the glaur of the pen.

'Ach, I'm right sorry, Pootie man,' Carnallachie apologized as soothingly as his gravelly voice would allow. 'It's jist – well I dinna ken if I'm coming or going myself and you upsetting my pigs was the last straw.'

For answer The Loon put his shaggy head in his arms and burst out crying. No amount of cajoling would get him to come out of the pen and in the end it was decided to send for Hinney, the only person in the whole of the place The Loon really trusted despite his exaggerated fear of her 'witchery'. She was the only one too who could control Dottie Drummond and as that awesome personage might likely arrive at any moment, Carnallachie went off post haste on the back of his horse. At the road end he came upon Dottie, collapsed with exhaustion on the verge, fanning herself with a corner of her apron, all the ire gone from her as swiftly as it had come.

Carnallachie muttered a few dark words at her under his breath and leaving her where she was made haste for Hill o' Binney. Hinney came, puffing, panting and grumbling but full of compassion the minute she saw the state the Drummond lad was in. She soon coaxed him out from the pen from which he extricated himself willingly, falling into her arms to cry his heart out against her warm, spice-smelling bosom.

'Would you listen to the smell o' him,' she commented, patting his head as if he was one of the local bairns. 'It's a good bath he's needing and the minute I get my hands on that Dottie I'll see he gets it too.'

Coulter chortled and couldn't refrain from saying, 'He must indeed be humming if you can hear him, Hinney.'

At which Carnallachie muttered darkly under his breath, 'My pigs are no' smelly and are cleaner than some humans I could name.'

'Ach, go away and fetch some things to hap the soul in!' ordered Hinney irritably and both men went off to rummage through Carnallachie's collection of ancient waistcoats and fungus-stained moleskin trousers. Between them they wrapped him in some bits of evil smelling Sunday best Carnallachie had had hanging at the back of his wardrobe from the year one and though they were anything but flattering they were better than nothing and The Loon was glad enough to shrug himself into them.

Bit by bit the story of his misdemeanour unfolded while Hinney tushed and tutted over Dottie's foolish handling of the affair and Carnallachie had the grace to hang his head in shame for putting the welfare of his pigs before that of a frightened creature whose only sin, if it could be called such, was complete and total innocence.

Dottie came leisurely along the track, apparently spent by her energies of the morning, her gaze lighting rather apprehensively on her son's tear-stained face and Hinney's angry one. She stood sheepishly while Hinney gave her a piece of her mind.

'It wis his pairts, Hinney,' she wailed, 'Surely no a fit sight for man nor beast and a sin to be seen like that in the eyes o' the Lord.'

'Ach, I'm sure the Lord saw plenty o' dowps in his day,'

Hinney scolded. 'And besides Himself you were the only one to see the poor cratur' and no seeing anything you didna see in your life before. Now the half o' Rothiedrum has set eyes on the affair and it will serve you right if you are never allowed to live it down. Go along, you silly woman and see and prepare a good hot breakfast for this laddie o' yours and make sure he gets a good wash for I'll be along later to see how you have been treating him.'

So saying she sent the shamefaced Dottie shambling home to Boglehowe, her son's hand trustingly in hers, a warm glow in his heart for Hinney who had protected him in her own gruff way since the day he was born, her adage being, 'Wise or simple, we are all Jock Tamson's bairns.'

Yet, for all he was supposed to be simple-minded, there was one thing he hadn't given away during all the drama. The secret meetings at the Kelpie Pool were as secret as they had ever been and one and all breathed sighs of relief when this fact finally emerged.

By the end of that memorable day the whole of Rothiedrum had heard about the affair. It was the talk of the place for years after, and a tale to be told at winter firesides long after The Loon and his mother had thrust it very firmly to the back of their minds.

In August Evelyn walked over the hills with her father, her hand tucked firmly in his as they wandered along picking great bunches of dew fresh heather, the clean sweet smell of it filling her lungs, the tough, gnarled stalks of it scratching her sun-flushed arms and making little snags on the bodice of her white cotton pinafore. The sound of guns came from low down in the houghs and she knew Evander Ramsey Forbes was entertaining a grouse shooting party, though he himself had never taken happily to such a blood-thirsty sport. Strange that, she mused, he was coarse and boorish in many ways, yet he truly liked animals and birds and never willingly did anything that might harm them. He had transferred these tendencies to Gillan who hated all blood sports and had vowed to her that he would never take a gun to the stags and the wild birds that delighted his heart.

The guns sounded again and in her mind she pictured a dying bird, blood staining the beautiful, mottled plumage which was such a fine camouflage in its battle for survival, yet counted for little when it came to the hour of dogs, beaters and murderous weapons. Yet it was a time too for the farmtoun lads to earn a few extra shillings while they acted as beaters to that privileged few, if such a world could be applied to men with so little compassion in their hearts for creatures whose right to live was as great if not greater, than theirs.

On the purple clothed hillsides that late summer of her thirteenth year Evelyn had been aware of certain things around her that she had never before noticed. She had thought she had taken in everything there was to know in her world, things that had been all around her yet tightly closed in, as if they belonged to her only and she alone was in possession of people, places, things.

That morning she had set off with her father on their annual pilgrimage to the heathery slopes and she had been walking along with her hand in his when the first of the big changes struck her. It was her habit when walking with him to pace out her territory, matching her stride with his, throwing one foot forward to its fullest extent, her head bowed, her finger pensively in her mouth. But today she began to notice that there wasn't the same need to step out in order to keep up with him. She was walking almost at his stride and glancing up quickly she saw that her head came well up past his shoulder, that he no longer loomed above her as in days gone by.

She had always thought of her father as a tall man but now he seemed to have shrunk – but it wasn't that. He was the same as ever, it was she who was changing. In the last year she had grown nearly as tall as he, and quickly upon that observation there came another. Ever since she could remember, his rough hand holding her smooth one gave her a sense of security. He was the man in her life and it was right that his skin should be rough. She had never stopped to ask herself why this should be so, but today she studied the big, workworn hand clasped around hers. She

186

saw the hacks on his knuckles, the purpled discolouration on his thumbnail where his hammer had knocked it. She saw a horrible pus-filled pouch below the nail of his index finger and a shudder went through her at the realization of how much punishment his poor hands must have suffered in the course of his lifetime. On impulse she lifted his hand up to her mouth and kissed it. Tears sprang to her eyes for which she could offer no explanation, neither to herself nor anyone else.

Laughing he ruffled her hair and asked her in his slow, quiet voice, 'What ails you, Princess? You're crying.'

'I dinna ken, Father,' she answered truthfully. 'I just feel – different about things.'

Bending his head he looked deep into her eyes and for the first time she noticed the tiredness in him. 'You're growing up, Evie,' There was a laugh in his voice but it didn't reach his eyes. 'My wee lassie, you're growing up,' he repeated softly.

Half shy of him suddenly she said wistfully, 'Am I, Father? Ach, you're full o' blethers today. I'm just a wee lassie yet.'

'Ay, but no' for long, no' for long, Evie.'

A great sense of sadness surged in her breast. She wanted to shake him, to make him take the words back even though she knew the truth of them. Ever since that day at the Kelpie Poll when Florrie had pointed out to her the beginnings of change in her body she had tried to shut her mind to reality. On bath nights she lowered herself into the water and washed herself as quickly as she could, never looking at herself, donning her clothes swiftly and carelessly. But now she knew there was nothing she could do about herself and she mourned for the childhood that was slipping away from her.

'It will no be for a whilie yet,' she persisted, hanging on desperately to the remnants of yesterday, willing herself to believe the words she spoke.

Tucking her hand into his once more he said softly, appeasingly, 'No, Princess, it will no be for a whilie yet, but when it comes you must welcome it – and yet – I ken fine

187

how you feel. The days o' childhood are sweet indeed but they flow past quickly, my lassie, and like the river, there's no stopping them.'

The leaves were turning red and yellow on the trees before she could bring herself to really face the fact that she was changing. On a cold night in September she went up to the little attic room she shared with Grace and stripped her body of its coverings. Her goose-pimpled flesh shivered a protest but she was used to the cold and with heart swiftly beating she went over to the full-length mirror on the door of the oak wardrobe. She stood for a long time with her head bowed, staring at her feet spread out on the bare floorboards.

'It's dirty to look at any part of your own body.' Nellie's voice spoke in her head. She trembled at her audacity but without being able to stop what she had started she slowly raised her head to stare in some trepidation into the glass. And now the secrets of her body were revealed to her, the firm buds of her breasts joyfully springing, the honing of her waist, the flattening of the ungainly pot belly, the curving of her hips that had once been as lean as a boy's. But most noticeable of all were the hairs. A fine but ebullient sprouting of tiny red-gold tufts at the pit of her stomach. She had known they were there of course, but never before had she actually looked at them, unwilling as she was to acknowledge their existence as if they were the start of some terrible disease she couldn't begin to face.

Now fascinated, she reached down to stroke them with one tentative finger. A sense of unease gripped her. She felt herself to be teetering on the brink of an unknown world and a tear squeezed itself from her half-shut lids. She didn't want to grow up. She wanted her life to go on as it had been. Always she wanted to walk as a child to the hills with her father; to run barefoot through summer meadows, to go back in time with Johnny Burns seated behind her in the classroom, tugging her hair and giving her big rosy apples at playtime. But even that was in the past now. Johnny had left school two years ago. He had changed in

188

so many ways. His voice was strong and deep, his body well-muscled and masculine although he was only sixteen. She couldn't go on pretending that he was a schoolboy any longer. Johnny too was growing up.

'Evie! You'll catch your death o' cold, lassie!'

Grace's voice behind her made her spin round, her face so hot she might just have risen from the fireside. For once in her life she wished she had the room all to herself. But Grace had come home on a well-earned holiday and it was really lovely to have her back – except at times like this . . .

Instinctively her hands came up over her small new breasts, feeling degraded beyond measure in her favourite sister's sight. Nellie was right after all. It was dirty to look at your own body – dirty and bad. Grace smiled rather mischievously, and going over to her sister's bed she retrieved her warm flannellette nightgown and helped her into it, pushing in her cold arms, settling the cosy folds of the material about her body. Grace's arms were gentle but sure. She smelled of lavender and a delicate suggestion of roses. Everything about Grace was chaste without being prim. She had grown even lovelier as she matured. Her eyes were great black pools, her skin as pale as alabaster, her body as willowy as the slender birches.

Evelyn gazed at her calm, sweet face and impulsively put her arms round her 'I'm sorry you saw me without my clothes, Grace. I just wanted to look – to see what I was getting to be like.'

Grace merely laughed. 'Ach, dinna fash your wee head about it. It's natural to wonder about such things at your age – to wonder about your body.'

Evelyn looked doubtful. She had never seen Grace without her clothes. Every night when she came up to bed she doused the candle and undressed in the dark and she was always up and fully clothed before Evelyn.

'Do you wonder about yours, Grace?' she asked daringly. As yet Grace had no steady young man though it wasn't for the want of male admiration. Kindly and firmly she rebuffed them all and seemed quite content with her

189

domestic pastimes as well as looking after her menagerie of small, wounded animals. Some said she was married to her job, for she was devoted to nursing – but that wasn't entirely true – always there was Martin Gregory. He would have been at her beck and call if she had been that type of girl, for it was plain for everyone to see that he was besotted by her and would have done anything for her. Grace took the relationship in her usual quiet way but told her mother that there was nothing serious between them. He was her friend, that was all, and Grace being Grace her mother was inclined and glad to believe her even though she knew Martin Gregory would never be content with such a relationship. He had attended college in Aberdeen in order to take an endorsement which would enable him to teach secondary level Supplementary Courses, and while this was an admirable enough thing in itself Maggie suspected that he had only done it to be near Grace. When she was away, he was like a man without a purpose and had changed a lot from the reserved Mr Gregory everyone had once known.

'Ach, never mind, Maggie,' Betsy O'Neil had consoled her. 'When true love comes to Grace everyone will know it for it will hit her like a bolt from the blue. These quiet ones are like that, they go along wi' their heads in the clouds and everyone thinks that's how they will always be – but there comes a time, Maggie. Ay, even for one so gentle as Grace. There's passion buried in all o' us and Grace is no different from the rest when it comes to that.'

Grace only smiled at Evelyn's question. 'Ach, I'm too busy wondering about other things, the world is full o' wonder. If I was as bonny as Mary I might pay more attention to myself, just now I prefer my life the way it is.'

'But you are bonny!' gasped Evelyn, amazed that such a beauty failed to see it in herself. She was too young yet to see that Grace's beauty came mainly from her serene, untroubled soul and her voice was full of indignation at the other's complacency on the matter. 'You're much, much nicer to look at than the rest o' them put together.'

'Blethers,' said Grace placidly. 'Look, I've got

something to show you – see – in this wee boxie.'

Inside the box was a small green frog reposing quite comfortably on a bed of wet leaves. 'He's twisted his wee leg,' Grace said tenderly. 'You hold him for me and I'll bind a twiggie round it till it's better.'

Evelyn held the frog while Grace put one of the strong back legs into a tiny splint. The frog then accepted a worm from the jar on the windowledge and was returned to his place on the drawer top beside other boxes and small homemade cages.

Evelyn pulled her sister's arm. 'Let's hang out the window to look at the Merry Dancers and I'll tell you the legends about them.'

Together they leaned from the window, craning their necks upwards to watch the breathtaking display of flashing lights streaking across the sky, Grace patiently listening while her little sister's voice prattled on, recounting the stories she had learned from her mother and which never failed to fascinate her. Her breath came out in swift, frosty puffs, she clasped her hands on the ledge and let the peace of the countryside wash over her. Grace was warm and sweet-smelling beside her, the world beyond the croft was wide and big and infinite. She was a child again, forgetting her changing body, knowing only the delight of watching the stars which appeared after the Merry Dancers had departed the heavens. She felt safe in the knowledge that everything in the world about her would remain the same, even though she herself changed.

It would always be like this, the old croft snug in the valley, the black silhouette of the hills, Johnny Burns up yonder at Birkibrae, Florrie whispering her secrets as they wandered together on the braes, Coulter coming along as he was now to sup a brew of ale with her father and take a fill of baccy. Reaching out, she clasped Grace's slender hand and felt safe and good in the world that would always be hers.

191

PART THREE

1912/13

CHAPTER TEN

The years that followed were to be among the happiest Evelyn was ever to know in her life. Later on, looking back on them over the distance of time, she would smile wistfully and remember the sunlight laving the fields of corn and see the fair heads of Johnny and Florrie, the dark one of Gillan, bobbing along together through heat-hazed meadows where the scents of summer hung sweet. Always when she thought back it seemed to be summer, as if her mind preferred to forget the harshness and the cold of a north east landscape covered in snow. Yet there was beauty in its very austerity, something cosy too in those long nights with the family gathered round the hearth, renewing the strong bonds of kinship that were apt to drift a little apart in the busy dys of spring and summer.

Often Alan Keith came with them on their outings, his long, clever hands sketching things to amuse them and, when they weren't busy with that, twining into Florrie's, who sometimes let them linger for awhile before impatience made her break away. During the last years of her growing up she had become thinner; a delicacy in her slender limbs lent her an air of ethereal mystery. But she had never been more active, a feverish activity that flashed out of her eyes and found expression in the acting and mimicry in which she had always excelled. Quite often she gave a little impromptu concert, sometimes in a hayloft, more often out of doors with the fields and woods as her props. They all loved those times, but Alan loved them most and then he would sit and draw the lithe, sweet figure and even capture the texture of her long bright hair . . .

Gillan – well – Gillan had changed so much from the polite, sober boy of Evelyn's first meeting that often she would look back on that day and hardly believe that this was the same person. His face filled out, grew alive, his eyes seemed to become deeper and darker and he walked so tall she fancied he had grown almost a foot from the Gillan of old. In his growing confidence in himself the passionate side of his nature was revealed and he would argue fiercely about everything under the sun though if he was in the wrong he was usually the first to admit it despite a strong streak of stubbornness that was very hard to withstand. It was never easy for him to get away from the confines of Rothiedrum House, but somehow he managed it though he was always uneasy that his parents might find out and would put a stop to his days of glorious freedom.

Sometimes on a Saturday they would take one of the carts and drive to the sea, Johnny at the reins, at seventeen nearly as tall as his father, his fair hair bleached white by the sun, his bronzed, handsome face thrown back in laughter so that the blue of the sky met the blue of his eyes, making them deeper and bluer than Evelyn ever remembered. Quite often too they would take the train to Aberdeen, there to wander around the marts and rake in their pockets for coppers to buy fruit or a loaf of new-baked bread to share between them.

Gillan became well known in the village of Lums O' Reekie. Bunty gave him her fusty biscuits as if he was one of the village youngsters and he bought strops of liquorice which they all ate together under the shade of the big oak tree which spread its cool bowers over the seat in the green. He spent a lot of time in the Smiddy, fascinated, as he watched George shoeing the horses or moulding cart wheels. He loved the dim, secret atmosphere in Souter Jock's and conversed eagerly with him, he who knew so much about the old days and the old ways from his early days in his grandfather's farm along by Stonehaven.

Best of all he loved Charlie Lammas and was totally enthralled at the things which went on in the Killing House in the yard behind the shop. Not that Charlie ever allowed Gillan to see an animal being slaughtered. He had far too much respect for life ever to think there was anything noble in the taking of it. It was the stories Charlie told that were so interesting; the pig who came to be made into ham but instead endeared itself so much to him he made it a sty in the yard and kept it as a pet; the white cow with the golden eye and eyelashes so long you could swing on them, who broke from her tether and went skelping up the street with half the village at her heels. She had put up such a good run for her money Charlie had reprieved her and sold her cheaply to a crofter friend who had lost his own cow through sickness.

As the autumn of 1912 drew near and with it the Forbes' usual trip to the South of France, Gillan begged to be allowed to stay on with Thoms at Rothiedrum. 'He can teach me all the French I ever need to know,' he earnestly told his father. 'I'm better when I'm here – really. I can't stand the heat in France at this time of year.'

Evander studied his son's face. The change in him this last year was markedly apparent. He had always wanted a good, robust son and heir and had never got over the disappointment of having one who was just a shadow of his imaginings. His wife had pampered the boy from the start, her anxious fussings exacerbating weaknesses instead of encouraging strengths. Evander had wanted another, but she had almost died in the effort of having Gillan and she was now past the age of childbearing. He sighed as he gazed at Gillan's anxious face. 'There's more to this than meets the eye, lad. You've changed this past year – haven't been slipping out to meet the servant girls, have you? Never too young for that – eh?'

Gillan coloured; his father's excesses were not a well-kept secret. Such a man wouldn't think it outrageous if his son was to follow in his footsteps. 'Good healthy fun,' Evander's gusty laugh boomed out. 'Still – you're not the type – eh lad? No. Well, I'll ask your mother, see what she has to say.'

Lady Marjorie was not at all keen on the idea but in the end capitulated to her husband's persuasive arguments. 'The boy looks better than he's done in years. Maybe we do drag him around a bit. Time he stood on his own feet, independence might do him the world of good and he'll have to learn a bit of that if he's ever to be strong enough to go off to school.'

'But what will he *do* with himself all day?' Lady Marjorie fretted, 'and who will look after him when I'm not here? Oh, I know he'll have Thoms and Mrs Chalmers runs the house so well she'll keep the servants in order, but there ought to be someone else just to make sure he's alright.'

In the end she sent for her old governess, a sweet, deaf old lady who spent most of her day embroidering hideous cushion covers, sucking mints and falling alseep by the fire. Old Moby, as Victoria Dick was affectionately known, was no threat at all to Gillan's independence and so his parents went off for two long months while he remained behind at Rothiedrum and was there as harvest time approached, a time when expectation and apprehension hung in the air of the farmtouns, as heavy as Sunday-best tweed.

In some of the cornfields of the bigger farms it was possible to bury yourself to the armpits in the golden waving grain, but the smaller touns and crofts, some of which sowed tattie corn year in and year out, couldn't expect such a fine yield, yet even so hopes anxiously cultivated through the bitter green of early promise, grew even higher as the green turned a fine golden yellow. All around Rothiedrum the days leading up to hairst hung hazed with warmth and on the smaller farmtouns half-forgotten binders were brought out from dark corners to be liberally squirted with oil.

Once harvest got underway it could last six to eight weeks if the weather was favourable, if not it could go on and on till tempers were sorely tried and folks began to wonder if the cornyards would be stacked before Christmas came along.

'We might be lucky this year,' said Jamie, each day anxiously scanning the blue skies for a sign of cloud. Gazing over his cornfields he felt a small thrill of excitement. The grain was rustling on the stalk and had turned a fine pale gold. 'We're ready,' he announced to his family with quiet satisfaction and one and all braced themselves for the long busy days ahead.

*

198

The kitchen was warm in the heat of the morning. All the windows and doors were thrown wide but even so hardly a breeze stirred the lace curtains. Evelyn hurried through her breakfast of milk brose, a treat that Maggie had prepared in place of the usual water brose, her idea being that they all needed to keep up their strength for the work that lay ahead. Milk was by no means scarce with two good milk cows giving several gallons a day but some of it went to the calves, some to the croft table, the greater amount was taken steaming hot from the udder to the chill of the milkhouse where it would be made into butter and cheese to be eaten at the table, the surplus sold to the grocer or the nearest market.

Pushing her plate aside, Evelyn helped herself to farls of oatcake and cheese, listening rather apprehensively to her father telling her mother that young Rothiedrum had been up to ask him when the harvest was starting as he would like to take part.

Evelyn fumed inwardly. He should have waited till she had had a chance to speak to her mother first. As it was Maggie's face was set and severe on hearing the news and Evelyn couldn't help wondering if it was because of her contempt for the gentry. But why Rothiedrum in particular? Why Gillan? Quite a few of the folk from the mansion houses in the area came and went from King's Croft, some to talk to Murn about chairback covers and anything else she happened to be working on at the time, others to discuss with Jamie the kind of shoes they wanted made. It wasn't unusual to find such folk seated in the kitchen, drinking tea and eating the buttery oatmeal shortbread Maggie had baked. Quite often too, some posh lady or gentleman was out there in Jamie's 'shoppie' the little hut he had converted into a workshop when he found it too inconvenient to go on making his shoes in the house.

Evelyn had seen that look on her mother's face before – the day Lady Marjorie had come to talk to Murn about embroidery. Maggie, normally so cool and collected in gentle company, had been flustered and strange – and terribly distant – even though Lady Marjorie had been at her most charming. She had certainly been anything but her natural self and had appeared most relieved when the visitor got up to go. Lady Marjorie had been several times to the croft since then and always Maggie behaved in the same distracted manner and there were times Evelyn saw her watching the visitor with an odd, indefinable expression on her face.

'And what made him pick our place to keep himself amused?' Maggie demanded, her gaze going from Jamie to Evelyn, with one guarded eye on Andy, the latest orra loon, who took his meals with the family which meant that the discussing of private affairs had often to be postponed. 'Are you at the back o' this, lassie?' Maggie asked through tight lips. 'I'll have a word wi' you later.'

Andy enjoyed the flush spreading over Evelyn's face. Lately he had begun to ogle her discreetly and now she stared back, indignantly at first then mischievously, delighted to see his own face blushing to the roots of his hair.

Col and Cal were making faces at one another at the other end of the table. At least Cal was, while the other gurgled in delight. Jeannie's son came regularly to spend the night at King's Croft. It was the highlight of Col's life and Maggie loved Jeannie for her attitude to her backward son. Others would have kept their children away, but not Jeannie. She seemed to love the little boy and did everything she could to make his life happy.

Evelyn watched them enthralled. Callum was such a bonny big boy for almost four. He had his father's fine physique, his mother's lovely laughing face. Colin, on the other hand, was small, more like two than four. The dark hair of babyhood had lightened to a deep golden red and his eyes were light blue. Both boys had the same colouring and might have been brothers – except for one thing – the lively intelligence in Cal's eyes was missing from Col's. They were deep tranquil pools with an expression in them that went back, back so that sometimes he seemed to be looking inward at his own puzzling, halting thoughts – and his mouth was too slack. He had a habit of gaping open-mouthed, for minutes on end, at some perfectly ordinary object which had attracted his attention.

Evelyn knew he would never be like other little boys, yet somehow the knowledge didn't sadden her. He would always be Wee Col, no matter what his age. He would never know the pain of raw emotion, he would gurgle and smile his way through life and never know any of its sadness. It was for her parents that Evelyn felt pain, even though they seemed to have accepted their son as he was, expecially her father who had endless patience with him and told him things about the croft and the countryside, even though half the time he wasn't taking much of it in.

Nellie came in, dressed for a day in the fields, one of her father's old wincey shirts tucked into the waist of her long black skirt over which she had tied a sacking apron made from a washed corn-seed bag. An old scarf was tied round her head, confining every fair strand except for an errant few which escaped round her ears. Clattering her plate on to the table she drew in her chair and snorted, 'Did I hear something about young Rothiedrum coming to help wi' the harvest? Hmph: It's a wonder the young gent wants to dirty his hands – him that's more used to holding a pen than a graip.'

'He's a nice lad,' said Jamie, despite Maggie. 'He has good manners on him and that is a thing missing from a lot o' his kind – talking o' manners –' he looked pointedly at Nellie, 'you missed Grace again this morning, Nell.'

He had always regarded as sacred these little rituals he carried out inside the four walls of his own home even though he didn't always attend kirk every Sunday. Nellie on the other hand went religiously to kirk and was wont to look askance at anyone who didn't. Yet, contrarily she had no patience with her father's insistence on giving thanks to the Lord for the meat set on the table. For one thing, she maintained she had worked too damned hard herself to get it there, and for another she was often too rushed or too busy to be always promptly at the table with everyone else. Over the years the matter had become a sore point between father and daughter. The years weren't softening her attitude to life; if anything she had grown more impatient, less forbearing and niggled at her father till Maggie sharply intervened and afterwards looked from one to the other in exasperation. Jamie got on well with all his daughters, only Nellie was a thorn in his side and Maggie would sigh to herself and wish her eldest girl could find a man she cared enough for to marry. But there seemed little hope of that now. Despite the valiant attempts of several young men she looked set on the road to spinsterhood and not even her love of children could shake her from the path she was very firmly treading.

She glanced sharply at Jamie. 'Grace! What time have I for the likes o' that? God knows well enough I'm mindful o' the meat I put in my belly! The only Grace I miss is my sister wi' a name the same. Pity she had to go away – and her the only one among us no' fit to be away from home.'

Jamie said nothing but pushed his plate away suddenly while Maggie threw Nellie a warning look. Evelyn sighed at mention of her darling sister whose spells at home were all too brief. Her room was so empty without Grace in the next bed and she had Florrie over to stay as often as she could. It was like having another sister snuggled next to her, talking and giggling, yet still she missed Grace and another sigh escaped her, making Nellie look at her sharply.

'What on earth ails you, child? Sighing and blowing down your nose like a broken-down cuddy. All you seem to do lately is moon around, dreaming and staring into the distance wi' your head in your hands – and dinna think I know you've been washing your face in the precious buttermilk. I've never heard the likes. What's wrong wi' good soap and water I'd like to know.'

'Ach, Nellie,' said Evelyn mildly. 'It was my share o' buttermilk to do as I like with – and if I want to wash my backside in it then that's my affair.'

Nellie almost choked while both Maggie and Jamie could not refrain from pressing their mirth into their hands.

'How can you laugh at that – that filth!' fumed Nellie, glaring at a sniggering Andy who immediately took himself outside with one ear pressed against the gently blowing curtains.

'Evie,' she appealed in some panic. 'What is happening to you, I'd like to know?'

Evelyn stood up and looked her sister straight in the eye. 'I think I must be growing up, Nellie.'

She said it without hesitation, a strength in her voice that amounted to pride.

There was an odd, stunned little silence, the same sort of silence that had greeted her announcement some years back of wanting to be a writer when she grew up.

'You'll have to work for that, lassie,' Jamie had told her solemnly. 'Try and get a bursary to college like your sister Murn.' But Evelyn's earlier thirst for academic learning had waned through the years; her romantic, idealistic nature finding its outlet in solitary writing and frantic reading of as many books as she could lay hands on, which to her was about the finest education she could ever hope to find.

Maggie and Jamie fell silent at this latest revelation and Nellie forgot her temper. 'Ay, you are that, you wee whittrock, I doubt you are at that – but that doesna mean you've to start behaving like your sister Mary – and you're no' too grown up to pack the basket for the midday break. There's some floury baps in the larder and all the usual things – and dinna forget a knife – and see and put in enough for everybody. That Andy has an appetite like a horse.'

Evelyn sighed again. There was always an orra loon to see to the hens and the cows and the pigs. The swill was waiting at the back door – still, she smiled, in a short while she would see Johnny working up there in the fields of Birkiebrae – and the pigs weren't so bad really. In fact she loved their pink, plump bodies and floppy silken ears and enjoyed it when the old sow farrowed and she could cuddle all those tiny, squealing piglets . . .

The basket filled, she drifted to the door.

'Dinna forget . . .' Nellie's voice followed her outside and she giggled as Andy caught her eye and sent her a slow, deliberate wink. Jeannie came in through the close and over the yard to the house, her dark hair caught up in a scarf much like Nellie's, her face breaking into smiles at sight of the youngest Grant girl standing by the door with a basket in one hand and a bread knife in the other.

'A fine way to greet a friend,' Jeannie chuckled. 'I'm late this morning. Tandy is back again and when he and Kenneth get together . . . Did Cal behave himself?'

'No bother. He and Col were out in the cornyard before breakfast, covered in stoor and hay but happy as kings.'

Evelyn stepped forward to allow Jeannie to pass, 'I'm no' that stout,' laughed Jeannie, calling attention to her five months pregnancy, discreetly concealed by her shepherd's tartan shawl, folded lengthwise so that its two ends fell longer down the front. She passed into the kitchen, her light voice coming back, the unsuppressed joy in telling of her gladness that another baby was on the way.

Evelyn moved away. Babies. They brought such happiness to women like Jeannie. She and Kenneth Mor had waited a long time for their second child and now that it was coming they were both delighted at the thought.

Evelyn swung the basket high, making Andy's eyes bulge at the thought of the midday repast landing on the dung-splattered cobbles. He rushed forward to grab at the basket and Evelyn grinned at him. 'Dinna foul your breeks, Andy lad, I'm no' daft enough to drop it. Here –' she extracted a piece of cheese from the pocket of her pinafore, 'take this, it will keep you from starving till dinner time – and don't dare say a word about it to Mam.'

'Thanks, Evie.' He took the cheese and eyed her slyly. 'and I'll no' tell either that you and young Master Gillan have been havin' a high old time to yourselves this past whilie.'

'Who told you that?' she asked sharply.

'Ach, the whole o' the place knows. Tis a wonder it hasna reached your mither's ears sooner.'

Evelyn tossed her head. 'Well, what if I have been seeing Gillie? We havena done anyone any harm. It's no worse and likely a whole lot better than you having the ben-the-hoose maid from the Mains up in the chaumer with you.'

Andy's eyes gaped saucer-like. He was a good-looking lad, a lot of the fee'd loons were, but Andy was the nicest yet. 'You winna tell?' he said cautiously. 'It was only for a wee whilie and nothing happened.'

'So you say, but I know all about Lizzie Scott and her reputation for getting the breeks off a lad before you can wink. Mam wouldna like to hear about it.'

'I winna tell aboot you and Maister Gillan.'

'I know you won't,' she smiled and Andy rushed away to get the horses from the stable.

At the window, Nellie craned her neck. 'That bairn is beginning to pass too much o' her time wi' the loons,' she observed, frowning.

'It's natural,' Maggie said meaningfully.

'But she's just three months past fourteen – she's a mite young for the likes o' that.'

'She's a bonny one,' nodded Jeannie. 'She'll have a wheen o' lads at her heels before she's much older.'

'Ay – and she's growing up,' Jamie put in softly. 'She has just told you so from her own wee lips – and proud o' it too. It was something she was aye a wee bit feared of for I mind fine when she just a wee thing saying to me that things would never change. Now . . .'

'Now they have and so is she,' Nellie finished for him. 'And starting to look at the lads. Nothing stays the same – does it? Only me . . .' She halted abruptly, but not before a bleakness in her voice gave away a lonely young woman whose capacity for loving had yet to be fulfilled.

Only the onslaught of bad weather hindered harvest once it had begun. For ten to twelve hours a day the whirring of the reapers, the swish of the scythe sounded over the countryside. Men, women and children swarmed busily over the fields, pausing only for dinner at midday and for tea or ale and a sandwich in the middle of the afternoon. And it was then that Maggie met her cousin, Gillan, for the first time. With wee Col happed at her back in her shawl, she came face to face with the dark haired, dark-eyed young Rothiedrum and Evelyn was to wonder then and many times in the future, at the wary, guarded look that came into her mother's eyes at that meeting in the cornfield with the honey-streaked morning sky above the patched golden fields below.

She said not a word at first, but took Col from her back and sat him with his back to a stook, then she straightened and came forward slowly, her calloused hand outstretched to the book-softened one of young Gillan.

'Gillan, tis pleased I am to make your acquaintance.' She never added a sir or master nor would she ever in all the time she was to know him, but he liked her the more for that and admired a pride and a gentility finer than his own.

Deep in his veins he felt that this wasn't gentry meeting humbler stock but like meeting like. To himself he couldn't explain it and the answer wasn't going to come to him in that hushed hallowed harvest field so he took her hand and held it, feeling briefly the rough skin, then he stood back and said respectfully, 'Mrs Grant, I'm pleased to meet Evelyn's mother at last.'

The reproachful look Maggie threw at her youngest daughter was interpreted only by her. Her mother hadn't carried out her earlier threat of 'having words wi' her', almost as if she didn't want to pursue the subject and so she had kept quiet about Gillan but wished now she had been more honest as she whispered, 'I'm sorry, Mam – I – I thought you would be angry.'

Maggie reddened. She realized how strange her attitude to the gentry must often appear to her family. Away in the beginning of their married life she had told Jamie about the circumstances of her birth, but never had she disclosed to him that her father was Lord Lindsay Ogilvie, uncle of Lady Marjorie Forbes and Gillan's great uncle. It didn't seem real to her that these two were her cousins yet it was a fact, one that made her awkward and strange in the presence of the laird's wife.

As a young woman she had resented terribly the idle rich, had despised her father for deserting her mother in her hour of great need. But in the busy hectic years of bearing and rearing children she'd had little time to reflect on much else so that gradually her attitude towards the gentry had grown more tolerant – until the day she found the pitiful little bundle of letters tied up in blue ribbon hidden away at the back of her mother's dresser. It was a month after she had seen her mother to her last rest and she had been clearing out her things.

Some of the letters were from her father to her mother, pledging his love for her, penning words that must have delighted the young Megsie Cameron, yet which had meant nothing. The other letters had been written by her mother, but they had never been posted. In them Megsie had poured our her heart to Lindsay Ogilvie, she had spoken of her terrible shame and fear on discovering that she was pregnant by him and almost humbly had pleaded with him to help her. The others had been written at a later date, telling him of her heartless eviction from her position, her employers' refusal to give her any kind of reference, her desperation in not knowing which way to turn.

Maggie had seen it all in her mind's eye. The frantic penning of words by a young girl unburdening her heart to a man whom she knew, deep down, had just been passing his frivolous time. She had known she would get no help from him and so she had never sent the letters. During her lifetime Megsie Cameron had never said a great deal about him. She had told Maggie the truth about her existence and that was that. No recriminations, no self-pity, just a quiet acceptance of how things had been. But the yellowed bundle of letters had said it all and Maggie's dislike of her father, her contempt for the gentry in general, had kindled anew. She had transferred some of her feelings to her older daughters; Nellie had scant regard for the higher classes, Murn took their money gladly enough but was wont to laugh at them behind their backs. Jamie had always got on well with them, treating them much as he treated his farming neighbours and they had always responded to his ease of manner with an affectionate tolerance. While sympathising with Maggie over her mother's treatment he had nevertheless disagreed with her vehement dislike of such people and many a heated argument they had had on the subject.

But try as she would, Maggie could never rid herself of her feelings and it had been with great misgivings that she had learned of Evelyn's growing friendship with Gillan . . .

'Mam – are you angry?' Evelyn's voice seemed to come from a long distance and Maggie pulled herself up sharply to look at her daughter's anxious face.

'Angry? Ay, maybe you're right at that. But it's too late for that now so stop your bletherings. We'll have our say later.'

At first Gillan was no more than a bystander, but Nellie soon fixed that. 'Here,' she ordered, pushing a rake into his hands. 'Even if you only gather a pickle o' corn you'll be far more use than just standing there wi' your hands in your pooches.'

The raker's job was one of the hardest in the harvest field and very soon young Rothiedrum's soft hands were scratched and blistered, but he made no murmur of protest and at the end of the morning even Nellie threw him a sidelong glance of admiration. After that he came whenever he could get away from Thoms and Moby and at gloaming he would ride home in the carts with the rest as the Clydes plodded through shadowed lanes and great yellow moons rose up over Bennachie.

But Gillan remembered best the celebration at the end of harvest when the last sheaf had been cut and everyone gathered in Maggie's kitchen for the harvest supper and then later, when all the sheaves were safely in the stackyard, the folk of King's Croft, met at Kenneth Mor's place for the traditional 'Meal-and-ale' celebration. Melodeons, fiddles, jew's harps, even the paper-and-comb sprang into joyous life and everyone danced in an abandonment of thankfulness for harvest safely gathered. The meal-and-ale, made from stout, whisky, ale, oatmeal and sugar, was supped from a communal bowl set in the middle of the table, followed by beef and plum-duff. Every toun had its meal-and-ale in turn, and though Gillan only managed to attend the one, he would never forget the camaraderie or the lads and lasses singing and dancing till the small hours of morning. Everyone forgot he was 'young Rothiedrum' and treated him the same as the rest for it wasn't so unusual for a farmtoun to entertain a member from the Big House at a meal-and-ale thanksgiving. The practice had been going on for countless years and when Rothiedrum himself was in residence at harvest time he joined the festivities at the Mains, accompanied by his wife who for once let her hair down and danced with the ploughmen. It was the first time for Gillan though and when it was ended he vowed that it wouldn't be his last.

Hot and dusty, he took Evelyn's hand and said earnestly, 'Now that I've had a taste of your kind of celebration you must come to the New Year ball at Rothiedrum. All the estate workers come but I've never yet seen any of the Grants'.

'We'll see,' she answered evasively, knowing fine her mother's aversion to attending such functions. 'New Year is a whilie away yet so wait till then.'

There followed a special time for her to look back on, the day it was just herself and Gillan at Rothiedrum House with Moby in bed nursing a cold and Thoms away in Aberdeen for the day. Martha gave them a marvellous tea after which they went to explore the grounds, then the house itself. It was a lovely, light, spacious house with vast windows that looked out across the whole of Rothiedrum and, nearer at hand, the woods, orchards, gardens and lawns of the estate.

The schoolroom fascinated her with its collection of books but Gillan's old nursery was neglected and empty and she didn't stay long there, preferring to wander through the downstairs rooms gazing at the paintings which hung everywhere. Mrs Chalmers fixed them with rather a steely eye when she came upon them in the dining room but Gillan soon appeased her and she departed with a finger at her lips saying that she hadn't seen them and therefore couldn't say anything in the wrong ears.

It was the portraits of Gillan's family which appealed to

Evelyn most, men and women of a bygone age who gazed down on her with keen, searching eyes that seemed to follow her around the room. Best of all was one of a distinguished looking gentleman with deep auburn hair and beard, a humorous mouth and the most brilliant eyes she had ever seen. He stood up there in the picture, one hand resting on a chair back, the other hooked into an embroidered waistcoat, his eyes going with her wherever she went.

'He's – he's so real,' she said in some awe.

'He isn't one of the dead ones,' laughed Gillan. 'He's my mother's uncle – my great uncle – Lord Lindsay Ogilvie. He spends most of his time in Capetown where he's a director of one of the big diamond companies. I've been over to see him several times and he's like no one I've ever met before – cares nothing for pomp and dresses a bit weird. I suppose you could call him an eccentric. He's been married twice but has no children, they all died in infancy which is a shame because he loves them. He comes over to stay here sometimes. I love the stories he tells about his life – he had quite a high old time when he was in Scotland as a young man, though of course he never tells me the tastier bits. He's done and seen so much – I wish I was a bit like him.' His tones were slightly wistful and Evelyn looked at him thoughtfully.

'You've been places too – more than I'll ever see in my life.'

'I didn't go to them by choice – you could say I was dragged.' He grinned ruefully. 'Half the time I'd much rather stay at home – I always think of Rothiedrum as my home, even though Father has other places we go.' He gazed around him. 'I like it best here – houses have a feel to them – some are friendly – others seem positively unfriendly – as if ghosts were there all the time, watching and disapproving.'

'Do you – believe in ghosts?'

He shrugged. 'I don't disbelieve in them, I've never really given it much thought.'

They went to sit on the window seat where Evelyn sat

gazing over the well kept lawns, tended by an army of gardeners working away unobtrusively despite their numbers. Clasping her hands round her knees she observed, 'You're lucky to have all this – so much room to enjoy yourself.'

A frown creased his brow. 'It's worthless if you can only enjoy it by yourself. You're the lucky one, sisters to talk to, a father and mother who listen to the things you have to say. Mine are always too busy or too engrossed in social niceties to let themselves go. Father's not so bad; he's more natural than my mother and has a lot of fun in him. He's disappointed in me, though. I'm the complete opposite of the kind of son he would have liked. He can't understand anyone who hasn't the same ox-like strength as himself. He can be pretty coarse too sometimes and rants and raves when he's in a temper. I keep out of his way when he's like that – we all do . . .' He smiled 'Perhaps with the exception of Mother – she can give as good as she gets and when they get together in a bad temper it's worse than anything you're likely to hear in the rowdiest of inns.'

Evelyn listened, fascinated, to these revelations of the people who lived behind plush curtains, finding them all the more interesting because they were about Gillan's parents.

When they came home in November she was invited along to the Big House for tea. Maggie looked askance when she heard this and for a moment Evelyn thought she wasn't to be allowed to go. Maggie looked over at Jamie who indicated his acquiescence with a slight nod so she counted the money she had got for eggs and cheese last market day and took Evelyn into Aberdeen to buy some material for a dress which Murn cut and stitched in six frantic nights in between correcting her class's homework jotters.

It was a blue dress of soft velveteen with ribbons of the same material to match. Johnny saw her in all her finery the night before the tea party. She stood in the kitchen, fidgeting a little as Murn fussed over seams and straightened the hem of the dress. Her father went to the

211

porch and, taking down the cracked mirror which hung above the marble topped washbasin, he brought it to her and held it while she stared in some embarrassment at an unfamiliar vision, so unlike the Evelyn she knew in workaday dress, long pinafore and long black button boots. The boots she could do nothing about, nothing fancier could be made or bought at such short notice, the rest was so becoming that for a moment she hardly recognized herself.

'Is it me?' she breathed. 'Really me?'

'Ay, it's you,' said Nellie dryly. 'Thanks to Murn, and to Mother for using up her precious sillar.'

'Ach, Nellie,' scolded Maggie. 'Must you spoil the bairn's moment? It's no every day she gets a new dress.'

'No,' said Murn quietly, remembering all the cast-offs and cut-downs she had had to wear while growing up. 'It's nice to see a young lass looking her best. You enjoy it, Evie, you deserve it.'

Shyly Evelyn kissed her sister's hot cheek and going to first her mother then her father she bestowed a similar offering of thanks.

The outside door rattled and Johnny came in, pausing in his tracks to stare at her as if she wasn't quite real.

CHAPTER ELEVEN

A look came into Johnny's eyes – a strange dark look which she couldn't define. She was skinny and leggy, small yet for her age but there was a promise in her of a beauty to come. She wasn't particularly pretty in her fifteenth year but there was a power in her face, a certain something that made one look twice and wonder what she would be like when she came to her full womanhood.

'Do I look nice, Johnny?' she asked, standing in front of him a trifle awkwardly.

'Ay,' he said briefly. 'Just you mind how you go – that's all.' And turning on his heels he went off without anyone knowing what he had come for in the first place, though Jamie looking after him felt something of the uncertainty he himself had felt as a young lad growing up quickly.

Murdo, the groom, arrived next day with the gig and Nellie watched from the window as it went spanking down the track to the turnpike.

'Our Evie is moving in high circles,' she said in some wonder. 'I just hope she doesna get hurt.'

'It willna last,' Maggie dug her darning needle into a holed sock with a touch of viciousness. 'She'll go there the day, they'll talk nice to her and all the while they'll be sizing her up and wondering what their son is thinking of hobnobbing wi' a crofter's daughter.'

She was right. Lady Marjorie and her husband couldn't have been kinder or nicer to the youngest daughter of King's Croft, yet the moment Evelyn sat herself down on the edge of a brocade chair she knew she had done the wrong thing accepting the invitation to take tea at the Big House. A starched and prim-faced maid brought in tea which Lady Marjorie poured into dainty cups. Graciously she passed them round. Wafer thin sandwiches appeared which wouldn't decently have filled a hole in a bad tooth.

Evelyn nibbled as fastidiously as she knew how and found herself thinking how much better she would have enjoyed being in the kitchen with the motherly Martha and her wholesome piles of thick, crusty bread and jam. Gillan too seemed ill at ease. She caught him eyeing her once or twice, wearing a look that said, 'We're here and we've got to go through with it but I'll be glad when it's over and done with.'

Lady Marjorie asked Evelyn politely questions about her schooling, her ambitions. When Evelyn blurted out that she wanted to be a writer Lady Marjorie's elegant eyebrows were raised so eloquently she might as well have said, 'Indeed, fancy a crofter's daughter wanting anything so high-flying.' She said nothing however, just cleared her throat and nodded rather patronisingly.

Evander was more forthcoming. 'Good for you, child,' he approved heartily, wiping his handsome black moustache with the corner of his table napkin. 'No reason why you shouldn't be whatever you set your heart on. Many a brilliant scholar has risen from the farmlands. I knew one myself when I was at school. His people were proud of him and almost killed themselves giving him a decent education. He didn't let them down and went on to become a surgeon of great renown.'

'Education is a fine thing in itself,' Evelyn spoke up, her fiery head well back on her shoulders though inwardly she trembled, especially when Lady Marjorie looked at her as if surprised she should express herself so clearly. 'But I dinna think you have to be academically clever to become a creative writer. If you read enough books in your life you can have all the literary education you want yet remain untrammelled by theory and palaver like that. I was writing poetry and stories when I was only an infant and what I put down on paper came from what I observed in the world and people about me . . .'

Evelyn stopped short, breathless suddenly. Lady Marjorie was staring at her, Gillan beaming in delight while Evander slapped his knee and boomed, 'By God, you're right, child! Couldn't have expressed it better

214

myself. You'll get on, gad and you will – that's if you don't let your heart rule your head. Nothing thwarts ambition more than marriage and children – if you don't have the money to back you up, that is.'

He was telling her that like married like, the poor stayed poor and knew their place. She was glad when it was time for her to go. With a few polite words of thanks she marched out of the elegant room with a straight back, unable suddenly to wait to get back to the cosy, homeliness of King's Croft. At the door Gillan caught her hand. 'I'll see you – whenever I can get away.'

His dark eyes were anxious, the sensitive face she had come to know so well, pale and slightly strained.

'Ay,' she nodded briefly and went off quickly while he went slowly upstairs to the lonely schoolroom and Moby sewing in her chair.

Evander stood with his back to the fire, coat and tails held up, legs apart. 'A clever, intelligent child,' he observed, wetting his thick lips as he thought about the girl's wonderful hair, the clarity in her green eyes, her burgeoning figure.

'Indeed she is,' Lady Marjorie turned away from his glinting eyes. 'But she's hardly Gillan's type, is she? I don't think we can allow the friendship to continue, Evander.'

'Havers, woman, what harm can it do? They're only children. Though mind, a lad of his own age would be better, whether he came from croft or castle. Might make a man of him if he had someone who could teach him a lesson or two about life.'

Lady Marjorie's nostrils flared. 'Gillan is a child, Evander, not a man – and he does have friends of his own age.'

Her husband's coarse laugh rang out. 'Those lily-livered cissies you picked for him to romp with! I don't blame the lad for giving them the brush-off. God, but it's been difficult to know what's best for a lad like him. When he was younger he was so damned delicate I used to think the slightest breeze would fell him. We can't go on trailing him about with us for the rest of his life. How old is he now, dear?'

'Fifteen – still very much a child,' she said through tight lips.

'Nonsense dear! If you had your way you would still be dangling him on your knee when he was forty. He's a lot stronger now,' he continued thoughtfully. 'High time he broke the ties, I've seen a great change for the better recently. Time he was off to school . . .'

'Oh, but I think . . .'

'Come now, Marjorie,' he broke in rudely. 'You've seen the boy lately. Running wild – from all accounts having a high old time by himself while we were away. I don't mind who he mixes with – it's good for a chap to discover what goes on in all worlds. After all we owe – or at least I do – what I am to the land and as my grandfather always used to say – good dung raises the best crops.'

He was positively revelling in the distaste showing all too plainly on her face. The love of the earth, of earthly things, was ingrained in his blood, and while he could be a perfectly courteous gentleman he also enjoyed just being himself and often wished his wife could allow herself to be more natural. But snobbery was too inherent in her for that. The refinements and the social graces were her world and he enjoyed seeing her squirm just now and again.

'Time for the lad to leave the stables,' he said firmly. 'I'll see to it right away – after all, Marjorie, we can't have him running about with a crofter's daughter – can we now?'

For a long time after that visit the echo of Evander's booming laugh surged in Evelyn's ears, that and the strange gleam she had noticed lurking in his eyes whenever they swept over her – eyes that undressed a lass. Some of the local lasses who worked to Rothiedrum said that, and now she understood why. As for Lady Marjorie she was a snob, attractive to be sure, kind enough in her own way, but still a snob no matter how you looked at her.

Yet the lure of Rothiedrum House was something Evelyn knew would always be with her. Gillan was right. It was a friendly house. There was an atmosphere about it of people who had lived there and had been contented with their lives.

Soon afterwards Gillan told her he was being sent away to school. 'I'm glad really, it's what I've always wanted,' he said enthusiastically, adding, 'But I'll miss you, Evie.' He took her hand. 'You'll still come and have tea in the kitchen? You and Johnny and Florrie? Say you will?'

'Ay, Gillie, I love Martha and Belle and all the others and would hate never to see them again.'

'Just them?' He smiled as he said it, a half-shy smile that filled his eyes with secrets.

'Ach well – maybe you too – just a bittie.' she laughed.

'Never as much as Johnny Burns?'

'I'll always see Johnny,' she answered seriously. 'He and I belong in the same world.'

'Don't shut me out of your world – Princess Evie,' he pleaded anxiously, the uttering of the pet name he sometimes used, displaying all the charm that was in his father though in Gillan's case it would never be overshadowed by coarseness.

'Dinna be daft,' she giggled, dropping a curtsy which he answered with a bow and they both fell laughing on to the hay of the Rothiedrum stables which was one of their favourite meeting places.

After that, Gillan was often to be seen with his father around Mains of Rothiedrum and some of the bigger farms, Evander having decided it was time his son saw where a good part of his bread and butter came from. He never pointed his horse's nose towards the crofts or the smallholdings. It was the job of the factor to keep an eye on such lowly places so that winter, prior to his departure to school, Evelyn saw less and less of Gillan.

'Just as well,' Johnny told her. 'You were getting too attached to people and things higher up. Better to bide wi' your own.'

'You mean I was getting too attached to Gillie,' she accused.

'Ay – if you like.' he replied bluntly and she felt suddenly as if a gust of fresh air had just blown over her face. He was

217

straightforward, almost rude in his frankness, so different from Gillie with his uncertain manner and shy approaches.

Life in the farmtouns went on for Evelyn as usual but there was a difference in it now, a subtle, intangible difference. It came to her one cold night a week before Christmas, that it wasn't the land or the people in which the differences lay but in herself. She was seeing it all, not from a child's point of view but from that of a girl on the brink of womanhood.

She was lying in bed, the moonlight streaming through her window, thinking how mysterious the dark shadows were, wishing it was next week when Grace would be home and she would have her quiet company instead of the empty bed so bare and alone in its corner. In the utter stillness of the frosty night, lying snug on the verge of sleep, she heard the Birkie hushing over the stones, purling insistently in her ears, lulling her sweetly and tranquilly to oblivion. And then another sound came filtering down over the hills and into the houghs of Rothiedrum, a lone, poignant yet triumphant voice, as of men and new life springing strong and sweet from the womb.

Sleep left her and getting up she padded to the window to wipe the steam from the pane and train her vision up yonder to Knobblieknowe hanging there on the very top of the hill. The night lay fair and dreaming under the moon, the low hills were silhouetted against the midnight blue of the sky, little woods huddled intimately into the bosom of the hillocks, the moon-laved parks stretched into eternity, hidden houghs were swallowed into inverted pleats of rich dark velvet shadows.

The sound reached her ears again. Putting her fingers to her lips she smiled even while she shivered with the momentous occasion of such a night. It was Kenneth Cameron Mor up there, striding up and down playing the pipes, proclaiming to all and sundry, whether they liked it or no, that Jeannie's baby was born. The glad tidings, now near, now far, borne on the frosty breath of the crisp hill air, sent shiver after shiver into the very marrow of the child-woman standing on the brink of the wonderful mystery of young adulthood. The pipes chimed again and again, ringing in the life of Kenneth Mor's bairn. She could picture him, proud red beard bristling, kilt swinging, joy racing through him as he marched up and down. The sound intensified, became stronger and she realized that Tandy had joined the master of Knobblieknowe and now they were both striding up and down, drunk or sober, announcing to the world that a child had been born – as it was on *that* night.

Evelyn stared up at the stars, looked into the eyes of the moon, held her breath till she felt she would burst with the pain of it – and cried. Pinpricks of light were illuminating the black eyes of windows all over the plains. Hill o' Binney – Alastair wakened from sleep and looking for Hinney who would surely be up there seeing the latest Cameron into the world. Dippiedoon – she could just hear Kirsty ranting on at Angus – 'Would you listen to that! That wild mannie from the Highlands – where he should have stayed so that decent folk could sleep at night.'

Evelyn laughed and cried into her hands while life surged into her, through her, over her, the life of a newborn baby, the life of King's Croft – of Rothiedrum – her own life. It beat and pulsed, merged and fused into her. She remembered looking down from this window on another night of new life – Wee Col's life. She had been a child then, silly and selfish, hating the thought of another being intruding into the ordered routine of King's Croft. But Wee Col had come and he was now, as much a part of the croft as any of them. He might never be like other children but he was life and that was all that mattered.

When Nellie and Murn came rushing through to look from her window and exclaim in loud voices all she could do was collapse on the bed and laugh for the sheer joy of everything that was good and wonderful in the world about her.

'The baby's come.' Murn sounded bleak, not at all glad that another child had been born to Jeannie and Kenneth Mor, as if its existence was a new threat to a cherished dream, like an heir to a throne being pushed further back

219

in line by another contestant on the scene.

'Ay, it's come,' Nellie said testily. 'And that Kenneth Mor is making sure the whole world knows it – though mind,' she added and her voice became softer. 'It will be nice for wee Cal to have a brother or sister – and fine to go visiting up there and hear a babby's cries about the place again.

The very next morning both Evelyn and Nellie went rushing up to Knobblieknowe bearing gifts for the baby. Kenneth Mor greeted them at the door, newly washed, hair like red silk, beard glossy and combed, face ruddy and glowing.

'It's a wee lass,' he said and his voice was filled with awe. 'Fancy me wi' a daughter – and one so like Jeannie I canna right credit it yet.' Blowing out his breath he emitted a great gushing of happy laughter and grabbing first Evelyn, then Nellie, he kissed them both soundly on the lips.

Evelyn reddened and grew still inside herself at her first experience of a man's lips on hers. Nellie too reddened and drew back, her fair skin stained from the neck up – yet she didn't bristle or say anything 'Nellie-ish'. Instead she stuck her work-reddened hand into his, pumped it up and down, uttered a few confused words of congratulation and marched straight-backed up to the bedroom.

Jeannie was like a little girl in the vast, smothering softness of the feather bed. Her dark hair rippled softly about her face and fell in glossy waves to her shoulders, the whiteness of her nightdress lent her a virginal innocence which no amount of babies would ever take away. Hinney had just bathed her and washed her face, the skin of it shone with a delicate transparency and added to the illusion of a child fresh out of school. Next to her, Hinney looked tired and old, her red hair was liberally sprinkled with white, her mutch cap sat tilted over one large ear but she was smiling and serene and hiccuped slightly as the Grant girls came through the door.

Jeannie giggled. 'Hinney, you old rascal – you should be ashamed of yourself – drunk at this time o' the day and poor

220

old Alastair wondering no doubt what's happened to you.'

Hinney had been called from her bed by an anxious Kenneth Mor at ten o'clock the night before. She had slipped away, leaving her husband slumbering on. After the arrival of the youngest Cameron she had dozed for a while then had celebrated the rest of the night away, seated round the kitchen fire with Kenneth Mor and Tandy.

'Ach, Alastair will keep for a whilie yet,' she said with asperity. 'The old goat will be out seeing to that daft cuddy o' his and will never miss me till his belly tells him it's feeding time.'

The black haired, delicately featured little girl was asleep by Jeannie's side. Evelyn stood back from the bed, hands folded behind her back, remembering last night and the welter of emotions she had experienced. The bedroom was warm and sleepy, the flames from the fire winked on Jeannie's treasured collection of small brass ornaments. In her childhood Evelyn had often laboured up the steep brae to Knobblieknowe with the offer to clean the ornaments just for the privilege of being there in Jeannie's room. Every aspect of it was stamped with her feminity, from the snow-white tatting bordering the chairback covers to the exquisitely crocheted doilies on the dressing table and the border of old Scottish lace on the bedspread. It might only be a small, rather poorly lit farmhouse bedroom, but to Evelyn it was a place of romance and suited well the handsome, bearded Highlander and his black haired, blue eyed Jeannie. Yet the room had also known pain – last night it must have been filled with it yet this morning here was Jeannie, a bit tired and pale but just as bonny as ever.

Nellie stood for a long time looking at the baby, touching the satin smoothness of its face. A ghost of a sigh trembled out of her. She bent down and kissed Jeannie on the cheek then sitting herself on the edge of the bed she took up the brush and began to do Jeannie's hair, brushing and brushing till the burnished waves streamed over the pillow. The two young women had become great friends over the years. Whether it was born of their mutual love for children or simply because they felt at ease in one another's company mattered not, enough it was that they could communicate effortlessly, not only about babies but about every topic under the sun. Nellie also tolerated Kenneth Mor better than any other man in the district, though it wouldn't have been Nellie if he hadn't come under the fire of her tongue from time to time.

Jamie and Kenneth Mor got along well too and it wasn't unknown for the latter to ask the older man's advice on farming matters. Never would he have lowered his pride to ask another but Jamie was different, he wasn't a man to indulge in idle gossip, so an easy friendship had blossomed between the two farms. No excuses were needed for a visit and a blether and Murn was often to be found up there, sometimes even taking a young man along with her, though when that happened he might well not have existed. She would compare him with Kenneth Mor and go home to sigh and dream her useless dreams for she had never got over her early feelings for the big Highlander.

Jeannie had been exclaiming over the beautiful baby clothes Nellie had knitted in her spare time but now she took the strong bonny hand in her dainty one and said with a glint in her eyes, 'Nell – I hope you will no be minding but I've called the baby Isla Nell Cameron. Yours is such a bonny name and I aye vowed if I had a wee lass her middle name would be yours.'

Nellie swallowed and reddened. Her name – bonny? She had never liked it – had always imagined it to be as bare and barren as she herself but now, hearing it coupled with Isla and spoken in Jeannie's lovely, lilting voice, it suddenly took on a new glad meaning, she didn't say anything, she couldn't but she squeezed Jeannie's hand and got up quickly to rush down to the kitchen, murmuring something about making tea.

Hinney paused in the act of shrugging herself into the heavy woollen cape she had fashioned from scraps of goat hair. 'You've made the lassie's day, Jeannie.' She shook her head sadly. 'It's a waste you know, a waste o' a good young woman. She should be having her own bairns and a man to look to her . . .'

She turned to Evelyn who was seated by the fire rearranging the brass ornaments. 'You'll beat your sister yet, Evie, lass. Just look at you.' She ran her fingers down the silken length of the girl's hair. 'It's as bonny as the birks in autumn. You're a sapling no longer but just coming into the blithe bloom o' your growing. I mind fine when you were just a wee fart o' a thing and that daft in the head wi' nonsense you were feared o' auld Hinney.'

Evelyn gazed into the fire, a wistful smile at her lips. 'It seems so long ago – yet so near. I thought I would never grow up, that I'd always stay a wee thing at my father's knee.'

'Ay, and before long you'll be breaking the loons' hearts – you wi' the gemstones for een and the sunshine for hair. Will it be Johnny Burns, lassie, or will he just break his heart in the running?'

Evelyn shook off her sober mood. Standing up she hugged the old woman, now smaller than she. 'Ach, Hinney, you're just a nosy old witch, that you are. I tell you this though, I'll no be for marrying or having bairns too quickly. I want to enjoy myself first and learn a lot more about life.'

Hinney winked at Jeannie. 'The fastest way to learn about life is to give it.' Pulling on her moleskin mittens she bade Jeannie goodbye with the promise to come back later. Taking Evelyn's arm she led her out to the landing, pausing at the top of the stairs to say in a quiet voice, 'You're a Grant and you can keep a secret. Speaking o' Johnny minded me o' something.'

'Ay, Hinney?' A tiny prickle of perception touched Evelyn then. It wasn't of fear but of something as yet outside the scope of her senses.

'Catherine is going to have another bairn,' Hinney said flatly.

Evelyn stared. 'Does Johnny know?'

'None o' them know yet – no even Catherine herself.'

'But how can you . . .'

Hinney gave her an odd look then. Deep in her eyes was the wisdom that had always been there but in her heightened awareness Evelyn glimpsed something else – something that had looked back at her from the mirror many times in the past.

'How can *you*, Evie – ask me that?' Hinney countered. 'When you were a wee lass you called me a witch. Hearken the day when a bairn might look at you and call you the same. In the Dark Ages you and me might have been burned at the stakes for the things we see and feel – that are yet to come.'

Evelyn stood very still though there was an awareness in her that had no name in the everyday world. 'You mean – you too feel the things that I feel?'

'Ay – and many's the time I've cursed the powers that gave me the second sight. Cursed them and feared them.'

'The second sight.' Evelyn spoke through numb lips. There was a name now to those visions she experienced from time to time. 'I dinna want it, Hinney.'

'Nor me – but I've got it and so have you. It won't aye torment you, just sometimes, and often when you're least expecting it.'

'I know,' Evelyn spoke tremulously. 'I – I'll fight it.'

'You will – I did – and in the end I learned to live wi' it.'

'Evie,' Jeannie's voice floated. 'Bring Wee Col to see the baby when you have the time.'

Evelyn shook herself, broke the spell the old woman seemed to have cast over her. 'Ay, Jeannie, I will.'

Normality returned. Nellie came up the stairs, a tray in one hand, Cal on the other, an excited Cal who could hardly wait to get upstairs to see his new baby sister.

Evelyn saw Hinney to the door. A bitter east wind was blowing, whipping up stoor and swirls of hay in the yard.

'It will be a white Christmas.' Evelyn gazed up at the grey clouds skudding over Bennachie's dour face.

'Ach, is it ever anything else in these parts?' Hinney was herself again, grumbling, worrying about Alastair, her lined face breaking into smiles at sight of him toiling up the brae towards her.

'You're here, wumman?' he greeted her sourly, his mane of white hair unfurling from under his cap as the wind

224

whipped it, his droll face showing nothing of the pleasure he felt at seeing his wife. 'I didna ken where ye were, Hinney, and me oot frae dawn seeing to the beasts and never a scrap o' breakfast to greet me on the table when I got back.'

'Ach, it's these blin' een o' yours,' she scolded warmly, taking his arm and giving it an affectionate squeeze. 'I left a wee letter for you on the mantelshelf telling you where I was going. You're such a hapless mannie I doubt you would just die on yourself if I wasna there to see to you. Come on, we'll go and find Kenneth Mor and get a lift home in the trap. My auld legs will no make that journey down to the turnpike without a cuddy's hooves under me.'

Grace came home for Christmas unexpectedly, not even a note to say when she would be arriving so that Jamie could meet her with the trap. She was looking exhausted and came through the door with a sigh of thankfulness to sink into the inglenook by the fire where she kicked off her shoes and rubbed at her cold feet.

Maggie came in from the milkhouse where she and Evelyn had been making butter. At sight of her second youngest daughter Maggie wiped her hands on her sacking apron and cried, 'Grace, you're peekit looking. Are you ill? And how on earth did you get here?'

Grace laughed and snuggled Tibby to her face. 'Dinna fash, Mam. I met Carnallachie in Aberdeen and he gave a lift all the way here. I came home a day or two early because – well – I havena been too well. Just my old trouble, my stomach. I'm fine now.'

'What old trouble?' demanded Maggie. 'It's the first I knew of it.'

'Ach, it's just pains I get, it's nothing serious.'

'And how do you know that?' demanded Maggie sternly. 'Have you been to see about it?'

'No, Mam, dinna fuss, it's nothing I tell you. I've always had them - at least this wee whilie back. It's just indigestion and I know what to take for it. I'm no a nurse for nothing you know.'

Maggie took the bright young head to her bosom. 'Lassie, lassie,' she murmured huskily. 'It's grand to have you home. It will be a real Christmas wi' all my bairns about me – as it was in the old days.'

It was a wonderful homecoming. Mary came rushing over from Rowanlea to join in the family gathering. They all sat round the fire, laughing and talking at once. Grace couldn't get over how Evelyn had grown in the few months of her absence. She also commented on Murn's changed appearance. No longer was she the docile, withdrawn creature of old. The years had filled her out. After an initial spell of unhappiness she loved her job at the primary school in Tillietoorie. She was enjoying several lighthearted affairs with young men who shared her tastes in politics and literature.

Grace questioned them all eagerly, thirsty for all the snippets of sisterly gossip she missed when she was away from home. Affectionately she tugged Evelyn's long fiery tresses. 'It will be nice to have you in the next bed, Evie, you can tell me everything you've been up to. I canna get over how you've grown, you'll be fifteen – let me see – next May. What will you do then?'

'Ach, I don't really know, Grace. I wasna clever enough to win a bursary like Murn so I'll just leave school and maybe find a job – and in my spare time I'll sit up in the hayloft and just write and write.'

Mary giggled. 'Ay, as long as Johnny Burns is up there with you. I've seen the way he looks at you, Evie.'

Evelyn coloured, but smiled with the rest. 'And didn't I have a few lessons about lads and haylofts from my very own big sister? It's a good job Greg came along when he did or heaven alone knows what kind o' reputation you would have earned for yourself.'

'Ach, he was as bad himself,' Mary said placidly. 'You could say we saved one another. Anyway,' she patted her stomach affectionately, 'we'll soon have a bairn to keep us in order – and this is only the beginning. After all, I'm nearly twenty-two – time such an old lady settled down to the drudgery o' hippens and feeding bottles.'

Nellie smiled sourly. Of them all her life was one which had undergone the least change. She was twenty-six now and people had almost stopped wondering if she would ever marry and settle down. Mostly she appeared contented enough with the way things were but there were other times, the bursts of temper, the bitterness, the harsh words thrown at her family in frustration.

'I'm no better than a doormat,' she frequently raved. 'Everyone who feels like it just wipes their dirt on me and I'm sick o' it.' It was then Maggie and Jamie would look at one another, saying nothing, for there was nothing to say to a daughter who had so determinedly carved out her own, lonely path.

Wee Col came crawling in among the girls and with a laugh Nellie snatched him up to crush her lips against his hair. Reaching up he took a strand of hers in his fingers and tickled his nose with it. He had never made any attempt to walk properly but shambled about, half-crawling, only pulling himself to his feet when Nellie came into the room. The only words he could utter with any clarity were the names of his own family and those of Knobblieknowe. Even then, only those used to him could understand the garbled words, Nellie's name being the clearest to come out of the slackness of his mouth. With all his heart he adored her. Often he would lapse into long spells of just staring into space, only the presence of Nellie having the power to reach him. Then a clear, bright awareness would pierce his vision and holding out his arms he would say her name in a queer, trembling nuance of love.

'Nella,' he spoke the name now, patting her face with his hands and she gathered him closer against her to kiss the tip of his nose. 'Ay, my wee man, I'm here, Nella's here.'

In his chair by the fire Jamie smoked his pipe and watched his children. The firelight played on the bright, young faces, lingered on shining tresses, sat hopeful and sweet on the tender curves of feminine shoulders. It was good to have them all gathered there at King's Croft fireside and he was sorry when the evening came to an end. Maggie put aside the socks she was always

227

knitting and got up to smoor the fire with damp dross.

Resting her head on one hand against the mantel she said softly. 'In the name of the Father, the Son and the Holy Spirit, Thanks be for our life, For peace in our home, And for matchless grace, This nicht and ilka nicht. Amen.'

The words of the old *smooring* prayer fell soft as snowflakes in the silence of the room.

'Amen.' The daughters of the house echoed in unison, all of them remembering themselves as children, hearing either their father or their mother repeating the words of the grace every night before bedtime. Now it held a deeper and more precious meaning as they looked at one another, each feeling a little sad that the days when they had all gone together upstairs were over.

Jamie rose somewhat stiffly from his chair. 'Come on, Mary lass.' He went with her to the door. 'I'll see you home before that good man o' yours thinks we've decided to keep you.'

CHAPTER TWELVE

Nellie was feeling good and relaxed as she picked her way over the endrigs of the stubble field which ran along by the edge of the deep, dark pinewoods above King's Croft. Near at hand a burn burbled its way down to the river, a cock pheasant uttered its rusty note as it ran for cover, a flash of purple and red against the rich brown of the forest floor. Looking down she could see the croft huddled into its cloak of winter white, the smoke spiralling lazily into the still day. It had been a good New Year as occasions like that went. Not that she approved of all that drinking and palaver with folks knocking themselves insensible in the name of celebration.

Still, she thought, with a touch of good humoured indulgence, the singing and the music had been good and it was lovely to have Grace at home. Somehow she always seemed to soothe any atmosphere. Men always behaved themselves better in her presence, though in no way did she inhibit their enjoyment. And of course Martin Gregory had helped too. His drinking was of the modest variety and he had a knack of engaging people in earnest conversation so that somehow they remained sober enough to be able to argue with him intelligently.

He had brought a sparkle to Grace's face too. Not that Nellie approved of her young sister's liaison with such a mature man but at least they were both sensible about it and as far as anyone could judge the affair had remained purely platonic.

Nellie hummed a catchy bothy ballad under her breath as, laying down her basket, she set about gathering kindling for the fire. There was plenty to be had under the trees and she wandered along, intent on her task, hardly pausing for breath or to take stock of her surroundings. It was her way to work at a fast pace and to be singleminded about anything she was doing, unlike Grace or Evelyn whose attention could so easily be diverted by flora and fauna.

It was dry and clear of snow here in the woods and soon she was warm enough to throw off her shawl and roll her sleeve to her elbows . . . A twig snapped somewhere close at hand and she froze, looking up to catch her breath and strain her eyes into the dark wood, the bundle of firewood tucked firmly under one arm.

Another twig snapped, then another, but still she could see no one in the dim, mysterious regions which surrounded her. She had strayed quite far from the path and a cold little tremor of foreboding touched her spine. Pushing back a strand of hair she called angrily, 'Who's there? Is that you, Pooty Drummond? If you're playing hide and seek wi' me I dinna think it very funny.'

Silence greeted her and she shrugged. A deer or some such creature. They were often to be found in the woods when the snow was on the ground, scratching and chewing at the bark of the trees. She bent to her task again . . . There came a stealthy movement behind her, a sound of heavy breathing – followed by a deep cruel laugh. Her heart galloped into her throat, the hair on her scalp crawled. She remained as she was, crouched low to the ground, one hand outstretched in the act of retrieving a twig. She knew that laugh, God how she knew it! The crude notes of it had made her cringe in disgust often enough.

'Well, well, if it isna Nellie Grant. All alone in the woods wi' the big bad wolf.' The mocking voice was immediately behind her. She straightened and swung round, dropping her bundle of twigs to the ground.

'Dinna be feared, Nell, it's only me. You're surely no feared o' me – are ye now?'

Peter Lamont swayed before her, a terrifying Peter Lamont with the drink heavy on his breath. She could smell the fumes of it, though he stood some few feet away from her. It was obvious that he had been out all night, his clothing was creased, caked with dried mud to which pine needles thickly adhered. His eyes were bloodshot and wild,

230

his face puffed and red, the black stubble of his beard shadowing cheeks, chin and upper lip. His thick lips were twisted into a mocking leer as he staggered about in front of her, an almost depleted whisky bottle dangling from his fingers.

'Come now, Nell, have ye nothing to say to me?' he grunted thickly. 'Here I am, complete wi' the very thing you've been needing all your empty life and ye dinna even greet me wi' a New Year salute. Most uncivil, lass. I'll have to teach ye a lesson in manners. You and me have an old score to settle – ye dinna think I'd forgotten what a bitch ye were to me the night o' Kenneth Mor's ceilidh – do ye now?'

He lurched towards her, sneering and grinning, saliva running from his mouth over his chin, his big hands outstretched towards her.

'Go away home, Peter,' she tried to speak evenly. 'They'll be looking for you over at the Mains.'

'Nell, Nell,' he chided. 'Am I seeing fear in ye? Fear in Nellie Grant o' the frozen heart and erse to match. Dinna let yourself down, lass, you mustna show such human emotions. Pride, Nell, dinna forget your pride.'

'Leave me be, you dirty pig!' she spoke desperately. 'I'm no one o' your kitchie deemies to be pawed and slavered over . . .'

He threw himself at her, his reeking breath washing sickeningly over her face, his grunts and snarls filling her ears. Pushing her to the ground he began to tear at her clothing, ripping apart the tight bodice of her severe grey dress, laughing with fiendish enjoyment at the sight of her wildly heaving bosom.

'That's what I like to see, passion. Ay, Nell, it's there, isn't it? You're no the frozen virgin you like to make out. See here, Nell,' he continued smoothly, 'it's no use your struggling or screaming – no a soul will hear ye up here. It's just you and me alone together – all alone – and I'm hot for ye, Nell, ye can feel the heat o' me. Feel it, lass, feel it and enjoy the thrill o' it while ye can.'

Terror closed her throat – the green canopy whirled and

blurred . . . She was a child again, alone in a dark room in the dead of night and in the stillness of dread shadows a male figure came towards her – it was alright – it was her father come to make sure she was alright . . . But no, it wasn't her father. It was some wild beast who reeked of drink and who lurched into bed beside her to lie next to her . . .

She was so terrified she forgot to scream and just lay where she was, sobbing out her father's name. But he never came and all the time the great rough hands of the man beast caressed her body and then came the pain, a pain that made her cry out in agony and over and over she called out her father's name while the great filthy beast slavered over her, his grunts filling her head while the pain went on and on till once more she was alone, alone and petrified in the darkness, wondering if the filthy creature who stalked the night would come back and get her again.

Come the morning she couldn't rise from her bed but lay there, sore, soiled, and degraded beyond measure. Her father had found her there, lying in her own blood, too shocked to talk to him at first. But gradually he had got it out of her and though the man he called Jake never came near King's Croft again she could never forget – nor could she ever forgive her father for not coming to her when she needed him most. She had never forgiven him – never – that was one of the reasons she hated drink so much, it could make even the most decent of men forget their reason . . . Peter Lamont was pushing her legs apart frenziedly pressing the heavy bulk of his body down upon her so that she could barely breathe. He was revelling in her passive terror. His wet, sweating face, inches from hers, exhibited such bestial enjoyment she knew without a shadow of doubt that he was beyond all pleas to whatever reason he possessed.

His meaty hands were on her, painfully bruising her breasts, her stomach, her thighs . . . And still she couldn't move, couldn't utter a single, solitary sound. She knew she was going to faint, blackness was rushing in on her, whirling her away into oblivion . . .

No! She wouldn't, she couldn't let this beast get away with this act of carnal lust – summoning every shred of her willpower she brought herself back – back to the awful reality there in the pine woods above King's Croft. He wouldn't get away with it – he wouldn't . . .

The weight of him was skewering her into the soft, dry earth beneath, the root of a tree ground into her spine. The pain of it spurred her to a desperate, vicious struggle – but he was strong – so strong.

Pinning her with one hand he tore his braces down and began ripping off his trousers. Rearing up he pulled both them and the long, woolly underpants down over his hips – she glimpsed the black hair coating his belly – and starkly pale against it that terrifying pillar of his arousal – she threw her head back on the earth and with all her strength began to fight for everything she held dear in her life. This drink-crazed pig would never rob her of all she had ever fought to retain – especially her pride – he would never take that – never . . .

'Lie still, you bitch!' he grated hoarsely, both hands free now to contemptuously tear at her undergarments, to pinion her while he threw himself on top of her once more and it was then she realized that what had gone before was nothing to what was happening now.

The sheer brute strength of him had doubled in force, his eyes were glazed, seeing nothing – her heart thundered in her ears – she couldn't get breath – couldn't . . .

From where she summoned the last remnants of her own strength she never knew, but at the last moment she opened her mouth and the screams came, one after the other, ringing and echoing through the woods till it seemed she would deafen herself with the hellish cacophony of them.

'Shut up – shut up, bitch,' he slurred as the sounds penetrated his maddened senses. His hand came down to crash into her face. The blow dazed her; she tasted blood and earth but still she kept on screaming and was so lost in her own petrified, dizzy world she was barely aware that the great weight of him was abruptly lifted from her as he was sent spinning against a tree several yards away.

Only half aware that something or someone had intervened, she raised her head to see a dim, blurred shape beating the living daylights out of her cringing, attacker. Once or twice he staggered up, his hands upraised to protect his face as blow after blow rained down upon him, pulverising him into a quivering, helpless jelly. Now she could hear the sound of flesh on flesh, of Peter Lamont's sobbing, rasping breathing and the even, controlled breathings of that tall, anonymous figure with fists of steel, magnificent shoulders – and a head that blazed as red as the dying sun at day's end. Nellie's focus became sharper. Painfully she raised herself on one elbow – it was Kenneth Cameron Mor of Knobblieknowe that she saw.

'For Christ's sake, man, enough, enough,' sobbed Lamont, a pitiful sight to behold in all the indignity of his bruised and beaten nakedness. Kenneth Mor stood there, hard, unbending, eyeing the snivelling grieve of the Mains with dangerous intent.

'Let me see the arse o' ye, man!' he roared derisively. 'Go on, waggle your skunk's arse into yon woods as fast as it can go. Run, rabbit, run! For all your bloody worthless worth!'

Lamont turned tail and ran.

'You've forgotten something, man!' Kenneth Mor's bellow stayed the petrified flight. Striding forward he rammed the other man's clothing into his shivering arms and poked his beard into his goggling eyes. 'Run, you good for nothing rat and dinna stop running till you're dead for the want o' breath or I'll come after you and ram your filthy arse down the back o' your throat till it chokes you. If I lay hands on you again I promise you'll no be fit enough even to sit down to pee – so, get going you, or I'll no answer for my actions.'

Lamont scuttled off, clutching his trousers to his heaving chest as a drowning man might clutch at straws.

Nellie passed a hand over her eyes, shame and weakness bowing down her head so that it sank fair and trembling to her drawn-up knees. At least she was still clothed, she

234

couldn't have borne the disgrace of Kenneth Mor seeing her without . . .

Strong arms were pulling her gently to her feet. Dear God, she could hardly stand, her knees were buckling beneath her – but she needn't have worried. It was a pillar that supported and held her, not a hard, unyielding tower but one that was warm and tender with caring arms that held her close and gentle hands that stroked her hair, and a voice that soothed as it crooned quiet comfort into her ears.

She lay passively against him, sobbing quietly and helplessly against the hard wall of his chest, wanting only to lie there forever, never to show him the tears that stained her face and ran unheeded on to him, soaking the coarse, hairy tweed of his jacket.

'There, there now,' he murmured and she felt small and helpless, not cheap and degraded as she had expected to feel the minute he turned his attention from Lamont to her.

'Greet, lassie, greet,' he advised sympathetically. 'Get it all out o' your system, it will do nought but good.'

How could this be? she wondered. He was speaking to her like a father speaks to a hurt child, the power of his kindness reaching down to soothe her very spirit, yet only minutes before, this same man had almost knocked another senseless.

She shivered and his arms tightened round her while his lilting Highland voice murmured soothingly on, like a tranquil river meandering peacefully between soft summer meadows . . .

Nellie knew a terrible and wonderful thing then. She loved Kenneth Mor. As surely as her name was Nell Christina Grant she loved him with a love that had somehow managed to remain hidden and secret even to herself until this moment – this earth-shattering moment with strong, protective arms holding her close, his beard tickling her face, his voice so soft, so lilting in her ears, the thudding of his fierce Highland heart against the wildly fluttering one of hers.

The knowledge of it devastated her. She felt weak with

the pain of it. It was too much, far too much to bear – first Peter Lamont – the hateful fear and disgust he had instilled in her – now Kenneth, big, powerful Kenneth Mor who could so easily squeeze her to death if he so wanted – who could easily do as he would with her in those weak, tremulous minutes.

A hatred of her own frailty rose up in her. She, who had imagined herself to be so strong, so remote from men. In the short space of half an hour one had almost overpowered her with his bestial strength, another had beaten her down into a wanting, willing submissive being, not by brute force but by the sheer magnetism of his manliness. She wanted to run, but was too physically and morally exhausted even to have the will to lift her head from his shoulders.

She hated herself then. How often she had preached her morals to Murn, thrown scathing insults at that quiet, white faced girl whose sufferings of heart had lain stark and bleak across her young, open face. She was no better than her sister, nay, a million times worse. At least Murn had recognized her weaknesses and in the displaying of them had somehow managed to keep going, even to begin to lead a normal enough life, while she – Nellie had smothered her natural instincts, locked them away and in those dark, secret recesses where they had been steadily smouldering, waiting for a day like this to bust forth and terrify her with the greedy, grasping strength of them.

'Nell,' Kenneth Mor's lips moved against her hair. 'Are you alright now? That swine, Lamont! Rothiedrum should hear o' this, the Mains would have another grieve before the month is out.'

'No!' Nellie pushed him away. Frantically she tucked away straying wisps of hair, straightened her dress, fingers shaking so much she had to batten them down with those of her other hand. 'No, Kenneth, he'll never try anything like that again, never wi' me or any o' mine. I – I dinna want this to be known – never – he will never open his mouth. He knows he would have you to answer to . . .'

She stumbled and would have fallen but his arms were

waiting, firm and sure about her waist – and it was the most wonderful experience of her life to be held like that in the protective circle of his arms. She could have lain there forever and never wearied, but the bitter sweet truth that lay, raw and exposed in her heart, was a force that she dare not tantalize.

A deep, penetrating sweetness touched her brow and with a sob rising in her throat she knew it was his lips and she tore herself away, feeling that she was wrenching the very soul apart from her body. She stood once more alone, feeling the chill of her loneliness sweeping round and about every aching, empty space in the heart of her, alone as she must always be now. For there could be no living comfort to be had in the arms of this tall red giant who stood with his rugged face to the red, living face of the sinking sun. He belonged to Jeannie and she had no right to any part of him. She began to walk away, exerting every shred of her willpower not to stumble on the rough, tree-rooted ground.

'Nell, let me see you home!' he cried and made to come after her.

'No!' She turned on him fiercely. 'I've managed all these years without the arm o' a man to hold me up and I dinna need one now. I'll no have family gawping at me and asking all kinds o' questions. So – so go away home and leave me be.'

She had picked up her shawl and was arranging it around her shoulders as she spoke, covering the torn bodice of her dress. Her hair had come loose in her struggles and she had no idea how attractive she looked standing there, the vulnerability of her womanhood lying vivid on her flushed, tear-stained face, her fine fair hair sweetly framing her face, making it softer, emphasizing the luminosity of her startlingly beautiful amber-green eyes.

He looked at her and recognized the appeal of a woman whose every defence had been forcibly ripped away. 'Nell,' he said and his voice was soft, persuasive. 'I'm your friend, lass, your friend.'

She bent to retrieve her basket, praying that he hadn't

noticed anything amiss, hoping that the craving she felt for him hadn't shown itself in her eyes.

'I know,' she whispered to herself, 'and would to God you were my enemy – I could live in a fool's peace then – and be happy in the hating of you . . .'

Soon after that Peter Lamont disappeared from the Mains. Nellie never knew how it had been achieved, no one ever spoke of it except to wonder at the reasons lying behind the dismissal. Everyone agreed it was high time Lamont had been sent packing and more's the pity it hadn't happened sooner.

Kenneth Mor never mentioned it to Nellie, she never asked. Once he smiled at her and said quietly, 'Everything's fine now, Nell lass.' That was all and she loved him the more for his diplomacy and silent, steady understanding.

Something happened to Nellie after that fearful, wonderful day in the pine woods above King's Croft, something that she was powerless to stop. She grew softer, more attractive, her fair hair had a new sheen to it, the expression in her arresting eyes became warmer, more sympathetic. There was something disturbing about her full, sensual mouth, as if it was waiting for an awakening, yet its tremulous softness displayed the lost hope of such an impossible dream. The gauntness of her figure was lost in a more rounded blooming of its natural contours. It was as if something held suspended inside of her had grown and blossomed into its natural awakening.

Nature had at last disobeyed the unnatural restraints that had stifled it for so long and was openly proclaiming its flowering to the world. Everyone noticed the change in Nellie and everyone welcomed it, not least Jamie, on whose conscience had lain the burden of guilt for his eldest daughter's aggressive dislike of all things womanly.

Nellie recognized the changes in herself and liked herself the better for them, though she lived constantly with the pain of her unfulfilled love. The flame she carried for Kenneth Mor must forever stay locked in her heart, unseen, unsung, a quiet, steady flame that would never be quenched but would always stay smouldering till the day her last breath would smother it for ever.

A month after the incident, Murn studied her thoughtfully as they sat together in the kitchen. 'Who is it, Nellie?' she asked quietly, 'Who, of all the men in Rothiedrum, has the power to make you look as you do?'

Nellie opened her mouth as if to make a scathing remark but said instead, 'We all have our secrets, Murn, and I have much a right to mine as any other body.'

Murn's eyes grew quizzical; she wanted to pursue the subject but knew that with Nellie she would be wasting her breath.

'Ay,' she murmured thoughtfully and turned away from the unflickering strength in the amber-green eyes of Nell Christina Grant.

CHAPTER THIRTEEN

Doctor McGregor closed his black bag with a snap and, patting Catherine's hand he said reassuringly, 'You'll be fine now, Catherine, just lie quiet and rest – doctor's orders.'

Her eyes searched his face. 'Am I – there's going to be another bairn – isn't that right, Doctor?'

Pushing his hand through his shock of black hair he nodded slowly, 'Ay, lass, you're right enough. You'll maybe know better yourself but I would say you're about four months on. It was a good thing you called me when the bleeding started or you could have lost it.'

She turned her head away from him. 'It might have been better if I had, Doctor. I don't rightly know how I'll cope with another.'

Gregor sat down on the bed and made her face him. 'Catherine, you've been a lot better these past years. When I first knew you, you could barely move from the house, now you're able to get about quite well.'

'Only with the aid of a stick, Doctor. How can I manage a new baby with the like of that? It's bad enough seeing to the other bairns, but at least they can fend for themselves to some extent, I don't have to lift and lay them.'

A frown creased Gregor's brow. He knew all about the Burns family, and like everyone else had wondered at the changes in Rob since the death of wee Janet. He wasn't altogether certain that they were changes for the better. Rob had become devout and made his whole family attend kirk every Sunday, rain or shine. Soon after losing his little daughter he had become a kirk elder but as he became more and more entrenched in his beliefs he had, much to the minister's consternation, taken to lay preaching, travelling far and wide to pour his thundering sermons into the heads of attentive audiences.

Folk filled kirk pews and barns to hear Rob Burns. He compelled, impelled, demanded attention though when people left the kirk behind they could never be certain if they were the better or the worse for having heard him. For there was something accusing in his all-embracing, glittering stare, something oddly disquieting in the clenched fist he thumped on the pulpit to emphasize his blood and thunder rhetoric. People squirmed in their seats and eyed one another, while each wondered if small, everyday misdemeanours warranted preaching of such violence. He knew how to disturb a body's peace of mind did Rob Burns, yet still the people flocked to hear him and to wonder if the big, burly giant's own lifestyle warranted such a puritanical approach to the Word of the Lord. The evils of drink was one of his favourite subjects, one that really got the men gulping in dismay as they thought back to the toddies and the drams of the night before. Women listened to such preaching with nods of approval and many a sober and chastened husband was poked in the ribs and for days afterwards bore the brunt of wifely naggings.

But folk nearer home were highly suspicious of the man and his 'holier than thou' attitude.

'He does it to ease his own black conscience,' sniffed Kirsty Keith. 'He canna pull the wool over my een or those of my man.'

'Ay, you're right there, Kirsty,' nodded Betsy O'Neil. 'It all came about after that terrible thing wi' wee Janet – poor, innocent cratur that she was.'

'He blames himself for that,' asserted Jessie Blair, chins wobbling in righteous indignation. 'Nary a word has he ever said about it, but it's there – at the back o' his black conscience.'

'Johnny got the brunt o' that,' rejoined Betsy. 'Poor laddie, tis a wonder to me he hasna left home years ago for he's no more than a skivvy up yonder. Strange how Babsie was never replaced, yet –' she lowered her voice, 'I heard tell years ago that the lass came back complete wi' her father, accusin' Rob Burns o' lying in sin wi' her. Imagine the likes! There in his very own home, whoring and lusting, his wife and all those poor bairnies under the same roof. The man's a hypocrite.'

That was the general opinion of Rob Burns of Birkiebrae and though some of it might be guesswork, the truth was hit on more times than Rob would have cared to hear.

For Babsie had indeed come back to Birkiebrae with her father – or, more accurately, she was dragged there by her father, five months pregnant, so tearful and terrified she hardly got two words in during the confrontation that followed. Rob had denied everything, stoically backed up by Catherine who, having got her man back, was prepared to defend him with everything she had – even to lie for him.

Scathingly she had informed Mr McTaggart that Babsie could take her pick of any of the farmtoun labourers and name any one as the father as she had flirted and carried on with them all.

Johnny had heard all the denials and the lying. He had stood outside in the passage, hearing all the hot protests springing from his father's lips, listening to the pitiless condemnation of Babsie.

A vision had come to Johnny, one that had never left him, of his father and Babsie lying naked together; his mother's shocked, livid face, her tears and her hopelessness. Now here she was, protecting Rob Burns, heaping all the blame on the slender shoulders of a little kitchen maid whose only real crime had been to fall for the flattering attentions of the master of Birkiebrae.

In the end, father and daughter had gone, the poorer for coming, Babsie tarnished forever in her father's sight, the innocent babe she carried given not one jot of consideration in all the lies and the arguing.

After all, Catherine Meiklejohn of Braemar, a respectable wife and a daughter of the Manse to boot, had pointed the finger of scorn and who could take the word of a servant girl against the likes of her? If Rob Burns had been to blame, no woman in her right senses would have shielded him with such indignant vigour.

At the time Catherine had not been in her right senses. She was a woman blinded by the triumph of having won her husband back, and she would fight tooth and nail never to lose him to any woman ever again. But it proved a bitter price to pay. In the years that followed she had never dared hire another kitchen girl and all the work of a person in such a position had fallen on her unwilling and inexperienced shoulders. For Catherine had never been nor ever would be a woman able to cope with domesticity. Her soft upbringing, coupled with her own inadequacies, had very efficiently seen to that. She only tackled as much as she could, the rest fell to Johnny, that sturdy, loyal son who had always propped her up with his protective shoulder.

This latest happening was more than she could bear. It was hard enough to contend with the house, the farmyard chores, the children – a husband whose increasing demands on her body often left her bruised and aching and crying into her pillow long after he had fallen asleep at her side. And yet he preached about the lusts of the flesh and the ungodly evils attached to them. To the good, honest, hardworking farmers he directed his attacks and while he ranted and raved at them they grew hot under the collar and felt guilty at having indulged in their honest, above board pleasures in the marriage bed.

Dr. McGregor himself had heard Rob at his most puritanical but neither he, nor the good folk of the parish, were terribly impressed or worried by him.

'A good shake o' the breeks is worth all the tea in China,' Danny the Fist confided once, and Dr. McGregor had rushed home from kirk with Mary to fly upstairs and get their clothes off as speedily as they knew how. Locked in their earthy embraces they would laugh and chide each other.

'This is the worst kind o' sin – take your hand from my bum this minute, Gregor McGregor.'

'No till you take yours from mine, Mary lass.' And they would clutch one another in laughter and renewed passion and forget all about Rob Burns and his lectures.

Gregor was thinking of all this as he sat by Catherine's bed and saw the glimmer of tears under her lashes.

'Catherine – it's none of my business I know,' he began carefully, 'but have you never considered getting someone in to help? A good kitchenmaid would take a lot of the work from your shoulders.'

'*No!*' She opened her eyes and hurled the protest at him, then realising her objection sounded too emphatic, she went on with studied calm, 'Ach no, Doctor, we're fine as we are. Johnny's a good lad and Jenny is coming up now, she's getting to be a good wee help about the place.'

Gregor thought about the impertinent, defiant Jenny and greatly doubted Catherine's words. He stood up. 'Right, Catherine, I'll go and have a word with Rob. Where is he at this time of the day?'

'He'll be up on the ley field – send Jimmy up to fetch him.'

'No, I'll walk up, it's a fine day and I could be doing with stretching my legs.'

The usual spring bustle was evident that day. A drying wind was sweeping up from the sea, the gulls were screeching in the smoke blue of the sky. Gregor breathed deeply as he walked leisurely along, revelling in the great awakening of the countryside. The wind tossed his hair this way and that as he paused for breath to look back down the steep hillside to the plains stretching away below. The fields looked like a vast brown and green patchwork quilt in which matchstick men, dogs and horses moved. The scent of turned earth was rich in the atmosphere. Far far away the silver grey ribbon of the North Sea glistened on the low skyline.

Gregor pushed back his shoulders. How good it was to be alive on such a day. Life was sweet, with winter past and the long days of summer to look forward to. Life could hardly be better since his marriage to Mary Rachel Grant, but this spring was particularly special for in May there would be a child, his and Mary's. After several years of waiting, no baby could be more eagerly awaited – unlike the wee mite growing in the belly of Catherine Meiklejohn. She was letting him tell Rob about it – as if she was afraid he might not be pleased with the results of his own intimacies.

Rob heard him out without a murmur. They sat together, backs to the sunny side of a dyke, Gregor puffing slowly at his pipe, Rob's idle hands picking aimlessly at the grass between his legs. Only the steady twitching of a cheek muscle gave any indication that he was not as composed as he was making out.

'Well, Doctor, I'll be honest wi' ye,' he nodded when Gregor's slow, pleasant voice had ceased speaking. 'I didna plan on another bairn, but if it is the Lord's will, then so be it.'

Tapping his pipe out on a stone, Gregor put it carefully back in his pocket and scrambled to his feet. 'That may be, Rob, but it's not quite that simple. Catherine almost had a miscarriage today, she will have to take things very, very easy if she's to keep the baby.'

Rob got up too, the great bulk of him blotting out the sun from the doctor's face. 'I'll see she does that, Doctor, never you fear.'

Gregor looked him straight in the eye. 'When I say easy I mean she'll have to stay in bed for a while, possibly till the end of her pregnancy – for at least five months, Rob.'

At last Rob seemed shaken out of his self-possession. 'Five months! But surely . . .'

'Five months,' emphasized Gregor. 'She isn't all that robust you know, – nor is she all that young.' He cleared his throat. 'You'll have to think about getting in some help – there's nothing else for it now.'

Rob pushed back his shoulders, a look of thunder on his brow. With a terse nod he dismissed the doctor. 'Thanking you for your time, Doctor, I'll be bidding you good day. Dinna worry about Catherine – I'll see she doesna rise out her bed.'

Gregor watched him striding over the rise of the field towards the harrowing ground, never a backward glance, self-possession in every iron hard muscle.

With a shrug Gregor went back to where he had left the trap.

'I've a feeling there will be ructions at Birkiebrae before

the day is much older,' he confided to Mary when he got home.

Standing on tiptoe she kissed the end of his nose. 'You've done your part, Greg, you canna do more.'

His hands moved over the swelling of her stomach. 'Ay indeed, I've done my part,' he said tenderly. 'And while I can do no more for Burns I can do something for my own wee wife. Sit you down and I'll get us a nice cuppy and then you can tell me what our wee lass has been up to this morning.'

'Our wee lad,' she corrected. 'Big and strong like his father.'

'No matter which,' he pressed his lips into her hair. 'It will be the most welcome bairn this side of the Birkie whether it turns out to be a loon or a quine.'

Johnny stared aghast at his father, hardly able to credit the news that had just been delivered to him in a series of abrupt sentences. Shock enough that his mother was pregnant again after a lapse of what must be more than nine years, but that she would have to remain in bed for the rest or her pregnancy was a blow that brought a curl of apprehension to his heart.

The house was very quiet. The younger ones were in bed, sent there early by Rob who was waiting for Johnny as he came in from the stables. Now they faced each other across the kitchen table. Wet logs hissed on the fire, the pendulum clock ticked lazily, the lamp cast a soft glow over the room. The illusion of peace found no echo in Johnny's heart. He sat there, saying nothing for a long time, fair head bowed, powerful shoulders hunched, strong brown hands clasped tightly in his lap. At eighteen he was as tall as his father, as broad and tight-muscled. There was a lot of Rob in him, the same blue eyes, the same startlingly handsome looks and fair Nordic colouring. But there was a sensitivity and kindness in his boyish face that had never been in Rob's, a depth of emotion in his eyes that Rob's icy orbs had never known.

He was conscious of those eyes now, boring into the top

of his head, waiting for him to speak. He knew what he was expected to say, knew what would be expected of him – but he couldn't, now that he had tasted some freedom these last few years since Janet's death. Life inside and outside Birkiebrae was a strange contradiction. The side Rob presented to the world was different from the one he showed to his family. In both worlds he was very much the self-assured master of his domain but at home he became softer, the hard façade was dropped a little so that occasionally you got a glimpse of a nicer being, the kind of man he might have been if he had been allowed to pursue the sort of life he had wanted.

These hadn't been easy years. Rob was difficult to live with and always hard to please, but he had seemed happier, more at peace with himself and his world. This attitude had shown itself in different ways. Though he and Johnny were never exactly close they worked well together. Gradually Johnny had been given more responsibility with the horses and had become such a good ploughman he had won honours at several ploughing matches. The walls of the stables were festooned with rosettes and other tokens, brought home by Johnny from various harness classes as well as the ploughing itself. There had been a light in Rob's eye then, if not exactly of pride then of satisfaction, as if he was thinking, 'Well, seeing he's my son'.

When the honours fell on Johnny, Rob would clasp him round the shoulders and say, 'No bad, man, you'll get better wi' practice, ay, you'll get better.'

He might well have said, 'Good for you lad, but you'll never be as good as me.'

Yet Johnny was not happy at Birkiebrae. His mother still heaped domestic responsibilities on to him so that at times he felt he was no more than a kitchen help and an orra loon combined. What she couldn't cope with fell to Johnny, and his resentment grew with the passing years. Somehow he couldn't bring himself to break away though he had lost count of the number of times he had thought of leaving home. He knew he could easily find work. The hiring fairs were full of grieves keeping weather eyes open for experienced farm hands but always he looked at his mother's weary face and knew he couldn't leave her.

The silence in the kitchen stretched. He licked his dry lips. 'You – Mother will have to get someone in to help.' His voice was very low, almost a whisper.

There were a further few moments of silence. Johhny's nerves tightened.

'She'll no do that, Johnny,' Rob's tone was expressionless but Johnny knew if he looked up he would see the tight jaw, the cold eyes.

He looked up then, straight into the blue, unflinching stare. 'She'll have to, all those months in bed – then a new baby to see to – she'll need a lot of looking after and so will the baby when it comes.'

'And you'll see she gets it, lad.' Rob's eyes narrowed to slits. 'She relies on you, you canna let her down.'

Johnny scraped back his chair and stood up, a wave of colour flooding the fairness of his face. 'No! I canna do it and I won't. I've had enough o' the apron strings. I – I'd rather leave home than face it all again. What do you think I am – what have you always thought I was? A damned cissy running around wi' an apron tied around me! I'm a man now, Father, a man! And if you were not so blinded by your own selfishness you would see me as such. You wouldna ask me to do a woman's work!'

Rob stood up too, his chair clattering backwards to go skating over the stone slabs. 'See here, lad,' he gritted, nostrils aflare, his face white with rage. 'While you're under my roof you'll do as you're damned well told, and be bloody glad to do it! Do you hear me, lad?'

'You're no in the pulpit now, Father, and I'm no one o' your open-mouthed flock soaking up every lying word that falls from your tongue –'

'Careful, lad, careful,' Rob warned in a low, threatening voice.

'Enough said, Father.' The colour had receded from Johnny's face leaving it deathly white. 'You've ordered me about once too often – and just remember this. Whatever happens – it is no fault of mine. You and Mother have made

248

your own bed and it's high time I got out from under you both and made mine.'

He left his father staring after him, a crouching panther who looked as if he was gathering himself for the kill. Any moment he expected the terrifying figure to follow him, to pounce. But nothing happened and he arrived in his room, weak and shaken but a resolve so strong in his heart he didn't pause for one moment as he reached up to the top of his wardrobe for a case and began hastily throwing things into it.

Jimmy stirred and sat up, small and slight for fourteen but with a wiry strength in him that was already proving its worth in the fields.

'Johnny, what happened? Why are ye putting your things in the case?'

'Go back to sleep, Jimmy.' Johnny heaved the case off his bed and shoved it underneath. 'You'll know soon enough, you're older than I was when I had to face it all.'

Stifling further questioning he undressed, blew out the candle and got into bed. He lay staring into the darkness, his heartbeat loud in his ears, expecting at any moment that the door would burst open to admit the raging form of his father. The minutes passed, laden with dread and all the while his emotions seethed, his pulse flew, his breathing was harsh.

Half-formed plans whirled in his head but none of them made sense and he was already regretting the hasty words spoken in anger. Where could he go? Who did he know well enough that would take him in, give him a roof till he was better settled in his mind? May 28th, was Term Day, the time of the hiring fair when men were engaged for farm work, and still a good way off. There were no near relatives, only distant cousins whom he barely knew. His mother's parents were dead, his father's mother alive but living in Canada – as remote as if she too were dead. She had come home twice to visit her son and his family and Johnny remembered her with affection.

'You come over and stay wi' me if things here get too bad,' she had told him the last time she left. He would write to her, find out if she still meant what she said but that didn't solve his immediate problem. There was no one – no one.

He tossed and turned. An hour went by. There came a soft padding on the stairs. His heart bounded afresh. How often had he heard that slow, stealthy, tomcat footfall?

The sound stopped and he knew his father stood outside the door, listening, waiting, like a creature who sniffed at the night and mingled with the black shadows all around. A board creaked. He let go of his breath. The steps padded away, a door opened, shut. Silence embraced the house. A watchful silence filled with unease.

Gradually he became calmer. He stretched his cramped muscles, feeling the power in them. Why was he so afraid of the man around whom everyone tiptoed as if he was some sort of god? Habit. The habit of years, conditioned in him from the cradle – and his mother's approach to life had never helped to make things easier. She had sat back, allowed it all to happen – taken him for granted. Didn't she – didn't they both realise how lucky they were to have a healthy son who was eager to work the land? Instead they allowed him to waste his strength in all the silly mundane woman's tasks around the place . . .

He turned to stare at the window. Rousing himself up on one elbow he saw the clouds floating over the face of the moon. Tossing back the covers he went to gaze into the shadowed night, his eyes travelling down to the velvet-wrapped houghs, pierced here and there by pinpoints of light.

Unerringly his gaze found one light shining from the window of King's Croft. He thought of the warmth down there, not just of bricks but of people. Maggie – Evie, so young and blithe and growing so fair and bonny. A sweet yearning gnawed at him then for Evie – for things that tormented him whenever he thought about her clean bright face, her lithe, blossoming body – and the wonderful hair of her – he could almost feel it, running through his fingers, yet he had only touched it briefly in the pretence of play. At school long ago there had been nothing to stop him from doing things like that, it had been innocent then, but growing up had erected certain barriers he had never yet crossed.

Jamie too was down there – an older, wearier Jamie, a man who had so sorely needed a son, yet had never shown by word or deed that his life was not the richer by the birth of Wee Col . . .

Johnny grew still and cold as he stood there looking below to the tiny light that was King's Croft. By the time he crept back to bed his feet and hands were numb – but his thoughts were crystal clear – for he knew now what he had to do – and where he was going . . .

Rob went away to the fields earlier than usual next morning. From the window Johnny watched him go before turning his attention back to the breakfast table. He had made the meal and Jenny had taken a tray upstairs to their mother. That would be the pattern for months now – the fetching, the carrying, the lifting, the laying.

Johnny ate his brose slowly and studied the faces of his young brother and sister. Jimmy's placid, friendly countenance was shining from its recent wash in cold water. He glided through life easily, peacefully, never brilliant at school but never too dim-witted either. Martin Gregory liked him and encouraged him, everyone liked and encouraged Jimmy, even Rob who had never kept him back in anything he wanted to do. Already he was guiding the plough, eager for the day he would leave school and work full time in the fields. His other love was football. Every evening in summer he was off on his bicycle to Lums O Reekie, there to play on the green with the village lads. Occasionally Rob took him to football matches in Aberdeen. Last Christmas he had brought him a coveted pair of football boots, a ball had been promised for his birthday. Jimmy would be alright. He was Jimmy and he would never be put upon.

Jenny was digging into her plate, elbows on the table, hair standing on end because she hadn't bothered to brush it before coming down. There was little in her appearance that was attractive. She hadn't inherited any of her father's fairness or her mother's fine features. She was coarse to look at, with lank dirty-fair hair, muddy skin and rather close-set eyes. She was short and stockily built with big feet and hands that incited her schoolmates to cruel comment. Perhaps because of this she was always on the defensive, ever ready with a smart answer from her abrasive tongue. There was a strangeness in her nature, a dark, moody stubbornness that made it difficult for people to take to her.

She was a child who craved attention and, unable to get it by normal childish wiles, gained it by fair means or foul. Some of the things she did to get her own back on a critical world were disquieting to say the least, and Johnny often looked back to that terrible day of Janet's death, trying to remember how it had been that morning before he left for King's Croft. He knew he had given Janet a lot of attention. At just four she had needed help with so many things, dressing, feeding and so on. Jenny had been sullen and morose, threatening dire happenings on Janet's innocent head because he was going off on his own and refused to allow her to come.

Occasionally he talked that day over with Jenny. At least he had talked while she appeared to only half-listen. But once she had got carried away with enthusiasm whilst describing the big chunks of ice she had thrown into the lochan.

'Of course, Jan got in the way,' she had said with such a depth of bitterness he had searched her face sharply. 'I aye had to look after her when everyone else was away enjoying themselves.'

'I suppose you had to push her a bit to leave the way clear?' he had queried conspiratorially and she had nodded.

'Ay, she wouldna move herself so I shoved her –' Checking herself she had turned on him a face so innocent he knew it was calculated. There had been an almost malevolent expression in her eyes and her lips were twisted as she continued calmly. 'Only a wee shove. I watched her well, Johnny, cross my heart and hope to die.'

252

Johnny never quite got over that careless slip of the tongue and ever after he couldn't be sure if Janet's horrific death had been purely accidental. After all, Jenny had threatened often enough to harm her sister. But at that he shuddered and turned his mind away from such evil. She was only a child. She would never have been capable of such a thing. Even while he tried to convince himself, he knew that a doubt about Jenny would fester away at the back of his conscience till his dying day.

She felt him watching her and she glanced up sharply. 'Did you and Father fight last night, Johnny? I heard you talking in the kitchen and things clattering about. I couldna sleep for ye,' she ended in aggrieved tones.

'We – were discussing things.' Johnny spoke slowly, deciding then and there he would tell them of his intentions, now, while they were asking questions. After all, they were old enough to understand. Jimmy was past fourteen, Jenny twelve. It was high time they had some of the responsibilities he'd had to thole for most of his life.

'Ye canna go!' wailed Jenny when he had finished speaking. 'How will we manage without ye?'

'We'll manage.' Jimmy spoke up, his oddly mature chin thrust out with a touch of aggression. 'You go, Johnny, I'd have went myself a long time ago in your shoes.'

'When are ye going, Johnny?' Jenny looked positively terrified.

Johnny stood up. 'Now – in a wee whilie anyway – after I tell Mother.'

Jimmy put down his spoon and looked steadily at his elder brother. 'Where are ye going, Johnny?'

Johnny gripped his shoulder. 'You'll know soon enough, Jimmy.'

'I want to come wi' ye,' It was an old lament, one Johnny had heard many, many times in the past.

Jenny's voice rose. 'Ye canna leave, ye canna! I'll be left wi' everything and I willna do it – I willna!'

'No you won't, Jenny.' Johnny spoke kindly but firmly. 'You're no the type to allow yourself to be put upon. You need a conscience for that and mine has been my downfall

253

all these years. Anyway, you're a big lass now, it's time you took your share of things.'

Leaving the kitchen he went up quickly to his mother's room before his resolution left him. She heard him out in silence then, as he had expected, the tears came, the trembling of the lips, the piteous pleas. When he seemed immune to those, the bitter accusations began, directed at his conscience, that part of him which she had always manipulated so successfully in the past.

'How could you, Johnny? Knowing how things are with me. Your father told you – he told you, Johnny?'

'Ay, Mother, he told me.' Johnny kept his eyes averted as he felt the old weakness taking hold.

'And still you tell me this. You tell me, Johnny.'

'It's because of it I'm going. I canna give any more of my life to you, Mother. You've had enough as it is, it's time I had it to myself and if you thought anything at all of me you would let me go wi' your blessing.'

Her haunted eyes raked his face. 'Thought anything of you, Johnny! You're my son, the only one I ever wanted or needed. You'll not do this to me, Johnny, you'll not forsake your own mother at such a time.'

He turned on his heel. 'You'll be fine, Mother. It's a daughter you need now. You've got Jenny, and Jimmy's a good lad. He'll be able to do all the things I had to when I was his age.'

'Johnny!' Her voice stayed him, sharp, tinged with dislike. 'Does your father know about this?'

'I told him last night – but no doubt, like you, he willna think I've got the guts to leave. Goodbye, Mother, and take care – I'll be along to see you whenever I can.'

Rushing back to the bed he kissed her briefly on the brow then, shoulders back, he went out of the room to go to his own and retrieve his case.

'Not much,' he thought as he made his way downstairs and out of the house. 'Not much to show for eighteen years of living.'

He took a last look back. It was a fine place. Someday he hoped to have a farm as good as it. His gaze took in the

254

well-kept fields enclosed in their dykes and hedges. Ay, it was a fine place – too bad the people in it couldn't appreciate it better. His father lived there on sufferance, his mother lived there and hardly saw the stark beauty around her she was so taken up with dwelling in the barren plains and dark houghs that were her own life.

A curtain twitched at a window. The faces of Jenny and Jimmy appeared. He waved but only one hand came up. A fine farewell, Johnny lad, he thought calmly, almost blithely.

He strode away down the track, swinging his case high, a happy whistle at his lips. The sun shone, the peesies birled in ecstasy in the spring sky, a breeze sifted through his hair, lifting the fair strands of it. He braced his shoulders, threw out his deep chest and sniffed the air appreciatively.

'A good time for a new beginning,' he thought as he marched down the track with his head high. 'And life has just begun for you, Johnny lad, just begun.'

CHAPTER FOURTEEN

'So you've left home at last, Johnny lad? A pity it had to be under a cloud but I suppose that's how it would have been no matter when you left. Maybe it's the best thing for everybody.' Jamie spoke slowly, trying to sort out his thoughts. He had been drinking heavily of late and it was taking him longer now to get over such bouts. They left his mind dull, his reactions to things and people slower than they had been. 'You're getting old, Jamie,' he told himself grimly. 'Too old for a lot of things.' He looked at Johnny's strong, serious young face. Lucky the man with a son like this: only that Bible-thumping bugger up at Birkiebrae had never appreciated the fact.

'Ay, maybe for the best, lad – but I'm no sure you did the right thing coming here.'

'I'm sure.' Johnny sounded more assured than he felt. Jamie might not want him at King's Croft – neither might Maggie. He hadn't thought of that possibility last night when his brilliant plan had come to him.

'You need another man about the place, Jamie. I'll work hard for my keep, you need never fear otherwise.'

'Ach, I know that fine, son, you have no need to justify yourself to me – the fact is I'm not a rich man. God knows it takes me all my time to pay to keep an orra loon about the place. I wouldna be able to pay you what you're worth. The hiring fares are not that long away. You could find a good place, earn yourself a bittie sillar.'

Johnny looked at King's Croft lying peacefully in its green and fertile hough. 'I've found a good place,' he said steadily. 'And I tell you this – I'll never go back home – not now I've made the break. My bed and board, that's all I ask. Give it six months, Jamie, and if it doesna work out then I'll away somewhere else and no hard feelings.'

Jamie took out his pipe and lit it with a slightly unsteady

hand. 'You'll have to sleep in the chaumer wi' Andy. Even wi' Mary and Grace away there's no spare room for all my lassies aye had to double up. Wee Col took up the only room left and that no more than a cupboard at the top of the stairs,' he explained almost apologetically.

Johnny grinned. 'I aye fancied the chaumer – and I hear tell Andy's a dab hand at roasting poached rabbits in the cinders o' the fire. It will suit me just fine, Jamie.'

Jamie held out his brown, sinewy hand. Johnny took it. 'Welcome to King's Croft, son.' His voice was slightly husky. 'Come down and we'll tell Maggie, then you and me will have a sup o' ale to celebrate.'

Johnny sat back on the bed, the bed he would share with Andy in the chaumer above the stable. Evelyn was putting his things away into a drawer she had cleared at the bottom of the dresser. Her hair was hiding her face, her movements were graceful and unhurried. She had taken the news of his coming quietly and he wondered what she was thinking as she folded his few possessions neatly before tucking them away.

Maggie hadn't said much either. Jessie Blair had been visiting, but later, when Maggie was alone with him in the kitchen, she had folded him to her bosom. 'I'm glad, Johnny, glad.' She had told him and he knew she meant every word of it. She had pushed him away to survey him at arm's length. 'I'm sorry for your mother, she has never been a happy soul. It wasna for her to become first the wife of a fisherman then of a farmer. She's had her heartbreaks but she had you, Johnny, she aye had you. Now she's lost you she'll not get over it so easily. Are you certain you're doing the right thing, lad?'

'I'm certain,' he had answered steadily. 'I know my mother. She seems soft but she's stronger than any of us know. She was strong when she lost Janet – great losses seem to bring out the strength in her. It might seem a strange thing to say but I think my going will bring out something in her that's just waiting to come out. She doesna need me anymore, Maggie – neither she nor my

257

father. Jamie does – and I need him.'

'You're a wise lad for your age, Johnny, there's a lot of wisdom in that young head of yours.'

He had eyed the soda scones Nellie had set to cool just inside the larder. 'And a hungry one, Maggie,' he said with a grin. 'I didna eat much at breakfast time.'

She had chased him then, round the table, and from that moment he felt at home in King's Croft and with its people – except for Evelyn. He wondered what was going on behind that smooth, untroubled brow.

'Evie,' he said softly. 'You – havena said much. Are you glad I've come?'

She turned to face him, but her eyes were faraway. 'Be quiet – I'm thinking.' Extracting a crumpled piece of paper and a stump of pencil from her pocket she sat down on the bed beside him and began to write furiously till eventually, flushed and sparkling-eyed she thrust the paper at him. He read aloud slowly.

'Johnny came today, here to King's Croft.

The sky opened wider, the peesies birled aloft.

My Father, oh my Father, his eyes were strangely bright.

And Mother, she was smiling, because it seemed so right.

Wee Col danced a Highland fling, sitting by the fire.

And Nellie she was singing, on her way out to the byre.

Murn threw down her pile of books to hang the washing out.

Jessie might have done the same except she was too stout.

Old Tat, the dog, and Tib, the cat, for once forgot to fight.

Instead they grabbed each other, and kissed well out of sight.

And Evie – well she disappeared to sit in the Wee Hoose.

So silent in her reverie she might have been a moose.

She couldna quite take in the fact that Johnny had come to stay.

Her heart, it felt like bursting, like a' the buds in May.

At last she sneaket back inside to see that all was weel.
And then she dashed outside again to dance an eightsome reel.
She couldna quite believe it, but it was really true,
Johnny Burns had come to stay to drink all Father's brew.'

Johnny threw himself back on the bed and howled with laughter. 'Was that Nellie singing?' he gasped at last. 'I thought she was moaning to herself! Oh, Evie,' he sat up. 'I'll treasure this for always. It's daft and it's wonderful.' He patted the bed. 'Come here and let me see you properly. I thought about you last night – and all the other nights before that – for as far back as I can remember, and now I'm here and I canna right believe it.'

She came to him, shy suddenly, a slender, small-boned young girl with grace in limbs that only last year had been coltish and awkward. Sitting down at a demure distance from him she folded her hands in her lap and gazed down at them. Rays of dusty sunbeams slanted in through the cobwebby skylight, setting the long bright hair of her on fire. A flush of pink suffused her cheekbones and all at once she wasn't a child anymore but a desirable young creature whose blossoming figure was oddly tender, yet at the same time unbearably appealing.

She was aware of his nearness, of his flushed, warm face, of his boy's hands reaching out to hold her close and stroke her hair – and suddenly they weren't a boy's hands but the strong, sure ones of a young man. The lean edge of his hip was hard against her soft one. His lips brushed her hair and a feeling rose up inside of her that frightened and thrilled her at the same time.

'Evie,' he whispered. 'You're such a bonny lass. You smile and you laugh and you write daft poetry. I love it all – just as I think I've always loved you.'

She faced him, shaking her head vehemently. 'No, Johnny, we're too young yet for that.'

'You might be, I'm not. I love you and I'll never stop thinking it or saying it. I think I've loved you ever since I

259

pulled your hair in the classroom and gave you apples. Remember that, Evie?'

'Ay – it's no all that long ago.' She wanted to hold on to it, that incredible wonder and innocence of childhood – but it was too late. It had slipped away like a ghost in the night and she knew she would never retrieve it again. The thought brought a poignancy to her heart. A tear glimmered on her lashes and tenderly he kissed it away.

'Dinna be sad, Evie. Growing up is pretty wonderful too.'

His lips travelled from her eyes to her cheeks. She felt hot and confused and somehow afraid. 'No, Johnny, no,' she whispered. His mouth came down over hers, cool, gentle, sweet. She lay against him, feeling her heart leaping in her breast, surprised at the rising tide of passion that rushed inside of her and made her forget all her yesterdays in this today, these moments of quiet intimacy in the arms of Johnny Burns. He was holding himself back, she could sense the wanting in his hard, young body, in the trembling of the arms that held her and when he drew away, she knew it had taken a great deal of willpower.

She laid her head on his shoulder, feeling contented and good. 'I'm glad you kissed me,' she confided. 'Up until last year the only man I ever kissed was my father and that was only on the cheek.'

'What do you mean – up until last year? I thought you and Gillan were supposed only to be friends – and if it wasna him then who –?'

'Ach, Johnny,' she pushed him away, laughing. 'Dinna fash yourself. Gillie never touched me in that way.'

He gazed sulkily at her amused face. 'Then who was it?'

'Kenneth Mor if you must know. He grabbed and kissed both Nellie and me the morning after the baby was born. He was that happy and excited he probably kissed Hinney too and maybe the dogs and cats as well.'

Relief washed over his face and he smiled at her. 'That's alright then. It's just – well, you're a mite too young yet to be going around letting men kiss you.'

She hid a smile. 'But no too young to be letting you do it?'

260

'That's different, I wouldna hurt you – others might.'

'You don't own me, you know, Johnny!' she said in a low voice.

He crooked his thumb under her chin and made her face him. 'No, Evie, not yet, but someday I hope you'll be mine. I've waited a long time for you to grow up and I'm not going to let go so easily. I'll fight for you if I have to – with every last breath that's in me.'

She was suddenly afraid of his intensity and breaking away from him she stood up. 'You'll no have to do that, so dinna look so fierce about it. I tell you this though, I'm no going to allow myself to grow up too soon and too quickly. I have a long way to go before I even think of marriage and bairns. I'm going to enjoy myself first and so too should you. You're too young yet to be talking so seriously.'

The tension left him. He smiled and once again he was the mischievous-eyed boy who had pulled her hair in the classroom. 'Ay, Evie,' he nodded. 'You're wise for a bairn of your years.'

She giggled and threw a pair of socks at him just as a head appeared over the chaumer hatch. Andy gaped into the room in some amazement. Quickly Johnny explained what had happened. Andy grinned. He was often lonely up here by himself and it would be good to have some company for a change, especially the company of Johnny Burns who he had always liked.

'I hope you dinna snore – I've enough snortin' and champin' wi' the horses down below.'

Johnny shrugged. 'Jimmy never complained, though mind, he told me I sometimes talk in my sleep.'

Andy chuckled. 'That makes two o' us. We'll have a fine time pourin' our secrets into one another's lugs and never the one able to tell the other what he's sayin'.'

Evelyn climbed down the wooden stairs and stood for a thoughtful few moments in the dim silence of the stables. It was lovely to have Johnny at King's Croft but she wouldn't visit him in the chaumer too often. There was danger now in such a cosy, intimate place and in the depth of emotion she had witnessed in a boy too eager to become a man too soon.

'Ach, Evie, you lucky thing! Fancy you having Johnny all to yourself at King's Croft. I wish he had come here instead.'

Florrie glanced round the cluttered, dusty kitchen of Cragbogie and tossing back her mane of hair laughed at such a ridiculous suggestion. 'We havena room here to even swing a cat – though mind, I could easily have tucked him in beside Maureen and me . . .' Her shoulders shook in a sudden bout of coughing and gasping for breath she lay back in her chair, pale and thin faced from a dose of flu which had brought back the bronchitis with which she had been plagued in the last few years.

Evelyn got up to go to the scullery and came back with a spoon and a brown bottle of cough medicine.

Florrie grimaced. 'I canna take any more o' that cat's piss. It doesna do me any good anyway.'

'Open up,' ordered Evelyn, pouring a good measure. 'Gregor wouldna give you anything that was bad for you. I want you well quickly. It's so bonny outside and Alan's been gey lonely without you. I saw him last night, mooning about by the river, all on his own.'

'Ach, Alan!' Florrie said impatiently. 'I'll be glad when he goes away to art college. He's too serious for my liking. Aye wanting to hold hands and gaze into my eyes when I'd far rather be doing something else – like gazing into Johnny's eyes and letting him hold my hand.'

'Boys are serious, aren't they?' Evelyn tried to divert the talk away from Johnny.

'Ay, at least Alan is anyway. I wouldna mind so much if he was in the least bittie interested in the things I like, but I dinna believe he's been once to the theatre and he doesna like singing or dancing very much either.'

A frown marred the perfection of Florrie's lovely face. She was growing into a real beauty, a willowy grace about her slender figure that was a delight to behold. She had left

262

school at fourteen, the dreams of childhood smothered by the demands made on her by an ever growing army of young O'Neils. There were twelve of them now, the youngest just two months old, and Betsy relied on Florrie's help as she was the only one of her older daughters remaining at home. Florrie seldom complained, but deep in her heart there still lingered a faint hope that one day she might escape the drudgery of her life. In her wildest dreams she saw herself on stage holding sway over an admiring audience. Her uncle still came to take her to the theatre and occasionally she and Evelyn caught the train into the city to sit up in the gods eating home made tablet while they gazed at the stage far below.

Evelyn only went to please Florrie. Her last year at school had been a hectic one. She had worked hard, more to please her father than to satisfy herself. She had passed classics, modern languages, maths and science in the leaving exam and come the winter intended going to night school in Tillietoorie to study English language and literature.

She could speak French with a reasonably good accent and often infuriated Nellie by replying to some curt request in the foreign tongue. 'Too smart for your own good, my girl,' Nellie would throw at her in red-faced chagrin. 'It's high time you had some of the nonsense knocked out of your head.'

Whereupon Evelyn would curtsy and reply in French, then rush from the room with a slipper whistling past her ears.

Much as she enjoyed school she was glad to be leaving in the summer for nothing was as good as the peace and solitude of the hayloft. There she could write and read to her heart's content until Nellie's shouts brought her back to reality and all the chores she had left undone. She studied Florrie in the chair opposite. Her fair beauty was very out of keeping with the squalor of her surroundings. Two of the younger children were crawling about the floor, bare bottoms to the wind, hands and faces smeared with coal dust and jam, a continual, irritating whine coming

263

from the smallest. The breakfast things had not yet been cleared from the table, the remains of the porridge congealed in the pan left lying on the hearth, partially licked and scraped by the abrasive tongues of the numerous cats which stalked in from the yard.

Florrie saw her friend's look. 'I'll never have a big family like my Mam.' She gazed round her with a shudder. 'It doesna bother her – all the mess and the snotty bairns, but it would me if it was my house. I like nice things about me and I'm going to have them, Evie, someday I'm going to have them – aren't you?'

'If I can. I've never thought that much about the future.'

'I have.' Florrie sounded fierce. 'It's all I think about when I'm in bed at night. That's the only time you get peace to think. I'm bonny enough to get a man wi' a good bittie money, somebody rich enough to buy me all the nice clothes I could ever want. As soon as I'm old enough I want to leave the farmtouns. I might never get to act on the stage but at least I'll be able to go to the theatre every night if I want to. The only thing is –' She sounded suddenly bleak. 'There's Johnny – and all he ever wanted was to be a farmer. He'll never even be that if he stays around here – he'll never make any money at – at your place,' she ended apologetically.

'Ach, it's only for a wee while. He has a lot to think about just now.'

'He should have left home long ago,' said Florrie, sighing a little as automatically she bent to pick one of the babies up from the floor. 'I'll no wait till I'm eighteen before I break away.'

She got up, staggering a little on shaky legs. Going to a drawer she came back and pushed a small parcel into Evelyn's lap. 'It's no much,' she explained off-handedly. 'I havena the money for grand presents – but happy birthday when it comes next week in case I don't see you then. I made it myself so dinna look too closely at the stitches. I never paid much attention when old Mrs Somerville tried to din thon fancy needlework into our heads.'

Despite her words of self-criticism Evelyn felt slightly

tearful when she removed the paper and looked at the sampler worked in cross stitch. 'Evelyn and Florrie – Best Friends. 1913 and beyond.' it said simply.

Memories came tumbling back. Carelessly scrawled words written in a field of snow. Far off it seemed now, yet as clear and bright as that day itself for the message of Florrie's words was etched in her heart and would be there always. Putting her arms round her friend's thin shoulders she kissed her on the cheek.

'Thank you, Florrie, I'll hang it above my bed so that I can see it every night and no matter where I go in my life this will go with me.'

Florrie grinned. 'Daft and romantic as always – but it's true – what I've said – even though Johnny might always like you better than me.'

'Havers, he likes us both equally – and what has Johnny to do with it anyway?'

Florrie ignored that. 'It was aye you. I knew it from the start and time hasna changed things.'

Evelyn folded the sampler carefully and put it in the basket she had brought filled with Nellie's baking for the O'Neil table. 'But it's changed other things. There was a time I thought all I wanted was to marry Johnny and have his bairns. Now I'm like you – I want other things out of life first.'

Florrie looked at her friend's glorious mass of tumbled hair, at the fine features and the green eyes so deep and filled with vitality. 'You'll get them all, Evie, if you're careful you'll get them all.'

Evelyn took Florrie's hands and laughed. 'We sound like a couple of old women blethering away like this.' She gazed through the window to the rolling hills on the far horizon. 'You take that medicine, Florrie O'Neil, so that you can be well enough to come wi' Johnny, Alan and me. It would be nice to go to the sea – that would soon clear your lungs.'

'Will Gillan come wi' us do you think? When he comes home from that fancy school he's at?'

'I think he might.'

'Then I'll be coming,' Florrie giggled. 'You never know,

him wi' all that money and me wi' my charms – it might work – stranger things have happened.'

Betsy came in, arms laden with an assortment of baby clothes given to her by a friend she knew in Lums O Reekie. She had no reserve about such matters, her philosophy being, 'Pride never covered a bare erse nor filled a hole in the belly.'

While the children clambered on to her knee she gasped, 'Get me a cuppy, Evie, there's a lass. That Bunty blethered so much my lugs are reeling wi' the din o' her. My throat's that dry it feels it's been rubbed down wi' emery paper.'

Florrie looked at Evelyn and they both laughed.

'Bunty did all the talking and your throat's dry?' nodded Florrie. 'Maybe I should take the teapot over to the Post Office while you give your lugs a rest.'

'Less o' your cheek, my lass,' grinned Betsy. 'Bring three cups through, Evie. You've surely time to spare while I tell you what Bunty was telling me about George the Forge. Would you believe, the dirty auld bugger was caught at the back o' the Smiddy wi' a young lassie – no more than sixteen she was. Himself as innocent as you like wi' his breeks at his ankles, a strop o' liquorice in one hand and God knows what in the other! It was Andra Dalgliesh who caught him, his bum to the four winds and the cheek . . .' Here she roared with laughter. 'The cheek to tell Andra that the lass was only mending his trousers.'

Evelyn squeezed Florrie's hand. 'He aye was an old rogue.' she said demurely and Betsy wondered why the two were suddenly convulsed with complete and abandoned laughter.

CHAPTER FIFTEEN

A few days later Rob came storming down to King's Croft to confront Jamie. 'What the hell do you think you're playing at, Grant!' he roared. 'Keeping my son here when he's got a perfectly good home o' his own.'

'Ach, stop havering, man,' Jamie said forcibly. 'Nobody *keeps* Johnny. He's got a mind of his own and high time too. He's been under your rule for too damned long. I didna ask him here, he came of his own accord but he's more than welcome to bide as long as he likes. We'll no make a fool out of him. He'll be treated like the man he is fast coming to be instead of a skivvy with an apron tied round his belly.'

Rob's fists bunched. 'Watch it, *King* Jamie,' he spat threateningly. 'You're too bloody high and mighty for your own or anybody else's good! No bugger makes fools out of me or mine for despite all your fine words you'll use him as much as anybody – ay, and for as much sillar as I could poke up my erse wi' a feather!'

'Hark to the man of God,' returned Jamie softly. 'Swearing and slavering like any ordinary heathen. It's well you're no in the pulpit now, letting folks hear the real Rob Burns. As for making a fool out of you – I wouldna waste my precious time. You've made such a good job of being your own fool there's not a soul hereabouts could better it.'

Rob's fists went up. 'Shut your bloody mouth! I'll no have a drunken tinkie speaking to me as if I was a bit of cow dung.'

He advanced on Jamie, a bristling, wild-eyed fury with thought for nothing but getting his revenge on the man who had lured his son away from him without any effort.

Jamie threw down the bundle of bedding straw he had been carrying through from the straw shed when Rob put in his appearance.

'I'll not fight with you, Rob, if that's what you're aiming for.'

'Is if feared you are, King Jamie? Going down the hill wi' all that boozing you indulge in?'

Jamie wasn't frightened but he knew he wasn't as fit as he used to be, and certainly no match for the powerful Rob Burns. Nevertheless he managed to say calmly, 'No, it isna that, man, I just wouldna like to hurt you, that's all.'

'*Hurt me*!' roared Rob incredulously. 'What happened that day at the loch was a fluke and bloody fine you know it.'

He froze suddenly as footsteps came over the cobbles. Father and son faced each other, the one red-faced and wild-eyed, the other pale but in control. It was a moment Johnny knew he would have to face sometime but he hadn't expected it now, at the end of the day when ever bone in his body ached with fatigue.

'How are you, Father?' he asked quietly, looking beyond the huge, threatening figure to the dim interior of the stables as if checking to make sure Jamie hadn't been hurt.

'How am I?' Rob's roar made the horses champ uneasily in their stalls. 'How am I? You've the nerve to stand there making polite conversation after what you've done! Made me and your mother the laughing stock o' the whole neighbourhood.'

'You're imagining it, Father. If you think I've done wrong you're the only one who does. Mother must know in her heart the reasons that made me go – just as you do yourself if you've any sense of decency left in you.'

Rob's colour receded leaving his face livid with fury. 'You bloody weakling, I'll pulverise you for that!'

He blundered towards his son, a furious mass of muscle and bone that might once have terrified Johnny. But not now, not when his own anger ran cold and controlled inside of him. He waited till his father was on him and at the last moment, before the great fist could get a chance to crash down, he warded it off with a powerful upward swing of his own. Rob's mad, sweating face was inches from his and pushing his own forward Johnny said steadily, 'Watch it,

Father. I promise you, if you start on me you'll never lift your head in pride again.'

For a long, tense moment the eyes of father and son held. Rob saw a young giant, as broad as himself, as tall if not slightly taller, cool, calm and controlled and infinitely more powerful in all the vigour of his youth.

Rob retreated slowly, every nerve tingling, beaten back not by the power of muscle but a few quiet words of warning. He drew air into his lungs, rasped the back of his hand across his mouth. A wild beast stared momentarily out of his eyes before it was extinguished by raw, bitter defeat.

'On your own head be it,' he gritted through clenched teeth. 'I hope you sleep well in your bed at night with the desertion o' your mother lying black upon your conscience. If anything happens to her I'll blame you, ay indeed,' he ended rather feebly.

For a moment all the lonely pain and grief of the past crowded in on Johnny, bitterness touched his soul with the misery it had endured in the days of his father's rejection of him following Janet's death. Then like a receding tide it left him, leaving him calm and peaceful and free.

'Go home, Father,' he said softly. 'Mother and the bairns need you. Your responsibilities are your own now. Look after Mother well, you owe her that at least.'

With a muttered oath Rob turned on his heel and went off into the night.

Jamie seized a dandy brush from the cornkist, slid his fingers into the splines and began to brush himself down vigorously. He cocked an eye at Johnny. 'Will you go and fetch Andy from the kitchen and we'll sort the horses for the night?'

Johnny squared his shoulders. 'Ay, Jamie, I will – there will be no bother now.'

'No, no,' agreed Jamie thoughtfully and with a smile added, 'We'll have a peaceful summer – a hard-working one as always – but peaceful.'

'Amen to that.' said Johnny and went to the house to oust Andy from the comforts of the kitchen.

Yet despite his feeling of wellbeing, a small part of him was with his mother up there in her lonely bed at Birkiebrae. Despite his father he vowed that he would go and visit her whenever he could. He loved her, no matter what, he still loved her. It wasn't in him to turn his back completely on a woman who had never been strong enough to run her own life.

It was only a miniature corn dolly, yet to Evelyn it was the most precious of all the presents she had received to mark her fifteenth birthday. It lay in her hands, so exquisitely fashioned she could hardly believe it had been made by hands as big and strong as Johnny's. Made of woven straw, hollow in the middle, tied with a blue ribbon above the hanging heads of corn, it was the most difficult of all the corn dollies to fashion and yet it was perfect.

'Who taught you to make such a beautiful thing?' she asked as they sat together in the hayloft, a place that had been her own exclusive retreat for as long as she could remember. It was cheek by jowl with the chaumer, divided from it by a communicating door which made it easy for Johnny to come through in the evening when she gave the special little knock they had concocted between them.

'Hinney showed me a long time ago,' he explained with a shrug of embarrassment. 'I used to make them for wee Janet but she didna appreciate them and usually fed them to the horses.'

'I'll hang it over my bed, where I can see it when I get up in the morning and when I lie down at night.'

'I got you something else.' He dug into his pocket. 'It isna much, someday I'll give you everything – everything I have.'

'Ach, don't talk daft, Johnny, if you did that you would be left with nothing.'

'Oh no I wouldn't.' He touched her hair. It was brushed back and held with a tortoiseshell clasp given to her by Maggie. She was wearing the blue dress Murn had made for Gillan's tea party and she looked so lovely he hadn't been able to stop himself staring at her when she had come downstairs to the parlour where everyone had gathered for the birthday tea. Nellie had baked one of her delicious fruit cakes. Covered with icing and decorated with pink sugar roses it looked as good as any of the confectionery Johnny had seen in the bakers' windows in Aberdeen.

The simple family celebration had been something of a novelty for him. Such things were unheard of at Birkiebrae, but no matter how hard it had been for her, Maggie had always tried to mark her children's birthdays in such a way.

Evelyn drew away from Johnny's hand and, flushing, he thrust a small parcel into her lap. Carefully she unwrapped it while he sat staring at his feet. It was a pair of silk stockings, gossamer fine and must have cost him a pretty penny.

She held them up, ran them through her fingers, stared at the shimmer of them in the last of the evening light filtering through the dirty skylight.

'Johnny –' she began doubtfully.

'Wheesht,' he said urgently, shyly, caught up in such a yearning to hold her he had to force himself to remain a little way apart from her. 'I thought, well I wondered if you would maybe come to a dance with me at Tillietoorie sometime. They have a good band there on a Saturday night. You could wear that dress and put these on and you would look wonderful. I have the good suit I bought last year with money my grandmother sent me from Canada for my birthday.'

'I'll ask Father.' Impulsively she put her arms round him and kissed him briefly on the mouth. His arms came up to hold her but she was already away and the moment was over.

Picking up the corn dolly she said thoughtfully, 'Johnny, would you make one of these for Florrie? She would love it – and I won't feel so bad about showing her mine.'

'Why should you feel bad? It's only a bittie straw.'

'I know, but och – you would have made it for her and she would treasure the thought of that – she loves you – did you know that?'

'No,' he said, surprised.

'You wouldn't, boys are like that. They never see what's under their noses.' For no real reason she felt annoyed with him.

'Don't you mind?' He frowned in the half-darkness.

'No, why should I?'

'Because I love you, that's why.' He pulled her to him and kissed her so fiercely she cried out in pain and tried to struggle free of him. 'Evie, I've something to ask you,' he murmured into her hair. 'Dinna try to break away from me – I won't let you go till you hear me out.'

'Let me go, Johnny. Nellie always looks at me suspiciously when I go into the house after seeing you. I'm supposed to be checking the henhouses and preparing the porridge for morning.'

'Evie, wheest and listen. Would you come away with me when you're a bit older? I mean far away – from Rothiedrum, from Aberdeenshire.'

'How far?'

'Canada. I wrote to my grandmother asking her if I could go out to stay with her when I've saved enough for the fare and she said yes. There's good opportunities there. If I worked hard I would have my own farm a lot sooner than I ever could here.'

'Everyone wants to leave – first Florrie and now you.' She sounded bleak and he held her gently and stroked her hair.

'I never wanted to leave,' he explained, 'but things have happened here. Now I must make a move if I want to get on – it's for you, Evie. I want to give you a good life.'

'I've got a good life. I never want to leave King's Croft.'

'You'll have to sometime.'

'Ay, but not now. Dinna ask me anything else, I've got too much here to ever think of leaving.'

'You mean you've got Gillan!' he said too harshly, and he knew it.

She stiffened and pushed him away. 'You're older than me, Johnny and yet you talk like a baby. It's not Gillie though I like him and will no say otherwise just to please

272

you, so just you leave me alone and dinna dare ask me about leaving again.'

'I'll ask you next year,' he said stubbornly. 'And the next and the next after that till you say yes.'

'I'll never say yes.'

'Never is a long time, and I'm prepared to wait.'

She got up. 'Goodnight, Johnny.' She marched to the stairs and put one foot on the top step.

'Evie.'

'Ay, what is it?'

'If you won't come to Canada with me will you at least come to a dance with me at Tillietoorie?'

She smothered a giggle. 'I'll think about it – and thanks for the bonny stockings.'

In the darkness he smiled. Rising he made his way through to the chaumer where Andy was already in bed, and snoring fit to blow the roof off.

CHAPTER SIXTEEN

Evelyn would never forget that long, golden, carefree summer – nor would she ever forget Johnny – Johnny so tall and fair and handsome in his nineteenth year, his blue eyes lighting with his love for her every time he looked at her petite body, tanned to a deep smooth brown. Sometimes when he ran his fingers through her hair an odd little shiver went through her and she would think back to other times when he had touched her hair. She had shivered then too but it had been different from now – now that they were grown and spent so much of their time together. Once he stood in front of her, hands at his back, laughing as he produced a rosy red apple. She had laughed too but in the laughter there were tears – tears for things past – for those yet to come.

Everyone seemed happier, more blithe that summer of Johnny's coming to King's Croft. Maggie and Nellie found themselves less burdened by the heavier tasks around the croft. Pails of water would appear on the slats in the wash-house. Without being asked, Johnny worked the churn for butter and cheese making, the fuel shed was never empty, a dozen smaller tasks were undertaken without question.

To have him about the place was an oddly comforting experience. He didn't talk a lot but went about his business, steadily, purposefully, a happy whistle never far from his lips.

Wee Col grew to love the tall fair young man who swung him up, carried him on his back and sat him on the horses. The little boy took his first real steps under Johnny's patient urging. He had a knack of tempering firmness with kindness and had only been at the croft a month when Wee Col was toddling gleefully all over the house, delighted as a baby in his new discoveries. Callum was overwhelmed when he first saw his friend walking unsteadily towards him then he let out a great whoop of joy and running forward embraced the little boy and told him, 'You'll be able to come out wi' me now, Col. We'll have a grand time together.'

As for Jamie, a change came over him that reminded Maggie of the vital young man she had married. His drinking bouts grew fewer then finally ceased altogether; his face filled out; the dark eyes she loved were filled with a new enthusiasm for living; his step was full of spring as every morning he strode out with Johnny to the fields.

Johnny took Evelyn to dances in Tillietoorie and Aberdeen. They rode the country lanes together as far as Stonehaven, but more often to their favourite haunts over by the cliffs at Culter. They walked hand in hand by the sparkling sea, talking or just being silent. Evelyn found a wonderful peace in the beautiful silences she and Johnny shared. They could sit for an hour or more, their bare feet in the sea, listening to the shingle rattling, the sea singing, hearing the great pulsebeat of life in the universe, the cries of gulls winging on sunbeams, their lone, plaintive voices so like those of a lost baby's cries.

Love for Johnny came to her gradually. It stole up on her like a gentle ghost and enwrapped her in a still, sweet wonder that made her seek times of solitude so that she could be alone with this strangely moving revelation that made her want to cry and laugh at the same time. Her diaries became filled with pensive thoughts that often made little sense because they crowded in on her so rapidly she could never put anything down in its proper order.

It was a quiet love that she felt for him. Not the mad, unsettling passion she had imagined love would be. There was a purity about it that was profoundly moving and appealed to her romantic, idealistic young soul. 'His hands touched mine,' she wrote. 'I look at them and see the strength in them and yet he touches me as if I might shatter before his eyes. His lips are warm and gentle on mine and yet the power and the passion that is in him reaches out to me. I am sometimes afraid he will sense my longing for hardness and passion and will stop seeing me as the tender, innocent girl he has imagined all these years. Often I have to get away from him to be myself again, to be as I was before Johnny came to King's Croft. I go up to the little pine woods above the house and look down on the moving figures far below – and I see him there, walking, his head in the sun, fair and bonny, and so tall I fancy he can reach up with one hand and pluck me down from my hiding place.'

That magical summer moved on, bringing its share of work and play. Each cool gloaming she and Johnny went on tranquil walks by the green-shaded Birkie, her hand in his, her head on his broad shoulder.

Sometimes Florrie and Alan came with them and they would all walk the summer lanes together, talking and laughing, throwing stones into the water from humpy bridges, lying on cool banks to gaze aloft through dappled canopies to quiet evening skies.

Florrie was very happy that summer. She had recently gone into service at a nearby mansion house and had confided to Evelyn. 'The dandy dowps are no so bad really. They treat me quite well and at least it has got me out the house. I couldna have borne to stay there much longer wi' squealing bairns about my knees and Mam lying back letting me bring them up. She didna want me to go at first but now she's glad o' the extra sillar and gives me the odd bob or two to spend on myself.'

Evelyn had looked thoughtful. 'I'll have to get a job now that I've left school. I didna fancy working to the gentry though, even as a child I used to think that.'

Florrie had looked at her quizzically. 'Ay, but you're no a bairn any longer, Evie and you canna live on dreams forever. You've always been cleverer than me wi' your books and your writing but in the end it's what keeps body and soul together that counts.'

'Working to the gentry wouldn't keep my soul together. I'd look outside and want to be running through the fields with my face to the sun.'

'Maybe, but the sillar might keep your breeks together

276

for without it you'd be running through the fields wi' a bare arse and a red face to match.'

They had laughed then, loudly and rudely, but Evelyn couldn't help thinking of the new wisdom in Florrie's thinking, of how, altogether she seemed to have changed. She had remained too thin after her last bout of bronchitis but she had never been lovelier, a tall, graceful beauty with life springing hectic in her blue eyes, roses staining her fair cheeks, her golden mane tumbled about her fragile shoulders.

Alan adored her openly, showered her with affection and a succession of small gifts. The dream of his life had been to go on to art college on leaving school. His proud parents had worked towards this end ever since learning how talented he was. They had scrimped and saved every penny towards his further education, often going without in order that their son might have his chance. When he won a bursary to college Kirsty had drawn herself up to her full, scrawny height and declared grandly to her husband, 'Of course, it was only what I expected o' him. Our laddie will have his chance and all our efforts will no go to waste. I will never stand in the light o' a laddie like our Alan.'

But in the light of his love for Florrie, Alan's enthusiasms for his future had deserted him of late. 'No matter how long it takes I'll wait for you to love me back,' he told her once and she had laughed, her white teeth flashing between her pale lips. 'There isna that much time left in the world – my world, Alan.'

Evelyn had puzzled over Florrie's words. How strange a thing from the lips of a young girl. With coldness gripping her heart she had asked Florrie what she meant.

'Ach, Evie, you know me,' Florrie had laughed. 'I never want Alan to get serious about me. He blethers on in that daft way o' his but he forgets he'll be going away to art college soon. He'll be too busy to have time to think o' me.'

The coming of the Cattle Show for a time cast all romantic notions from young minds. It was a colourful event and in the week leading up to it the evenings of all the farm folk

277

were taken up in preparation. Kenneth Mor always entered, horses, cattle and sheep, and Tandy arrived in time to give him a hand. Jamie sometimes entered one of his cows but this year he decided against it. With Coulter, the Loon, and half of King's Croft, he took himself up to Knobblieknowe to assist Kenneth Mor in giving his animals an extensive beauty treatment.

'Are you not going?' Murn asked Nellie. 'You dinna go up to Knobblieknowe as much as you used to.'

'I have quite enough to do here,' Nellie answered off-handedly, every fibre in her longing to run up there to Knobblieknowe just to be near its master. 'And I dinna ken why you're so keen to help with things you never bothered about in your own place.' Her face softened and she put her hand on Murn's shoulder. 'You go along up. I would be going myself but I have a lot to do here. The Cattle Show is the one time I actually get paid for my baking and it will not get done just thinking about it.'

Knobblieknowe was alive with people that week before the show. The horses were groomed till the electricity came out of their hair. Feet and fetlocks were washed, combed and brushed till they were as soft and tempting to touch as a young girl's tresses. Harness and halters were cleaned and polished till you could see your face in them.

The sheep were washed in a deep pool and it took strong men like Tandy and Kenneth to manhandle the stubborn Border Leicesters and throw them in the water. They went wild at being subjected to such indignities and once out of the water everyone had to run to catch them and bring them back for their fleeces to be washed with soap and water. Thrashing and kicking they were thrown in the pool again and ducked down with long poles till all the soap was rinsed from their fleece.

The next day, after the yellow dip treatment, the shears were brought out to clip them into a shape that would appeal to the judges' eye. On the morning of the show everyone appeared in their best clothes. In every croft, cottage and bothy, the scrubber and the dandy brush had been busy. The men stepped out from their doors, the

278

ploughmen in tight trousers, white collarless shirts fixed in place with brass studs, shapeless cloth jackets and new caps set at jaunty angles on close-cropped hair, the women in their Prussian-collared long dark dresses, the skirts of which were well puffed out with two petticoats, the outer one fully pleated and made from wincey. Some wore mutch caps tied under the chin with ribbons, the younger ones saucy little straw boaters bedecked with flowers or ribbons.

Maggie tutted and fussed over Jamie in his dark green tweed suit, wielding the dandy brush so heartily he was moved to protest though he was well pleased with his reflection in the mirror and paused for a moment to wet his fingers and apply them to the little quiff at the front of his hair. Maggie came up at his back, the dandy brush poised ready and he cried in mock sternness, 'Will you take that brush off me, woman or I'll use it to skelp your erse.'

Nellie turned a scandalised face on him. 'Father!' she intoned primly. 'We all know you're excited but there's no need to let your tongue run away with you.'

But her words had an empty ring to them. Nellie loved the Cattle Show as much as anyone and was so restless to get going she almost forgot to put on her hat. Attractive she looked too, with a flush on her face and a dark green, high necked blouse bringing out the amber in her eyes.

'Do I look alright?' Maggie whirled round in the centre of the kitchen, plumper in her later years but still trim and eye-catching enough for Jamie to grab her round the waist and waltz her round the room. Mary and Gregor were gathered there, their two-month-old son decked out in a frilly cotton bonnet that shaded his rosy face, the little decorative holes on the frill filtering tiny spots of sunlight onto his cheeks and chin.

Murn came flying downstairs, eyes sparkling, skirts swirling as she rushed off to meet the young man who was taking her to the show, her hopes high that at the dance later Kenneth Mor might have consumed enough whisky to forget he was a married man and spend some of his time with her.

'We're all here,' Maggie plucked a washed and shining

Col from the inglenook and looked round at her family gathered there in King's Croft's kitchen. 'All except Grace – it's strange – she's such a quiet lass yet when she isn't here I miss her. She fills the house somehow with her peacefulness.'

'She'll be here soon enough, Mam,' Mary consoled. 'She's happy doing what she's doing. Although she loved the crofting life it wasna for her.'

Standing together by the door, Johnny and Evelyn looked at each other. He was wearing his good suit and looked slightly uncomfortable but she squeezed his hand reassuringly and whispered, 'You look – fine, Johnny Burns.'

He looked into her face, sun-kissed and rose-flushed, her nose sprinkled with tiny freckles, her eyes the sparkling green of the sea over by Culter. 'And you're beautiful.' he said simply. She blushed deeper and disentangling her hand ran outside to the cart.

Nellie came struggling out with her baskets full of baking, the others at her back with various things they hoped to sell at the show. They divided themselves between Jamie's cart and Gregor's phaeton. Wheels rattled over the cobbles, churned up the dust on the track. The turnpike was alive with herds, teams, and flocks, here and there a lone crofter driving a single cow or a best mare.

On the way they met the O'Neils, and Florrie made her father stop the cart so that she could jump out and squeeze in beside Evelyn. Dippiedoon and The Mains were entering a good number of beasts in the show and they all met and passed, met and passed along the way, Alan gesticulating at Florrie, Kirsty nudging him and telling him to behave like a gentleman in public.

Johnny hadn't seen his father since that last confrontation but as they reached Tillietoorie he saw him ahead, riding his best mare, his cattlemen and ploughmen following along with their herds and teams. Jimmy and Jenny were in the thick of the melee but Jimmy turned and spotted his brother and his face lit up. He had been a regular visitor at King's Croft, bringing Johnny the news that their mother was well and actually looking forward to the baby coming. Jenny had never once appeared and now she threw Johnny a belligerent look which couldn't quite disguise the hurt in her sad, plain little face.

'See you there!' Jimmy yelled. Rob turned then, his eyes boring directly into Johnny's though he was some distance away. There was no forgiveness in his glance. Johnny might have been some stranger who shared no ties with him or his.

'All these years,' Johnny murmured. 'And he looks at me as if I had never existed.'

'He'll get over it.' Evelyn put her hand on his arm. 'He knows he's wrong and if he's the big man he likes to make out, he'll get over it.'

Gregor came clattering alongside in the phaeton, Maggie, Jamie, Nellie and Col all waved and shouted and the moment was over for Johnny. He forgot his father in the task of guiding Fyvie through the seething streets of Tillietoorie. Flocks and herds were pouring into the narrow lane leading to the showyard. The animals were confused and excited and crowded past in a baaing, slavering, bellowing mass. Town dogs barked, children shouted, dung flew free and wild while drovers and stewards went frantic trying to guide and regulate the flow of traffic.

The judging ground was in a field made blessedly cool by river breezes. The animals were in pens all round it, the middle roped off into several rings for judging the various breeds of livestock.

The folk of Rothiedrum mingled with the crowds, The Loon in his element playing with the children and dodging his mother who stomped around looking for him, puffing her clay pipe and hurling vitriol at anyone who got in her way.

Carnallachie had the audacity to enter Trudge in the horse judging and when his turn came he stalked round, pulling the animal along, making him stop at regular intervals to show his points. Of course the inevitable happened. Trudge stopped dead in the middle of the ring and refused to move. Nothing would persuade him to budge, no amount of cajoling, threatening or abuse.

'Try the Horseman's Word,' someone dared to suggest in a breathy snigger.

'Get that bloody cuddy out,' mouthed a stern-faced steward, full of his own importance and very conscious of the silver cardboard badge pinned to his lapel.

Carnallachie's face turned purple, oaths flowed from his twisted lips into Trudge's calmly flicking ears while from all quarters the spectators laughed, jeered and made rude suggestions.

'Serves the bugger right,' wheezed Coulter, hugging himself with delight, relations between him and Carnallachie being somewhat strained since the latter's suggestion that Coulter spent so much of his time talking about fairies he was beginning to act like one. 'The damned cuddy's ready for the knacker's yard and he puts it in the ring like it was star quality.'

In the end Trudge lifted his tail, sprayed the shoes of the steward with a stream of molten dung, and with a nonchalant flick of his ears walked calmly out of the ring to thunderous applause and cheers.

Despite Carnallachie, Rothiedrum came off well in the final judging, Kenneth Mor winning red and silver tickets for his two pairs, The Mains and Cragbogie gaining similar honours.

Johnny, Evelyn, Florrie, on a day's holiday from the nearby estate where she was now in service, and Alan strolled round together, arm in arm, into the refreshment tents and along by the river banks. Men got drunk while wives cringed in shame, old friends met and young people renewed pledges of love.

Towards the end of the day, when the sun blazed red between the trees and the breezes carried the scent of crushed grasses far and wide, the band played eightsome reels and waltzes. Evelyn danced in Johnny's arms, the echoes of the day good and lasting and etched in her heart for all time. All around her homely country faces came and went, those of her own family in amongst them till, tired out, they set off for home.

And still she and Johnny danced, to a rhythm that came from within and was all their own, the rhythm of heartbeats meeting and mingling and sweet, quiet whisperings that fell like music into ears that tingled and ached for more, yet longed for the stillness of solitude so that each could think back and remember with yearning all that had been said and left unsaid.

And then the night and the music was over and all of them strangely quiet on the journey home through roads still and empty, but alive with a million hopes and dreams and heavy with the nectar of wild honeysuckle and shy dog roses.

Johnny was warm and comforting beside her. Florrie and Alan talking quietly in the pile of hay at the back of the cart.

'It was a good day.' Florrie's voice rose out of the darkness, quiet and thoughtful, unlike the Florrie of the bygone days who sang and laughed on the road home from marts and fairs and cattle shows.

Alan laughed. 'Carnallachie didna think so.'

'Everything was good,' Florrie spoke as if to herself. 'There will never be another like it.'

'There's always next year.' Johnny's deep voice rose above the clatter of Fyvie's hooves on the road.

Florrie didn't say anything and something cold and empty stabbed the warmth in Evelyn's heart. Johnny's hand curled into hers, strong and firm. She held on to it and didn't let go till they came to Dippiedoon and watched Alan walking away up the track to home. Then Evelyn climbed into the back of the cart to put her arms round Florrie and hold her close, not letting go till the pinpoints of light from Cragbogie's window appeared and Florrie reluctantly untangled herself from her friend's embrace and whispered, 'Come and see me soon, Evie.'

'Ay, soon,' promised Evelyn, unwillingly letting go of Florrie's thin hand.

Towards the end of August Catherine gave birth to a son. When Johnny heard the news he went to see her, surprised to find her up and seated in the cool parlour with the blond, blue eyed baby to her breast. She greeted Johnny with pleasure and he was amazed at the change in her. Her face had grown fuller, with a new, soft colour in it that made her instantly attractive and combined agreeably with the brightness in her eyes.

He had been right about her after all, the strength that had lain latent in her was at last coming to the fore and the knowledge of that took away some of the guilt he'd felt since leaving home.

'Sit you down, Johnny lad,' she said rather dryly. 'You're such a big giant of a loon I get a crick in my neck looking up at you.' She studied his face. 'You look well. Are you happy?'

'Ay, Mother, very – are you?'

She looked down at the baby nestling in her arms. 'When you left I thought I could never be happy again. I will not deny that things were hard and at times I almost hated you for what you did.' She looked directly into his eyes, shame on her face. 'Imagine that, a mother hating a fine lad like you. I think in a way it was because I was afraid, afraid of being left to cope on my own for the first time in my life. But I need not have worried. I have good neighbours, I never knew how good till then – and they way they spoke about you, Johnny, never a bad word, just what a fine son you were to me all these years and how it was time you had a life of your own.

'And Jenny was a rare wee help about the place – strange that – I – well to be truthful, of all my bairns she was the one I never took to very well. But I discovered she was a lonely soul, as much afraid of being left unloved as I was myself. That's why she took your going so badly, Johnny, she aye needed you in her life, like me she needed you but now she's had to cope with things she's a changed bairn and seems happier than she's ever been, so in some ways your going has done us all a power of good.'

'Father will never forgive me,' he said with a touch of bitterness. 'He blamed me for all the nasty things that happened here and he hates me for leaving the way I did.'

'Your father has changed too,' she said softly. 'He's grown quieter – more thoughtful this past while and he's not going around preaching as much as he did – thank the Lord,' she said fervently. She looked at him and said hesitantly. 'He had not spoken of you since you left – until the birth of his son and then he said, "I wish Johnny was here to see his new brother but I don't suppose he'll ever come back here again – not after the way I treated him."'

'Is he glad about the baby?'

'Ay, at first he didn't want it but in time it became important to him that nothing happened to make me lose it. It's given him a new lease of life.'

Jenny came into the room, an unusual hesitancy in her manner at the sight of her big brother seated by the window.

'Johnny,' she spoke his name uncertainly then, as he held out his arms, her plain, aggressive little face lit up and she threw herself at him. 'Are you coming home, Johnny? I've missed you and I promise I'll be better and take my share of the work.'

'No, Jenny,' he said gently. 'I'm not needed here anymore but I am at King's Croft. Jamie wasn't as lucky as our father with his sons and I'm going to stay and help him for a whilie.'

'Will you come and see us then?'

Having extracted that promise she surveyed him slyly. 'Are you in love with Evie Grant? Everybody says you are.'

He laughed and stood up. 'Still a nosy wee whittrock! You come down to King's Croft and find that out for yourself. Evie will not eat you.'

Jenny made a face. 'She never liked me.'

'Only because of your cheek. You've changed a bittie though; she might like you better now.'

'I'll come and see her then,' she said solemnly as he went to the door.

'You come back now, Johnny lad,' Catherine told him quietly. 'As often as you can.'

'Ay, Mother, I will.'

He went outside and stood undecided for a moment then bracing his shoulders he walked quickly to the fields. Jimmy saw him first, then Rob who straightened up slowly to shade his eyes and stare. Jimmy came running over, his manly face shining. 'I knew ye would come when ye heard about the baby.' He gripped Johnny's arm. 'I'll away and leave you two in peace – and dinna forget to come back now you've made the break.'

Johnny walked steadily over to his father. They stood for a long time looking at one another, two tall men with hair the colour of ripe corn and eyes as blue as the August sky above.

'I'm glad you've come,' Rob spoke haltingly, uttering the words of peace with difficulty. 'Your mother will be happy now.'

'And you, Father?'

Rob took a deep breath. 'Ay, me too, it's no a good thing for families to break up wi' bitterness in their hearts.'

'I never felt that – only anger that you never gave me my place in your life.'

'Ay, it was wrong of me and –' Rob drew another deep breath – 'I'm sorry for it.' He looked at his son standing quiet and still against the sun. 'Can you ever understand, Johnny – about your mother and me?'

'How can I? Neither of you ever confided in me and that's how it should be between husband and wife. I only know some of it – the bits I saw and heard, the rest is just guesswork.'

Rob's eyes glittered strangely. 'You'll know someday, lad how a woman can drive a man to do things he doesna want to do.'

'Maybe – but I'll know what I'm doing and what I'm feeling while I'm doing it. You knew, Father, and you never did anything you weren't keen on doing.'

'I took on Birkiebrae – for *her* sake – your mother's. That was something that went against the very grain of me, lad. I didna want that. God knows my life was the sea, not the land.'

'Then you did it for love. That canna be wrong, Father.'

Eyes of father and son met, both of them remembering the years of misunderstanding that marched back into the dim, half forgotten past.

'Never lose yourself for the love of a woman, Johnny.' Rob's advice was terse, tinged with all the regret that had embittered his own life.

'I would lose myself without it, Father,' Johnny said simply. Taking his father's hand he gripped it strongly before turning and walking away, his heart light as he strode down the brae to King's Croft – and Evelyn.

CHAPTER SEVENTEEN

The halo of light from the lamp on the dresser cast dark shadows over the room, its feeble glow filtering over the bed in which Florrie lay under an untidy jumble of patchworks. She had returned only yesterday from the house where she was in service, sent home by her concerned employers. She was thin and hollow-eyed, racked with coughing, purple smudges under eyes which were over-bright with fever. Gently Evelyn brushed her hair, running the long tresses of it through her fingers and arranging them so that they fell thick and golden about her friend's thin shoulders and down over her breasts.

One hand came out to catch Evelyn by the wrist, a hand that was without flesh, the long, pale fingers bony and fragile. 'Evie,' she gasped urgently, 'Do you think I look any better?'

Evelyn heard the fear in the young, trembling voice and she drew in her breath, the pain in her heart swelling and bursting. 'Ay, Florrie,' she lied painfully. 'Better than the last time I came. Just you lie quiet and get better. You're as well cooried in there anyway. It's so cold outside I doubt we'll get snow soon.'

The November wind keened at the windows, rattled the loose sashes, added to the sense of desolation that lay bleak and stark in Evelyn's breast.

'I dinna feel any better.' A touch of the old Florrie sparkled in her eyes. 'But I'll take your word for it. You never lied as good as me but you're doing no bad this time –'

She reached a shaking hand to the bed rail above her head. 'Get it down for me, Evie. I want to look at it.'

Evelyn unhooked the exquisite little corn dolly and placed it in Florrie's hands.

'Johnny made it for me,' Florrie gazed at the straw

288

ornament. 'I think it's the loveliest present anyone ever gave me. Fancy Johnny being able to make a bonny thing like that. Hinney taught him –' Her eyes sought Evelyn's.

'Remember, Evie, how feared we were of her when we were bairns? Now she comes up here and bathes me and strokes my brow wi' hands so gentle and all the while she talks to me in such a soothing voice I often fall asleep in the middle of it. I still think she's a witch, but a nice one – she has a way of bewitching people wi' her voice.'

Evelyn nodded, not saying anything, remembering, remembering Florrie of the golden days of summers past, filled with entrancing life that shone from her sparkling face and lit her eyes with mischief . . .

'How is Johnny?' Florrie's sudden switch of mood made Evelyn start and say quickly, 'Oh, he's fine. He and Father get on so well and even Nellie likes him.'

'Who in their right mind wouldna?' Florrie spoke dreamily, her gaze fixed on the corn dolly nestling in her hands. 'Are you going to Canada wi' him, Evie?'

'Did he tell you that?' For a moment Evelyn was angry at Johnny. He had known of Florrie's feelings for him and yet he had obviously confided his dearest hopes to her. But the anger left her. She saw in a flash that he hadn't deliberately set out to hurt Florrie, but had trusted a dear childhood friend with the things closest to his heart.

'I'm no ready to go anywhere yet, Florrie,' she said quietly. 'I'm too young to know my own mind and so too is Johnny.'

'I know mine.' Florrie took Evelyn's hand and held on to it. 'Where Johnny's concerned I've always known – I love him too, Evie, but I'm glad for his sake he never loved me – I wouldna have been much good to him like this – would I?'

'Has Alan been to see you?' Evelyn changed the subject, a feeling in her of such inadequacy she wanted to flee the room. Florrie had said such strange things of late and now she was saying them again – an odd, quiet acceptance in her that was frightening.

A spasm of coughing shook her and when she drew her

hanky away from her mouth Evelyn was horrified to see that it was flecked with blood.

'Dinna look so shocked, Evie,' Florrie said weakly. 'I'm used to it by now – thought when it first started I was as frightened as you. Ay, Alan has been to see me and that awful mother of his came wi' him, fussing and skirling in my lugs till poor Alan told her to be quiet and she stomped out o' the room in a fair tissy.' She moved her head restlessly on the pillow. 'Alan's a nice lad, I wish I had been kinder to him. He was aye that good to me, giving me presents and drawing things to make me laugh.'

'He always loved you, Florrie.' Evelyn recovered herself with an effort. Florrie's hand was so thin in hers, so burning hot. Florrie pulled it away and drew it over her brow.

'I know. It's funny, isn't it, him loving me, Johnny loving you – and you, Evie, never knowing if it was him or Gillie you cared for.'

'I never thought of Gillie in that way.'

Florrie smiled. 'Ay you did – and you still do. There was a time I thought of him in that way too but –' she giggled, 'only for his money. I thought of all the nice things he could give me and the places I could go. It's nice to dream of things you know you can never have.'

Evelyn picked up the brush again and resumed her attentions to Florrie's hair. The room grew silent, outside a dog barked, the wind whined through the trees, soughed mournfully in the lum, making the feeble flames in the grate cringe against the onslaught.

Florrie's lids came down. 'I want to sleep now, Evie,' she whispered. Evelyn fastened the neck button of the voluminous rough cotton nightdress that made Florrie look thinner, more fragile than ever. Tucking the covers round her she got up and crept to the door.

'You would make a fine nurse, Evelyn Grant. Just too bad your head is filled wi' all that palaver and nonsense about writing and love.' It was Kirsty's high, insistent pipe that filled the room. Evelyn stopped in her tracks and looked back at the bed. A smile hovered at the corners of Florrie's pale mouth.

'I havena lost my touch, Evie,' she said without opening her eyes. 'Kirsty and Jessie – they were aye my favourites – Jessie wi' her fleerin' skirts and wobbling chins – Kirsty wi' her sharp nose and fixed smile – ay, perfect they were for the likes of me – to imitate.'

She was asleep, an uneasy sleep in which she seemed not to be able to draw enough breath into her lungs.

Evelyn shut the door softly and went downstairs. The family were gathered round the fire, an assortment of bodies, Betsy and Danny in the midst, Danny's slippered feet on the hearth, Betsy's bare, mottled legs spread with uncaring immodesty to the blaze.

'Would ye like a cuppy, Evie, the kettle's on the boil?' Betsy turned a friendly face, hospitality oozed from every benign pore.

'I'll be havin' a cup while you're at it,' grunted Danny, sucking at his pipe, removing it at regular intervals to hurl his spit into the fire. Evelyn opened her mouth to ask what they thought about their daughter lying so desperately ill upstairs. But she thought better of it. Betsy would just start to cry again, Danny would grow red faced and stare into the fire wordlessly because illness was something he had never understood. It made him uncomfortable to talk about it.

'No, thank you, Mrs O'Neil,' Evelyn went to the door. 'I'd best get along home before it gets too dark – look after Florrie – she's – she needs a good bit of attention just now.'

'Dinna you worry your wee head,' Betsy's voice followed Evelyn outside. 'I'll see she takes the medicine the doctor left. She's a stubborn wee whittrock – ill or no – but I'm firm wi' her, Evie, that I am.'

Her easygoing laugh instantly belied her words. Evelyn shook her head helplessly and pulled her shawl closer as the wind screeched over the hill.

At the gate she turned and looked back. The feeble light from Florrie's room flickered, seemed to go out, flickered again. With a shudder she pulled the gate to and walked away down the track to the turnpike as fast as her shaking legs would take her.

291

A week later, on a night of bright stars and snow capped hills, Florrie died peacefully in her sleep without ever leaving her bed again.

'How am I going to tell Evie?' Gregor, white-faced and weary after a night spent at the bedside of the dying girl, appealed to Mary. 'She and Florrie were inseparable.'

Mary put her arms round him and held him close. 'We'll tell her together, in the morning – after you've snatched a few hours sleep. There, there, my dearest Greg,' She stroked his dark head gently. 'I know how you feel, how you hate losing a patient – especially one so young as Florrie.'

'If only I could have done more,' His voice was low with the pain he had felt ever since Florrie's thin little hand had let go of his for the last time. 'She was too far gone – and too weak to fight. This is when I hate my profession, Mary. That poor beautiful wee lass, she just slipped away without any fuss or struggle – yet when first I knew her she was so bonny and so filled with life it was all she could do to contain it inside herself.'

'Bed.' Mary bent and took off his boots. 'Once you've had a good sleep you'll be better able to face my dear wee Evie.'

Evelyn stared at Gregor as gently he broke the news to her.

'I knew she was very ill – but I never thought she would die.' She spoke the words like a protest, every fibre in her resisting the truth.

'She's been ill for a long time, Evie,' Gregor pulled her down on the inglenook and put his arms about her. 'She had tuberculosis – by the time I discovered it she was too far gone. Pneumonia set in a few days ago and she was too weak to fight it.'

'But her family! They must have known how ill she was.'

He shrugged. 'You know Betsy; a good, kind soul but easy going to the point of carelessness, and Danny with all those bairns to clothe and feed. He couldn't have afforded the proper medical treatment even if he had known how ill his daughter was. Perhaps that was why Florrie didn't say anything – yet I don't know if she had any idea herself just how bad she was. She was a dreamer, her head in the clouds, dreaming about the stage and living in fairy stories.'

'She knew,' Evelyn's voice was flat and dull. 'She was – strange for a long time – she said things that just weren't Florrie.'

A numbness was coming over her, a sensation of withdrawal from everything that was real in her life. She wanted to be alone, to get away from her mother's sympathetic glances, her father's anxious eyes, Nellie's awkward condolences.

Gregor and Mary seemed to stay for a long time, drinking tea, talking, trying to be sober but unable to smother their laughter at the antics of their little son who was already crawling about getting coal dust on his face. It was right that they should laugh yet they were all trying too hard to be discreet, talking in hushed voices because it was the right and proper thing to do when death intervened in day to day living. She sat silent and lost, her hands folded in her lap, only half-listening to the murmur of their voices. They didn't know, they couldn't know what it was like to lose a best friend who was young and vibrant, who had ran and laughed and whispered secrets to her – and who had died at just sixteen years and two months old.

Bleakness engulfed her, raw, stark emptiness swallowed her up until she felt she wasn't there in the kitchen at King's Croft but somewhere far away where a great void of darkness stretched away into nothingness. Eventually she could bear it no longer. She stood up. 'Mam – can I go now – please?'

They all looked at her then, really looked at her instead of pretending that everything was normal and that she was there with them as the Evelyn they knew and felt at ease with. The love in their faces reached out to her yet couldn't touch the sore, hurt spirit that lay buried in the shell that was the living part of her.

Maggie touched her shoulder gently. 'Ay, lass, away you go – we know how you feel – we've all been through it. It's the first time for you, Evie – and my heart aches for you in your loneliness.'

She fled outside, feeling not the wind or the stinging hail that slashed her with its cruel bite, her steps taking her to that haven of comfort and solitude that had been hers since she was a tiny girl.

It was quiet in the hayloft, the kind of timeless quiet that dreamed the days and nights away and never stirred in its slumber. She fell on to the hay, curling herself up like a small animal who has crept away to lick its wounds in peace. For a long time she lay there, hearing Florrie's voice inside her head, her thoughts taking her back to the past and all the times of childish joy they had shared. It was gone now, all gone, those days she had thought would last forever . . .

Cold seeped into her, she grew stiff and sore, but still she lay curled into a ball and felt she would never move from this place, never face the world again.

Johnny found her there. He said nothing but took her in his arms and held her so close she could hear the beating of his big, gentle heart. He cradled her, stroked her hair, crooned words of love and comfort into her ears. And in his arms she cried, helplessly and quietly against his chest and he said nothing, but let the tears wash some of the pain from her heart. When she eventually lay weak and depleted in his arms he took out his hanky and wiped her face as if she was a little girl and tenderly kissed her swollen eyelids.

How beloved was Johnny Burns to her then, how precious his gentle, undemanding love. No one else in the world could have soothed her so completely, not even her father whose manly arms had held her and comforted all her childhood fears. But she wasn't a child any longer, she was nearly a woman and now Johnny was the only one who had been close to her in her growing, who had touched her in the way a young man touches a girl he loves more than he loves himself.

She allowed him to lift her to her feet, to help her down from the hayloft, back over the cobbles to the kitchen where he sat her down and stood over her while she spluttered down a small dram of whisky. She was aware of her mother then, doing things, making tea, filling the whisky pigs with hot water which she carried away upstairs.

Her father came to her, his dark, velvet eyes moist with love and pain. 'I'm sorry, Evie, my wee lass,' he murmured helplessly.

She reached up and touched a lock of his hair. It was threaded through with white and she bit her lip. 'I know, Father.'

Johnny led her upstairs, kissed her, handed her over to Murn and Nellie who said nothing but were just there, loving sisters who had always been in her world when she most needed them.

The sampler above her bed caught her eye, Florrie's birthday gift, so painstakingly worked. 'Evelyn and Florrie – Best Friends. 1913 and beyond.'

Had that just been last summer? And now – beyond. She wanted to cry all over again but there was nothing left, only weariness and a longing to sleep forever.

The bed was warm and enveloped her in a cloud of comfort. There was nothing in the world she wanted more than to close her eyes and forget the grief and pain of her reality.

Arms came around her, arms that were sparse yet filled with a softness that brought her an unexpected sense of peace. Nellie's arms that had long, long ago nursed her when she was a baby and impressed themselves upon her memory for always.

'Will you stay wi' me, Nellie?'

'I'll stay, babby, never fear.'

'Thanks, Nellie,' she murmured, and slept.

A few days after the funeral she came upon Alan Keith walking alone by the cold, lapping waters of Loch Bree. It was a bright, bitterly cold day, the Grampian hills were covered in snow, remote and beautiful against the deep blue of the sky.

'Alan, how are you?' she asked, going up to him and

295

taking his arm. He looked up, seemed to come back from a long, long distance. His fine, sensitive face was tear-stained and she knew that he had recently cried.

'I – dinna ken where I am, Evie.' He sounded dazed, as if he really meant what he said. 'I came here to be alone to think – you know what it's like at Dippiedoon. My mother means well but she fusses so.'

'I came to be alone too.' She stared unseeingly over the loch. 'We can be alone together. That sounds daft but I'm like you – I don't want to talk.'

'I dinna mind talking to you, we both loved Florrie – we each understand how the other feels.'

'I think we were the only people who really ever did love Florrie the way she deserved to be loved,' she said slowly.

He nodded, his fine artist's hands clenched at his sides. 'Ay – that might be – there are so many O'Neils and though they're a close enough family there was so much they had to share.'

He faced her, his dark eyes pain filled. 'I loved her but I always knew she never felt the same way about me. You're one of the lucky ones, Evie, you and Johnny know where you stand wi' one another.'

She frowned. 'I'm no so sure about that, Alan – I canna think of my life without him – but I feel there should be more.'

'Then you've still to find the right one for you.'

She stared at him. Alan had always been the deep thinker among them. When he said a thing he usually meant it and almost always he was right. 'Time will tell, Alan, right now I'm too mixed up to think much of the future. Everything's changed so much.'

'Ay, nothing will be the same again, will it?' His voice broke. She turned her head away, allowing him to show his grief without embarrassment.

'Will you go to art college next year?'

He pushed his hands into his pockets and kicked the frosty sedges at the lochside. 'It canna come fast enough now – yet – before I wasna looking forward to going away.'

She took his arm again. 'Time will help, Alan. I don't

think I believe that myself just now but I hope the pain will get less – it's got to or I don't think I can bear it,' she finished bleakly.

'There will be other friends for you, Evie.'

'But none like Florrie,' she smiled shakily. 'We were best friends – from the beginning. None can ever compare with the best friends of childhood. We shared so much – and now it's gone.'

He pulled her to him awkwardly, his arm going round her shoulder. 'You still have Johnny, at least you have someone.'

She sniffed and drew out her hanky. 'I know, I'm lucky.'

Kissing him on the cheek she drew away from him. 'You'll find someone else too, Alan. You're too nice to be lonely for long.'

'I'll never find anyone like Florrie – even when I'm old and maybe married I'll always look back and remember her – how it was – how it might have been.'

'Childhood friends, childhood sweethearts – they go – yet they're everlasting.'

She smiled at him and left him there, thinking of his Florrie – grieving for her – probably to the end of his days.

PART FOUR

SPRING/SUMMER 1914

CHAPTER EIGHTEEN

Gillan came back into her life in the spring of 1914, a handsome, assured Gillan, strong enough and able enough to direct his own life to a large extent. She was down by the burn, soaking salt herrings in a wire cage, anchoring it with a big stone in a cool, deep little pool where it would lie for two days before the fish were considered fit enough for the table. It was a method every croftwife tried to make the monotonous diet of preserved fish more palatable for eating, yet even so they often tasted like boiled socks and could only be got down by liberal coatings of mustard sauce. She was up to her elbows in the burn when he came riding along and she was annoyed and flustered at being caught with her skirts tucked up and her hair in disarray despite the scarf tied round it. Gillan got down and came towards her, leaving his horse to wander to the roadside grasses. It was a beautiful horse, its coat polished to a rich chestnut which gleamed in the bright light pouring over the edges of the clouds.

Drawing a self-conscious hand across her hot face and leaving a muddy smear in the process, she squinted up at him, brows down against the glare. He was dressed in sand-coloured jodhpurs and a well-cut tweed sports jacket. His shoulders were broad, his chest solid and deep, his legs so long that when she scrambled up the bank to stand beside him she only came up to his shoulder.

'You smell of fish,' he teased, his dark face creasing into a delighted smile at seeing her again.

'And you smell of horses,' she threw back at him, unable to understand why she felt so annoyed at his intrusion or why his obvious enjoyment of her untidy appearance should irritate her so much. With Gillie she had never cared about looking too tidy or too groomed. In fact she had revelled in making him feel stuffy and conventional in her company and had often tormented him to fury by teasing him about his manicured appearance.

'Princess Evie.' He grinned down at her and she noticed that the beautifully modulated voice had grown deeper, with a timbre to it that made her realise he was no longer the boy she had known but a youth fast growing into a man. 'It's wonderful to see you again.' His eyes twinkled. 'Dirty face and untidy hair and all.'

'You've changed,' she said curtly, gathering up her basket and tucking it under her arm. 'I dinna ken you at all with all that smart sophistication you have about you now.'

'And you're exaggerating that Aberdeen twang of yours in order to try and accentuate the differences you imagine between us.'

'We are different.' She glowered at him, annoyed at herself for her ungracious welcome but unable to stop herself from carrying on, 'You're young Rothiedrum, the laird's son, while I'm just plain Evelyn McKenzie Grant, a crofter's daughter. I'm sure your mother must have pointed out the differences to you as many times as she drinks champagne with her dinner guests.'

'She never touches champagne – it's against her principles.' He laughed then grew suddenly serious. 'Oh, Evie, the times I've thought about seeing you again and all you do is snap my head off and try to make me feel guilty because I don't end my day with soil on my boots. It's been a long time, Evie.'

Her head went up. 'It didna have to be, you were the one who kept away – I couldna' very well go marching up to Rothiedrum House and ask if you were coming out to play, could I now?'

His eyes crinkled. 'Fresh air, that's what you are, Princess Evie. I didn't come because I heard Johnny had come to live at King's Croft and that you and he were – well – for want of a better expression – sweethearts.'

She was lost for a quick reply to that so she said nothing. A silence sprang between them, one laden with a strange suspense, then before she could move away he took the basket from her and laid it on the grass.

He gathered her in his arms, staying her struggles by holding her so tightly she couldn't get away. His mouth sought hers. His lips were cool and firm but in seconds charged with warmth. The arms that held her were unrelenting, his body hard but supple, moulding hers to it with little effort because she found herself responding to him. Against all her better principles she gave in to the persuasive demands of his mouth. He kissed her deeper and deeper till she felt reality slipping away. Over and over they kissed, there in the dip of the field with the burn purling in their ears and the corncrakes rustling in the long grasses.

With a great effort she tore herself free, breathless, bewildered, looking swiftly round in case anyone had witnessed their passionate exchanges. But there was no one, only the sylvan fields all around, empty but for cattle and sheep.

Not looking at him she demanded furiously, 'If you know so much about Johnny and me why did you come over here today? You should have left us in peace – you don't belong here,' she finished miserably.

His eyes flashed. 'I belong as much as you – don't forget, Rothiedrum is as much in my blood as it is in yours – and I came because I only just got home and heard about Florrie. I wasn't here at Christmas – Mother wanted to spend it in London – so I only just found out – Evie . . .' His voice changed and he looked at her with such tenderness she felt tears pricking her lids. 'I can't say how sorry I am. I know what she meant to you. I understand how much you must have suffered – and I came to try and make you a little happier.'

She bit her lip. 'And all I did was snap at you. It's good to see you again, Gillie, really good.'

He took her hands. 'Then will you come and see me sometimes? I've got the house to myself just now. Father's away on a business trip and Mother's staying with friends in Edinburgh. She wanted me to join her but I said no – I'd rather spend my holidays in Rothiedrum.' His face was glowing as he continued, 'When I say I've got the house to myself I use the terms loosely. My great uncle's here – the one in the picture you liked so much. He lost his wife recently and has come home to get over it. He's in Edinburgh with Mother but is travelling down here tomorrow on his own. I'd love you to meet him – he's such an interesting person. Why don't you come the day after next? He'll have settled in then.'

She gazed at his shining face and didn't hesitate in her reply. 'Alright, I'll come –' she giggled, '– and I promise I won't come smelling of fish. I'll wash my face and even comb my hair so that your uncle won't think I'm a tinker.'

His dark eyes studied her assessively. 'You're beautiful, Evie, whatever you're wearing, however much mud you've got smeared on your face. When I saw you at first I couldn't believe it was the same skinny little girl I saw last. You've grown, Princess Evie, and I can hardly take my eyes off you.'

She flushed. 'Ach, get away, Gillie, before I duck you in the burn.'

Laughing, he mounted his horse. 'See you the day after tomorrow. I'll send Will down with the trap.'

She thought of Johnny then, of how he would feel seeing Rothiedrum's gig pulling up at the door. 'No, I'll walk,' she said quickly.

'Suit yourself. As early as you like, it can't be too soon for me.'

She watched him go, wondering if she was doing the right thing encouraging young Rothiedrum into her life again.

Evelyn faced her mother, feeling for the first time in her life that a chasm of misunderstanding separated them.

'I will not forbid you to see Gillan, Evie,' Maggie told her daughter in a hard, unfamiliar voice. 'But I am hoping you will use your own commonsense in the matter. He isn't for you and fine you know it too. He – people like him only play for themselves. He will soon grow tired of you so it's up to you to stop it before you get hurt.'

'Life is hurtful, Mam, no matter which way you handle

it,' Evelyn said quietly. 'And I don't think about him in a serious sort of way. We're just good friends.'

'A woman can never be just good friends with a man,' Maggie said scathingly. 'It's no in a man's nature to be satisfied with a bit of talk. They soon want more and you've grown to be a bonny young woman. Gillan will take what he can from you and leave you in the lurch when he's had his fill.' Her voice was tinged with such bitterness even Jamie looked at her in some puzzlement. But wisely he held his council, knowing in his heart that she was genuinely concerned for her youngest daughter's welfare and was trying to guide her as best she could.

'That can apply in all walks of life, Mam,' Evelyn argued, her hands moving restlessly in her lap.

'Ay, but it applies more to them than to us. There's a different set of rules for the gentry, Evie,' Maggie retorted fiercely.

'It's Johnny, isn't it, Mam?' Evelyn said coolly. 'You always set your heart on Johnny for me.'

Maggie nodded. 'Ay, it's Johnny. He'll be the one who will be most hurt by all this. He's a good lad, you'll not find another better – and he comes from the kind of world you know best, Evie, just you remember that.'

'I know, Mam,' Evelyn answered gently. 'And you need never fear for Johnny and me – it's just that I have to take some things while I can. I'm young yet and it will be a long time before I allow myself to get serious about anybody.' She looked at her father sitting quiet by the fire, puffing worriedly at his stubby Stonehaven pipe, his brown fingers working nervously on the bowl. 'When a man marries a woman the ties that bind them to the home are as tough as the hawsers they use to tie up the great ships in Aberdeen Harbour.' She spoke softly, meeting his dear, dark eyes in a moment of love. 'I never forgot that, Father, and I never will.'

'I taught you well, lassie,' he said huskily. 'Maybe too well.'

She shook her head. 'No, Father, you taught me a wisdom that will sustain me wherever I go, whatever

305

happens to me – and it canna be wrong to teach a child that.'

With an odd little apologetic glance at her mother she got up and left the room. Jamie looked at Maggie. 'She's right you know, Maggie – and if you forbid her to see young Rothiedrum you will only succeed in making her all the more determined to go on as she's doing. Let the matter rest for a whilie. It will turn out right in the end – she's having her fling, she'll come to our way o' thinking in the end.'

'Time will give us the answer to that,' Maggie said heavily and with a sigh got up to help Col down from the table where he was aimlessly playing with the cutlery.

Gillan had been right about his great uncle. He was a tall, distinguished looking gentleman dressed in plum-coloured plus fours, a deerstalker hat and a tweed jacket he might have picked up at a bargain stall at a cattle show. His eyes were a piercing grey-green, his skin was fair and fresh, his deep auburn hair was turning grey at the temples while his big, bushy beard was almost entirely white.

'So, you're Evelyn,' he greeted her warmly, holding out his hand to take hers in a crushing grip. 'Gillan has spoken of very little but you and I'm glad to make your acquaintance at last.'

'You're just like yourself in the painting,' she told him, rubbing her hand behind her back.

'Oh, I've changed a bit since those days, Evelyn, I was young then and ready for anything. I think it's safe to say I've quietened down a good deal – despite what this young rascal may have told you,' he laughed, catching sight of his great-nephew's amused face.

He took more note of Evelyn and reached out a long delicate hand to touch her hair. 'Such colouring,' he told her appreciatively. 'I always had a soft spot for young ladies with red hair.'

'It runs in our family.' Eveyln found herself opening up to this striking looking man who was utterly natural in his approaches. 'I took it from my mother, she from her mother.' She showed him a tiny picture of her grandmother that she carried in a locket round her neck. 'This is my grandmother – she's lovely, isn't she?'

Lord Lindsay Ogilvie looked at the minute oval picture set in the locket. A strange look came into his eyes, his face blanched and he put out a hand to steady himself against the back of a chair. 'Your – grandmother you say?'

'Ay, she was young there of course. She's dead now. I didna really know her at all but my mother often speaks of her. When her husband died she and my mother were left with the croft so it was a good job my father had came along and married my mother.'

'What is the name of this croft?'

'Mossdyke – but better known as King's Croft because . . .' she reddened. 'Well, it's a long story and I'm sure you dinna want to hear it.'

'And – is your mother still living there?'

Evelyn laughed and looked at him curiously. 'Ay, of course she is – where else would she live?'

Almost unwillingly he let his gaze travel back to the tiny cameo picture hanging round the girl's neck. A feeling of great sadness washed over him. His thoughts took him backwards, back over the years, back to Megsie Cameron. He had never forgotten that bonny, laughing, red-haired little servant girl whom he had first noticed at a Balmoral house party. He had been very young at the time, no more than twenty. He would never forget her beguiling smile, those big green eyes of hers looking at him with mocking laughter. He had lost his head over her and for one brief, wonderful month they had been lovers.

Then he had had to go away and when he returned Megsie was gone and no one knew where. Later he learned she had been dismissed because she was carrying a child and he had told himself it could have been anybody's, even though he knew in his heart of hearts it had been his. But he hadn't gone looking for her; she was a servant girl after all and these things happened, and anyhow, he was married by then to his first wife who had later died in childbirth.

His second marriage to the daughter of a Duke had

produced three children, all of whom had died in infancy – now his second wife was dead and he had come back here – back to his roots to try and get over it. Yet all through his life he had never got over the shame or the sadness of abandoning Megsie, of never even making the effort to enquire about her and the child. At least he could have offered some financial assistance, anything to rid his conscience of its burden of guilt. When his children had died he had felt somehow he was being punished for what he had done, that life for him would never know the fulfilment of having children that were his own flesh and blood – and now, here was a lovely, laughing child, with Megsie's hair, Megsie's eyes, looking at him in a bemused fashion – his granddaughter – and not more than a mile away was his daughter, living the life of a humble crofter's wife – when he could have given her a life of ease – of riches.

'Are you feeling alright, Uncle?' Gillan was watching him and with an effort he shook himself and said heartily, 'Of course, lad, just needing my tea, that's all. I was under the impression that Martha had made a special cake for this occasion. Ring the bell, Gillan and you sit down by me, Evelyn and tell me everything about yourself.'

At the first opportunity he took himself to King's Croft. The place looked deserted but then he remembered it was spring; everyone would be out in the fields getting them ready for sowing. A movement in the little garden at the front caught his eyes. Maggie was there, pegging out the washing in the walled-off drying green. Col was toddling about at her skirts, handing her pegs, every so often pausing to gaze vacantly up at the clouds meandering across the sky.

Maggie paused, feeling she wasn't alone. Turning slowly she saw a tall, distinguished looking man watching her and something in her froze. She didn't know why. He was obviously gentry, though what he was doing here she had no earthly idea.

Very deliberately she picked up her basket, held out her

hand to Col, and made her way through the gate to where the visitor was standing.

'Ay, can I help you?' she said politely, self-consciously tucking away a strand of snowy hair.

'I wonder,' he smiled at her rather nervously. 'Could I come inside for a little while?'

He offered no explanation as to the reasons for his visit but she invited him in, going immediately to put the kettle over the fire. There was silence in the room while she made the tea. Col was gaping at the visitor but Lord Lindsay didn't notice. He was looking at the woman who was his daughter. That carriage! That bearing! That strong, proud, determined profile. She was his alright. The same nose, the same keen eyes – and though her hair was so white a few bright, fiery strands still gleamed.

She served him tea; something about her attitude suggesting she didn't exactly relish giving her attention to this particular visitor. Taking the cup he stirred his tea thoughtfully, his eyes on her as he wondered how best to approach this proud stranger who was his own flesh and blood.

'Mrs Grant,' he began, then clearing his throat, 'don't you have any idea who I am?'

She glanced at him sharply. 'Why don't you tell me?'

The whole story came out then, hesitantly at first, then in a rush, as if he was getting something off his chest that had lain heavy on it for a long time. When he was finished he looked at her rather apprehensively. A dark gleam of bitterness shone in her eyes, masking so many emotions she couldn't pick out any one that made sense.

'Just why have you come here?' she got out at last. 'Do you expect me to throw my arms about you and call you "Father"? Just tell me why you've come and be sharp about it for I have no wish to have you here in my kitchen when my family come in.'

He looked round the simple, homely room with all the marks of poverty stamped upon it – if only she would allow him to help, but she was proud this woman, it flashed in her eyes, bristled in every taut bone.

Tentatively he asked her if she would allow him to give her some financial help – to make up for all the time that had been lost.

Her nostrils flared and, as he had expected, she refused in no mean manner.

'The child then,' he persisted, 'Evelyn – she's a bright, intelligent girl. I could see she gets a proper education – a decent start in life.'

Maggie's thoughts flew helter skelter. It was everything she wanted for Evelyn – what she would have liked for all her children. She hesitated, sorely torn between pride and temptation. Then a picture of her mother flashed into her mind, workworn, careworn through a life of struggle to make ends meet.

She stood up, drawing herself to her full height, unconsciously pushing out the generous swell of her bosom.

'So you want to help Evie,' she said softly. 'All very grand and noble. Has it struck you yet that she is not the only grandchild you have – there are six of them – including this wee mite here who gawps at you for the stranger you are. Your sudden sense of responsibility comes a bit too late, my noble lord. My dear mother died in poverty, worn out with the struggle to feed and clothe the bairn she bore you in shame and degradation. Where were you then? You must have known she was dismissed from her position because she was carrying a child, yet you turned your back on her and went on your merry way. Of course, you're no worse and no better than any of your sort and that's about the only excuse I can make for you. You came here today because your own life is as barren as the northlands o' the Dark Ages. Suddenly you have flesh and blood and though it would be too harmful to your name to declare it openly you think to salve your conscience by offering the one plentiful thing you have. I cannot think of you as my father. You are as real to me as the forgotten hobgoblins of my childhood nightmares. And now this sudden interest in a bairnie you would like to claim as your grandchild – just as long as she is kept secret from your fine feathered friends.

It is conscience money you are offering, sir, and I will have none of it. But before you go, hear this – I have never made any difference between my daughters and I have no intention of starting now – so, good day to you, and I will thank you not to come back here bothering us again.'

He stood up, his fingers working on the ebony handle of his cane. He opened his mouth to argue further but one look at her thunderous face decided him against it.

'Very well, Margaret, if that's your attitude there is indeed nothing more to say. But know this, wherever I go, whatever I do I'll remember my granddaughter, Evelyn – and one day she will know who I was to her, one day she will know that the Ogilvies and the Forbes were as much family to her as the Grants were.'

'Never while I am alive,' she said through livid lips.

He smiled strangely. 'Nor I myself. But things can be done beyond the grave, Margaret, and those that are left behind are powerless to stop them – and I'm not talking about hauntings and ghostly happenings either. Evelyn shall come into her own one day and my only regret is that I won't be alive to see her face when she does.' He raised his hat and went out, his back as proud and straight as that of the daughter he left at the door staring after him.

Lord Lindsay Ogilvie looked searchingly into the scandalized face of his niece.

'Well, Marjorie,' he said quietly, 'What have you to say? Shouldn't I have told you?'

Lady Marjorie's nostrils were pinched, her nose slightly red though the rest of her face was pale. 'You – if what you have just told me is true – it means that she – your daughter is my cousin – my *first* cousin?'

He nodded and she went on in a shaken voice, 'How – how could you, Uncle? Why should your sins be visited upon this family? The disgrace of it!'

His keen eyes glittered strangely. At one time she had been a very dear niece to him but the years had changed her and he was seeing another side to her now – one that he didn't in the least care for. 'You're a snob, Marjorie, my dear. Margaret may be a crofter's wife but she's as good as you any day – ay, and maybe a whole sight better.'

'How dare you say that to me! You – you that have whored with a servant girl with this – this scandal as the result.'

'Scandal my big toe,' he retorted scathingly. 'Only you and I know of it – and Margaret too of course – and I'll wager everything I have that she will never breathe a word of it. She's kept quiet all these years and isn't likely to start spreading the dirt now. She's a mite too proud for that – ay, proud. As for me and my whoring – it runs in the family, Marjorie. You should know better than most what I'm talking about.'

'Indeed I do not!'

'Oh, stop hedging, Marjorie. Although I'm safely tucked away in Africa I still have friends here with whom I correspond regularly. There has been talk of an unsavoury nature and not just about Evander. I believe you have avenged him nicely with some little indiscretions of your own. So far you have been clever enough to avoid the usual tittle tattle but you should be careful in your choice of playmates – one at least has a big mouth and the circles you move in can be pretty small. A word here, and innuendo there – you know the sort of thing.'

She paced nervously, twisting her hands together. 'Never mind that now, Uncle, it's you we're talking about. You must keep quiet, if only for Gillan's sake. If it's money your daughter wants you must see that she gets it.'

It was his turn to go pale, only in his case it was in a mixture of rage and regret. 'You don't know Margaret or you would never utter such words. She wants nothing from us – more's the pity. I tried to get her to accept something and she sent me packing with my tail tucked between my legs.'

She threw up her head to stare at him desperately. 'Neither Evander or Gillan must ever find out about this.'

'They won't,' he cut in harshly. 'Not from me and not from my daughter.'

'Tell me one thing,' she said. 'Why did you tell me all

this? You didn't have to burden me with your troubles. You could have gone away and none of us need ever have been any the wiser.'

'Because, Marjorie,' he said heavily, 'I happen to be aware of your attitude to Evelyn. I know all about the little tea party you and Evander threw for her so that you could size her up and consider if she was a worthwhile companion for Gillan. Obviously you found her lacking because soon after that you packed the boy off to school. And don't look like that. Gillan never said anything. Walls in these big houses have ears, Marjorie, and it's only natural that the servants should talk among themselves. Evelyn is my granddaughter. Stop and consider that if you will. To you she is just another daughter of the farms but she is my flesh and blood and I don't like the idea of you looking down your uppity little nose at her. That's why I told you. I just wanted you to know who she is, so let's all keep it nice and cosily in the family, even though there are some members who may never find out the truth.'

'May?' she said sharply. 'You mean they certainly won't.'

'Have it your way,' he said coolly. 'But I tell you this, Marjorie, if you have any plans in your head about getting the Grants evicted from Rothiedrum you can forget it. You would really be putting the cat among the pigeons then.'

She forced a smile. 'Alright, Uncle, I'll stick to my bargain if you stick to yours – and now, can we forget about the Grants? You and I were friends before all this and Evander will suspect if we go about avoiding each other. Let's enjoy your time here. When Gillan goes back to school I want you to come to London with me. Most of my friends are there and –'

'In other words you want to get me out of here as quickly as possible,' he grinned, admiring her for her tenacity if nothing else.

She smiled back, all at once the cool, collected lady that he knew so well. 'I never could fool you, could I?'

'Always did read you like a book,' he told her sourly.

'My dear brother, God rest him, used to say I knew you better than he ever did.'

'At heart I'm still the child you once knew and loved,' she said, sounding relieved at his obvious change of mood.

Pity you hadn't stayed that way,' he grunted. Dashingly he crooked his arm. 'Come on, let's go and find Evander. If my stay here is to be such a short one I'd better make the most of it while I can.'

CHAPTER NINETEEN

Gillan went back to school after Easter and normality returned to the busy routine of King's Croft. Maggie had never mentioned Lord Ogilvie's visit to any of her family, not even Jamie, and from time to time she was overcome with the enormity of the secret she carried. Every time she looked at Evelyn she felt guilty for having denied her an opportunity to make something of her life. She was also apt to go over in her mind all that had taken place between her father and herself, and to wonder wistfully if she had been right to deny herself the chance to get to know him as she had imagined, in her most fanciful dreams, she one day would.

Then she would pull herself up sharply. Such things could never be for her. It was too ridiculous even to consider. She had done the wise thing sending him away like that. It was no more than he deserved. She had heard that Lady Marjorie had trailed him off to London and she had wondered if he had told his niece about the affair. It made no difference if he had. She was just relieved that Gillan had gone back to school and now maybe Evelyn would stop hankering after things that were so far out of her reach – yet, what a nice lad he was – different from what she had expected. If he had any of his mother's snobbery he had certainly hidden it well enough, especially that morning out in the cornfield when she'd had to treat the blisters on his hands so willingly and uncomplainingly had he worked.

Johnny, who had been prone to fits of moodiness during Gillan's short, upsetting stay, changed back to the Johnny everyone knew, his steps light as he went about his daily tasks, a tune never far from his lips. He and Jamie were like father and son, working harmoniously in the fields by day, talking together by the glow of the evening fire.

Sometimes Jamie got out his fiddle, Johnny his

melodeon, Evelyn her comb and paper, and they would have an impromptu ceilidh round the fire. These were the times of laughter, of bothy ballads, of well worn and much loved stories from Maggie and Coulter. Nellie would sit knitting by the lamplight, fair hair shining, long, bony fingers flying busily, Murn beside her, sewing her exquisite stitches for the gentry.

Mary and Gregor came often to visit, Grace came home for a long holiday and for Evelyn it was just the old days again – only now there was Johnny, Johnny in firelight, Johnny in sunlight, his fair head shining, his blue eyes deep and warm with his love for her.

He had never mentioned Canada again and she had thought he had given up the idea of it till she asked about it.

'I'm still going someday,' he told her, 'but I'll wait till you are ready to come with me – meanwhile I'm happy here at King's Croft – so happy I know that even if I do go away I'll come back one day to Rothiedrum. If we get a farm nearby I'll be at hand to help Jamie. He helped me when I most needed help. I'll never forget him for that.'

She noticed that he had said 'we' quite naturally and her breath caught on a tear. She loved him, she would always love Johnny Burns but she wished she could be as sure about the future as he was. The uneasy rumbles of war had been in the air for quite some time now. Johnny himself had mentioned it several times and she had looked at him in dismay and demanded angrily, 'One minute you talk about Canada and the future and the next you go on about a war that might never happen – and yet if it does, you and and all the other young men from here will march away – and what of the future then, my bonny Johnny Burns?' she had finished bleakly.

He had taken her in his arms then and kissed her fears away but not even his warm, safe strength could shut her mind to the talk of the men at the ceilidhs.

'It's brewing – as sure as that tea stewing on the hob,' Danny the Fist had stated whilst seated at Knobblieknowe's hearth.

316

Coulter spat into the fire and for a long time contemplated the sizzling gobbet. 'Ay,' he agreed sagely, nodding his white head slowly up and down. 'It's been brewing for a long time now and something in my old bones tells me it will no be long afore it reaches boiling point.'

After that all the men and boys in the room had gathered into a close circle to discuss what the newspapers were saying, and Evelyn looked at Johnny's earnest young face and felt shivers of apprehension along her spine.

These were the times she had to be alone and she would take her bicycle and follow the Birkie to Culter, there to stand on the windblown cliffs and try to think what she really wanted from her life. She wasn't yet sixteen, there was so much she didn't know, so much she wanted to find out. Her father's dreams of sending her to college had never come to fruition. Unlike her sister Murn she had failed to win a bursary and so she still went to night school, still frittered her time away in writing poetry and stories. But she knew it wasn't enough. She would have to get a job to help the family make ends meet.

Jamie no longer made his beautiful shoes for the gentry; he was older now, the energies of his youth were on the wane. Grace sent as much money as she could spare, though her wages were poor enough. The thought of her gentle sister always brought a warm smile to Evelyn's mouth. She had never been strong enough to help with the heavier croft work but somehow she had always managed to contribute to the home. Even while still at school she had worked evenings and weekends as companion to a rich old lady who had shown her gratitude to the bonny young crofter's lass in many different ways, not the least of them being gifts of such bounteous food baskets that Maggie had been moved to protest though in the end forcing herself to swallow her pride in order that her daughters should never go hungry.

Murn too had worked for the family from an early age, handing over any money she made from the embroidery work entrusted to her by ladies of big houses. Now she gave in her bed and board with a little extra besides, though she

317

was careful to save every spare shilling for her future. Evelyn understood her attitude. A sense of security was important to the girls of the farmtouns and if you didn't look after yourself no one else could afford to do it for you.

Jamie no longer hired an orra loon to lighten the work load. Johnny had brought that about. He had insisted he was as good as two hired hands rolled together and though Jamie had been adamant about raising his wages, it was still less than paying two lads. Things were no better and no worse than they had been and for a long time Evelyn had felt uneasy about not bringing home a wage so she planned to ask Gillan, next time he was home, if he could see his father about getting her a job at the Big House.

She smiled wryly to herself, remembering her vows to her father concerning work for the gentry. How long ago it seemed, all that childish vehemency – all those passionate, unrealistic declarations. Florrie had worked at a nearby big mansion house since leaving school at fourteen – Evelyn smiled wistfully at the memory. She had been like her. 'I'll never work to the Dandy Dowps,' she had said, tossing back her mane of hair. 'I'll make more money in a week on the stage than they could pay me in a year – and just think,' she had added in an awed voice. 'They'll pay to come and see *me* and throw themselves at my dressing room door begging for my autograph.'

But she had grown up and though she had never discarded her dreams she had gone to work for 'them' and, being Florrie, she had thoroughly enjoyed it and had come home, proud of earning her daily bread, brimful of wicked mimicry and imitations of everything her quick mind had absorbed at 'the house over yonder'.

Evelyn didn't mention her plans to anyone, knowing how much her father had hankered after a better way of life for her, and she didn't tell Johnny because then he would have spoken of Canada again and while it might prove to be a better way of life it wasn't one she wanted. As for Gillan, she knew that a life with him could never be yet she couldn't bring herself to part with him. A job at Rothiedrum House might just be the thing to help them both get things into their right perspective – and if Johnny didn't like it – well – she couldn't please everybody.

Gillan studied her for a long time when she put her request to him. His strong, handsome face, tanned and glowing from all the outdoor things he did while he was away at school, grew dark with the thoughts that travelled through his mind when she had finished speaking. The long summer holidays stretched before him and he had come home to Rothiedrum full of enthusiasm for all the things he had hoped to share with her.

'I can't see you as a servant girl somehow.' He spoke at last, a frown on his brow. 'I don't like the idea of it – not for you, Evie, you're different somehow, I can't explain why. I just don't like the idea of you tending people hand and foot.'

'Well I have to like the idea of it!' she flashed angrily. Strange how angry she got with Gillan – she was seldom like that with Johnny – but somehow there was a passion in Gillan that found its echo in her. Johnny was too quiet, too gentle to ever really kindle ire in her, her times with him were peaceful and reassuring, but she never felt the same peace with Gillan. He made her feel alive, more aware of her own restlessness and in many ways that was what she liked most about him – his ability to stir fires in her that slumbered tranquilly with Johnny.

'It's alright for the likes of you,' she continued, 'you'll never have to work if you dinna want to – you can be as idle as you like all the days of your life.'

'But I do want to,' he flashed back. 'For your information I'm set to study law when I go on to University. And you're doing it again – exaggerating that north-east twang of yours – you always do it when you're with me and I don't like it.'

'Hmph! Thank the Lord we dinna all speak with marbles in our mouths! I dinna ken half the time what you're saying so don't you dare criticize my honest to goodness tongue.'

'I didn't mean I don't like it, I mean I don't like the way you put it on for me.'

319

They looked at each other and burst out laughing.

'We always do this,' he grinned and she noticed how white his teeth were when he smiled. 'From the first time we met at the Smiddy you've snapped my head off – while I –' he smiled again, 'I've somehow managed to remain the perfect gentleman.'

'You impudent snob,' she laughed and this time made no resistance when he took her in his arms and hungrily sought her mouth. She melted against him, eagerly and willingly. A fire leapt between them, compelling them to touch one another with a naked urgency that made them forget everything but the excitement they induced in each other. His hands explored her body, moved up to brush her breasts. Temptation sweet and dangerous rushed through her.

'Please, Gillie,' she pushed him away. They stared at one another, dazed with longing.

'Evie, Princess Evie,' he murmured tenderly. 'You're the loveliest thing I've seen in a long time – since the last time we met in fact. I've never met anyone else like you.'

Without warning her mother's voice pulsed in her head. 'People like him only play for themselves. He'll soon grow tired of you . . .'

'I told you before, Gillie, I'm not a princess, I'm an ordinary farming girl, born of the soil. I've no place in your life nor you in mine. I need to earn some money to help my father keep a roof over my head – so are you going to ask your father about that job or not?'

He looked at her quizzically, the flush of passion staining his suntanned skin.

'If that's what you think you really want.'

'I don't think it, I know it.'

'Alright, Evie, I'll ask him – if you promise me you'll come out with me on your time off.'

She returned his impudent smile. 'Ay, I promise, though of course Johnny will want to see me in my spare time too.'

'Two strings to your bow, eh?' The anger was back in him and without being able to help herself she reached out and touched a lock of his hair.

'Dear Gillie, you don't hide your feelings, do you? Your moods are like the northern sun, out one minute, in the next. You'll have to try and understand about me and Johnny – he's a part of my life – and I canna hurt him just because you've made all your summer plans in advance.'

'But you can hurt me,' he returned bitterly.

'I don't want to hurt anybody, Gillie.'

'Maybe you don't but it happens all the time – and one day you'll hurt one of us more than the other! Which of us is it to be, Evie? Answer me that.'

'I can't,' she said slowly, 'I don't know the answer. I never set out to hurt anybody – but I think in the end it might be you, Gillie – your mother will make sure of that.'

'Mother had me tied to her when I was too young to do anything about it,' he said scornfully. 'I don't have to answer to her anymore.'

'Oh, but you do, Gillie,' she said gently. 'Your mother and your father. You're their only son, remember. They'll expect you to make a good marriage when the time comes – with a girl of your own sort.'

'Then – if you think that – is it worth our while to carry on as we're doing?' he asked forlornly.

'Oh, Gillie, don't take it all so seriously. When we're young like this we're only really playing. We'll both change as time goes on – but meanwhile, it's up to you to decide – so what do you think?'

He gazed at her, at her slender, enticing figure, at her mouth slightly parted in expectation, at the sunlight laving her hair, turning it the colour of beech leaves in autumn. 'I think it's worthwhile, even if I have to share you.'

They moved away then, away from the little hollow by the river where the lacy trees patterned the grass, Gillan to mount his horse and ride back to Rothiedrum House, Evelyn to make her way back to King's Croft – back to Johnny who worked in the fields in the heat of the day and who watched with darkened brow the red-haired girl walking over the ridge of the hill, the kisses of young Rothiedrum fresh and sweet on the dew of her lips.

*

Evander heard his son out, his hands folded at his back as he gazed out of the long window in the drawing room to the sweep of lawns in front of the house. As Gillan ceased speaking he turned his head slightly and said thoughtfully, 'Evelyn Grant – she's the lass who lives at Mossdyke, isn't she – the one you brought to tea some while back?'

Gillan nodded, a slight uneasiness in him as he noted the sudden gleam that came into his father's eyes.

'Hmm, that one,' Evander turned back to the window again. 'You been seeing something of her then, Gillan?'

Gillan shifted. 'A bit. I like her, she's full of fire and independence. I know fine her father would have liked to send her to college but there's no money there of course. She feels it's time she earned her keep – though I tried to persuade her against a servant's job. She's got pride in her has Evelyn Grant.'

Evander swung round. 'Pride doesn't fill the belly, lad, only the mind. Independence is another thing altogether, that's the kind of resolution that counts –ay,' he continued heartily, 'let's have her over and see what she's made of. I'm sure we can find something for her to do in the kitchens.'

'The kitchens!' Gillan said sharply.

'Ay, ay, the kitchens! What lines were you thinking along, lad? Would you see her in a frilly cap and apron in the bedrooms? Maybe bringing you up your morning tea?' His coarse laugh rang out. 'Wouldn't say no to that myself but I doubt if your mother would approve. She's hung on to that frumpy Minnie for years now and I can't see her making way for a slip of a farm girl, no matter how pretty or independent. Beggars can't be choosers, Gillan, so rid yourself of your fancy ideas and take what I suggest or leave it.'

Gillan turned on his heel. 'When do I bring her?'

'Tomorrow morning. I'll see her in my study around ten. Be sharp about it too. I've some people coming to lunch.'

Evelyn sat on the edge of a plush red leather couch, feeling herself growing hot with humiliation under Rothiedrum's admiring stare.

'Whew, a change from the little lass Gillan brought to tea. You've grown into quite a beauty, my dear.' He sat back, ogling her with rude enjoyment. 'No wonder young Gillan's taken a shine to you. Still, he's only a lad and must have his fun. Young blood and all that. Remember myself at his age, couldn't get enough of it, the more the merrier.'

'There is nothing like that between Gillie and me,' she said coldly, quite unconscious of the fact that her flushed indignation only served to make her more attractive in Evander's appreciative eyes.

'So, it's Gillie, eh? And you tell me he's only a bosom friend. No need to be so reticent about it, lass. Take your enjoyment where you can – as long as you're careful about it.' He grinned at her, his teeth showing between thick, sensual lips. 'You young people, all innocence on the outside, but put a lad and a lass together and whoosh! Fireworks!' His brows came down over his dark, flashing eyes. 'Silence, eh? The best defence, I suppose. Gillan tells me you're looking for a job. If I'm minding correctly weren't you the one who wanted to make a career out of writing? All het up about it last time we spoke.'

She pulled her skirt more decorously about her knees and looked at her hands. 'People need money to pursue an ambition like that. It takes time to get started, even more to get established – and I dinna have any time to spare at the moment. I need to get a job, Mr Forbes and I thought you might be able to help.'

He rose up from his desk and came to sit beside her on the couch, throwing his arm carelessly over the back so that it was inches from her shoulder, one thumb ever so gently touching her hair. 'In a house like this there's jobs and there's jobs, Evelyn – if you see what I mean.'

He moved closer, one big knee brushing one of hers. 'It's entirely up to you to decide. I could find something nice and easy for you – what do you say, lass?'

His hand slipped further down the couch till the weight of it was resting on her shoulder. She could feel the heat of his big, bulky body, smell the animal scent of him as his

323

legs caressed hers suggestively. For a moment she was at a loss as how best to handle the situation, all her instincts making her want to get up and run from Rothiedrum House and never come back. Her head went up. Why should she? She had come here looking for a job and she wasn't going to flee meekly away like some frightened rabbit just because some moneyed barbarian was making sexual advances towards her.

'I'm no looking for an easy job, Mr Forbes. I came to ask for work and if you haven't anything suitable then I'll be bidding you good day.'

He slapped his knee, making her jump. 'Be God! No wonder young Gillan likes you! At last, a pretty face with brains at the back of it. The kitchens for you, my lass, what do you say?'

'What can I say – except thank you.' She stood up, surprised to find that her legs were trembling. 'When can I start?'

'Right away if you're so keen. We'll go and see Martha now and she can tell you what's expected of you. Mind you, I'll have to let Mrs Chalmers know about you. It's her job to interview intended employees, but Gillan seemed to feel you were a special case so I thought I'd have a look at you myself.' He took her small hand and she stared at the thick dark hairs on the back of his. 'We're going to be friends you and I, Evelyn.'

'I – I hope so, Mr Forbes.'

'Good friends,' he emphasised. His hand lingered in hers, his thumb stroked her palm in an obviously suggestive gesture. 'We must enjoy ourselves while we can, Evelyn.' He sounded so serious suddenly she brought her head up to look into his face. 'War, my dear girl. The Germans have advanced into Belgium, there's going to be an ultimatum.'

She shivered and felt strangely afraid. People had been talking about it for some time. Old Carnallachie, a keen supporter of royalty and an avid devotee of Queen Victoria during her reign, was always to be seen outside the Smiddy these days, his specs on the end of his nose as he devoured the newspapers. 'Ay, ay,' he had muttered sadly to a gathering of his cronies. 'Victoria wouldna like it if she was alive now. She thought the world o' that grandson o' hers and now the bugger is raking up all sorts o' trouble.'

'Ay, is it no terrible' sympathized Betsy, pausing on her way to the Post Office, 'if she was alive she would be turning in her grave, ay she would.'

She had stared in genuine bemusement as everyone roared with laughter and Carnallachie had shook his fist at her and roared so furiously she had vacated the scene with alacrity. It wasn't till she was in the Post Office, recounting Carnallachie's reactions to her words, that she realized what she had said and both she and Bunty had sprawled over the counter, helpless with laughter, made all the more enjoyable everytime they looked from the window and saw Carnallachie glowering in their direction.

Evelyn had heard the story and somehow it had taken the sting out of the newspaper reports but now, seeing Evander's unusually sombre look she faced the seriousness of the situation. 'I know,' she said in a low voice. 'It's in all the papers. My father has talked of nothing else this while back. Do you – really think it will happen?'

In her anxiety she forgot his lecherous tendencies and spoke to him quite naturally.

'Oh ay, lass,' he said softly. 'I have no doubt of it – and all the young men will go away – there will be no one left except older, more experienced men.'

His abrupt change of mood nonplussed her. His booming laugh surged in her ears and she realized that he took a delight in switching suddenly from one topic to the next – yet she had glimpsed something more in him and looking him straight in the eyes she told him, 'You're a very nice person – when you want to be. At least you dinna put on any acts for anybody. You're like your son that way – or should I say – he's like you in that respect.'

Taken aback he stared at her. 'No one could be as straight as you, lass. I take what you've just said as a compliment – one of the nicest I've ever been paid.'

His black eyes were raking her face and she experienced a moment of panic wondering if he was seeing her frankness as some sort of encouragement.

He saw the apprehension in her eyes and smiled. 'For heaven's sake, girl, I'm not going to eat you! You remind me of a hind cornered in some dark place in the forest. I might be a bit of an ogre but I can assure you I'm not such a bad one once you get to know me.' He took her arm. 'Come along now, I've got people waiting and can't spend the entire morning in your company.' His gaze swept over her. 'More's the pity,' he grinned and laughed again as she tossed her red head and marched in front of him to the door.

Lady Marjorie was furious with her husband. 'Evelyn Grant – coming here to work! You might at least have had the decency to ask my opinion on the matter, Evander.'

'Tosh, woman,' he told her carelessly, 'why worry your pretty little head about such lowly matters? It was between Gillan and me anyhow. He asked if I could find the girl work and to please him I did.'

She stared aghast. 'Gillan asked you! And like a fool you saw fit to encourage his whims. You know my feelings about this girl. I warned you not to let her come here again – and now you coolly inform me she's actually starting work at Rothiedrum. Are you blind, Evander?'

'Anything but that, Marjorie.' He was watching her suspiciously, his black brows gathered into a frown. 'And if you ask me there's more to this affair than meets the eye. You aren't just afraid that your son might get himself entangled with a farm girl – it's something more than that. Why are you afraid of the Grants, my dear? I've sensed it for some time now. Is there something I should know about them?'

A tremor of apprehension shivered through her. He must never know that Margaret Grant was her first cousin. Evander was many things that weren't to her liking but he had always been fair in his dealings with his tenants and, unlike her, could mix freely with people from all walks of life. In fact he seemed to prefer quite ordinary company and much to her annoyance took himself off on occasion to the various inns around the district. He revelled in marts and cattle shows and the like, where he mixed agreeably with all sorts of characters, at times behaving as coarsely as any of them.

Whether he would think it a disgrace having crofting people as relatives she didn't know, and she was certainly not going to take the risk of finding out. The Grants would never get their hands on the family fortunes, not if she could help it. Despite what her uncle had said about Margaret and her pride she didn't believe for one moment that it was true. Give these people an inch and they would take a mile! The very idea of a scandal leaking out was enough to make her feel faint and so it was a sweet and innocent face she turned to her husband though what she knew she had to say went against the very grain of her.

'Don't be silly, Evander darling. If Evelyn is so desperate to find work, then of course, if you have already employed her, there's nothing more to be said on the matter.'

He grunted. 'As well, Marjorie. The girl starts in the kitchens tomorrow and that's final.'

Lady Marjorie wasn't the only person opposed to the idea of Evelyn working at Rothiedrum House. Maggie too was furious when she found out.

In bewilderment Evelyn listened to her mother's words of outrage until finally, with tears in her eyes, she cried, 'But why, Mam? I have to go out to work sometime. We need the money and I need to find a bittie independence. I canna go on living on dreams forever, I have to make my own way. You never behaved like this when Grace or Murn spread their wings.'

'This is different,' stated Maggie flatly.

'Is it, Mam? Or is it because you can't bear the idea of a daughter of yours going to work to the gentry? You've always had it in for them yet you took enough of their sillar from Murn's sewing and Father's shoes!'

'That's enough from you, you impudent wee upstart!' raged Maggie, her face livid. 'Go you up to your room

327

this minute. You'll hear more of this later!'

Evelyn fled sobbing and Jamie took Maggie by the arm and made her sit down. 'Calm yourself, Maggie, the lass is right. I myself canna think what ails you about the Forbes family. I know how you feel about what happened in the past but it has nothing to do with them. What's past is over and done with and it's time you stopped feeling so bitter.'

'You dinna understand, Jamie.' She sounded exhausted and he looked down at her with concern.

'I've tried to understand, Maggie, but it's beyond me now to know what lies in your mind.'

She looked into his honest brown eyes and for a moment she was tempted to tell him the truth. But what good would it do, she thought wearily. It would only complicate matters further and would place him in an unbearably shaky position. A simple crofter married to a woman who had family ties with Rothiedrum and financial claims on their estate, the irony of that might be too much for him to bear – he who had worked all his life to give her everything he had. He had as much pride as she herself and if he knew her secret it might only serve to make him give up his tenancy of the croft – and she was damned if she would be driven away from her home for anybody!

She took his rough hands in hers. 'Go up to her, Jamie, tell her it's alright. If she wants to work to Rothiedrum I'll not stand in her way.'

At the door he paused. 'I wish I could have given her a better start in life, Maggie.'

Guilt tore at her. If she hadn't been so proud – so bitter – she could have taken her father's offer and there would be none of this now . . . 'You've done your best Jamie, my man,' she told him quietly and with a sigh he went out of the room and closed the door softly behind him.

CHAPTER TWENTY

Despite everything Evelyn found herself enjoying her work at Rothiedrum House. Martha and the rest of the staff made her feel welcome, though the old cook made it plain from the start that she was matriarch of her own domain and woe betide anyone who stepped out of line.

Evelyn didn't mind. She sang as she worked, bringing life to the monotonous routine, making Martha smile at her and praise her work with a few dry words. Even though she spent most of her time in the kitchens there was the strange, quiet thrill of being inside Rothiedrum for she couldn't deny it to herself that the house fascinated her. Right from her first sight of its gracious façade and magnificent grounds she had admired its dignity, its timeless air of peaceful elegance. Only once had she felt an intruder into the place and that was when she encountered Lady Marjorie one morning as she was making her way round to the servants' door. The frosty, almost belligerent expression in the woman's dark eyes had made her hurry away and for the rest of the morning she had been in a mood of such pensiveness Martha had been moved to rebuke her for dreaming.

Evander Forbes had come upon her once or twice and had asked quite kindly after her welfare. But he had seemed preoccupied and distant, with none of the sly flirtatiousness of their last meeting and she had breathed a sigh of relief and had begun to relax more whenever she encountered him.

'I haven't forgotten you, Evelyn,' he had grinned at her once. 'It's just his war business has gone to my head you might say. A terrible, terrible thing war but –' he had laughed wryly – 'there are those among us who take advantage of the opportunities it brings, and I'm afraid I'm going to be one of them. One or two of my little business

329

ventures were all set to take a nosedive but I suspect now they are on the way up. I'm a rogue of the worst kind you see, my dear.'

His booming laugh rang out but somehow she didn't mind it so much now. He was frank to the point of indiscretion but she admired his honesty and liked him the better for it.

And there was always Gillan, coming down to the kitchens to throw himself on to a chair to pass the time of day. He drank tea and ate biscuits and pinched Martha's bottom as she bustled past, an action which made her take the dishcloth to his ears as if he was the stable boy instead of the young master of the house. Somehow, with Gillan, things like that didn't matter. The servants were perfectly natural and at ease in his company and he would sit with them all at table, the gardeners, the stable hands and the kitchen staff, and the little kitchen maid with the glowing red hair and the air about her of never quite belonging below stairs, though it wasn't a studied or deliberate aura but one that seemed to surround her quite naturally.

'You don't belong down here, Princess Evie,' Gillan told her continually. 'You're too refined somehow.'

At that she would exaggerate her 'twang' and the usual arguments would follow then the passionate, breathless kisses that left them both trembling.

A few weeks after her starting work at Rothiedrum Johnny confronted her in the yard and, seizing hold of her arm rather roughly, marched her up to the hayloft and made her sit down to face him. He was breathing heavily, as if he had been running, but she knew him and saw that he had worked himself up to this meeting.

'I'm no going to beat about the bush, Evie,' he told her harshly. 'I dinna like the idea o' you working to Rothiedrum but more, I hate the idea of you and Gillie being thrown so much together, and I'm no going to stand for it much longer!' He held up a peremptory hand to ward off her protests. 'Just hear me out, for I'm in no mood to listen to a lot o' excuses. I ken fine you like him – fascinated might be a better word. He's different from anyone else you've known and in a way I can understand all that grass on the other side business.'

He was really getting warmed up. Evelyn looked at his flushed face, the barbs of ice sparkling in his blue eyes and the thought came to her how like his father he was when in a temper.

'I've thought a lot about what I'm going to say, Evie,' he continued heavily, 'and I'm no going to waste my breath on any fancy words. If you won't marry me I'm joining up, going some place where I'm really needed instead o' staying here to watch you make fools of both of us. You dinna have to say anything just now. I'll give you a day to think it over and if you canna come up with a good answer then I'm off and I'll no be sorry to shake the dust o' Rothiedrum off my heels.'

Very straight and dignified he left her. She sat where she was for a long time, her brow furrowed in deepest thought...

Evelyn turned her face away from Gillan's kisses and frowning, he told her, as if excusing himself for his healthy desires, 'I'm not like my father you know. I wouldn't ever do anything to hurt you. As a matter of fact you're the only girl I've ever kissed.'

He had looked at her quickly as he mentioned his father. 'He – hasn't done anything to annoy you – has he?'

'Ach no, he's a nice man really – once you get to know him. He's been very kind to me – though I canna say the same for your mother.'

'Oh, don't mind Mother, she can't help being the way she is. She just can't be natural the way Father can.'

'Your father is a very honest sort of person. He told me he's going to make some o' his businesses pay owing to the war.'

'Father always had an eye for opportunity. He likes making money and the war has given him plenty to think about.' He laughed. 'At least it takes his mind off other things.'

'I hate all this war stuff!' she cried passionately. 'It's all everyone ever seems to talk about. It changes folk – even the ones who aren't away fighting in it – and the farms are already losing the young hired hands. Some o' them are only fifteen but lied about their age just to go and fight – and maybe even get killed! Why do they do it? Why do they, Gillie?'

'For King and Country I suppose,' he said quietly.

'Ach, you would say that!' she cried scathingly, the bright light of fear staring stark from her eyes. Her voice changed and she said almost pleadingly, 'You won't go away, will you, Gillie?'

He gathered her into his arms and in her terrible uncertainty she made no protest. 'Would you really care if I did?' he asked lightly.

'You know I would.'

'I have thought about it – quite a lot in fact,' he confessed at last. 'Since going into senior year at school I've been a member of the Officer's Training Corps and loved every minute – at least I wouldn't go to war a complete novice.' His eyes were shining and she saw the same enthusiasm on his face as she had seen on those of Jock Gilchrist, Iain Galbraith, John Jamieson; lads she had known all her life and who had gone away proudly wearing uniforms that only served to emphasize their youth.

'But you're going to college to study law – only a short whilie ago you were all keen on the idea – and now you too have changed,' she ended miserably.

His arms tightened round her. 'Evie, oh Evie,' he said tenderly into her bright hair. 'I'm not quite eighteen, I'll have plenty of time for all that. The war might not last all that long and then I'll be back to bury my head in my books. Can you imagine the Gillan Ogilvie Forbes of the future? A sober and respected citizen in my pinstripes and bowler hat.'

'It sounds sophisticated – and a bittie boring,' she couldn't refrain from saying impishly. 'All those fusty books and fusty people with wigs and flapping black cloaks like Coulter's witches.'

'That part won't come for a long time – and only if I'm clever enough to make it.'

'You will, Gillie, you're the brainy sort.'

He grinned ruefully. 'I need brains to help me fight my father. He and Mother have been planning things for little Gillan. He's so anxious to keep me from joining up he wants me to get involved in family business, mentioned something about a managerial position in his munitions factory. Somehow I can't see myself doing that.'

Restlessly she moved away from him. 'I wish Johnny had the chances you have; he deserves so much more than he's got.'

'Johnny again! Why can't we have a conversation without him coming into it?'

'He's part of my life, that's why, a big part.'

'And I suppose that means the little part that is left is mine, eh?' he fumed angrily.

'You and I were always just good friends,' she spoke slowly, searching her mind for the right things to say because everything in her rebelled against hurting him even though she knew he was going to be hurt – and she could hardly bear the thought of that.

'Good friends!' he hurled the words back in her face before she could speak further. 'Like sticks to like, eh? Is that what you're trying to tell me, Evie? A farmer's son, a crofter's daughter! And never the twain shall look any further than their own cabbage patch!'

'Bugger you, Gillie,' she told him fiercely. 'You always try to belittle Johnny – and me too whenever I mention him.'

'Maybe I'm jealous!'

'Ay, and what if you are? At least marriage with Johnny is possible – it could never be with you.'

'Stranger things have happened, Evie,' he told her angrily, his young face dark and sullen. 'Just give me time, that's all. I won't always be reliant on my parents for everything. I'll come out to be a lawyer one day – I'm bloody sure of that – and then I can marry who I like and to hell with all this!'

333

She took his hands and looked at him rather sadly. 'I canna wait that long, Gillie. Johnny's been acting strange lately – ever since I came here to work. He told me only last night that if I didn't promise to marry him he'll forget all about Canada and go to the war instead – and I canna allow that to happen – no to my Johnny.' she finished softly.

'So – that's that.' He drew away from her and pulling up his knees stared moodily down at his feet. For a long time he sat immobile while the September sun slanted its rays through the slats in the hayloft above the stables. A spell cast itself over them. They both withdrew into their own particular worlds while the harvesters whirred in the fields of Rothiedrum. The familiar scents of late summer pervaded the countryside, the lone haunting cry of a curlew winged over from purple shadowed haughs, mingling with the sadness of the lark's late song, a mere echo of ebullient spring days long gone.

'I won't see you again after this summer.' He eventually broke the deep, dark silence, his voice husky and low, so unlike the passionate Gillie she knew. She could have loved him then – could have allowed him to make love to her there in the hot sweet hay that engulfed them with enticing scents of summer past. She was torn – torn between her love for Johnny and her deep, warm, lasting affection for Gillan the younger of Rothiedrum . . . The finality in his next words came almost as a relief, absolved her from making a move that would only have plunged them into further confusion.

'Maybe you're right, Evie, maybe our worlds could never come together – though if you'd let me I'd have done my damndest to try and make it happen.'

He glanced at her, a hurt in his eyes that made her turn quickly away. 'So, it's Johnny for you and God knows what for me. I'll never forget you, Evie, no matter how far I travel or who I may meet. It's been wonderful knowing you – you made me live when I needed life most. I promise I won't bother you again or try to touch you. You belong to Johnny and I have no part of you now. I'll make damned sure I don't come back here – I couldn't bear it – to see you, to be near you knowing you can never be mine. I only have a week or two left of my holidays – a bit of time for me to make up my mind about my future. Would you let me share what's left of my time – with you and Johnny? The best man has won, so surely you wouldn't grudge a drowning man his last wish – and after all, it's you I'll be fighting for when I leave these shores far behind.'

She couldn't see him for the blinding tears. 'Must you be so – so melodramatic!' she burst out in anguish. 'No wonder you and Florrie got on so well – she loved acting too!'

She dissolved into tears, burying her face in her arms so that she was hidden from him. He didn't move, didn't touch her though every fibre in him cried out to stroke the rich shining hair of her and to kiss away the tears that shook her slender shoulders.

'Of course you can come with us,' she spoke at last, shakily, wiping her eyes on the hem of her dress, grabbing his proffered hanky to blow her nose resoundingly. 'And dinna be daft saying you won't come back here because of me. I'll get a job somewhere else – the gentry places are ten a penny round here.'

'No,' he replied bluntly. 'I've had enough of Rothiedrum for a while. I might try France for a change – find out if all that smoke and stink has blotted out the sun I used to find so uncomfortable.'

'Stop it, please, stop it Gillie.'

'Why, why should I? Oh, don't worry about me, Evie, there are plenty of places for me to while my idle hours away – and plenty of Father's money for me to do it efficiently and well.'

'It's not like you, Gillie – to throw your position in my face.'

'No,' he said grimly, 'but it is like you to throw yours at me – and you've done that today – very thoroughly.'

Johnny was waiting for her as she came walking along the road from Rothiedrum House, a very different-looking

Johnny from the gentle one she knew. His face was thunderous as he apprehended her, taking her arm in a painful grip and grinding out 'Just what the hell are you playing at, Evie? I know where you've been, who you've been with. I was up seeing Will and I saw you and Gillan disappearing into the stables. You're having a fine time to yourself, playing one off against the other!'

'Johnny, let go of me,' she panted, 'you're hurting my arm . . .'

'I'll hurt a lot more than your arm before I'm through!' he retorted, his blue eyes dark with the anger and hurt that had raged inside him for weeks now.

With a sob she tore herself free from his grasp and turned away but his arm shot out once more, fingers of steel clamped themselves over her wrist and, whirling her round, he brought her hard up against him so that the rigid wall of his chest was close against her face. She felt the tensile power of him, saw the naked urgency stark and deep in his eyes. A small thrill of awareness trembled through her. This was the Johnny she didn't know, the one he had kept hidden from her till this moment. And now his hurt and anger were spilling over, erupting in waves of fury from every muscle of his body.

'Johnny,' she breathed. 'Nothing happened between Gillie and me – and nothing ever will! It's you I love – I know that now – I've loved you for a long time – I don't think I knew how much – till now.'

He didn't say anything. Still holding on to her arm he propelled her through the gates of Hill O Binney's lower fields. It was as deserted as all the other fields, everyone having abandoned work to go home to tea. Golden acres of newly cut corn stretched for as far as the eye could see.

Without a word Johnny led her along, stopping only when he came to an uncut stretch of waving corn, so high it came up to their armpits and only their heads were visible above the heavy ripe heads.

Slowly and deliberately, his hands slid round her waist, she placed hers on the bare flesh of his arms, feeling the heat of it, seeing the fine furring of fair hairs glinting in the mellow September sunshine. Her pulse trembled, the sweet warmth of her love for him filled her with new and wondrous sensations. Tossing back her hair she looked up at him. He towered above her, his wide powerful shoulders silhouetted against the blue sky, his head a sheaf of white-gold, matching that of the heads of corn which swayed all around them.

'Evie, I have to ask you something.' His voice had lost its harshness, it was filled with a husky urgency, it flooded out of him, filling her senses, making her shiver suddenly.

'Ay, Johnny, what is it?'

'Will you marry me? Even if you won't come away to Canada for a whilie it doesna matter. I want you to belong to me, Evie, to have you and hold you as my own darling wife. I love you so – I – I canna live without you.'

'Johnny,' she traced the firm, sensuous line of his mouth with one trembling finger. 'Yes, oh yes,' she whispered, loving him so much in those intimate moments she felt the tears springing to her eyes. 'I'll marry you and I'll love you back – to the end of my days I'll love you back.'

Gathering her to him he pressed his lips to the top of her head, she felt her hair falling loose and free about her shoulders as he untied the ribbon that held it. He let the long bright strands of it glide through his fingers, kissing each one as they whispered over his skin to fall sweet and glorious down her back to her waist.

'Such bonny hair,' he murmured reverently, 'I always loved it – even when you were a wee lass in school.'

Her cheek was pressed against the rough fabric of his shirt. His heartbeat surged in her ears, the strong, beloved sound of it reverberating through her, making her very aware of the deep powerful forces that were the man of him. He smelled of the earth, the sun, the fresh clean smell of everything they both loved in their world. She looked up into his darkening eyes and saw the mist of tears glinting on his lashes.

His mouth came down on hers, softly, caressingly, and as her lips parted, the gentleness in his became something

337

more. She gave a little cry at the back of her throat and kissed him back, the passion that had lain latent in her inexperienced body now springing up to engulf her with longing. He felt the response in her and his mouth became rough, demanding, his tongue exploring the moist, secret recesses of her mouth. As one they sank down into the cool damp shadows of the corn stalks, the fragrance of it enveloping them as over and over they kissed. Desire welled into her being. He had never kissed her like this before. The urgency of his mouth unlocked fires in her that flickered through every fibre of her body. The last remnants of sweet and innocent childhood flew unheeded away from her. Johnny's hands brushed her breasts. She felt her nipples tautening, an ache of yearning shivered into her very marrow.

Hardly aware of what she was doing she was helping him to slide her dress off her shoulders, her shaking hands were unbuttoning his shirt, her fingers curling into the springing hairs that furred his broad deep chest.

'Evie,' his voice seemed to come from a long way, a husky deep sigh that throbbed passionately into her. 'Evie – are you sure?'

An echo of childhood rang in her mind – 'I'll never do things with boys . . .'

And Florrie, 'Course you will, and you'll do it right well Evie, cos your father's hot blood is in you . . .'

She smiled at Johnny through a sudden mist of tears. 'Oh, Johnny, I love you,' she whispered huskily, 'I want you to love me.' She took his head between her hands and looked at him for a long, tremulous moment before bringing his mouth down against hers.

He removed the last of his clothing and she gave an involuntary gasp of admiration. He was both beautiful and devastating in all his masculine nakedness. There was an untamed strength in the steely hardness of his muscles, his deep chest plunged down to a narrow pelvis – and his legs! Long and lean and lithe and stirring so passionately against her soft ones.

With a shiver she caressed his broad back, enjoying the

338

feel of the smooth brown skin, the hard edge of his shoulder blades moving under her touch . . .

His naked flesh was hard against hers, his magnificent body covered hers. For long, unbearable moments his eyes worshipped her body, then his lips were moving over her high young breasts, caressing each taut nipple with his tongue, moving down to the silken skin of her belly . . .

'Johnny . . .'

He cradled her head in his hands, gazed deep into her eyes. For a split moment in time there was clarity in the deep blue orbs. She gazed back, aware of the scents around her, of the rhythmic swaying of the corn above their heads – of the muscles rippling under the bronzed skin of his arms. Gently he merged with her, his body moving, quickening. His eyes darkened with pleasure, became abstracted. She closed her own. Pain washed into her and through her as he plunged deep inside her body. She strangled a little cry. Then with the pain came a sensation of such unbelievable pleasure it brought a dew of perspiration to her brow. She clung to him as she felt herself drowning in a wild, rapturous sweetness that carried her with him to crests of an almost unbearable ecstasy . . .

An eternity later she lay in the safe warm circle of his arms, trembling softly with fulfilment, her moist cheek pressed against his heaving chest. From the deep caverns within, his heart was thundering and she listened to it till the beat of it slowed, became normal. His fingers were stroking her hair, tenderly, lovingly, his powerful limbs were quite still and peaceful against the softness of hers.

'Johnny,' she raised herself to look at him anxiously. 'You're very quiet, what are you thinking?'

Snapping off a piece of corn he tickled her nose with the feathery head. 'I was thinking . . .' He paused and grinned, his teeth very white in the tanned fairness of his face. 'I was thinking, Evelyn McKenzie Grant, we ought to get married quite quickly after today. I'll have to make an honest woman of you.'

She sat back on her heels, her slender body cool and

white against the shadowy corn. 'A woman,' she spoke slowly, her young face pensive. 'I suppose I am a woman now. Yet . . .' she giggled suddenly. 'I still feel as daft as I did when I was just a girl, way way back in time – an hour ago in fact . . .' Grabbing a handful of corn heads she began to tickle first the soles of his feet then his legs. Shouting with laughter he caught her. They tussled for a while then became still again as passion leapt between them once more.

'I was wondering,' she demurred as his lips brushed hers, 'what I'm going to say to Mam.'

He stared at her aghast. 'You're no going to tell about us – surely?'

'Daftie,' she snuggled against him. 'I was just wondering what excuses to make for being late in for tea – because,' she put her arms around him and smiled. 'I'm going to be very very late.'

His mouth moved over her smooth shoulders. 'Ay,' he replied thoughtfully. 'You might be right at that, Evelyn Grant.'

The September sun dipped lower, the cool breath of evening blew over the countryside but there in the little hollow of the cornfield all was warmth and delight for Evelyn McKenzie Grant and her Johnny. So enraptured were they with each other they forgot all about time there in the sylvan fields with the sweet and wondrous promise of their future lives together just one kiss away – and the next . . .

It was her day off, a still, warm day with a humid atmosphere and the threat of thunder in the purple clouds piling up over the low-slung hills. Gillan and Johnny trudged beside her, the former carrying a large picnic basket packed by Martha, the latter walking along, hands in his pockets, fair head bent, hardly a word out of him since leaving King's Croft an hour earlier.

They had come on bicycles as far as the track leading up to the old mill where they planned to have a picnic. Gillan had borrowed Will's ramshackle old bike with its little carbon lamp tied to the handlebars with string and one mudguard flapping loosely on rusty stays.

It had been strange to see Gillan riding a bike instead of a horse and she had wanted to laugh at the sight of him wobbling along, every muscle taut with concentration. But Johnny's black mood hadn't allowed for laughter. He hadn't wanted to come at all, telling her that if young Rothiedrum had had any decency in him he wouldn't have intruded into the one day in the week when they both had time to be alone together.

She hadn't told him about the talk she had had with Gillan, fearing that he would see it as an admittance that something more than friendship had existed between them, but now, seeing the mood lying over his set face, as dark as the thunderclouds gathering on the horizon, she wished heartily that she had. None of them was enjoying the day very much, certainly not Johnny, and Gillan looked as if he would like to turn and go back the way he had come.

'There's a storm coming.' Johnny studied the sky. 'We'd better get back.'

'Och, we've come all this way. We can shelter in the mill if the rain comes on.' She spoke rather sharply, angry with him for behaving so childishly. 'You never wanted to come in the first place, did you, Johnny?'

He glanced at her sideways. 'Too bloody true. Do you think I enjoy being pig in the middle? You two have a nerve expecting me to trot along meekly at your side. Do you think I'm daft enough no to see what's happening before my very eyes?'

Gillan was walking ahead and though he turned at the sound of their raised voices he went on, slightly faster than before, as if conveying that he had no wish to intrude upon a private argument.

'Johnny Burns,' she said breathlessly, half-running to keep up with his long stride, 'you're growing more like your father every day – the same moods, the same anger, the same way of glowering beneath your brows.'

'And what if I am! Maybe he was driven to behave like that,' he hurled at her icily. 'I'm beginning to think he was

341

right about one thing – women can change a man – they can make them do and say crazy things – they can drive them crazy wi' their flirting and their wiles – they can make them do anything they want.' His voice changed and he sounded so miserable she made him stop in his tracks and face her.

'Johnny, stop it! Stop that this minute and listen to me. The other day I said I would marry you – I said it because I love you – in fact – I love you so much I'll – I'll even come to Canada if you want – though mind, I want to come back here in the end – that's my one condition – or I'll not go with you.'

The thunder left his face, to be replaced by a look of such joyous disbelief she giggled.

'Evie.' He drew her to him and his lips claimed hers, passionately, demandingly, never a thought for young Rothiedrum walking on ahead, knowing what was happening and almost too sick with hurt to care anymore.

'Johnny,' she took his hand. 'We have a lot to talk about and plenty of time to do it in – but for now, will you be in a better mood for the rest of the day? Gillie has only a few days left before he goes away – you and I have all the time in the world together.'

'The rest of our lives.' That was the Johnny she knew best, the Johnny of their schooldays, blue eyes shining, the dear smile of him lighting his face with a happiness that came deep from within the big, generous, gentle heart of him. 'I've got something for you, Evie.' From his pocket he withdrew a huge rosy red apple and tossed it in the air.

'You're daft, Johnny Burns,' she giggled.

'Ay, daft on you.' He tucked the apple inside his shirt. 'You'll get it later – I canna have you crunching in my ears and driving me any dafter than I am.'

Taking her hand they went after Gillie who had disappeared down a dip in the track.

It was peaceful by the mill, a gaunt old place which had long ago fallen into disuse but for all that still retained a certain charm, reflected as it was in the deep calm pool over which it stood.

They had explored it somewhat half-heartedly and having eaten now sat awkwardly beside one another, Gillan throwing stones into the water, Johnny hunched up, staring at the ripples, every so often glancing at Evelyn as if he would like to be alone witn her.

A rumble of thunder came from the hill peaks, followed a few seconds later by a flash of lightning. Johnny scrambled to his feet. 'Better get back before we're soaked.'

'Wait a wee minute.' She had spied some harebells growing in the long grasses some way off from the ruin. 'Let me go and pick them. Mam loves wildflowers. I can wrap them in wet paper and they'll last till we get home.'

She darted off, soon immersed in picking the delicate flowers, mixing them with purple scabious till she had gathered a great armful. It was very hot and sultry, yet even so she shivered as a cold tremor of premonition went through her. Icy fingers seemed to clutch at her heart, squeezing it so that it seemed to stop beating for a few moments before it went racing on.

'No,' she whimpered, 'Oh, God, please no.'

She heard the raised voices above the thundering of her heart in her ears, Gillan shouting, 'You've got her – what more do you want?'

And Johnny, 'For you to stay out of our lives – that's what! She doesn't need you or your kind, Rothiedrum, she never did and she never will!'

She raced back to the mill, the flowers squashed to her breast, her breath swift and painful in her throat. But she was too late to stop them coming to blows. They were at each other's throats, too incensed with rage to heed her pleas. She could only stand by helplessly, watching them hitting out, seeing the dark fury in their eyes while all around the thunder snarled, the lightning lit the lowering skies. The rain started suddenly, teeming down, blotting out the fields and the trees, pitting the calm surface of the pond.

In moments they were soaked. Through stinging eyes she saw them struggling, hair plastered to their heads, shirts clinging to muscle, bone, sinew, a terrifying spectacle against the sodden landscape. Then Gillan's foot slipped on the treacherous wet earth at the pond side and suddenly he was in the water, his white, frightened face bobbing for a few moments before he went under.

'Johnny, he can't swim!' she screamed, staring through the blinding rain.

Without hesitation Johnny plunged in. He was a strong swimmer and in seconds had reached the struggling Gillan, grabbing him by his collar and holding on to him. Gillan was pulling him under, but with a great effort Johnny hauled him up, hardly seeing where he was going for the rain and the hair spiking down over his eyes. Slowly he dragged Gillan to safety, shoving him on to the bank where he lay gasping and coughing. Johnny grabbed a tussock of grass, the earth crumbled away and he slipped and fell back, cracking his head hard on the paddles of the mill wheel.

'Johnny!' Evelyn screamed. 'Johnny!'

Horrified she watched him disappearing under the water and then her pertrified limbs sprang into life. Tearing off her skirt and her petticoats she was about to jump in when the surface broke and Johnny reappeared. His hand came up and he hoisted himself aloft, holding on to the slippery wooden paddles, his knuckles white with strain. For a moment she glimpsed his face, saw the last vestiges of consciousness draining from his eyes. In that split second he seemed to look directly at her before the wheel carried him under, the last thing she saw of him the blood staining his thick, fair hair.

The thunder growled, lightning lit the scene, then everything abated and suddenly there was silence, broken only by the hiss of the rain, the shudder of the wheel as it found its way back, empty now, a watery pink stain on one of the paddles washing away rapidly in the rain. It creaked for a while then it became still. The flowers that had fallen from her grasp floated on the surface of the water, blue and purple blobs, bunching together then spreading out one by one. Something bobbed to the surface near the wheel, a rosy red apple – floating, floating, bringing with it a

344

thousand tears, those past, those she would shed for the rest of her life whenever she thought of the tall, fair young giant that had been Johnny Burns.

Gillan was hauling himself upright, staring over his shoulder in horrified disbelief. The pool was calm again, pocked by the rain and a swirl of green water below the gaunt paddles of the wheel. The flowers were floating towards it, then as they became trapped in the miniature whirlpool they bobbed round and round in a crazy little dance that mocked their own innocence for quite unintentionally they had become blossoms of death strewn on the watery grave of a young man who only just recently had talked of a future that he had thought would last forever.

Evelyn covered her face with her wet hands. 'Johnny,' she whispered. 'Dearest Johnny.' Arms came around her, Gillan's arms. Her shocked body cried out for the comfort of them but her mind pushed them away. 'Don't touch me, Gillie,' she sobbed.

'Evie,' he cried through clenched teeth as he shivered in his soaked clothing. 'You surely don't blame me for what happened!'

'Ay, I blame you,' she said, softly, bitterly. 'But more than you I blame myself. I shouldn't have allowed you to come with us, I should have finished with you instead o' letting you follow – and now Johnny's dead and I just want to be alone.'

Picking up her skirt and her petticoat she fumbled into them while Gillan looked on, his face white, his body trembling. She left him there by the gaunt ruin of the old mill as she ran from the place, never a backward glance, never stopping till she reached the road, hardly remembering anything of the journey home through the blinding, lashing rain.

The little wood by the lochside was alive with birdsong. The sweet sounds of it pulsated in the air, beat into Evelyn's heart as she stood, a slender girl of sixteen, hands folded restfully in front of her, looking down on Johnny's grave. The September sun played on her hair, hair that was the same shade as the beech leaves now turning to bronze on the trees. Tiny strands of it lifted in the playful breeze, shimmered and glowed before it fell back unheeded on to her brow. The sun was shining, the birds were singing – and Johnny Burns was dead. It was a week now since the funeral, Rob Burns had cried, openly and shamelessly into his big hands, his great shoulders shaking with his grief, and she had wondered then if he was realizing too late how lucky he had been to have had a son like Johnny. Everyone had cried for him, everyone had liked the big, gentle lad with the generous heart and the kindly words for all who chanced along his way.

Yesterday Evelyn had silently walked along the heather braes with her father, each saying nothing, too lost in their individual thoughts to care where they were going, what they were seeing. Then Jamie had taken her in his arms and they had both cried, father and daughter, sharing their grief as they had shared so much throughout their lives.

'He was a son to me, Evie,' he had sobbed.

'I know, Father,' she had wept, clinging to him. 'I loved him but I didn't do right by him. I blame myself for what happened. It was my fault.'

'No, lass, no,' he had said urgently. 'It wasna your doing. We were all pushing you too much, Johnny, me, your mother. You rebelled against it and just wanted to go your own way for a wee whilie. You're only sixteen, Evie, for God's sake dinna blame yourself for any of this.'

'I was going to marry him, Father. I told him so – before – before . . .'

'Evie, you mustna torture yourself,' he had urged, holding her tightly in his arms. 'You have all your future in front of you. You will never forget Johnny, but you must go on, Evie, you must go on.'

'Ay, I'll go on,' she had whispered, 'but not just now, Father. I must stop for a wee whilie and remember – I have to look back before I can go forward.'

She thought of that now as she stood at the graveside, letting the peace of the place wash over her. She felt that her life was finished, first Florrie, now Johnny, her mind took her back over the years she had shared with them, remembering, remembering the days of yesteryear when they had all run wild together through the summer fields of childhood. As children they had come here to play in amongst the stones of the kirkyard, death a thing that happened only to the old, none of them dreaming in those far off, carefree days that two of them would lie too soon in the cold dark earth, the sad leaves of autumn covering their graves.

Sinking to the ground she put her face in her hands and burst into helpless, hopeless tears and when she was spent she sat back on her heels looking at the grey old walls of the kirk. A shadow seemed to detatch itself and she fancied it was Florrie standing there, pain in her lovely face, the laughter still now, the young mouth set in its own expression of grief.

'Florrie,' she whispered. 'Is that you?'

Something touched her then, she felt as if young arms were around her, helping her to her feet. She felt no fear. Always she had been aware of a spiritual world running parallel with her own earthly one, some part of her knowing that if she was to allow it, she would find no great difficulty in communicating with that other existence beyond the grave. Now she was wide open to anyone trying to get through and in her vulnerable state of grief she felt that she wouldn't mind glimpsing something of what lay beyond.

The feeling of Florrie grew stronger and then somehow she was there, not ill or intangible but very real and clear. They seemed to stand looking at one another for a long time while the whisper of autumn laughed in their ears and touched them with long, golden fingers.

'Evelyn and Florrie, best friends – 1913 – and beyond.' The epitaph grew up before them, misty, transparent, yet burning brightly like a flame. They saw each other through a veil of tears.

'I loved him too, Evie, I always did.' There was no speaking voice but Evelyn knew that her friend had spoken.

347

'You have him now, Florrie,' Evelyn spoke aloud clearly. 'You have him forever.'

They cried then, each in the arms of the other, their childhood gone now, and with it the echo of ghostly dreams and yearnings. And then Evelyn knew that she was alone once more, her thoughts quite still and peaceful, not thinking beyond that sunlit day in September when young Johnny Burns lay quiet and still forever.

Another shadow detached itself from the walls of the old kirk, a tall, dark shadow. For a moment she thought it was Johnny coming back to her but as it came out into the sunlight she saw the dark hair, the sad, handsome face of Gillan.

He came towards her, hands outstretched. 'Evie,' he murmured. 'I heard you talking – I thought you were with someone.'

'I was, I was wi' Florrie,' she said simply and without embarrassment.

He showed no surprise. 'I know – I always knew there was something about you that went beyond the understanding of most mortal beings.'

'But not you, Gillie?' she said softly.

'I can't pretend to understand – but I accept the things you know that I don't.' He took her hand. 'Evie, you don't still blame me for what happened – do you?'

'No, Gillie, I'm sorry for saying such a thing, at the time I didn't rightly know what I was saying.'

'I knew I would find you here. Mother is closing up the house for an indefinite period, she wants to go to London and do her bit for the war, and Father has some business things he has to see to there. One or two of the staff are staying on of course and I'm going to hang around for a few days before I have to go back to school. Will I see you before I go? I thought – well – I would like to try and take your mind off all this.'

'Ay, Gillie, you can see me. I dinna suppose I'll be seeing that much of you from now on.'

'Oh, I'll be back, Evie,' he assured her softly, his hand tightening over hers. 'Come on home now – I met your